NON-RECOURSE

NON-RECOURSE

William A. Thau

To Paul —
With best wishes —
Wm Thau

iUniverse, Inc.
New York Lincoln Shanghai

NON-RECOURSE

iUniverse, Inc.

For information address:
iUniverse, Inc.
2021 Pine Lake Road, Suite 100
Lincoln, NE 68512
www.iuniverse.com

ISBN: 0-595-32719-2 (pbk)
ISBN: 0-595-66671-X (cloth)

Printed in the United States of America

To my wife Jane, without whose years of love, encouragement and support this book would never have been written.

There are places
within a man
no woman could ever know.
At the bottom of himself...somewhere
broken faces
and dreams he's nourished
....

Tears can't always fall from eyes,
and some things are just too deep
or quiet
to be talked about,
maybe only thought about
when he's alone
on a plane,
or looking out
any window.

If you love him,
let him go
to those places within himself
where he can never take you
and where
you must never ask to go.

—Merrit Malloy
Human Subways

PROLOGUE

▼

The old priest picked up the brass flask of incense, shook it three times over the flower-laden casket, and stared briefly into the mournful eyes of the onlookers.

"Into your hands," he began, "O merciful Father, we commend your servant Julia Lawrence. Acknowledge, we humbly beseech you, a sheep of your own fold, a lamb of your own flock, a sinner of your own redeeming. Receive her into the arms of your mercy, into the blessed rest of everlasting peace, and into the glorious company of the saints of light. May her soul and the souls of all the departed, through the mercy of God, rest in peace. Amen."

The bronze casket, covered with lilies, lilacs and roses, seemed to disintegrate as the torrent of rain increased. The priest brushed back the shock of white hair that had fallen across his brow, gently wiped the rain from his glasses, and walked slowly over to us. He then extended his hand. I took it, and he reached his other arm around my shoulders, pulled me to him, and whispered, "Matt, I'm so sorry. May God bless you and Angela, all the days of your lives. Take comfort that Julia now rests in the hands of the Lord."

I stood in a daze, looking over the rolling hills and the endless tombstones, and then down at the casket that would soon be lowered into the ground. My daughter, Angela, held my hand and quietly sobbed.

After acknowledging the friends who had gathered, we were taken to a black limousine where we found refuge from the crowd and the rain. I held Angela close, trying to give her the comfort I couldn't find to give myself. As the limousine wound slowly down the long drive through the cemetery, the only sounds were the whining of the windshield wipers and her continued sobbing.

"Dad, why...why?" she asked.

I didn't answer. There wasn't a reason. Julia was gone. Forever. And I didn't know why. Not then.

PART I

CHAPTER 1

▼

Bangor, Maine, 1992

Strong winds and heavy rain lashed the east coast as my American Eagle plane landed in Bangor, Maine. Occasional bursts of lightning lit up the sky, followed by rolling and then loud claps of thunder. Overhead, I stared at screeching seagulls as they circled around the coastline, pummeled by the torrential rain. The sky was dark and ominous, stirring within me a feeling of dread. I was there to confront a man I had never met, Julius Freytag. I tried, hopelessly, to lay out a plan, but I had no idea what would happen.

The airport was small, with only a handful of arriving and departing passengers and ticket agents. Sheets of rain drenched everyone leaving and entering the terminal. I found a hard bench, waiting both for the arrival of my small baggage and the storm to subside. I stared vacantly at the luggage trams, thinking of times long past and a life I thought would last forever. Visions of Julia constantly blurred my mind. What was the last thing I remembered about her—other than the funeral? I couldn't think. When I first saw her, it was at a distance and only a glimpse, but I was mesmerized by her radiance. I mistook her at once for a young Catherine Deneuve. It was her blonde hair curled in a cluster around her delicate face, like a fine piece of porcelain. Her alluring smile, shining turquoise eyes, and deep red lips—she was breathtakingly beautiful and elegant. She wore a shimmering black satin evening gown, cut somewhat low at the neck and moving ever so gently with the curves of her figure. A single strand of pearls circled her neck and she wore diamond and pearl earrings. She was captivating, regal and unobtainable. But it was more than her beauty—there was a feeling of serenity and gentleness about her. We later exchanged several glances, and then she looked deeply into my eyes and gave me a glimmer of a smile. I understood. Without a word being spoken, I had fallen hopelessly in love.

I was then a young lawyer with a small Dallas law firm, barely out of law school, attending an affair given by a partner. There was very little I could offer her, but after four months of dating, it seemed to be enough. In the first ten years of our marriage, I think the most endearing times were the struggles. She wanted so little but gave me so much. And now that I had become a highly successful partner in what had become a major law firm, it was gone, every vestige of the happiness I had known. I was left alone, with my bitterness and anger, to face a man I had never met, hoping to find the reason why—why she had to die and why my existence seemed to hang by a single thread.

All I had was a phone number, one that was taken several months before from the pocket of a dead man in Rome, Italy, a man who had tried to kill me. Through a man linked with the Mafia in New Orleans, Raymond Jarrett, it had been connected to Freytag.

My bag arrived drenched in rain. I carried it to the nearby Hertz counter, got the keys to my car, and walked cautiously without feeling to the garage. After first removing the pieces to my Beretta handgun from my bag and then assembling those pieces, I loaded the bag into the trunk of the red Chrysler. The stained velour seats had a musty odor. I sat for several minutes in solitude, saying a small prayer to a God I had ceased to believe in long ago. My stomach was churning as I pulled out my cellphone and dialed Freytag's number. Following six rings, I heard the receiver being lifted off the hook and a deep but soft voice say, "Yes, what do you want?"

I hesitated. "I'm looking for a friend. I was given your name as someone who might help."

"A friend? I don't know what you're talking about."

"Mr. Freytag, I've come a long way. Could I spend a few minutes with you?"

"I'm very busy," came the reply. "Who are you and what do you want?"

"I'm a lawyer and would like to use your services. I understand from an acquaintance that you might be of particular help to me."

There was a long pause, followed by a click as if another phone had been lifted off the hook, and then he said, "Tell me, who is this friend?"

I breathed deeply, trying to calm my shaky voice. "I met him in Rome.... I won't need much of your time."

"This afternoon, at three," he said. "Have you been here before?"

"No."

"Take the old Habersham Road, east until you reach the coast. Then turn right on Pelham. I'm in a white, wood frame house at the end of the street. The number is 109. Can you find it?"

"Yes," I said, and the phone was disconnected.

Bangor was old, Victorian and gloomy. It's a small town of 35,000 people on the cold Atlantic shores. The beating it takes from its exposure on the coast was apparent to me not only from its weathered buildings but also from its weathered inhabitants. The house where Freytag lived fit perfectly into the landscape.

I was met at the door by a small oriental woman who showed me into a study on the side of the house. It was decorated in brown velour and cheap furniture, and was littered with old newspapers and books. The house had a pungent smell of old food. Freytag appeared in a black turtle neck sweater, gray slacks and worn loafers. He had a speckled unkept mustache and wore small reading glasses. His overall untidiness made him look much older than I suspected he was.

"I'm Julius Freytag," he said, extending his hand. "And you are...."

"I'm Matthew Lawrence, an attorney from Dallas." My mouth was dry. I paused to regain my composure. "I appreciate your taking the time to see me."

"Not at all," he said. "Guests are always welcome here. It can be quite lonely. Tell me, what can I do for you?"

He motioned me to sit on a worn sofa as he sat across from me. "You mentioned a friend, in Rome?" His voice was quite remarkable, like that of a college professor or an announcer.

"Yes, a friend in Rome. I met a man there last month, who had an unfortunate accident. He gave me your number when he died, and I thought it important to contact you."

"Died?" He looked at me with a very puzzled gaze, and then motioned for the oriental woman. "Would you like some tea?" he asked as he studied my question—and me.

"Please."

"You say he gave you my number. For what purpose?"

"He didn't tell me. I thought that maybe you could."

He shook his head. "I'm afraid that I don't know any Italians," he said. "I have no idea why this man had my number."

"What do you do?"

"I'm a freelance writer, magazine articles and that sort of thing."

"By the way," I said quietly, "he was not Italian. A large American."

"What was his name?"

"I don't know."

A look of irritation came across his face. "You had a friend in Rome who died and you don't even know his name. That's very strange, wouldn't you say?" He paused, looking for a reaction. I avoided his eyes. "Mr. Lawrence, I don't know what you're up to, but I don't appreciate your games," he said glaring at me. "I suggest we end this meeting."

I swallowed and stared back, putting my hand into my jacket pocket. "No...not until you tell me your game."

His face twisted into a scowl. "I don't play games."

"Mr. Freytag, this man tried to kill me in Rome. He was connected with you. How do you know me?"

Seconds passed in silence, and then he rose to go to his desk. "You're very perceptive, Mr. Lawrence," he finally said. His eyes remained fixed on mine, but I could see him slowly reaching to open the middle drawer of his desk.

"I wouldn't do that," I warned. He froze and watched as I raised my Beretta where it would be unmistakable to him.

"You're a damn fool! Do you really think that will work…here in my house?"

"Someone killed my wife and I want to know why…and I want to know why someone is trying to kill me. I think you can tell me." My heart was pounding in my head and I looked down momentarily in an effort to catch my breath and steady my voice.

He sat back, studying me intently, and then said, "I'm a businessman. I make arrangements for people, but I don't kill people."

"Is it possible, in your business, that maybe someone wanted you to make arrangements to kill me?"

He sipped his tea, gently rubbed his forehead, and reached for his pipe. Sucking on it, he looked up directly at me and said slowly, "Anything is possible. Mr. Lawrence, I don't get involved in the business of my clients."

"What is your business, Mr. Freytag?"

"I told you," he answered.

"No, no you didn't. Let me guess. Is it brokering mailmen—are those the buzz words of the trade?"

He seemed temporarily amused. "Buzz words? What happened in Rome wasn't my doing. I had no idea what would happen." He narrowed his eyes, showing his lack of patience. "I provided a name to a customer—nothing more."

"Consider this," I said. "My wife and a good friend are dead. Probably because someone provided the name of a mailman. Maybe you. I want you to know that unless you tell me, within the next two minutes, who your customer is, you will also be dead. That's not a threat, it's a promise." I glared at him, waiting for his reaction.

"Put your gun down. You won't shoot. If you do, you won't walk out of here alive. You know that don't you?"

"Try me." I deliberately jerked back the slide on my gun and leveled it at his head.

A worried look crept imperceptibly across his face. "You know, for some reason I believe you might."

"Think, Freytag, because your time is running out. Is your customer's identity worth your life?"

"I've tried to tell you," he insisted, "I don't know his identity."

"Then how does he use you?"

"If you'll let me reach into my desk drawer, I'll show you."

"Slowly," I warned as I kept the gun leveled at his head.

He produced a manilla folder, opened it and handed it to me. The first thing I saw was a picture of me taken from the Dallas Bar Journal. There were other pictures of me, at various places, and with Julia. As I flipped through the file, carefully watching Freytag, I stumbled upon an advertisement torn out of a magazine called *Guns&Danger*. It was listed under the heading "Miscellaneous" and read-

> "*Services required. Delivery special. Top price. Message for two. Respond Dallas P.O. Box 9112. Requirement urgent.*"

Beneath it were wire instructions and a typed resume, describing in detail information concerning my personal life, travel plans, contacts, and physical attributes.

I closed the folder, laid it next to me, and refocused my full attention on Freytag. "Does this mean what I think it does?" I felt the blood rush to my head and took a deep breath, anticipating his response.

"It's a contract…dealing with you," he said, clearing his throat.

"A death warrant—you bastard! I should blow your head off now and end it."

"That won't end it. I gave you that folder because it will end it with me. But not my customer."

"End it with you! Do you think it's that simple?"

He shifted in his chair, keeping his eyes on me and the gun. "I've told you, because now that you've discovered me, it will serve no purpose for me to be involved with it. I have no desire to be killed by you or anyone else if another attempt is made on your life."

"Who do you people think you are? You place ads in magazines and kill people. Do you think you can get away with this?"

"I don't kill people! All I do is bring the buyer and seller together. They don't know me and I don't know them." He hesitated and said softly, "Except the man in Rome. I was careless. It won't happen again."

I sat back, stunned. A network of killers who obtain contracts through middlemen and magazine advertisements. I was incredulous. "How do I find and stop this customer of yours?"

He leaned forward, hesitated, and then said in a subdued voice, "You're searching for death, Mr. Lawrence. You needn't waste your time—it will find you."

For a moment, I considered shooting him. The sweat of my palm felt clammy against the metal grips of the gun. My mind was filled with rage and the sounds the gun would make if I squeezed the trigger. I breathed deeply and then slowly lowered the gun to my lap.

The strain began to ease from his face. "If your choice is to persist, I can only give you leads—you'll be on your own. As a beginning, I suggest you try to trace the post office box and the wire transfer origination."

"What if that doesn't work?"

"Then I suggest that you go into hiding, at least until you find out who wants you dead. I'm not the only broker."

"Go into hiding? You must be kidding!"

"Mr. Lawrence, you can do what you want. But if I were you, and someone was intent on killing me, until I found that someone I would make myself very scarce. The file is yours—please keep it in good health. You have my personal assurance that I will no longer take part in the determination of your future. Now, I must excuse myself. I have many things to do today."

Freytag got up, walked over to the worn sofa, and extended his hand to say goodbye. I looked squarely into his solemn gray eyes. "You're very interesting, Mr. Freytag. You act as a middleman to arrange for my death, and then you show me all the courtesies of an old friend. Why?"

"You're not getting my point," he said, taking a long drag on his pipe. "There is nothing personal in my profession. It's only business, and nothing else. I wish you a long life. Goodbye."

I heard a double click at the door as I left. My hands trembled as I opened my umbrella and walked down the cobblestone path. When I reached my car, I leaned against it for several minutes, gulping the cold wet air, unable to move or calm my nerves. What had I become, and what was I doing here? I had been a lawyer and family man, not a target for an assassin. I suddenly found myself thrust into a world where I didn't belong. I knew then that I had to either quickly find my way...or face a certain death.

Two hours later my plane took off from the Bangor airport, shaking violently from strong head winds that carried over from the storm. Once airborne and above the clouds, the plane leveled off and I laid my head back and closed my eyes, wishing that it had all been a horrifying dream that would soon go away. But I knew it wouldn't. My thoughts drifted to the day my nightmare had begun.

CHAPTER 2

▼

Dallas, Texas, 1990

It was on a Wednesday in May, of 1990, that my secretary burst into my office with the early edition of the Dallas Times Herald. She held it in front of her, displaying the headlines which were easily readable from across the room. "*Braxton Indicted—49 Felony Counts*", it read.

I was startled, but not surprised. Leigh lowered the paper and placed it on my desk, giving me a look that anticipated a strong reaction. I gave her none.

Still waiting for a reaction, she moved to the chair across from me and sat down, carefully adjusting her blue knit skirt. "Can you believe that?" she said, holding her breath and giving me the feeling that she had just swallowed a mouse. Her eyes momentarily darted around the room, looking to be sure no one was listening.

Shifting in her chair, she pushed her hair away from her eyes and leaned forward. "Matt, aren't you shocked by this? It's incredible that they could do this to Mr. Braxton."

I couldn't hide my lack of surprise or the numbness in my brain. "Not really," I said. "When you live in the fast lane, you're bound to have some crack-ups. It had to happen, sooner or later." It occurred to me how predictable it had all been.

*   *   *   *

Dallas, Texas, 1986

When I first met Braxton, it seemed like divine providence, that idea that everything happens according to a plan. But time proved that it wasn't like that at all. It was more like the theory suggested by a German philosopher, called synchronicity. He speculated that events occur, randomly, by themselves meaning nothing. But subtly, at a particular time, place and order, synchronicity raises its ugly head. And without warning, in a fleeting moment, an event happens which changes everything. That's how it began, in a millisecond of time.

It was four years before, in the late fall in 1986, and my patience had been wearing thin. The client who had asked to meet me for lunch at the Knox Street Bar never appeared.

I remember gazing at a glass porcelain globe hanging from the middle of the ceiling on three brass chains. There was a light in it. Around the edges it was perforated, with small colored bubbles that changed colors alternatively from blue to green to orange, and then back again. Underneath hovered a cloud of smoke, hanging motionlessly in the stagnant air. The light flickered back and forth on the source of the smoke, a medium-built muscular man in his forties, with ragged gray hair, bushy eyebrows and a thick mustache that exaggerated the ruddiness of his hard-muscled face. He took a long drink, and then nodded to the bartender for another.

I stared at him for a moment, thinking of how unusual he looked in that dim light. His eyes caught mine, and then he lifted his glass and smiled. "Hey bubba," he said in a throaty voice. "We know each other?"

I smiled back and moved in his direction. "No, I don't think so, but you look familiar. My name's Lawrence, Matt Lawrence."

He shifted his drink from one hand to the other and extended his free hand. "Braxton—my friends call me Bic. You look like a lawyer."

That made me laugh. It wasn't funny, but I couldn't stop. He laughed.

"I'd give you a card," I said, "but I passed an accident on the way here and handed them all out."

He was amused. Pointing to the bar stool next to him, he said, "Buy you a drink?"

"Scotch and soda. Thanks. You spend your afternoons in bars?"

"I could ask the same of you," he answered. "No, not usually. I needed a break from the merry-go-round of my practice. This is it."

"Don't tell me, you're a doctor."

"Close. An architect. Don't despair. I use a lot of lawyers."

"Not as much as doctors."

"Wrong." He smiled again and took a long sip of his drink. "You haven't seen my buildings."

It then hit me. "Charity Square!"

"Right on," he said. "I'll bet you don't like it."

"How could I not like it. Best architectural design for 1980—you're famous."

"So was Adolph Hitler. I can tell we're going to be close friends. Not many people like twisted drain pipes surrounding aluminum scaffolding."

"It's a hell of a lot more than that," I protested. "Your peers sure as hell liked it."

"But not the general public. A little avant-garde, I think is what the critics said. But it's my last."

"Your last? Why?"

He raised his foot and placed it against my bar stool, exposing a highly polished alligator cowboy boot. The light caught the diamond in his gold ring as he lifted his hand and extended a finger towards me. "Money," he whispered. "Not enough of it in what I'm doing."

"But that's what you're trained for, and you're damn good at it."

He narrowed his eyes at me, showing his disagreement with what I had said. "I'm trained to think," he shot back. "Do you remember what Willie Sutton said when they asked him why he robbed banks?"

I shrugged and reached for my drink. "You got me. What?"

He smirked. "Because that's where the money is. Get it?"

"Not quite. Are you telling me you intend to rob banks?"

He showed a wide grin, exposing well groomed and perfectly straight teeth. "Not the way you think. I intend to buy one. By the way, do you know anything about banks?"

"Yeah, a little. I represent a few."

He was pleased. "Perfect. I just found me a lawyer."

Leaning forward, he extended his hand, as if to seal the bargain. I felt the uncomfortable stirring of wondering what it was I was getting into. He shifted his eyes around the room, searching to be sure no one was listening. Having confirmed that we were alone, he moved his eyes back to mine and sighed, letting the air out slowly.

"Years ago," he said, "I decided to build a homebuilding company. The ingredients were there, every one of them. I had the right people and ideas—not mine, you understand. Compliments of my competitors."

"Your competitors?"

"Oh, it wasn't a gift. I stole them, so to speak."

He saw the displeasure in my eyes at that statement and grinned, wide and sheepishly. "All legal," he added. "You're a good lawyer, and I suspect a very shrewd one. You above all should know…there are areas, of black and white. They say you should know the difference, not cross the line. Well, I live in the gray."

He studied me for a moment, with a self-satisfied smile, waiting for a reaction.

"Gray," I finally said. "Isn't that what they dress prisoners in?"

"I knew you were clever," he responded. He took a long sip of his drink, and then turned to study a couple in the corner, holding hands. Turning back to me, he nodded towards the couple. "There they are, two gray people enjoying the afternoon. Why do you suppose they're sitting there in the corner, holding hands on a rainy day?"

"You tell me."

"Because they're meeting secretly. You can see from their rings, they're both married. I'll bet you ten to one—not to each other."

"You don't know that."

He momentarily closed his eyes. "That's one thing I know a lot about. Not hurting anyone, at least when they can't see you. But in the gray. Get my point?"

"I'm listening."

"So," he continued, "I built this company. Second biggest home-builder in Texas. But the market went south, the banks took my company, and I made a promise to myself."

"And what was that?"

"Next time, I promised, I'll own the bank. Well, this is next time."

"That takes money."

He laughed. "No…banks have the money. It only takes imagination."

Suddenly, he turned silent. Looking through me, he mumbled, "You're with Milbank, Brewer and Daws."

"I'm one of the many."

"You represented the banks that took my company—and forced me into bankruptcy."

"What was your company?"

"Monolith Homes. Familiar?"

"Yes, it's familiar. But we were only representing our clients," I said defensively.

"And damn well. It's O.K. I'm impressed with your work. The company deserved to be taken. Now I know you're the lawyer I need!"

I sat, silently, thinking of what he was saying. I wasn't sure that I liked him—or disliked him, but I knew I was impressed. In parting, we shook hands without any plans to see each other again.

Three weeks later, I received a call. He had found a bank to buy, Congress had just eased regulatory controls, and I had just landed the biggest client of my legal career.

Cities Savings Bank was made to order. So were the monogrammed cars, watches and women. With virtually an unlimited right to sell certificates of deposit to an unsuspecting public, backed by guaranties of Uncle Sam in the form of the FDIC, Braxton's tiny bank grew by over 1,000% in less than two years. He found borrowers by the scores, and I closed loans at a dizzying rate, involving billions of dollars. With those loans and that growth, he rapidly expanded his toy chest to include jet planes and yachts.

As time went on, I found that I had little time for other clients, but I didn't mind. Braxton was a genius, or so I thought then. He always seemed to be two steps ahead of everyone, and most of the time they never knew it. That brought admiration and enemies—lots of enemies. But it never bothered him. And I never thought to ask him why.

CHAPTER 3

▼

Dallas, Texas, 1990

"Matt!"

I snapped out of my daydream to see Leigh, protesting my lack of attention. "How can you seem to be so uninterested? You haven't read what the paper says," she protested. "They're claiming that he stole millions of dollars, that he used the taxpayers' money to hire prostitutes and bribe government officials. That can't be true! Can it?"

"Anything's possible." I flipped through the paper and skimmed Braxton's indictment, which was reprinted in full. It detailed abuses that I had long suspected, but could never verify. Before I could finish the article, we were interrupted by Harry Stanton, my long-time friend and partner. He stood at the doorway, puffing on a large cigar.

"Leigh," he said, motioning towards her desk, "out."

"You want me to leave?"

"You got it."

She protested with her eyes and then left. Harry shut the door with his foot and leaned against the wall. "Great figure. You ever want to—"

"I'm married," I interrupted. "And very happily."

"Matt, did you ever take a close look in the mirror. D Magazine says you're one of the ten best lawyers in Dallas. You have movie star looks, you have lots of money, you're in great physical shape, and women actually turn their heads to look at you when you enter a room. My God man, you could have any woman in this town and Julia would never know. Are you going to live like a hermit the rest of your life, or are you going to sample what's out there? Let me tell you buddy, it's a great big wonderful world."

I stared at him in silence. His blue striped shirt, yellow bow tie, red suspenders and thick gray hair made him look more like someone in his fifties than forties. He took another puff, waiting for my response.

"You're wasting my time Harry. I married for life. And by the way, aren't you also the guy who said your marriage was made in heaven?"

"Yeah, I'm the one. But I discovered that so are thunder and lightning. Let's change the subject. Your buddy—so he met his Waterloo."

"Not my buddy, Harry. Our client. Don't forget, this is the guy who helped send your kids to college."

"Did you read the whole article?"

"Almost," I answered.

"How about the end, where the Justice Department mentions us?"

He suddenly got my full attention. "Us?"

"Yep—us. This guy McAlister says we were his lawyers, that we must've known what was going on."

"That's dead wrong. We didn't.".

"You tell him that. I'll make a prediction," he continued. "We'll get sued, and they'll ask us to put the money back they think Braxton stole."

"You're crazy. Not a chance. We didn't see any of that money. We were only his lawyers. That doesn't make us liable if he embezzled money."

Harry loosened his tie, took a deep drag on his cigar, and shoved his feet on my desk. "You wanna bet? Do you think McAlister's comments to the press were just passing the time of day? Come on, Matt. This guy's serious!"

Harry was one of our best and brightest attorneys. Phi Beta Kappa, Harvard. Overweight and intense. He headed up our litigation section and had developed a reputation for being tough and ruthless. I headed up the banking section. I suspected he knew what he was talking about.

Before I could answer him, we were interrupted by Leigh. "Sorry gentlemen," she said quietly. "Firm meeting in ten minutes. Mr. Milbank says you two must be there."

We looked at each other as she left. Simultaneously we both said "shit."

Conference room three held forty people—max. When we walked in, there must have been seventy. Harry leaned over and whispered, "Did you know we had this many partners in our Dallas office? Where in the fuck have we been?"

Herb Milbank frowned at his comment. He was standing near us, at the end of the massive table. Milbank was what a managing partner should be—short, heavy set, bald, and no nonsense. He cleared his throat several times in a futile effort to get everyone's attention, and then finally pounded on the table with his fists. "Quiet!" he demanded.

Milbank fidgeted with his glasses as he waited for everyone to get seated. Showing his impatience, he finally said, "Be seated!" The room became quiet and all eyes focused on him, standing alone at the end of the table. "I want to read you something," he began. "It was hand delivered to me this afternoon by the U.S. Justice Department."

He cleared his throat, placed his glasses on the end of his nose, and slowly looked around the room, daring anyone to say a word. "This is addressed to me, as managing partner. I'll not read every word, but just the important parts. It references Mr. Lawrence's good client, Bic Braxton, and the indictment you should all by now be familiar with. It says, in the third paragraph-

"Milbank, Brewer and Daws served as counsel for both Mr. Braxton and Cities Savings Bank, a direct conflict of interest. During the period from January 1986, through May 1990, Cities Savings, with the legal assistance of your firm, closed in excess of two billion dollars of loans. Those loans violated Federal regulations and were unsafe and unsound.

Those closings should have been stopped by your firm, but were not. Milbank, Brewer and Daws chose to look the other way."

He paused and again looked around the room, this time for a reaction. His gaze was met by a stunned silence. Looking back at the paper, he continued—"Fourth paragraph-

"The United States of America hereby makes formal demand on Milbank, Brewer and Daws for full restitution of all lost funds, totaling in excess of one billion dollars, plus interest from the date of each illegal loan at the rate of ten percent per annum. In the event restitution is not made by 5 P.M. on Friday, July 30, 1990, then a suit will be filed to recover those sums and to enforce all legal rights and remedies of the United States of America."

He carefully removed his glasses, placed them on the table, and folded the letter. His eyes glistened with anger. "Anyone have any ideas?"

A voice from the back of the room said, "Herb, they can't mean that. We acted as the attorneys for Cities Savings—nothing more."

"That's damn sure our position," Milbank responded. "But you try to convince the Justice Department we're right."

"What about our E and O insurance?" someone else asked.

Milbank's eyes drifted towards the ceiling. "Errors and omissions," he repeated. "Unless Lloyds of London refuses liability—fifty million. And we may need every penny of it!" He stopped, pulled a yellow sheet of notes from his coat pocket, and continued. "I've made a little outline here of what we have to do. It's my judgement that we must first hire the best attorney available to represent us. My suggestion is John Barrie of Barrie and Williams in Washington, D.C. He's handled some major malpractice litigation and been very successful. He wrote the book on bank white collar crimes and malpractice. Anyone got a better idea?"

Milbank shifted his gaze from face to face around the room, and after receiving no response to his question, said, "Then it's settled. I'll call Barrie this afternoon."

Before he could proceed further, a young attorney on my right expressed his strong views. "Herb, let's fight the bastards. We're up to it. We did nothing wrong, and they know it."

Milbank looked at him with an exasperated expression. "Sounds simple, doesn't it? Fight the bastards. Well let me remind each of you of something. Twenty five percent of this firm's client base is tied up in government related work, particularly insured financial institutions. Now ask yourselves a simple question. What do you think will happen to that work while this thing is pending? I'll tell you what—it will go away. Fellas, we're going to be blacklisted! So you better think twice when you decide to get tough with Uncle Sam."

I could see the blood drain from the faces around me with that statement. "Herb," someone else said, "if we're going to be blacklisted, what's the alternative? What do we do next?"

He shifted to look at the person asking the question, maintaining his agitated look. "What we do next," he said softly, "is keep our mouths shut. Do each of you understand that? I don't want to pick up tomorrow's paper and see a quote from anyone around this table. If I do, it'll be hell to pay for the person who talks. You got it?"

There wasn't a sound in the room. Harry leaned towards me and whispered, "He's really pissed."

Milbank stared at him. "You're damn right I'm pissed. Either we get this thing settled, and quickly, or this firm may be out of business. I have no desire to be managing partner of a defunct law firm!"

Milbank picked up his glasses, returned his notes to his pocket, and turned to look out the window. Turning back to the meeting, he said, "That's it. Meeting's over. I want each of you to go back to your offices—and back to work. No closed door meetings, and no private conversations with your secretaries. Understand?"

The entire room nodded its understanding.

He then turned to me. "Matt, I want to see you in my office." He then left.

Herb Milbank's office occupied an entire corner on the sixtieth floor. It was decorated in early battleship, probably pre-World War I. The floors, walls and furniture were various shades of gray.

Milbank was in his third year as managing partner, primarily for two reasons. No one else wanted the job and no one else was mean enough to deal with the politics of a major law firm. He looked up from his desk as I entered and motioned with his eyes that I sit while he finished reading papers lying in front of him. After several minutes, he crumpled the papers, tossed them into a waste basket, and rose to sit across from me.

"Matt, you've been with this firm for over twenty years. A long time. You've been good to us, and we've been good to you. Do you agree?"

"What's the point, Herb? You didn't call me in to rate the firm's performance."

"So right you are," he conceded. "The point is this. We have to make some major decisions if we're going to survive this government suit. Frankly, right now you're a liability. You were Braxton's lawyer, and while I know you did nothing wrong, the connection hurts us."

"How do you know I did nothing wrong?" I asked, my blood beginning to boil.

"What...?"

"Let me sum it up for you. Twenty years with the firm and you want to use me as your scapegoat—correct?"

He removed his glasses and lightly rubbed his eyes. "I wouldn't put it that way exactly."

"Then how would you put it? I'm all ears."

He cleared his throat, showing his discomfort with the way the meeting was going. His eyes closed briefly, then squinted at me. "If you took an indefinite leave of absence until we settle with the Government, fully paid for at least one year, our ability to settle with them might be improved."

"How?"

"How?" he repeated. "It would show them that we have distanced ourselves from Braxton."

"Settling with the Government could take years. You want to force me out of the firm. You know what Herb," I said, standing to face him more directly, "you can go fuck yourself! Bic Braxton paid this firm over twenty million dollars—twenty million! I don't recall you or anyone else refusing to take his money. And by the way, I wasn't his only lawyer. As I remember, his deals kept about twenty-five lawyers employed."

"Matt, you have a point. But I hope you can see mine."

"You want me to leave? You got it. On one condition. I want not only my full salary, but all bonuses I might have earned, guaranteed for not one but two years, and I also want Leigh's services, part time when I need her."

"That's pretty strong."

"Not for twenty years. Herb, you owe me that much."

He gave me a severe look and then grabbed a pen and paper. "You made $650,000 last year. Correct?"

"With bonus $800,000."

"And you want that much to take a leave of absence. Matt, the partners will never go for it."

"They don't need to go for it—you have the authority. And let me remind you of something. You're going to need my friendly help in getting this thing resolved. I know Braxton better than anyone. That's the price."

He paused and made some notes on the paper. "Suppose we pay it monthly?"

"No. Quarterly, and in advance."

"You want the first payment now?"

"No, not now. Herb, I'll give you thirty minutes to get a check."

My anger was seething, and he knew it.

"Done."

"Yeah, O.K." And so my twenty year career seemed to have ended with a twenty minute meeting.

CHAPTER 4

▼

Julia was waiting for me at a quiet corner table in the rear of the Crescent Bar. The apprehension showed in her face. She knew something was wrong. We never met in the middle of the afternoon, especially not in a bar. As I entered, my eyes first caught the light filtering through her shimmering light blond hair, and then to the expanse of the windows surrounding the bar.

She shifted her gentle eyes from a glass of wine to me as I got seated. She looked stunning, so much like the day I first met her. "I'm not sure if I want to hear this," she said.

"What are you afraid I'm going to tell you?"

"Matt, are you having an affair?"

Her question took me totally by surprise. "You must be kidding! Where did you get that idea?"

She gave me a distressed look. "From you. You did say that what you had to tell me was serious, that it would affect our future. What else could it be?"

I grabbed her hand and kissed it. "Sweetheart, I've been told to leave the firm. I've been fired!"

She tightened her grip on mine and stared at me, wide-eyed and in shock. "That's impossible," she protested. "They love you at the firm."

"Loved—past tense. The exact words were I'm a liability."

She peered at me, sympathetically, searching for the right thing to say. "Whose words…and why?"

"Our friend, Herb Milbank."

I sat back and signaled the waiter for a glass of beer. "Why? Because I represented a man named Bic Braxton, who you know well."

"Maybe not well enough," she mumbled under her breath. "But that's no reason to push you out of the firm. He was the firm's client, not just yours."

"Milbank doesn't exactly see it that way. With Braxton's indictment, he thinks the firm would be better off to distance itself from Braxton and me."

She looked at me with forlorn eyes, and then said in a subdued voice, "After all these years."

"Yes, all these years," I repeated.

She shrugged. "I know how this must hurt you, but we'll survive. At least it wasn't an affair."

I smiled and leaned over and kissed her. "You couldn't really have thought an affair—could you?"

She sat back and tightened her lips, and then smiled gently. "Well, in that firm, it wouldn't be the first. It happened to Maggie Duncan."

"But I'm not Maggie's husband."

"Thank God," she said softly to herself. She looked down, fixed on her glass of wine. Slowly raising up, she asked, "Now what?"

"I have a few ideas. Why don't we take that honeymoon we never had. Let's travel to Europe and stay in that hotel in Burgundy where we've stayed so often."

"The one in Beaune?"

"Yes."

"You know how I love that hotel—I will never forget our times together there. But Matt, after that—what will you do? Your career has meant everything to you."

"Maybe I'll just spend time with you and be happy for a change."

"Can you do that—really? For all these years, you've been consumed with your work. You know that. You go to work at the break of dawn, and I hardly ever see you on weekends."

The guilt feelings were beginning to rise. I knew she was right. I took her hand and held it tight. "I haven't been a great husband, have I? But I'll change, I promise."

"You've been a good husband and a wonderful father to Angela. I'm not trying to make you feel guilty. It's just that your obsessive nature took over, years ago, and you couldn't let go. Can you now?"

"I can, and I will. I promise." I don't think she believed me.

At first she gave me a doubtful look, and then she changed her expression. "This may be a blessing in disguise," she said with a devious glint in her eyes. "Angela is settled in Duluth, and we're free as a bird. Maybe I do believe you. Wouldn't it be ironic if, after all my years of trying, it was finally Herb who forced you to refocus your life." Her voice trailed off. "But can we afford it?"

I thought about that. "Actually, I've made some good investments we haven't talked much about. We're very well off financially, and the firm will pay me my full salary and bonus for two years. I raised my glass, kissed her again, and toasted, "To a new life?"

She hesitated, and then raised her glass. "To a new life."

She stood up, turned and raised her eyebrows, again showing her doubt. "And you won't be bored?" I didn't answer.

When we left the bar, a dark sky was descending on the city. It was beginning to rain. Fixed on the storm clouds, I didn't notice the black car sitting at the curb. Everything happened so fast. I jumped back when I heard the screeching tires and tried to grab her. It was too late. In a flash of a moment, the car had disappeared and she was lying in the street. Her twisted body lay still, blood seeping across her once beautiful face.

Paralyzed, I screamed for help. The roaring of the car was an echo in my head, and the figure lying in the street was only a blur. I felt sick to my stomach, and prayed to God that it wasn't true. But it was. She was dead.

The pain, that enormous pain, wouldn't leave. I felt I was going mad. I couldn't forget the cluster of graves, or the rain. The sudden rain, crowds of mourners in black around a burial site, the snapping of umbrellas. And a man in a robe, holding me, and people muttering brief apologies. Rain and the clapping of thunder. And no one would tell me that it hadn't happened. For months I was obsessed with all the images of my past, and my inability to deal with reality.

CHAPTER 5

▼

Three months after Julia's funeral, I received a letter. It was labeled "Official Business," and contained a summons for me to appear at the offices of the FBI in Dallas. The building was a converted warehouse on the corner of the west end, an area littered with bars and restaurants. After waiting thirty minutes, I was taken into a large conference room, brightly lit but empty except for a lone man peering out of an angled window at the skyline. He turned towards me and began arranging a stack of papers laid out on the table before him. Seeming to carefully choose his words, extending his hand he said, "I'm FBI agent Tom Archer. You're here because of your client, Henry Braxton. Please be seated, Mr. Lawrence." He nodded at a chair at the end of the table.

He turned slowly to face me, and studied me for several minutes. "Mr. Lawrence, we've been looking into you and your relationship with Braxton for some time. Successful lawyer, prominent law firm—why?"

It was an old question, one that I had heard many times. And one that I had asked myself over and over. "Because I didn't know."

"Do you want to explain that?"

"At one time he was well thought of. I liked him; he was talented and a good businessman. I had no idea what he was doing. I was his lawyer, and it stopped there. He never let me into his inner circles."

He cleared his throat, giving me no indication of what he was thinking. But I suspected he didn't believe me. Rearranging the papers in front of him, he said casually, "You lie down with dogs, you wake up with fleas." I had a strong sense of being transparent.

For a moment his eyes darted among the papers. Then they focused directly on me. "So you didn't know? That simple? Well unfortunately, Mr. Lawrence, it's not. Before Henry Braxton took control of Cities Savings Bank, he had taken bankruptcy, left his creditors with losses in the millions, and had begun to establish his connections with the New Orleans Mafia. And then he went to work looting Cities Savings. But then, you were just his lawyer. Is that what you want me to believe?"

He didn't wait for an answer. Without looking up, he slowly and deliberately pulled a chart from the stack of papers lying on the table and slid it in front of me. It looked like a tower built with an erector set, with boxes and lines moving up and down the sheet. At the top was the name Raymond Jarrett. Underneath that name was a labyrinth of other names, people and companies.

"Recognize any?" he asked.

"A few. This man Jarrett, and of course Braxton. But most of them, I've never seen before."

He suddenly stopped and turned towards the door. Standing there was a tall thin man, slightly balding with gold rimmed glasses and dark, beady eyes. He adjusted the watch chain hanging from his vested gray suit, closed the door and, without saying a word, moved to the chair across from me.

"Mr. Lawrence," Archer said, "this is Buckroyd McAlister, U.S. Attorney for the Northern District."

McAlister only nodded, making no attempt to be courteous. In a subdued voice, he said, "Do you want a lawyer?"

"I am a lawyer." I studied him for a moment and then said, "You want my cooperation, and I'm willing to give it. I have nothing to hide. I want to know all the facts, as I know you do. But I will not tell you anything else unless I have immunity from prosecution."

"Why should we do that?" McAlister said.

"I just told you why. I've done nothing wrong, and I think you must now know that, or you would have named me in the Government's suit long ago."

They both sat in silence for a long several minutes, thinking of my demand, and then asked me to step out of the room. Thirty minutes later, I was called back in. After being seated, McAlister stood up and walked to the window.

"They say you are one smart lawyer, and that's coming through to us. We know of your reputation, and we also know of your involvement with Braxton. I'll have to tell you that giving you immunity in this case flies against my better judgement, but we need you. You've got your immunity, but only within the sphere of the questions we ask you. If you ever lie to us, we won't hesitate to prosecute you for perjury and obstruction of justice. Understood?"

"Understood," I said.

"OK, let's be frank," he said, "this is not about you, but it's about these people here," he said, pointing to the chart. "We understand that you have, or should I say had, an attorney/client relationship with Braxton, and that's a fine line. What we'll ask you will not cross that line. If you think it does, you'll have the right not to answer. Agreed?"

"Agreed. What do you want to know?"

He smiled, imperceptibly, while Archer chewed on his finger nail. "Everything you can tell us about these people." His voice was deep and raspy, very unpleasant. "Start with Raymond Jarrett."

"Jarrett. I met him once in New Orleans. That's all. I don't know much about him, except that he did business with Braxton."

"What kind of business?"

"I have no idea. Braxton never included me in any of his dealings with Jarrett."

"Do you know that he has connections with the Louisiana Mafia?"

"No. I told you, I have no idea what he does."

He seemed to accept that. "And the others?"

I looked back at the chart, seeing that it highlighted a long list of foreign offshore companies, an accountant named Alan Crone, some wine merchants in Bordeaux, France, and the names of some Catholic priests. "Who are these people? And the priests, what are they doing on this list?"

"You tell us."

"If I knew, I wouldn't have asked the question."

McAlister began tapping his pencil on the table, showing his impatience with my answers. He shifted his glance to Archer, who remained silent, and then back to me. My hands started to feel clammy. "You want to tell us about the Vatican?"

"The what?"

"The Vatican," he repeated. "Home of the Pope, in Rome. Ever heard of it?"

"Don't patronize me! What are you getting at?"

He gritted his teeth and stood to confront me. "What am I getting at? Don't play games with me, Mr. Lawrence! You knew Braxton's connection with the Vatican."

"All I knew," I said slowly, letting out air, "was that he had friends in the Vatican. He made them gifts. That's all. Nothing more."

He returned to his chair, closed the file in front of him, and looked away. Adjusting his glasses, he momentarily pulled a pen from his pocket and made several notes on the paper in front of him. He puffed on a cigarette and I watched a thin stream of smoke escape through his nose. Looking up directly into my eyes, he said, "I have one more question, and then you're free to go. Tell me what you know about a company called Great West Properties."

I loosened my tie and thought deeply about his question. "Great West Properties was a company owned by some of Braxton's cronies. It owned large amounts of real estate in the southwest. In 1989, it had huge losses in those properties. Cities Savings had a large portfolio of loans it made to Great West, secured by those properties. Unless Braxton got them off the bank's delinquent loan list, the regulators would have declared the bank insolvent."

"Why the bank?"

"Because the properties couldn't be sold after the changes in the tax laws, and their market value had dropped by over 50%. So I was told he invented Sugar Daddy."

"Sugar Daddy?"

"Yes. It was the name he gave to his scheme to bail out the bank. It had a great many borrowers who were in deep financial trouble. Their loans were in default and they faced bankruptcy. Braxton had his cronies unload Great West's properties on them at inflated prices, and then showed the sales on Great West's books as profits, not losses."

"Why in the world would they do that?"

"Simple. To get their loans renewed and extended—and to avoid financial ruin. They had no alternatives."

"That still doesn't make any sense," he said. "In a falling real estate market, they couldn't finance their purchase of those properties."

"No, they couldn't," I agreed. "But the bank could, and legally, if it had appraisals showing values in excess of the loans."

"Were there appraisals?"

"I was told there were. Those sales to the bank's borrowers gave the bank a basis to substantially increase its appraisals. Braxton arranged for them."

He sat back in his chair and gave me a disbelieving look. "I'm still confused. Each borrower had to be buying a property with a built in loss—and a substantial one at that. Eventually, it would have caught up with him."

"You're right," I said. "So Braxton became their Sugar Daddy. He gave each buyer a side letter agreeing to personally cover their losses. When I heard about it, I knew it was illegal—but it was too late. He had already done it."

"You knew? But you did nothing about it. Why?"

"I didn't know for a long time. Braxton delivered those letters after the closings, without my knowledge. As far as I knew then, the properties were worth the values shown on the appraisals. I never knew, not until recently, that Braxton had the bank finance properties that had been owned by Great West and sold to the borrowers."

"Then how did you find out?"

"About a year after the collapse of the bank, last October to be exact, I got a call from a man named Charles McWhorter. He was one of the delinquent borrowers in the Sugar Daddy deal and was worried about being indicted. I met with him and he told me about Sugar Daddy, secrets I had never known because Braxton kept them from me. Braxton did it all without lawyers."

"Why would McWhorter want to tell you about all of that, particularly when it would incriminate him?"

"Because he was desperate and hoped I could help him. I couldn't."

"So what did you tell him?"

"I told him to take his story to the FBI."

"Why didn't you do that?"

"Why? Because I wasn't sure he was telling me the truth. And as a lawyer, I had ethical problems, like attorney/client privilege. I couldn't offer evidence against my client."

McAllister gave me a suspicious stare. "I want to talk to this McWhorter. Where can I find him?"

"At Restland. He died shortly after I met him. A car accident or something."

He smiled. "Why am I not surprised?" He jotted down a few notes, then stood up, and turned to face me. "They tell me you were close to Braxton—real close."

"Who are *they*?"

"Some of your partners. Were you?"

"No. Except for the work the firm did for the bank, I had no personal relationship with Braxton. We ran in different circles. It's interesting, but every time I tried to have lunch or dinner with him, he refused."

"Refused? Why?"

"I don't think he felt that comfortable with me. We were too different. Whatever the reason, I was his lawyer, but it ended there."

He seemed to accept that, paused and then whispered something to Archer. He flipped through some notes lying before him and then pointed his pen at me. "You personally closed some forty loan transactions involving Great West Properties, Cities Savings and a variety of borrowers. Correct?"

"I believe that's right."

"In those transactions," he continued, "over $200 million was funded by Cities Savings to Great West. That money disappeared. We've traced it to DFW Title, and from there to Barclays Bank in the Cayman Islands. There we lost it. It was wired to Barclays at your instructions. We want to know where it ended up."

"Barclays had second liens on the properties. The money went to pay off those liens."

"Wrong!" he said.

"Wrong? It's on the closing statements."

"You're right about that. The closing statements do show Barclays," he confirmed. "But Barclays held those liens as an agent for an undisclosed third party who got the money. We think that third party was Braxton. He's very clever. He concocts this plan, apparently to take bad properties off the balance sheet of Great West, and uses innocent borrowers who can't talk as his go-betweens. But you know what? That wasn't his plan at all. He fooled everyone, including you, his lawyer. He was laundering embezzled money off-shore."

His statement left me groping for answers. "Why don't you ask Barclays?"

"You ever heard of bank secrecy laws? Well, the Caymans have the toughest around. Impossible. Those funds disappeared, Mr. Lawrence, and we were hoping that you knew where."

"Why should I know?"

"Because you were his lawyer and because you're smart. Surely you suspected something fishy."

"I told you—I didn't. He gave me no reason to believe he was a crook."

He took a deep breath. "Braxton stole more than $200 million of the taxpayers' money. We intend to get it back. And his crooked loans left his bank with over $1 billion in losses. We intend to send him up the river for the rest of his life. You have limited immunity. If you want to clear the slate, search your brain and your files, and find the $200 million. Until then, Mr. Lawrence, you've got a problem with the Justice Department." Without another word, he gathered his files and left with Archer.

I sat for several minutes, alone, trying to assemble in my mind all the things I had just heard. And then I left.

Nine months later, Braxton was convicted of 10 counts of embezzlement and obstruction of justice. He was sentenced to fifteen years in the Federal penitentiary at Big Spring, Texas. I was constantly harassed by McAlister, but for some reason he never asked me to testify. I felt a great sense of relief when I heard about the sentence, but it didn't end my nightmares. Several weeks later I awoke at 2 A.M. in the morning, in a cold sweat. I knew I had to see Braxton.

CHAPTER 6

▼

Big Spring, Texas, 1991

Big Spring, Texas, is a desolate little community about one hour from Midland/Odessa. Although small and remote, it's known throughout the state as the white-collar country club for criminals. It houses the minimum security facility that's become home to the convicted bank felons in the southwest. While it's surrounded by barbed wire and guard towers, it doesn't look like a prison. It's more like a military base, which it was at one time.

The head librarian at Big Spring is the former chairman of a bankrupt Texas utility, the athletic director a former lineman for the Dallas Cowboys, and the prison electrician is Bic Braxton.

I was struck by the sobriety and starkness of the prison as I entered the main gate. Inside, I was taken to the main visitor area to meet Braxton. It was a sharp contrast from the lap of luxury he had been used to. Whitewashed walls, light fixtures with exposed light bulbs, uneven wood floors, and a smell of Pinesol. The furnishings were sparse, old wood chairs and tables, and the walls were dotted with small windows covered with iron bars.

The door opened and prisoner number 454 entered, dressed in gray prison fatigues. I expected to be greeted by a tired and older looking Braxton, but instead I was met by the indomitable Braxton. He still had his salt and pepper mustache, but his hair had become grayer, hinting of a man moving into his fifties. He appeared to have lost some weight, but his six foot frame gave every indication of a man at the peak of his health.

He let out a low belch as he approached. Same old Braxton, I thought to myself.

"How are you, Matt?" he asked. "Nice of you to finally visit me. What's it been, over a year? I know you want something, or you wouldn't be here."

"I'm in trouble. I need your help."

"Trouble? The whole world's in trouble. But don't let it bother you. You'll never get out alive."

"Bic, I'm not here to make jokes. I want some answers."

He pulled up a chair and placed his feet on the table that separated us. Lighting a cigarette, he blew a large smoke ring in my direction.

"Do you remember Sugar Daddy?" I asked.

He gave me a broad smile, and blew another smoke ring. "You had nothing to do with that."

"That's what you'd like me to think. But you had me close those deals."

"Yeah, but you didn't know what was going on behind the closings."

"You set me up, didn't you?"

He raised his eyebrows and looked to his right. "No. I didn't set you up." Then he slowly looked back at me. "I kept you out of it. Don't you know that?"

"Well, it didn't work. I'm right in the middle. They say you laundered over $200 million through a Cayman Islands bank, Barclays. Is that true?"

"What are you doing, working for Uncle Sam? Do you think I'll tell you what happened? If you do, you're fuckin' crazy."

"Is that what all my years of loyalty mean to you?"

He took his feet off the table and leaned across towards me. "Look, Matt, I've been sentenced to fifteen long years. I'm 50 years old. They've told me I can't get paroled, and they're threatening me with another indictment. I'm not going to spend the rest of my life here, not for you or anyone."

"Tell me what happened to the money. They know a lot. Maybe I can work a deal for you."

"A deal?" He laughed. "They don't know shit, they only think they do. Those assholes, who do they think they're playing with? Those deals were legal, on paper. We had appraisals."

"Bullshit! If they were legal, what are you doing here. Those appraisals were phonies, and you know it. And what about those side letters, Bic? They have them!"

"I've got a word of advice for you pal. Leave it alone. You don't want to know what happened." He got up to leave.

"Where are you going?"

"Meeting's over," he said as he walked away. He suddenly turned, and asked, "How's Julia? Send my best."

"She's dead, Bic."

A stunned look came over his face, and he slowly walked back. "How?"

"Hit by a car, over a year ago. I thought you knew. It almost killed me. I wish it had."

"I'm sorry. I really am." I knew he meant it.

I suddenly felt a wave of depression come over me, and I stood up to leave. "Sorry to bother you, Bic. This was a wasted visit."

"Wait. Matt, I do owe you a lot. If you haven't heard anything I've said, listen to this. I don't think Julia's death was an accident. I think they were trying to kill you."

"Oh God." I felt tremors throughout my body, and an overwhelming nauseous feeling. After regaining my thoughts, I turned to him. "Who are they? Why would they want to kill me?"

"I don't know who they are—if I did, you'd know." He put his cigarette down and rubbed his eyes. Shifting his eyes around the room as if to be sure no one was listening, he continued. "Why would they want to kill you? It's obvious to me. They think you know where the money is. Get away from it—far away. Do you remember Raymond Jarrett, that bastard in New Orleans? He's involved. And so is the Pope."

"Jarrett and the Pope? You're talking in riddles."

"You want answers," he said with a slight smirk on his face, "go see Jarrett and the Pope, but don't come back here. Get religion. You're going to need it."

With that, he was taken by the guards back through the gates, and I was left in a daze. I had nowhere else to turn. My law firm had kicked me out, Julia was dead and now I heard that someone wanted me dead. I drove slowly back to Midland, through the west Texas dust, constantly looking in my rear view mirror and wondering if *they* were out there. At times, my thoughts drifted back to Julia, and then to my meeting with Bic, and I remembered the only time she met him.

CHAPTER 7

▼

Dallas, Texas, 1987

It was in the early part of June in 1987. We had been invited to Braxton's house for a dinner party, and were entertained by politicians, movie stars and Braxton. Julia didn't like the dinner, his friends or him, but she was fascinated by his knowledge of wine.

It was on a warm night in June, late in the evening, that we sat in his massive bar with its twelve foot ceiling and twenty bar stools, surrounded by guests waiting to go home. But he wasn't ready for the evening to end. The room had an unreal greenish color, like light filtered through a fish tank. I found myself staring at him, watching his faint smile tug at the corners of his mouth. Slowly twisting the ends of his gray mustache, he flashed his dark eyes at me, winked and then broadened his smile, preparing himself for his audience.

"You see," he began, as he reached for one of hundreds of wine glasses hanging upside down in his bar (to avoid dust), "Jesus Christ should have been French. The wine served at the last supper must have tasted like crap." He then let out a low belch.

Julia stared at him, offended by his irreverence. She frowned, twisting on the edge of her chair and pushing back the curl of blond hair that had fallen across her forehead. Eyes flashing, she tucked her lower lip under her bright white teeth. "French?"

"Yeah, French. The world's worst soil—and best wines.

"There isn't bad soil in Israel?" She had decided to take him on.

He slowly twisted a cork screw into a thirty-year old bottle of wine and peered at other guests chuckling at the conversation. "What's it been?"

"What's what been?" she asked.

"Two thousand years since the death of Christ. Well the French have been busy since then. Two thousand years of trial and error, matching hundreds of different grapes with different soils and microclimates. Only the French did that! Did you know that grape varieties in France are specified by law?"

"You've got to be kidding," someone in the back mumbled.

"No, I'm not kidding," Braxton responded. "Geological composition of soil has been studied, meticulously, and marked out by experts. What's more, the area of production for each vineyard is carefully marked and controlled. And the government tells you how and when to prune. You can't go to the john without their O.K."

"So what?" Julia slightly rolled her eyes towards me, as if to say "What's with this guy?"

His audience was growing and he loved it. "Let me tell you something," he said. "If you don't do it right, like pruning and harvesting at the right time, the vines will overproduce and grapes will develop so little sugar that the wine will taste like cow manure. The French government isn't going to let that happen. Every factor that contributes to the wine, every process, every detail literally from the ground up until the bottle of wine is sold, is controlled by law. And so…you get the best wines in the world."

"How do you know so much about wine?" Julia asked, beginning to show that she was fascinated.

"Because wine is a true love of mine. I've been fascinated with it for years. When something gets my interest, I make it my business to get to know it—every detail. Your husband knows about that. He's the best, the very best, at what he does, and what I pay him for. If you've got a legal problem, he knows what to do. Why do you think he's so good?"

I blushed with embarrassment as half the room turned to look first at me and then at Julia.

Not waiting for her answer, he continued, "Because he's driven. You can't learn just a little about anything. Either you know it or you don't. In this life, you don't guess. You better know—and I do—and so does your husband. We just concentrate on different subjects, that's the only difference. But he knows."

Julia squinted at him. "How do you know he's that good?"

He shifted his gaze from the people around us directly into her eyes. In a low voice, he answered, "Because we've been in the trenches together—many times."

"The trenches?"

I nudged her. "It's just an expression," I whispered. "Drop it, please."

Julia squeezed my hand and then leaned towards me. "Are you that good—really?" she whispered back with a grin.

I ignored her question.

Braxton smiled at Julia, then me. "Yeah, he's that good. He's not recognized as one of the ten best lawyers in Dallas for nothing. Your husband's a genius. I hope you know that."

Julia gave me an approving smile. Later, as we drove away, she leaned against the door and asked, "All that money, and his love of wine. My God, Matt, why does he dress in a robe for a party like that, and why that sleazy woman?"

"Sterling?"

"If that's her name, it sure fits."

"Well, it wasn't a robe. It was a silk smoking jacket. As for Sterling, who the hell knows. That's his taste."

She adjusted her seat belt and then said dryly with a faint hint of sarcasm, "Do you want to tell me what you two have in common, if anything?"

"That's easy."

"I'm waiting."

"Brains."

*   *   *   *

I suddenly snapped out of my daydream to see the sign saying "Midland Airport—Next Exit". I returned my rental car and walked the long distance to the terminal, stopping frequently to see if anyone was following. I had an ominous fear that I was being watched. Thirty minutes later I boarded my flight back to Dallas. Landing at DFW airport left me with an immense feeling of sadness and aloneness. It no longer felt like I was coming home. The airport felt foreign and uninviting.

CHAPTER 8

▼

Dallas, Texas, 1991

My apartment in Dallas is on the twentieth floor of a high-rise known as the Athena. After Julia's death, I boarded up our house and its memories, and leased a furnished apartment. When I returned from Midland, I was met by Frank, the lobby guard.

"Hey Mr. Lawrence," he yelled out as I approached. "You got a message." He handed me a note from Claire Sorrell, Julia's best friend. It read "If you are lonely, please call for a free meal. Concerned about you. Claire."

Claire had been married to a successful doctor—too successful. It seemed he had no time for her, and their marriage dissolved. She was a dark eyed, very attractive brunette, in her early forties. Her skin was soft and creamy, and she had a face that could brighten the cover of any fashion magazine.

I entered my apartment, picked the mail off the floor, and disgorged my suitcase. The apartment was still and lonely, and I sat for a minute and stared at the blinking light on my answering machine. I hit the message button and heard the soft voice of Claire. "Matt," she said, "I'm very concerned about you. Are you O.K.? If you're lonely, please call me. A free dinner and a warm fire aren't bad on a cold night."

I unpacked, took two Excedrin for my throbbing headache, and dialed Claire. Before she could plead, I said, "Not tonight, Claire. I appreciate your offer more than you know, but I'm really exhausted."

"Matt," she said in her soft southern voice, "it's only five o'clock and you have to eat. Just come for a quick dinner at seven."

I hesitated. "OK, but I won't stay long."

"See you then," she said. "Goodbye, Matt."

*   *   *   *

Claire lived in an area of Dallas known as Bent Tree. It was a cluster of townhomes surrounding one of Dallas' most exclusive country clubs. Rolling hills and look-alike million dollar homes. The winding pebble walk led me behind a clump of six-foot shrubs to the front door, where she was waiting, dressed in a black skirt and beige silk blouse. Her house was very French, filled with antiques and furniture reflective of a wealthy former husband. She embraced me when I entered, flooding me with memories of Julia.

"You look wonderful," I said, staring at her radiant brown eyes and sparkling smile that were framed by her thick brunette hair. She was beautiful.

She winked lovingly and held up a drink. "Beefeater martini, straight up. I believe that's your drink?"

"Thank you. This may put me right to sleep."

She gave me a suspicious stare and then a slight grin. "You don't know how happy I am to see you. Over the past year, I've kept reminding myself that all things get better in time. You seem to have gotten so much better. Have you?"

"No, not really."

She rose and narrowed her eyes. "I'm sorry. I had hoped you would. In case you're wondering," she said, "I feel as bad as you do. Julia was my best friend. She's gone now, and Matt, nothing will bring her back." Her voice drifted off. "Nothing."

"I want to tell you something," I said, ignoring her question. "This is painful, but I have to tell you."

She stared at me for a moment, showing her surprise at the sudden change in my expression. "What is it?"

"Claire, Julia was murdered."

"Oh God!" she whispered, holding her hand over her mouth. "How do you know that?"

"Braxton told me."

"How does he know?"

"He wouldn't say—but he's in the middle of it. He knows. He said they were trying to kill me."

There was an infinite sadness in her eyes. Then she said in a barely audible voice, "But why you? Matt, what have you done?"

I watched her fidget, struggling with what I had said. "I've done nothing, except act as Braxton's lawyer. I was in the wrong place at the wrong time. There are people out there, without names or faces, who want the money Braxton took from his bank. They must think I know where it is and that by killing me they'll remove an obstacle to getting it."

She looked at me in exhausted disbelief, completely stunned by what I had said. "Surely you must have some idea who they are. Call the police or the FBI! You can't just do nothing and wait for them to kill you!"

I paused, wondering if I had told her too much. "I have no idea who they are—absolutely none! If I did, I *would* do something. Calling the police or the FBI is a waste of time. Braxton said that I should get far away from it, and he told me to get religion and see the Pope." I shrugged. "That's where he lost me."

She cupped her chin in her hands and stared at me. "None of this makes any sense. Why don't you start from the beginning and tell me everything that's happened."

"This could take a long time."

She came to me and took my hand. Squeezing it, she said, "I have all the time in the world."

"I'm hungry. Is dinner ready?"

Surprised by my question, she hesitated, and then said, "Yes. But I'm not sure I can eat after what you've told me."

We sat near the crackling fire, on big over-stuffed pillows. I sipped slowly on the crimson wine, staring in a trance at the broiled lamb chops and scalloped potatoes. The searing hot embers, surrounded by dancing flames, cast shadows through the old iron grate—and on the inner sanctum at work in my mind. I stared at the shimmering fire reflecting in her dark eyes, alternatively changing them from brown to amber. She adjusted her skirt and looked up at me, inviting a comment on the dinner. "It's perfect!" I said. I wondered as I watched her why she had never remarried. After dinner she asked again for the whole story.

"Another time," I pleaded. "I really am tired."

She persisted. "I'll give you a good piece of advice. Share it with me—all of it. Maybe I won't be of great help, but I'm a good listener."

"I give up. Where do I begin? I need to get from A to Z, but I can't seem to get past B. I'm stuck."

"When did you see Braxton?"

"I saw him today at Big Spring. He talks in riddles. I thought he would try to help me. He wouldn't talk much about it. In our thirty minute meeting, he told me very little."

She looked at me oddly, confused. "I thought the two of you were close."

"Close in a strange way, but that was a long time ago. He warned me to leave it alone. He mentioned a man named Jarrett, Raymond Jarrett. And the Pope."

"Tell me about this man Jarrett. Who is he?"

I swallowed hard, trying to recall what I knew about him. "I met him on only one occasion, about five years ago. Braxton and I went to his offices in New Orleans to close a loan. He's a huge, enormously unpleasant man. I hear he's connected with the Louisiana Mafia. He's very influential, politically and otherwise."

"Mafia?" She pursed her lips tightly and frowned. "That's scary! How did Braxton get involved with him?"

I thought about her question and tried to recall when their relationship began.

"In the early 1980's Braxton was broke. He lost all of his money in his homebuilding company. I heard that it was then that he met Jarrett. One of Jarrett's banks held mortgages on some of Braxton's properties. I think Jarrett saw in Braxton a way to get into the Texas business scene with some respectability. Braxton was respected, in those days, and was looking for a way to regain his fortune. Jarrett offered one."

Her eyes glittered as she continued grilling me. "But what could he possibly have given Braxton?"

"Money, pure and simple. He provided it to Braxton through companies he controlled. That enabled Braxton to buy Cities Savings."

"And what did Jarrett get out of it?"

"Who knows—but I can guess. Financing for his deals through Braxton's bank and buyers for his properties.

"What's wrong with that? It all sounds very legal."

"Oh, it was legal, at least on the surface. But there were rumors that Jarrett had secret interests in Braxton's bank."

She leaned over and placed her hand on mine. "Was it illegal for him to have an interest in the bank?"

"It could have been, if Jarrett was restricted by the Feds from owning a bank. And I suspect he was."

"So how did he get away with it?"

"For him, it was easy, He was too smart. He was implicated, many times, in illegal schemes. But they could never prove a thing."

She stood gracefully and removed our plates to the kitchen. "Coffee, decaf or espresso?" I heard her ask from far away.

"Coffee please, and very black."

"She returned briefly carrying porcelain cups of her strong coffee and sat next to me as she continued her questioning. "What do you think he meant by saying you should get religion and see the Pope?"

"Beats me. He damn sure isn't religious. But it's interesting. He did see the Pope."

"You're kidding!" she said in amazement. "Why in the world would the Pope see Braxton, or want to have the slightest thing to do with him?"

"He was a different person then. Many people, in fact, admired him. Before he was indicted, he went to the Vatican on a trip through Europe. If you want one reason why the Pope would see him—they're both Polish. And there's another one. Braxton gave the Pope a wood carving of Jesus from the twelfth century—evidently enormously valuable."

"Why would he do that?"

"Who knows, maybe to buy his way into heaven. It won't work, not for him!"

"Anything else?

I was beginning to get tired of her questions. She detected my impatience. "Would you like a brandy?"

"No thank you. Claire, I'm exhausted. Please, and no more questions. I have to go."

She left the room briefly and returned, swirling two curved glasses of Remy Martin, and handed me one. "I'm sorry," she apologized. "I know you said no, but this will do you some good. I don't mean to put you through the third degree, but I'm fascinated and terribly worried by all that you're telling me. Do you really mind that much?"

I looked into her pleading eyes and knew that I didn't. She also knew. I sniffed deeply the fumes from the glass and then refocused my attention on her. "He had nothing else to say," I assured her. "Nothing! I love you for your interest in my problems, but this discussion is not going to solve them."

"How can you be so sure?" she protested. "Maybe Braxton gave the money to the Pope."

"Now that's a crazy idea! Are you suggesting that he simply handed the Pope $200 million?"

"You shouldn't rule out any possibility—should you?"

I dismissed her question. "Let's make a list," she suggested, "of the people you should talk to. Her dark eyes glistened as she grabbed a pen and paper and began to write. "Who's number one?" she asked.

"Marianne Sandler, Braxton's secretary. She and I were good friends once, before his world came apart. She knows a lot."

"Good," she said, making careful notes. "And next?"

"Maybe his wife, Sterling." Then I thought about her and said, "Forget it. She won't help. But there's always Jarrett. Who knows, if it suits him, he might help."

I gazed at my watch. It was past eleven. "Why don't we continue this later," I suggested. "I'm really very tired."

As I rose to leave, she smiled sweetly and said, "Where and when do we begin?"

I gave her a wooden expression. "We don't! This is my nightmare, not yours. I'm not going to get you involved. Just be here when I need a kind ear and someone to lean on."

She embraced me as I started to open the door. Peering at me through half-closed eyes, she said tenderly, "Call me whenever you need someone to talk to or lean on. Matt, I'll always be here for you. And Matt, please be careful. I'm terrified thinking of what might happen to you."

I thanked her and left.

Driving away from her house, I was suddenly drawn to the rearview mirror. There was a hint of a speck of light, an image of something, a black shape. And then it was there. Far away, down the street, a car was following me. There were no headlights, just a dark moving shadow in the distance. I accelerated rapidly, made a quick turn and pulled in behind a service station. The other car flew by. I grabbed the wheel, trying to steady my nerves. "This can't be real?" I asked myself. But it was.

CHAPTER 9

▼

When I returned to the Athena, I was disappointed that Frank wasn't there. I handed the keys to my Jaquar to the security guard and walked into the empty lobby. It was eerily quiet. I ascended in the elevator to the twentieth floor. My apartment was dark, and I stood for a moment looking over the partially lit Dallas skyline and the bright red horse on top of the Mobile Towers. In the corner of my eye I saw the blinking light of my answering machine. For a brief second I thought of erasing all messages—but I didn't. I pressed the play button.

"Matt," I heard Leigh's voice say, "you have several messages from former clients. What do you want me to tell them?" Her message was followed by silence and a click, and then the voice of Harry: "Matt, are you O.K.? Please let me know how you're doing."

The third voice was my daughter Angela. "Dad, how are you? I haven't heard from you in days, and I'm worried about you. Please call me soon."

At the end, I heard a voice that sent my mood spiraling downward. "Lawrence, this is Jarrett." The message was interrupted by a series of hoarse coughs and wheezing. "I want to see you. Come to New Orleans. Tomorrow! Call me. 504-696-5000."

In the distance, I heard the roar of a jet leaving Love Field, and felt the walls slowly closing in around me. I picked up the phone book and looked up Marianne Sandler. When I dialed, I was told that Marianne's number had been disconnected. There was no forwarding number.

The next morning, Leigh was more help. She told me that Marianne had moved back to San Antonio, and that she would try to find her.

After talking to Leigh, I called Angela. She was a late bloomer, an average student with few friends who, after several rough beginning semesters in college, blossomed into a very bright student. She caught the eye of a local news director after graduation and found a career.

After two hard years of apprenticeship, she had become a lead TV news anchor in Duluth, Minnesota. Over the years, she had also become stunningly attractive. Her strawberry blonde hair and light complexion served her well before the cameras. She was approaching 24 years old, but had never married and rarely dated. I never asked her why. I think I knew that her answer would have been that her career took all of her time.

"Dad." Her voice was subdued. "I've been so worried about you. I haven't heard a word from you for over three weeks. Are you O.K.?"

"Of course. Tell me about you. I've missed you."

I could hear her quiet sigh. "Me too. Dad, I've got to tell you. I feel like I've let Mom down. She would've wanted me to watch over you. I haven't done a very good job. You never level with me. Are you really O.K., I mean really?"

My eyes closed involuntarily. "Level? No, I'm not O.K." I let out a deep breath of air and my pent-up frustrations. "How can I be? But I'm trying my very best. And I hope you are too."

"Daddy…I think every day about Mom, and I miss her terribly. But it doesn't bring her back, it just never does." She stopped and cleared her throat. Then silence.

"We've got to take care of each other, we just have to," she whispered. "So, when can I see you?"

"I don't know, but soon. I promise."

*　　*　　*　　*

That night I awoke before 5 A.M. from my troubled sleep and tried to recount all the events of the past several days. Streaks of lightning began to appear across the early dawn, followed by sharp bursts of thunder as the rains began. I shaved, showered, and surveyed my list of priorities for the day. Marianne Sandler was my first. She was the one who knew Braxton best, other than his wife.

Marianne was in her early forties and was thin but attractive. Her years with Braxton had somehow taken her through two unpleasant relationships, in both cases with bank employees. She had never married and seemed to have a callous attitude towards men.

Her former apartment manager told me she was having her mail forwarded to her mother's home in San Antonio. I called San Antonio information, asked for a Sandler on Forest Circle, and was given her number. After a number of rings, the voice on the other end said with futility, "How did you find me?"

"You shouldn't have left a forwarding address for your mail with your apartment manager. Marianne, I'm desperate. I've got to talk to you about Bic. Soon. Can I come to San Antonio?"

"No!" she screamed. "Don't you have any idea what I've been through? For the past year I've been harassed, night and day, by the FBI. They took all my records. They've threatened to indict me if I didn't cooperate. I've told them everything I know. Matt, I'm exhausted. I just can't take any more of this. Please…leave me alone."

"I can't. All I need is a few hours of your time. Please, Marianne."

She took a deep breath. "I was warned not to discuss Bic with anyone."

"Who warned you?"

"The U.S. attorney, McAlister."

"I've met with him. He won't know. Everything we discuss will be between the two of us. Please see me."

She hesitated, and I prepared myself for rejection. "If you can be here by 2 P.M. today, I'll meet you at the bar in the Menger Hotel, next to the Alamo. But Matt, you've got to promise me—this is it. One time, and then you leave me out of it."

"I'll see you then." I breathed a sigh of relief.

I hung up, finished my coffee and dressed. Several hours later I caught the Southwest Airlines' commuter flight to San Antonio.

CHAPTER 10

▼

San Antonio, Texas, 1991

Traffic on the highway between the San Antonio International Airport and downtown San Antonio was unusually heavy. At my urging, my taxi driver speedily maneuvered from lane to lane while I continually looked for anyone who might be trying to follow me.

The drive to the Menger Hotel took me past blocks of decrepit buildings, cheap tourist shops and discount stores. In the middle of it all was the Alamo, unchanged since Santa Ana. And then to its right I saw the hotel, also appearing unchanged. Neither belonged with the surroundings. The driver took my fare and tip without comment and pulled away quickly, leaving me in the middle of a blustery wind and centuries of Texas history. I buttoned my overcoat, looked around for any signs of Marianne, and walked to the entrance.

I brushed past a short balding man with a scrubby goatee as I entered the lobby. He was in as much need of maintenance as the hotel. The bellman directed me to the walnut paneled bar, with its dark red carpeting and green and blue plaid upholstered chairs and booths.

As I entered the bar, precisely at 2 P.M., I couldn't help noticing the pictures of Teddy Roosevelt that were everywhere. The bartender looked up, surprised to see anyone in his bar, and mumbled "Rough-riders."

"Excuse me?"

"Roughriders," he repeated. "Roosevelt—he organized them here, right here. See the pictures?" He pointed a glass in his hand at the wall.

I nodded my understanding and glanced around, hoping to see Marianne. The bar was empty. The feeling began to creep into me that this was a mistake, that she wouldn't show up. Two beers later the time was 2:30. Just as I motioned to the bartender for a check, a slightly built woman, dressed in an expensive fur coat draped over a dark green sweater and matching wool skirt, appeared at the door. Her sunglasses seemed out of place in the dim lights of the bar, but she didn't remove them.

Marianne had aged since I saw her last. Her hair was beginning to turn gray, and the rough life she had led showed in her weathered complexion and wrinkled skin.

She looked very worried. "Matt, I don't have much time. I'm here against my better judgment, but you've been a friend. I guess I owe you this much."

She slid into the booth across from me, and I signaled to the bartender. "Perrier," she requested. "With a lime, please."

I looked at her for a moment, feeling a twinge of regret for the passing years. "You look well." She knew I lied. "Thanks for coming. Let me get to the point. When we closed the Great West Properties' sales, a large amount of money slipped through the cracks, about $200 million. I was told that by McAlister. We wired the money to Barclays in the Caymans."

I looked at her for a reaction, but got none. "Do you remember anything about that?"

She gave me a very agitated look. "Some Federal Prosecutor! He's tapped my phones, had me followed, threatened me with criminal charges, and made my life hell. He's a bastard! He won't give up. And if you think you can cooperate with him, that he can be trusted, you're wrong—dead wrong."

"I get the feeling you're angry."

She wasn't amused. "Matt, grow up. He'll screw anyone, including his own mother, if it serves his purpose. You'd better understand that before you talk to him again—or you'll live to regret it."

"Relax, I don't like him either. Can you put that aside, just for a moment? Think back to December 1986. What were Bic's connections with Barclays?"

"He dealt with a man in London. I think his name was Alan Crone. I remember that there was a company involved with Barclays—Fidelco, or something like that. Fidelco had second mortgages on most of Great West's properties."

"Did you tell McAlister that?"

"No."

"Why?"

"You may not believe this Matt, but with all his questions, he never asked me about Barclays or the money."

I looked at her through my glass of beer, wondering if she was telling me all she knew. "What did he ask about?"

He asked about every relationship and transaction Bic was involved in, but when it came to Great West, he seemed to already know, or didn't care. It just never came up."

"Then why is he so adamant about my telling him where it is?"

"I don't know. You tell me."

I watched her fidget with her scarf, knowing she was uncomfortable with my questions. "Where do you think the money is? With that company you mentioned, Fidelco?"

"I have no idea. Bic kept a lot of things close to the vest. You knew that. Particularly money."

"Could there have been more than $200 million that disappeared?"

She responded with silence. Sipping on her Perrier, she gave me a very uneasy look. "The years have been good to you. Most men in their forties begin to look their age. You don't have a single gray hair—not one. How do you do it?"

"You're changing the subject. Answer my question."

"You must be joking!" she answered. "Where were you all those years? Matt, I swear to God, for being a brilliant attorney, you're one of the most naive persons I've ever known. Cities Savings Bank had assets of over $3 billion in 1986. In 1989, it was put into receivership. In 1990, it was liquidated. Only $300 million was recovered! Where do you think it went?"

"Where did you get those numbers?"

"From *Time* and *Newsweek*." She gave me a look that questioned my intelligence. "You really should read magazines. You might begin to learn what the world is all about. Now you answer my question. What do you think happened to all that money?"

"The collapse of the real estate market had to account for most of it."

"You know, Matt," she said as she sat back against the wall, "you always believed in Bic—to a fault. For some reason, you never asked where he got all those cars and planes. They don't come out of thin air, you know. He had so many schemes, Perry Mason couldn't figure them all out."

"Tell me about Raymond Jarrett."

"Now we're getting into dangerous territory. That man is deadly. Jarrett was Bic's tutor. Bic was always smart, but not really devious until he met Jarrett. Jarrett had the criminal mind. Matt, down deep, I don't believe Bic is bad—he's just greedy. Jarrett is scary. Stay away from him."

"That may be hard. He wants to meet with me."

"I wouldn't go, not if I were you. Not if you value your life," she mumbled, staring down at her drink."

"How much money, Marianne?"

"What do you mean?"

"How much has disappeared?"

"I don't really know or want to know," she said, showing her discomfort with my questions. "But a whole lot more than $200 million."

My stomach was churning. I was hearing things I should have known long before but was too busy to stop to examine. Another thought suddenly popped into my mind. "What was Bic's connection with the Catholic Church and the Pope. He seemed fixed on that when I saw him in Big Spring."

"He used the Church. Somehow, he got himself ingrained with Cardinal Cress in Dallas. I think he made some big donations to the Cardinal, and in turn got some big loans from the Diocese fund. The Cardinal got him an introduction to the Pope." She looked away. "Matt, there's nothing else I can tell you."

She looked so forlorn, I suddenly felt very sorry for her. "What are you going to do?"

She sat staring at me, slow to respond. "Become invisible. I thought I could come to San Antonio and escape it all, but it hasn't worked. You're here. Next time, I may leave the country. I'm just worn out. What are you going to do?"

"I don't know. Try to find the truth. And find out who killed my wife."

"Your wife? Oh no! She wasn't murdered? I thought it was an accident."

"I did too, until I talked to Bic. He thought they intended to kill me, not Julia."

She looked horrified. "Matt, I'm so sorry." She looked down, as if to avoid my eyes, and said under her breath, "If they would want to kill you, they would probably as much want to kill me. There's so much money involved, and you and I were involved in so much of what happened."

"But neither of us knows what really happened."

"You know that…and I know that. But Matt, I don't think they know that."

"Who are *they*, Marianne?"

"If I knew that, I wouldn't be so terrified. It could be Jarrett, but it could be others. Bic did business all over the world."

We finished our drinks and our conversation. I was painfully tired. She only nodded when I thanked her again for seeing me. We shook hands as she walked away, leaving me with an overwhelming feeling of sadness.

CHAPTER 11

▼

New Orleans, Louisiana, 1991

With great apprehension, I rang Jarrett the next morning and agreed to meet with him in New Orleans. I kept reminding myself that meeting with him was inevitable. But so is death.

I was met at the New Orleans airport by his driver, a husky young man with too pretty a face marked by a jagged scar across his right cheek. "I'm Bixler," he said, as I followed him to the jet black Lincoln Towncar waiting for us in the drive. It was meant for evening gowns and tuxedos. The bar was stocked with the best liquor and Tiffany glasses. I pushed the button on the television screen, and in an instant it showed, on a split screen, a view of everything in front and back of the car. Bixler stared at me through the rear view mirror, showing his displeasure with my probe. I stopped. After that, our entrance into the city was solemn. I tried to ask a few questions but he remained silent.

Jarrett lived in the center of the French Quarter, on Bourbon Street. What was once an elegant testimonial to the city had begun to show its degeneration. Old unkempt buildings were interspersed with bars and nightclubs. We passed the Royale Orleans, one of the city's great old hotels, and drove through narrow one-way streets to an old warehouse. A large door was opened and Bixler drove our car onto a huge elevator. After ascending one floor, we left the car and I was taken by Bixler down a long corridor to two large steel doors. They opened and my eyes were met by those of Raymond Jarrett.

He must have weighed more than 300 pounds. He sat in the living room, sipping on his coffee, in a silk green robe trimmed in gold piping. His thick, clawlike hands were wrapped loosely around the coffee cup. One was pulled loose as I entered the room, motioning me to sit in a large, overstuffed chair across from him.

The building had given no indication of the elegance of his apartment. The highly polished dark wood floors gleamed underneath the off-white painted walls and the expensive cream and pink old French rug. The antiques and paintings that filled the room looked priceless.

"Hey, Lawrence," he said with a faint smile, "make yourself at home." To his right was a young woman, also in a robe. There was an emptiness in her eyes. To his left sat two muscular thugs dressed in black pants and T-shirts. "You've ignored me, fella, and I don't like to be ignored."

I sat across from him and ignored his comment.

"I want to tell you a story, Lawrence," he began. "Entirely fictional, you understand, but of importance to our discussions. There was this guy, you see, who was dead broke and in great need of a backer. There was another guy, with all the needed financial resources, who wanted into certain financial markets with the right connections. He couldn't do it on his own because of what, shall we say, was a somewhat dubious reputation with Federal regulators. So they struck a deal. This second guy provided the money...and the first guy got rich. But the deal was, Lawrence, that the money would be split 80-20. The second guy, of course, to get 80."

"But do you know what happens?" he continued, his black eyes boring into mine. "This first guy gets himself in prison, but before he goes he sends the money to parts unknown—for safekeeping, he says. When the second guy says where's my money, this little shit says he's not sure but is thinking about it. He sits in his little cell and tells me, Raymond Jarrett, that he will think about telling me where my fuckin' money is!"

Jarrett began to wheeze and cough, and then rasped, "I'm an asthmatic, Lawrence, and excitement brings on attacks. Excuse me—don't leave." With that, he quickly exited to the next room, and I sat under the scrutiny of his two toughs. Minutes later, he returned with an inhaler and motioned for his servant. "Mr. Lawrence," the servant asked, "can I bring you a cup of chicory coffee, cappuccino or tea?"

"Coffee, please."

When the servant returned with the silver serving tray carrying the coffee, Jarrett had regained his composure. "Lawrence, you represented Braxton in his deals. He funneled the money, my money, through those deals and out of sight. Do you remember Sugar Daddy?"

"Yeah, I remember it. But I never saw the money."

"You're too smart for that, Lawrence. You knew!"

I looked up and caught his stare. "Go to hell! I'm sick and tired of being accused of knowing what happened to the money."

He gritted his teeth in anger. "Who was the first?" he shot back.

"The U.S. Attorney in Dallas, McAlister."

"Shit!"

He sat back, first watching the servant refill his coffee, and then staring at the woman next to him. "I might be inclined to believe you," he finally said. His wheezing started up again. "Forget where the money is—for a moment. You damn sure know the people involved, the wiring instructions, the banks. Ever heard of Alan Crone?"

"How do you know Alan Crone?"

"Answer the goddamn question!"

"I heard of Alan Crone, but I never met him and don't know him."

"Where'd you hear of him?"

"I don't remember." I lied.

"You had better not lie to me, Lawrence," he warned. "I'm in the financial business, not the killing business, but business plans change. You understand what I'm saying? I want my money! Make it easy on yourself, life's too short. Who is Crone?"

"Don't threaten me Jarrett! The only thing I heard is that he was connected with a company named Fidelco."

"Why do you say was?"

"Because that was five years ago."

"Where was he then?"

"I was told he was in London."

"London. What's our friend's connection with London?"

"I have no idea. But I want to ask you the million dollar question. If Braxton has the money, which you say is your money, why won't he give it to you?"

I could see him becoming very flushed, and he sucked deeply on the inhaler he kept cradled in his hands. After several minutes of wheezing and coughing, he said quietly, "The little bastard is going to use the money as a bargaining chip with the Feds. He thinks he can buy his way out of jail with it."

"Did he tell you that?"

"He doesn't have to. I know how his mind works. They'll keep him in for life, with one charge or another, and he knows it. There's no other way out for him."

I fell momentarily silent. "Jarrett, I'm going to ask you a question, and I want a direct answer. Did you hire someone to murder me?"

A startled look came over his face. "What in the hell are you talking about?"

"In Dallas, last year, my wife was murdered. They meant to kill me."

"Are you fuckin' crazy? Why would I try to kill you? I need you. That should be pretty obvious. Where did you get that idea?"

"Braxton."

He narrowed his eyes, showing me his wrath. "That's bullshit! If I had wanted to kill you, you'd be dead!"

I don't know if I believed him or not. "What do you want from me?" I finally asked in a low voice.

"Work for me. Get Braxton to tell us where my money is, and I'll make you rich."

"Why in the world would I *ever* want to work for you! It's common knowledge that your connected with the Mafia, and you're looking for embezzled money. I've been told by the Feds that there is $200 million or more, somewhere. You say there's a lot more. How much is there? And where is it? You're out of your goddamn mind if you think I'm going to help you find money Braxton stole from the bank."

"I guess you need to know that if you're going to help me," he mumbled. "But if this information gets past the two of us, you won't live long enough to think it through. Cities Savings made loans, about 900 of them, to about 300 borrowers in the 1980s. Your law firm handled most of them, I believe."

"As far as I know."

"Those loans," he continued, "amounted to about $3 billion. Each of those borrowers had, shall we say, a special relationship with Cities Savings. They were permitted to draw exorbitant management, leasing and development fees, not to mention brokerage commissions when the projects were sold. All legal, mind you, because each of the projects had a value substantially in excess of its loan."

"If you're trying to tell me Braxton bribed those borrowers to get fees, you're crazy," I interrupted. "And there is no way in hell Braxton—or anyone for that matter—could get three hundred different borrowers to enter into any kind of a fraudulent scheme. What could be their incentive? They each wanted their projects to succeed!"

He smiled sarcastically. "Of course they wanted their projects to succeed, but what if they didn't? What's the worst thing that would have happened if they didn't?"

"They would've had to pay their loans back. That's obvious, and that's a lot of liability."

"Did you ever carefully read your own loan documents?" he barked. "For all intents and purposes, those borrowers had no liability—those loans were non-recourse."

I sat back and thought about his analysis—and nodded my understanding. "Let me refresh your memory," he continued. "Each loan you closed for Cities Savings was with a standard loan document package. Personal guaranties ended when either the loan was paid down

20% or breakeven was met. Breakeven was met when each project made enough to meet its expenses. Every fuckin' project met the breakeven test, and every fuckin' loan became *non-recourse*! You remember what *non-recourse* means, don't you?

He glared at me for a reaction. I gave him none. "No liability...no fuckin' obligation to pay the money back. Only the projects were at risk, and they were usually underwater." I stared at him with my mouth wide open. He nodded, pleased that I had gotten his point. He ground his cigarette stub out with his huge hand and continued. "We played with those tests, Lawrence, enough to guaranty each borrower that he had nothing to worry about. So we had borrowers who would take the money whether or not they needed it—just to get the fees."

"And what did Braxton get out of it? He's smart enough to know that eventually the loans would go bad."

"There was always an outside chance," he said, licking his lips over and over again, "that property values would continue going up and the loans would be repaid. But that wasn't the reason they were made. The bank got fees for each loan, substantial fees, and they were legal. They were booked and certified by a big eight accounting firm and accepted by the regulators."

"Are you telling me," I said slowly, "that in all the years we closed loans, pouring over loan documents, Braxton never really cared if they were repaid? That he was just generating front-end fees?"

He gave me a self-satisfied grin and took several large drags on his cigarette. Then he began to wheeze and choke, and grabbed for his inhaler. "You're killing yourself," I said. "You'd better give up those cigarettes while you have the chance."

He glared at me. "Keep talking Lawrence, you're killing yourself, too."

We sat in silence for a while. The woman on his right looked paralyzed. She had hardly moved during the entire conversation. Her eyes had remained fixed on Jarrett. I wondered what kind of drugs he had her on. Eventually he looked up, made some mental calculations, and said, "Four to five points a loan. Figure, for hypothetical purposes, 4½% of each loan. I think that works out to about $135 million, not to mention other fees and income, like interest, that Cities Savings got with each loan."

"But that money couldn't be taken out without violating capital and dividend regulations."

"Wrong," he said flatly. "Since the fees were booked when they were received, they were legitimate income, income that qualified for dividends unless there were losses. There were no losses then. So the money was taken out. All legal."

"Where'd it go?"

"That, my friend, is what you're going to find out. Those funds were controlled by Braxton, but were subject to our agreement."

"What agreement?" I asked.

"We had a gentleman's agreement to avoid, shall we say, certain niceties of the law and scrutinizing by the regulators. You see, in regulatory circles I don't enjoy the best of reputations. I could have never been approved as a shareholder of Cities Savings. So we had a handshake, which is good to my death—or his."

"What about Sugar Daddy? Why so much attention to that deal?"

"Because it's the only one the Feds could prove was illegal. It was a minor rung on a big ladder, and they couldn't begin to figure out what was really going on. I trust you're beginning to see why Braxton won't get away with this. Now, will you help me or shall we discuss the alternatives?"

"What alternatives?"

He gritted his teeth and glared at me with his beady eyes. "You don't want to know, Lawrence. Let me lay it out for you. You don't have any!"

I sat there, drained. "How do you know I won't take this to the Justice Department?"

"You won't, that's the least of my worries. What would you tell them? That Braxton has money somewhere that he got legally and that part of it's mine, under a gentleman's agreement. Come now, Lawrence, you're smarter than that."

With that, he adjusted the ties on his robe, took another sip of his coffee, and said, "Lawrence, I want you to meet someone. Monica, go fetch Oetting." The woman next to him clumsily stood up and left the room. A short time later she returned, followed by a thin, cheaply dressed man. His nose and chin seemed to protrude at the same extreme angles, and his dark eyes were set far back into his head.

"Oetting, meet Lawrence. He'll be your responsibility for a while. Lawrence, this is Bird Dog. He gets his name from his extraordinary abilities. They really are peculiar. He tracks people—and sometimes kills them. He'll be your shadow until you find and return my money to me."

Bird Dog showed a brief grin, exposing yellowed teeth that perfectly fit the rest of his appearance. I glanced at him briefly and sighed in frustration. "You're missing the point, Jarrett. I'm not going to work for you."

He grimaced. "No, it's you who's not getting the point, Lawrence. Wherever you go, Bird Dog won't be far behind. Just in case you ever get it into your mind to double cross me, Bird Dog will be there to change it. He'll be my eyes, so to speak. Ever worked with a killer following you?"

I stiffened, trying to decide how to respond. He didn't wait for my answer. Turning to Bird Dog, he said, "Bird Dog, I believe Mr. Lawrence can find my lost money. You see that he does—and don't let him out of your sight until I have it."

"Mr. Lawrence," Bird Dog said with an enormous amount of severity, "Yo' understand what I got to do. It'll make yo' life mo' pleasant if yo' cooperate. My momma didn't raise no dumb Cajuns! Wherever yo' go—look 'round. I'll be there." He finished with a disgusting grin.

"Well said, Bird Dog," Jarrett murmured with a slight cough.

I smiled at both of them. "Too bad yo' momma was poor," I said.

"Huh?" Bird Dog flashed a confused expression.

"So she could fix yo' teeth."

CHAPTER 12

▼

London, 1991

Everything was beginning to seem completely unreal. In many ways, my life had changed so dramatically that it took on a dreamlike quality. When I left Jarrett, I couldn't remember a time when I felt so completely exhausted. The terror of thinking that any moment I could die was beginning to fade. Julia was gone. The only thing that mattered now was finding who had her killed.

Leaving the country and finding Alan Crone suddenly struck me as a very good idea. I had Leigh book me on British Airways from Dallas to London. My plane touched down at 6 A.M. on December 1, a cold and damp Monday at Heathrow. I hadn't seen Bird Dog, but whether he was there or not was unimportant.

In London, I began my search for Alan Crone. I found out that he had been employed by Barclays for over thirty years, but was now a part-time accountant with Bristow Limited near Picadilly Circus. The Circus, of course, is no circus at all, but an old area of London comprised of aging buildings and aging people. Crone was no exception.

I found his offices on the top floor of the Bristow Building, an antiquated walk-up in the tradition of 19th century London. The three flights of stairs were especially grueling after my long flight. On the third floor landing I stopped, out of breath, and listened for any sign of activity. There was none.

An array of early roll-top desks and wooden chairs caught my eye when I entered the office. The lone receptionist, a woman who must have been in her seventies, directed me behind a glass screen to a small corner office that had a view of the adjoining roof top. There sat an elderly gentleman with small black spectacles and a whiff of white hair. He spoke in a fragile and weak voice. "I say, gov'nor, are you the chap from Dallas?"

"I am," I said.

"And what brings you here?"

My gaze drifted first around his sparse office before settling on the mouse-like man before me. His face was long and thin, and a little flushed. He had easily passed sixty, and looked like someone with high blood pressure who was too fond of whiskey. His coloring, to an untrained eye, gave a false impression of health. He looked more like a farmer than an accountant.

"Mr. Crone, during the period of 1986 though 1989, you were employed by Barclays, or was it Fidelco?"

"Barclays," he answered dryly. "I handled the wire transfers for certain U.S./U.K. transactions. Fidelco was not my company. We just officed in the same building. What is it you want?" His bloodless lips turned down, waiting for my answer.

"I'm an attorney in Dallas. I'm trying to piece together a series of wire transfers involving Cities Savings Bank and its borrowers during that period. I was told you could help." His lack of interest was apparent as I spoke, and he added to my concern by ignoring my question and walking across to a water cooler to obtain a drink.

"Thirsty, Mr. Lawrence?" he asked.

"No thank you. Do you remember those transactions?"

He shook his head and looked at me with blank eyes. "No I don't. I bloody well handled hundreds of wire transfers each week. My memory isn't that good."

"Maybe this will help you. There was a lot of money involved, in excess of $200 million. It would have come through your branch in the

Cayman Islands for the account of Cities Savings or possibly Fidelco. There were probably a number of these wire transfers, all taking place in 1986 through 1989."

"I remember transfers involving Fidelco, but I can't tell you about them. You 'ever heard about the Bank Secrecy Laws? I'm bloody well bound to them." He then lowered himself into a wooden chair across from me.

"Mr. Crone, you're no longer with the bank. I'm not asking for confidential information—just information. I'm sure you're a pensioner. Life must be difficult with inflation at such a high rate here. I could make it worth your while."

He parted filthy blinds next to him and momentarily peered out the window. Looking back at me, he said flatly, "How much? It will do me no bloody good to get caught up in a bank scandal."

"There won't be a bank scandal. I'll pay you 1000 pounds, cold cash. Just tell me about those transfers."

"That's a lot of money." He pensively scratched his chin, thought for a moment and nodded his approval. "What I remember is that funds were routed from Dallas through the Caymans to London, for the account of Fidelco. There were about 40 transfers in all, each one greater than $5 million. All of the transfers took place in 1987 and 1988."

"Was Fidelco an affiliate of Cities Savings?"

He thought about my question and fidgeted with his pencil. "Not that I know of. I told you, I was not connected with Fidelco."

"How do I find them now?"

"Beats me," he answered in a distant voice. "Any address they had then would be in the files at Barclays. No one can see those files without proper authorization."

"Can you get it?"

"Maybe. It would take a lot of risk on my part. What would it be worth to you to see the whole file? Another 1000 pounds?"

"Mr. Crone, you'll have the money when I get the files."

Our meeting ended with his assurance that he would contact me the next day at my hotel, the Grosvenor House near Hyde Park. When I finally checked in, exhausted, it was nearly noon, which was 5 A.M. in Dallas. I immediately went to bed and slept soundly until I was awakened by the shrill sound of the telephone ring near 5 P.M. The voice on the other end was Leigh. "Matt," she said with a startled voice, "Marianne's dead. She was murdered!"

"What? How do you know that?"

"I was glancing through the Dallas Morning News. There was a story, buried in the back pages, that a Dallas woman had drowned in San Antonio. It was Marianne. They found her floating in the canal." There was a moment of silence, and then she said quietly, "Matt—please be careful."

"I will," I mumbled. I was suddenly overcome by feelings of sadness and futility. "Listen carefully, Leigh. I want you to go to Buckroyd McAlister at the Justice Department. Tell him what happened. Tell him I need his help."

"What help? What should I ask him to do?"

"Tell him that Marianne has been murdered and that I'm in London at the Grosvenor House. Ask him to get me whatever he can on a British company named Fidelco. Tell him that Fidelco is somehow involved with the money taken by Bic Braxton. Will you do that?"

"Yes, of course," she said. "Where do I find him?"

"He's at the Federal Courts Building, downtown. Don't call, he may not believe you. Go see him in person."

"I'll go now if he's there. Please be careful. I'll call you as soon as I meet with him."

I hung up and tried to collect my thoughts. Dead...she only tried to help. Deep inside I heard my pulse pounding in my ear and a distant voice saying, "Because of you." But why? The evening sky had darkened and I looked out on the orange cast of the moon as it slowly drifted behind a thick layer of clouds. London, seemingly always overcast and damp, added to my feeling of gloom.

Two martinis removed a lot of pain. I followed them with a dinner of steak and kidney pie. My spirits lifted, I walked across the street into Hyde Park. Still no sign of Bird Dog—I couldn't decide if his absence was good luck or a bad omen. I sat on a park bench, in the dark mist of the London night, watching normal people carry on with their normal lives. It was inconceivable that mine would ever be normal again, if I could manage to preserve it. Suddenly it occurred to me that if someone had wanted to kill me then, I was a perfect target. I rose and quickly returned to the safety of my hotel, challenging my sanity every step.

The concierge met me as I entered, with a message. It was from Crone, and said simply, "Meet me at 9 A.M. Bristow Building. I have what you need."

What I needed was sleep. I was physically and mentally exhausted. But as I drifted off, I was again jarred by the phone. It was Leigh. "Matt, he wouldn't listen to me."

"What do you mean, he wouldn't listen?" I said amazed. "I'm just asking for his help."

"He...he told me it was a mistake for me to be involved. He said they now have evidence—he said hard evidence—that you lied to them about Braxton. He said this was your attempt at a smoke screen, that the Justice Department doesn't cooperate with people it's targeted for criminal investigation. Why would he say that?"

"That's ridiculous," I said, fumbling for words. "Leigh, just forget it. Thanks anyway."

"Matt, I don't have any idea of what's going on. Is there anything else I can do to help?"

"No...nothing. Thanks." And our conversation ended.

*   *   *   *

The next morning, as I tried to hail a cab, I was drenched with sheets of wind and rain as I was introduced to the worst of London.

Finding a taxi in good weather, when it exists, is a severe challenge. But in the rain, it's impossible. I began walking in hopes of finding a ride, and shortly saw a black cab releasing its passenger. I quickly jumped inside and asked for the Bristow Building. "Where you from, mate?" the driver asked.

"From the colonies."

"The colonies? Cute, mate," he said. "In this gale, you may never find another cabbie. You want me to wait, or will you be a while?"

I considered his suggestion and asked him to wait. "What's your name?" I asked.

"Edwin Hagan.

"Well, Edwin," I said, as I shook my soaked umbrella all over his seat, "I'm in a hell of a lot of trouble."

"Ain't it what I told the misses this morning. Daedra, I said, this world's a bloody mess. What with the IRA and all those lunatics, you never know when your time's up."

"Do wait," I reminded him as we finished our short ride. "I won't be long."

The downpour had subsided as we pulled in front of the Bristow Building. Andover Street in the rain gave the appearance of an old master's painting—multi-colored umbrellas dotting the skyline along the old shops with their black and green awnings, framed in old brick and stucco. The Londoners, in their Burberry coats and wool caps, moved quickly along the slick sidewalks in their typical British fashion. It was a scene I held onto as I again climbed the three long flights to see Crone. He was waiting for me—alone. For some reason it did not occur to me, in our first meeting, to ask why the offices were empty.

"Mr. Lawrence, sir," he said with obvious anticipation of his expected reward. "Are you prepared to pay me for my troubles?"

"I am, but first let me see the file."

He reached into his bottom drawer and placed a battered thick manilla folder on his desk. It was marked, in black lettering, "Barclays—Fidelco IAT." I noted with interest the apparent authenticity of the file and asked, "Is this all of it?"

"It is, and now the money."

I withdrew 2,000 pounds from my wallet, handed it to him, and opened the file. As Crone verified his payment, I scanned the 30 or more wire transfer confirmations, instructions from DFW Title Co. and a number of rerouting instructions authenticated by Crone. My quick addition resulted in an amount in excess of $150 million. "What does IAT mean?" I asked.

"International account transfers," he answered. "A label placed on all wire transfer files for funds originating outside the U.K."

The confirmations in the file all showed, as a first destination for the money, an account with Barclays styled "Fidelco A.G." Why, I thought, would the money have been placed in a British account, not subject to international secrecy restrictions, when they might have been sent to a Swiss or other numbered account? "Mr. Crone, this isn't much help if I don't know who Fidelco is or where the funds ended up," I said as I tried to show some disappointment.

"I thought you might ask, so I had the account file of Fidelco pulled up on the computer. It's a Dutch company. Shareholders are not disclosed, but the Managing Director is Sir Phillip Hollaway, a local barrister. I doubt you'll get much from him, though. He died last year. If you'll look closely at the file, you'll find that Sir Phillip authorized further transfers of the funds."

My interest peaked as I thumbed through the communiques and wiring instructions signed by Hollaway. The file was littered with some forty communiques instructing Barclays to transfer funds to three French banks: Credit Agricole, Banque Paribas and Societé Generale. The transfers were made over a four month period, each was to a different account, and each was code named "YANOU". "What is YANOU?" I asked as I continued to sift through the papers.

Crone frowned and gave me a very puzzled look. "I don't have the slightest."

"But you approved those instructions. Surely you knew what they meant?"

"Those code names were identification for the receiving bank—they were of no interest to us. I approved the transfers because they were properly authenticated."

"Authenticated? How?"

He yawned. "See the Power of Attorney—signed and sealed. That's the authentication."

I pulled out a document at the bottom, stamped with a red wax seal. It was labeled "Irrevocable Power of Attorney," and was signed by Sir Phillip Hollaway. It read that Sir Phillip was the person authorized to sign wire transfers. Attached were the articles forming Fidelco as a limited liability company under British law. Its shareholders were not disclosed.

"Why in the world would you accept an authorization of Hollaway designating himself?" I asked, shocked at the shabbiness of the transaction.

"Because he acted in two capacities, one for the company, and the other for himself. Perfectly legal and backed by proper company documentation. Look, Mr. Lawrence, I've done my part of the bargain. No more questions. I've taken enough chances just getting this file. As far as I'm concerned, I've never heard of you or the file. Good day sir."

With that, he made it clear that I was invited to leave, and I did. I tucked the file under my arm and descended the creaky staircase to the first floor, where I was pleased to see Edwin and his cab. The rain had stopped and the air had become brisk. I glanced in the back seat and saw a figure slumped in the corner. The door of the cab was thrown open as I began to retreat, and there sat Bird Dog.

"Hey Lawrence," he said, "how'd we do. I'm past due to repo' to Mr. Jarrett."

"Dead end, Bird Dog."

"Get in," he said, and I did. He smiled as he pulled the Fidelco file from under my arm, and repeated "dead end?" He nodded to Edwin to drive off, and then he turned to me and said, "Hey Lawrence, 'splain this 'ere file to me."

"'Splain it?" I thought out loud. "To a retard?"

"Look 'ere," he said, pointing a gun in my direction.

"Is it loaded?" I asked, flipping it up towards his face. His eyes pierced me like a dagger, showing his intense anger.

After a few tense moments, I told him a little about Crone and he scratched on a piece of paper. He then motioned to Edwin to pull over. "Yo' runnin' out of time. Mr. Jarrett is a nervous dude. I ain' goin' to wanna be 'round when he hears ma' report—yo' may have no mo' future. Yo' get my point? If I were yo', I'd sure 'nuff concentrate 'ard on telling me where Braxton stashed the loot." He stared at me and threw the file across the seat. His finger shot up into my face and he grimaced. "Get off yo' mound of bullshit!" The door slammed and he was gone.

"Some bloody bloke, that one," Edwin mumbled. I nodded my agreement.

At the Grosvenor House, I laid out the file and again searched for any clue to the missing funds. I felt completely stifled. The only person connected with the transfers was Hollaway, and he was dead. I carefully placed the instructions and communiques across the bed, by time sequence. First, the twenty odd original wire transfers from DFW Title to Barclays, then the forty odd rerouting instructions from Hollaway sending the funds to the French banks. Each one had a date, the amount of the transfer, the sending and recipient banks, account numbers, and the international routing numbers. In addition, the first twenty bore the contact name of Alan Crone, and the forty rerouting instructions had no contact but only the code "YANOU."

I then examined several notes and pieces of correspondence which referenced the transfers and confirmed various dates and sums, all seemingly consistent with the transfers themselves. Then I chanced upon a scrap of paper on which was jotted "Institute for Religious Works." What was the Institute for Religious Works? It seemed hopeless. While Crone had secret access to the file through evidently his old contacts at Barclays, I had no access at all to the French banks. And even if I found access, the likelihood of locating any of the money, after four long years, had to be non-existent.

After pouring a mini-bottle of Bombay over ice, I turned on the television and laid back on the bed, surveying the scraps of paper and feeling the enormity of my isolation. I closed my eyes and thought of Julia, Angela and even Claire, as the BBC reported on an IRA car bomb in the financial district. In stark contrast to the realities of life, Princess Di was next interviewed, radiant in a black silk evening gown, as she exited a royal limousine for the one millionth royal affair.

I was jolted out of my stupor by a brief report of local interest. London had just experienced its two hundredth homicide for the year. An almost insignificant crime rate. An aged accountant, the report went on, was found shot to death in the Bristow Building. I jumped up and stared at the screen. It was Crone. He had been murdered, the reporter said, at the end of the day by a burglar in the empty third floor offices. Nothing of value was taken, but the offices were left in disarray. I was stunned. It was no chance incident. I felt a sudden chill.

In desperation, I picked up the phone and dialed Claire. The voice at the other end said, "Hello, this is 967-4412. We're not able to come to the phone at this time. If you'll please leave a number, we will return your call shortly." The voice was a man's voice.

"Claire, I need you," I said. "Please call when you can," and I left my phone and room numbers. I walked to the window and stared out. Marianne and Crone had been murdered, both a short time after meeting with me. Why? And why not me? I was scared and knew I couldn't stay in the Grosvenor House. Checking out quickly, I left by the rear of the hotel and grabbed a cab for the Dorchester.

When I was settled in the room in the elegant old hotel, I double locked the door, searched my cellphone for the number of the Hotel de la Poste in Beaune, France, and dialed (33) 80 24 19 71. The assistant manager was an old friend from the trip Julia and I had taken to the hotel. "Martine Paulet, s'il vous plait." I didn't expect to find her in—it was 8 P.M. in Beaune—but the response was "Attendez."

Within a short time I heard her soft voice. "Allô."

"Martine, this is Matthew Lawrence. Do you remember that my wife and I have stayed at your hotel?

"Yes, of course I do. It's good to hear from you. Do you need a reservation?

"No, I'm calling for a different reason."

"How is Mrs. Lawrence?"

I took a deep breath. "She's dead."

"Oh,…I'm so sorry. Is there some way I can help you?"

"Actually, you can. If I provided you with account numbers at three French banks, could you help me find out who owns them?"

"Mr. Lawrence, do you know what you're asking? French banks are controlled by the government. No one has access to accounts—I can't even deal with the hotel's account without special authorization, and I'm an assistant manager."

I accepted her rejection. "Have you ever heard of the Institute for Religious Works?"

"No. What is it?"

"I don't know, but it seems to be connected in some way with a series of wire transfers I came upon."

"Where is it located?"

"I assume France."

She paused, with a deafening silence, and then said, "I really don't know, but I'll ask my stepfather when I talk to him next. He is an editor for the British Economist."

"When you talk to him," I said, finishing our conversation, "please have him FAX any information to my secretary Leigh in Dallas. You have my number in the hotel files."

*   *   *   *

My next call was to Harry. He was my last close friend at the firm. Harry was loyal to the core—to the firm and me, but not to his wife. I had always wondered why.

"Hear you're building up a lot of advantage miles, Matt," he said.

"Yeah, a lot!

"Fill me in. What's going on over there.

Before I could answer, he said, "Oh, Matt. Did you know the San Antonio police want you for questioning?"

"I'm sure it's about Marianne Sandler. Do me a favor—stall them."

"How?

"Easy. Tell them I'm in England and that I won't be back for a month."

He mumbled something, and then said, "Is it true?"

"Would I lie to you?"

"I'll cover for you. So what have you found out about the money?"

"I've traced it part of the way, at least to three French banks. There's a lot of money involved—in excess of $200 million was evidently sent over here by Braxton. Right now, I've reached a dead end. I got a file from a former employee of Barclays that details a lot of the transfers. But I don't know how to get past the French banks. The only clue I could come up with is a code name for the rerouting transfers— YANOU. And I came across a name in the file, the Institute for Religious Works. Whatever that is, it may be an important piece of the puzzle."

"Can't this guy help you with the French banks?"

I took a deep breath. "He's dead, Harry, killed within hours after I met with him."

"Jesus! Sandler and that guy. Matt, you're the angel of death."

"You've got a point, and believe me, it hasn't escaped me."

"So who's doing it?"

"Harry, I don't have a clue. Maybe Raymond Jarrett and a creep he has tailing me, named Bird Dog."

"You must be kidding."

"I'm not."

"I'm going to get one of our paralegals to run YANOU and the Institute through our Lexis research system. It may give us nothing, but you never know. Where can I reach you?"

"Lee knows. See her. But Harry, keep it to yourself."

At 7 A.M. the next morning two messages were slipped under the door. The first was from Claire. It read, "Dear Matt: Leigh told me where you are and what has happened. I am booked on the evening flight to London. Will arrive at Heathrow 9 A.M. I need a change. What you're doing sounds exciting. Claire."

As I began to read the second message, I was totally flabbergasted.

CHAPTER 13

▼

The message was from Harry. It was stamped "LEXIS RESEARCH CENTRAL" and read:

Copyright (c) 1987 The New York Times Company;
The New York Times
July 18, 1987, Saturday, Late City Final City Edition

"SECTION: Section 1; Page 2; Column 4; Foreign Desk
"HEADLINE: Institute for Religious Works—Top Italy Court Annuls Warrants Against 3 Vatican Officials
"BYLINE: By ROBERTO SORO, Special to the New York Times
"DATELINE: Rome, July 17
"BODY:
"In a major legal victory for the Vatican, Italy's highest court today annulled arrest warrants accusing an American Archbishop and two other Vatican bank executives of fraudulent complicity in the billion-dollar collapse of Banco Ambrosiano.

"The warrants, issued in February, have strained relations between the Italian Government and the Vatican, which asserted that its sovereignty was under assault and that the investigation of the 1982 collapse of Banco Ambrosiano, a Milan-based bank with close ties to the Roman Catholic Church, was not being conducted in good faith.

"The ruling today comes as Italy's powerful magistrates, who combine the roles of judge and prosecutor, face widespread accusations that their decisions are often arbitrary or politically inspired.

"Responding to an appeal filed by the Vatican, the Supreme Court of Cassation in effect nullified all existing accusations against the American, Archbishop Paul C. Marcinkus, and his two colleagues at the Institute for Religious Works, which operates as the Vatican's bank.

"Now Free to Leave Vatican

"The three officials, who have lived behind the Vatican's walls for almost five months to avoid arrest, are now free to leave the tiny city-state.

"'I am happy,' Archbishop Marcinkus said. 'I have always had faith in justice.'

"Neither he nor the Vatican offered any further comment.

"The 26-page arrest warrant signed by two Milan magistrates asserted that three people—Archbishop Marcinkus, who is president of the Vatican bank, Luigi Mennini, the managing director, and Pellegrino de Strobel, the chief accountant—had taken part "in the diversion, concealment, dissipation and in any case destruction" of Banco Ambrosiano's assets.

"When Banco Ambrosiano went under and its chairman, Roberto Calvi, was found dead hanging from Blackfriars Bridge in London, it left debts worth $1.3 billion. In their warrant, the investigating magistrates argued that the Vatican officials had "full knowledge" that their dealings with Mr. Calvi were helping him to secretly divert Ambrosiano's funds to a string of shell companies in Europe, South America and the Caribbean.

"These allegations, which have not been in the form of a judicial indictment, are supported by many documents, according to the magistrates.

"Vatican Agreed to Pay

"In 1984, the Vatican bank, a major shareholder in Banco Ambrosiano, agreed to pay Mr. Calvi's creditors $250 million as part of a bankruptcy settlement but insisted this was not an admission of guilt in any misdeeds.

"Archbishop Marcinkus, who cooperated with the investigators by providing them with documents and memorandums through his attorneys, has told recent visitors to his office that he put his trust in Mr. Calvi, as did many other bankers as well in the Italian state, and that Mr. Calvi betrayed them all.

"In April, Pope John Paul II criticized the "exclusive and brutal" treatment of Archbishop Marcinkus, a 65-year-old native of Cicero, Ill. Several Vatican officials have recently expressed a suspicion that the arrest warrants were designed to embarrass the church, which remains an influential force in Italian politics.

"The court said its ruling today was definitive and thus beyond appeal by the magistrates. But following a common practice, the court did not immediately reveal the reasons for its decision, and lawyers close to the case said it was unclear whether the Vatican officials might be liable to further legal action in the investigation of Italy's largest postwar bank failure. The court is expected to announce its reasoning within several weeks.

"SUBJECT: Institute for Religious Works

"ORGANIZATION: Banco Ambrosiano; Roman Catholic Church

"NAME: Soro, Roberto; Marcinkus, Paul C.

"GEOGRAPHIC: Rome (Italy); Italy"

I flipped the page and came upon copies of magazine articles from *Time, Newsweek* and U.S. *News and World Report*, all dated in 1987, which gave more details to the bank scandal involving the Institute for Religious Works. It involved two suicides, both of which could be murder. As much as $1.4 billion in lost funds. The failure of Banco Ambrosiano, one of Italy's largest and most prominent banks, which left more than 200 international financial institutions holding the bag. A scandal that threatened the stability of the entire international banking system, and a secret plot to undermine the government of Italy and to change the shape of politics in several Latin American countries.

The involvement of power, mysterious deaths, corruption at the Vatican—it had all the ingredients of a mystery thriller, but it was real life. I noted that when Roberto Calvi, the 62-year old president of

Banco Ambrosiano, was found hanging from Blackfriars Bridge, they found some $13,000 in various foreign currencies in his pockets, as well as 12 lbs. of bricks and stones.

I learned that Instituto per le Opere di Religione (I.O.R.), referred to in English as the Institute for Religious Works, was founded in 1942 to invest and increase the funds given to it by the Holy See (a synonym for the Vatican) for religious works. In time, it began to operate like any other international commercial bank. It accepted savings and checking accounts, and transferred funds in and out of the Vatican. But in international circles, it remained "offshore and unregulated."

I also discovered some interesting differences between I.O.R. and other banks—tucked away in the medieval tower of Sixtus V. Depositors must be connected with the Vatican. The list of those eligible included members of the Curia (the Pope has a personal account, no. 16/16), the 729 permanent residents of Vatican City, and a small group of clergymen and laymen who have regular business dealings with the Vatican. No others could apply.

Archbishop Marcinkus, according to the articles, was alleged to have issued letters of patronage, indicating that the Vatican stood behind Calvi's ventures, which included some ten dummy companies. Calvi, who was dubbed by the Italian press as "God's banker", was thought to have been murdered. His secretary had died a few days before in a plunge from the fifth floor of the bank's Milan headquarters. The church was dragged into the mess with Sicilian financier Michele Sindona—convicted of fraud in the collapse of the Franklin National Bank of New York—who was Calvi's partner and mentor.

I searched for further information about Sindona and discovered that he died in a jail cell after drinking coffee laced with cyanide.

Throughout the entire investigation, the stories read, the Vatican declined to cooperate—citing its status as a sovereign state. It had managed to keep the entire affair veiled in secrecy! And it was never established whether the multiple deaths were murder or suicide.

*   *   *   *

I glanced at my watch, noticed that Claire's plane landed in less than an hour, and quickly dressed and left to meet her. The day was beautiful—the air crisp and clean, but cold. I hailed a cab and was delighted to see my friend and former cabbie, Edwin. "Edwin, what a coincidence. Can you get me to Heathrow by nine?"

"No problem, mate," he said. It struck me briefly that maybe this wasn't a coincidence.

The American Airlines' flight from Dallas was within minutes of being on time. My feelings were mixed as I watched Claire walk down the ramp towards me. She looked tired from the long flight, but stunning. Her beige wool slacks and silk blouse, with a black and orange beaded necklace, were draped in a full length black mink coat. She said hello with a broad smile.

"What a surprise, Claire."

She shrugged lightly. "I hope you don't mind that I'm here. The message on my answering machine was too intriguing." She gave me a cool level stare.

"Do you really know what you're getting into?"

"Matt, we don't need to debate this. The simple truth is that I'm bored in Dallas, and being here to help you sounded incredibly exciting. You and Julia were always dear friends to me, and with Julia gone, I didn't want you to be alone. I felt I could help. So where do we begin?"

"At Barclays, in their wire transfer section," I answered, taking her arm. "I want to learn more about some wire transfers."

We grabbed a cab, and I was relieved to find the driver was not Edwin. I filled Claire in on what I had found out since we met last on the way to Barclays. At Barclays, we were ushered into the wire transfer section and introduced to Ms. Clarissa Boles, an assistant controller for the bank. Her dark hair was combed tightly against her head. Oversized dark shell-rimmed glasses made her eyes look vague and empty. She wore a one-piece linen dress with no ornaments of any kind, not even earrings. "Mr. Lawrence?"

I nodded yes, introduced Claire as my assistant, and tried to smile. "Ms. Boles, I represent an American investor about to transfer large sums of money in an acquisition of a London firm. It's our intention to use your bank. Could you please explain to us your wire transfer procedures?"

"The procedures are elementary," she said. "In addition to the funds being on deposit with us, we require only the name of the transferee bank, its address or routing number, the beneficiary's name or code, the account number to which the funds are to be sent, and the originator's complete name."

"And who can give those instructions?"

"Anyone. Anyone whose authorization appears in the files." She added that all wire transfers internationally made by Barclays were made and settled by SWIFT.

"SWIFT? What's that?" Claire asked with a heightened sense of interest.

"SWIFT is an acronym for the Societe for Worldwide International Financial Telecommunications. It was organized under Belgian law and is the international communications system for messages among its member institutions. Its members are banking organizations engaged in transmitting international financial messages. Unlike Fed-Wire and Chips," she went on, "which are facilities for communication and settlement, SWIFT is purely a message facility. It links members, national communications' centers and regional processors devoted exclusively to the transmission of SWIFT messages."

"Does that include wire transfers?" I asked.

"Of course. Settlement between members is made through offsetting debits and credits to correspondent accounts maintained with one another or intermediary banks. Unlike FedWire, settlement occurs through arrangements external to the system."

"External?"

"Yes, in other words, secretly."

"As in codes?"

"Yes."

We sat in a moment of silence as I contemplated my next question, but before I could speak Claire asked, "Is the Vatican bank a member of SWIFT?"

"Do you have business with the Vatican bank?" she asked.

"We might," Claire answered.

"Yes, the Vatican bank is a member, but we rarely see its transactions."

"Why?" I asked.

"Because its purposes are limited. It's not open to general depositors, but serves exclusively the Pope and his chosen few."

"Have you ever heard of the code name called YANOU?"

"No, why do you ask?"

"Because I have seen that name on wiring confirmations. I thought it might mean something to you."

"If you want me to check on it, I'll be happy to do so provided it's not classified in the bank."

"What would make it classified?" I asked.

"Only if the transferee requested that it be." After a slight pause, she added, "I'll check and contact you if you'll tell me where you'll be. In the meantime, if we can be of assistance to your client, please call on us. Good day." And she excused herself.

I had the curious feeling that she knew we were lying. As we left the bank, I took Claire's arm. "I'm impressed—Dr. Watson would have been envious."

"Would you have expected less?" she smirked. "Now, I would like some rest and a charming dinner with you tonight. Is that a fair bargain?"

"It is," I conceded.

Our rooms at the Dorchester had adjoining doors—she closed hers. I took two Excedrin and rested, in dead silence, staring at the ceiling and asking myself "why?"—over and over.

I was jolted out of my trance by a sound. Metal turning, squeaky hinges, and a soft voice. "Matt...are you awake?"

"Oh yes, only thinking."

"Well, it's time to get dressed for dinner."

She left and reappeared forty-five minutes later in a red silk crepe cocktail dress with a gold amethyst necklace and diamond earrings.

I took stock of myself as I tied my yellow silk tie and put on my double-breasted blue blazer. My eyes looked tired, but otherwise I was pleased.

"Will you tell me our plans?" she asked, taking my arm.

"For tonight, tomorrow or next month?"

"Just like a lawyer! Tonight will do for now."

"A quiet evening. Dinner at Chanterelle. And if you're up to it, dancing at either Tokyo Joe's or Stringfellows."

She frowned at me. "Tokyo Joe's sounds dreadful. Do they require bomber jackets? Stringfellows, please!"

There are two ways to make sure a restaurant is always crowded—either build it too small or serve marvelous food. Chanterelle did both. The restaurant was like a courtyard of flowers under the moon, and the candles on the white table cloths flickered as we were escorted to our table in the rear. It was the first time I had had dinner with a woman since Julia's death. I felt very uneasy, but Claire was radiant. Her long brunette hair was swept back across her forehead, exposing her soft brown eyes and full red lips. I glanced at her as I reviewed the wine list. "How do you manage to be so beautiful after such a hard trip?"

She peeked back at me with playful eyes. "I thought you were depressed. Could it be that it's passing? And to answer your question, you give me good reason to be beautiful—and thank you for the lovely compliment. I'm glad you think I am." I had a very difficult time taking my eyes off of her. She looked back at me, with half-closed eyes, giving me the sensation that I was being manipulated. It was a feeling that I had known before. But I didn't mind.

After two martinis and a bottle of wine, the Lobster Bisque, Rack of Lamb and Grand Marnier souffle were like an afterthought. My memories blurred with my vision, and the past disappeared into the present.

She looked at me and smiled. "Shall we go dance? The evening's still young."

I paid the check, retrieved her fur coat, and we took a taxi to Stringfellows. Stringfellows is one of the most distinguished clubs in London—dark, private and understated. It's frequented by politicians and royalty, carefully chooses its' members and permits outsiders in only if vouched for by members. When I called, I used as my sponsor Sir Sidney McGarrety, a highly respected London barrister I worked with in the past. Sir Sidney and I had become good friends, and he had encouraged me to use Stringfellows whenever I was in London. I frequently took him up on his offer. It was easily my favorite club anywhere.

"Good evening, Mr. Lawrence," I heard as we were greeted at the door by the maitre d', Joseph. "So good of you to join us tonight," he added. "May I take the lady's fur?"

"You may, Joseph. A quiet table, away from the dance floor?"

"Of course, sir." He led us to a remote table, lit only by a small candle.

"Matt, it's perfect!" Claire remarked as Joseph showed us to our table. A single piano player, Marie Osnevour, played and sang the old favorites. As we were seated and ordered our drinks, a Bailey's Irish Cream for me and a Cognac for Claire, she sang *I Wish I Didn't Love You So*.

She smiled. "I don't want to appear forward, but would you like to dance?"

I took her hand and led her onto the tiny dance floor. Marie sang *"Will this be moonlove, nothing but moonlove, will you be gone when the dawn comes stealing through. Are these just moondreams, grand when the*

moonbeams, but when the moon fades away will my dreams come true."
Claire melted into my arms. I closed my eyes and felt the warmth of
her body as we swayed across the floor.

When I opened them, I noticed a single flame in a dark corner,
someone lighting a cigarette. It was past midnight and Stringfellows
was virtually empty. The song ended as we walked to our table. I said,
"I've got to get up early in the morning. Shall we call it a night?"

"So early?"

"I'm going to the Vatican in the morning."

"The Vatican. Why?"

"After tonight, I want to make a confession."

"Matt, be serious."

"I am serious, Claire. Very serious," I said, still watching the cigarette in the corner. "There are people there I want to talk to—if they'll
talk to me. I'm hoping for a change that I'll get some honest answers."

"OK. What time does our plane leave?"

"At ten."

"I'll be ready," she declared, as she picked up her purse to leave. I
noticed that the cigarette in the corner was being put out and I
motioned to Joseph.

"Joseph, the person in the corner. Who is it?"

"Not a member, Mr. Lawrence. He's alone, sponsored by one of our
American members. A strange fellow, indeed. He seems to have developed a great interest in the two of you—he's been watching you all
night."

"I want to leave without him seeing us. How can I do that?"

"Walk down the back hall, past the rest rooms. I'll have a cabbie
waiting."

I leaned towards Claire and motioned her to follow me. "Don't ask
any questions," I cautioned, "just follow me. Quickly!"

We both exited down the hallway as Joseph detained the stranger
with what had to be amazing small talk. I pushed Claire into the wait-

ing taxi as she grabbed my arm and demanded, "Now, Matt, explain. Who was that?"

"Jarrett has had a man following me. He goes by the name Bird Dog. I know that was him."

"Are we in danger?"

"I don't think so, at least not until I find the money."

"If he found us at Stringfellows," she suggested, "don't you think he knows where we're staying?"

"It's possible. Tomorrow we'll check out early. Maybe we'll lose him on the way to the airport."

"Maybe? What if we don't? You haven't so far."

"Let's worry about that tomorrow," I said while I constantly looked over my shoulder all the way to our rooms. When I tried to deposit Claire in her room, I was stopped by her protest. "Oh no you don't," she said. "You tell me we're in danger, that we're being followed, and then leave me to sleep alone? Not on your life! You can sleep on the sofa."

CHAPTER 14

▼

Italy, 1991

The cloud cover was heavy as our Air Italia 727 descended to land at the Rome airport. We caught a glimpse of the Colosseum and then Saint Peter's Basilica as we landed. Within and beyond its seven hills, which lay along the winding Tiber River, were scattered the old Roman imperial ruins. The ancient churches and monuments, surrounded by a modern metropolis, were an incredible sight.

Vatican City covers 108 acres sprawled over a hill west of the Tiber River, separated by a thick, high wall from the City of Rome that surrounds it. The Lateran Treaty of 1929, signed by the Holy See and Benito Mussolini, established Vatican City as an independent and completely sovereign state. It was this declaration of sovereignty that made possible the Vatican bank, and the veil of secrecy that surrounds it.

As we drove along the Via della Conciliazione and approached St. Peter's Square, I was in awe of the enormity of the square and basilica. Claire reached for my hand as we pulled in front of the I.O.R. for our meeting with the Monsignor. I paid the driver and we stepped out into the magnificence of the Vatican. The doors to the Institute of Religious Works were bronze, towering over my 6'1" frame, but they opened with a slight push. There we were greeted by an attractive receptionist who directed us to a massive marble lobby. We were seated in large red velvet chairs facing an old tapestry of the death of Christ. She asked us to wait there for her further instructions.

After almost 30 minutes, she reappeared and asked that we follow her into a large oak paneled conference room. The silence was deafening. A large mahogany table sat in the middle of the room surrounded by eighteen red leather chairs. The floor was dark green marble, overlaid with what appeared to be a very old and valuable oriental rug. Old tapestries hung from the walls, depicting religious history from centuries long past. We could hear the echoes when we whispered, the room was so cavernous. We spoke softly.

My call the day before to Monsignor Bertellini had seemed, at first, futile. He was the Assistant Director of the Vatican bank and told me unequivocally that no one of significance at the bank could meet with us. It was not until I mentioned Braxton, and my suspicion that he was connected with Roberto Calvi, that the Monsignor agreed to see us.

Eventually the large oak doors opened and we were introduced by the receptionist to three men, one of whom was dressed in a flowing red robe with a black sash, the other in white, and the third in a conservative blue suit with a striped English spread collar shirt. The first, we were told, was Cardinal Ramoni, the second Monsignor Bertellini, and the third Angelo Braschi. They were solemn and reserved, and remained silent as we all became seated. We faced them across the wide expanse of the massive conference table.

The Cardinal had thick lips and furrowed eyebrows. He looked at us, cautiously, and lit a cigarette. I guessed his age at 60. The Monsignor appeared to be quite a bit older—probably in his seventies. His shock of white hair hung over his forehead and framed his gentle, but tired looking, blue eyes. He slumped in his chair, seeming to take no pleasure at being included in our meeting.

Angelo Braschi was far younger than the other two—at least in his early forties. His jet black hair was combed to a point above his forehead, slicked down by hair lotion that he must have saved from his childhood. His face was puffy and tanned—looking like he had been bitten by a bee. His brown eyes glared at us through heavy rimmed glasses while he tapped lightly on the table.

"Gentlemen," I began, unsure of how to address the Cardinal and Monsignor, "I'm the attorney for Bic Braxton. Mr. Braxton, as you may know, is in prison at the U.S. penitentiary in Big Spring, Texas. He had substantial dealings with the Vatican in 1986 through 1989," I bluffed, "and through his London barrister wired a sizable sum of money to the Vatican bank. As his attorney, I'm here to verify the safety of the funds and their location."

"Signore Lawrence," declared Angelo Braschi with a thick Italian accent, "I'm the Controller for I.O.R. We agreed to meet with you only because you raised the specter of a connection between Signore Braxton and Roberto Calvi. You mentioned nothing in your previous conversation with Monsignor Bertellini about any funds. The dealings of the I.O.R. are, of necessity, extremely confidential. We do not, under any circumstances, discuss them with private individuals. I'm afraid you made your trip for nothing."

Claire stared at him, incredulous, showing her disdain at what he was saying. "Mr. Braschi," she said in an extremely agitated voice, "I'm Mr. Lawrence's assistant. I assure you we did not make this trip for nothing. Did you happen to read the Friday edition of the Wall Street Journal? If you did, then you must have noticed the front page story concerning Olivetti's Chairman Carlo De Benedetti. He was just convicted and sentenced to six years in prison for aiding a fraudulent bankruptcy in Banco Ambrosiano's collapse."

"That had nothing to do whatsoever with the Vatican bank," Cardinal Ramoni quickly interjected.

"Whether or not it did is not the issue," Claire replied. "The issue is Banco Ambrosiano is still front page news, and the Vatican bank was unquestionably connected with its collapse. If you have no interest in talking to us, maybe the Italian press would. Bic Braxton and his dealings with the Vatican would surely be of interest to your local papers."

Her timing was perfect. The hostile looks we had received from our hosts quickly turned to surprise and then obvious fear. I was totally astonished by her revelation, and particularly by her source of information.

After a short huddle, we were addressed by Cardinal Ramoni. "Our committee exists to protect the bank. The bank has suffered from the publicity surrounding Calvi and Banco Ambrosiano. Within bounds, we'll try to assist you, but we must have your assurance that our discussions will never leave this room."

"You have our assurance," I promised. "Tell me, what is this committee you refer to?"

"It's known in the Vatican as the Shadow Committee. It was formed by the Holy See to monitor the events surrounding Banco Ambrosiano, Roberto Calvi, and the I.O.R." His voice became barely audible. "Mr. Lawrence, the very foundation of the Catholic Church and its sovereignty are at stake. The bank scandal is intolerable to the Holy See...surely you see why it's within our power to take whatever steps are necessary to protect the Vatican."

"Of course," I said, "but you have absolutely nothing to fear from us. I have only one concern—to confirm the location and safety of Mr. Braxton's money."

"How do we know that you act for him?" Braschi said in an agitated voice. He sat hunched forward, waiting for my answer.

I offered my business card. "You're more than welcome to contact him in the Federal penitentiary, but somehow I don't think that would be good politics for the Vatican. Do you?"

Monsignor Bertellini cleared his throat and then answered in a distant voice. "It wasn't good politics that our bank ever dealt with him— we know that now."

"Then why did you?"

"Why?" He let out a deep breath. "Because we had no reason to question his credentials. He was introduced to us by Cardinal Cress of

Dallas. He made several substantial gifts to the Vatican, gifts that were very much appreciated."

Claire eyed him suspiciously. "And what did he get in return?"

"You don't know?" Braschi seemed surprised.

"No, we don't. Are you going to tell us?"

His response was interrupted by Cardinal Ramoni. "This money you refer to," he said, "why don't you know where it is—why do you come to us? Surely Mr. Braxton knows where his own money is."

"He can't get to it while he's in prison. That's why he sent me." I lied. "The funds were wired to your bank, by code. But why don't we get to the point—where are they?"

"What if we told you we can't help you?" Braschi said, fidgeting with his pen.

"We'd think you were lying," I answered.

Claire sat quietly, taking notes and nodding occasionally.

"Mr. Lawrence," said the Monsignor, "suppose you provide us with what you want. Give us the details of these so-called funds belonging to Mr. Braxton. We'll let you have whatever information we feel at liberty to give you."

"Have you got a pencil?" I asked. Braschi was the only one to reach into his pocket, and he removed a gold plated pen.

"Take this down." I continued. "About $200 million was wired to accounts in three French banks in 1987 by a company called Fidelco. The funds came from Barclays in London. The French banks were Credit Agricole, Banque Paribas and Societé General. They were simply way stations. The funds left those banks, evidently within seconds, and were wired to either the Vatican bank or accounts in the name of the Vatican bank. Fidelco was controlled by Sir Sidney Hollaway, a London barrister acting for Mr. Braxton who died last year. We want to know where those funds are now."

"You've given us little information," Braschi complained. "What else can you tell us?"

"There was a code on the wire transfers—YANOU. Does that mean anything to you?"

They each shifted in their seats, looked at one another, and together nodded no. "We'll check for that code," Braschi said. "Give us several days to get back to you. And by the way, don't get your hopes up." He stared into my eyes—belligerently. "Where can we reach you?"

"I'm not sure," I replied. "I'll be back in touch with you in 48 hours. Please don't disappoint us. We have a common goal. We're not trying to harm the bank or the church—we're simply here representing our client, Mr. Braxton."

With that, we exchanged formal goodbyes and left the conference room for the long walk down the entry hall. As we left, Claire whispered, "Where did you learn to lie so well?"

"And when did you start reading the Wall Street Journal?"

She smiled, with an apparent sense of satisfaction, as we pushed through the doors onto the street. Rome was beginning to look dark through a dense cover of clouds, and a curtain of rain started to descend on us. "Stay under the overhang," I yelled, as I ran into the street to hail a taxi. I immediately saw a cab, sitting on the opposite curb, and rushed to the driver. He rolled down his window and stared at me, indifferently.

He nodded to the back door, but when I reached to open it, he pulled an object from his coat. Suddenly, I heard a sharp crack and felt a blast of cold air. "What?" My knees slowly crumpled beneath me and my vision blurred. I tried to get up and run, to shout to Claire, but I was paralyzed. In the distance I heard shouts and the pounding of feet…and people screaming. The pavement pounded against my head, and I heard the driver gun his engine and race away.

My shirt was slowly turning red and I knew, lying in the wet street, that I was dying. In the far distance I heard a voice shout "un' ambulanza". My world turned into darkness.

Several hours later I woke up, in a dim hospital room, with my arm and chest bandaged tightly. A nurse was nearby, and I tried to speak, but my throat was too sore. My flesh felt clammy, and my head throbbed. "Claire," I whispered, but no one heard. I felt panicky, dizzy—I couldn't breathe.

"Matt, I'm here." I felt a tight grasp of my hand.

"Claire," I whispered, "are you alright? I thought they might have killed you…like Julia."

"I'm OK, Matt. Please be quiet. The doctor is on his way. I won't leave you."

"I didn't want this to happen, not now…not this way."

"Please don't try to talk. You were shot in the chest, very near your left shoulder. The doctors removed the bullet. You were very lucky. They tell me the bullet didn't hit a vital organ. You're going to be alright. Matt…. if you had died," she said faintly, becoming very choked up, "I don't know what I would have done."

She continued to hold my hand while we waited. I could hear the sound of rain running down the spouts, dripping off the eaves of the building, and her quiet sobbing. Her wet hair dangled across her shoulders, and stains of blood were smeared on the front of her coat. After a while an attendant in a white uniform came in, hurriedly talked to a nurse in staccato Italian, and left as she gave me a shot.

I slept through the night, waking at times to feel the pain shooting through my head and shoulder. In the morning I woke to see an exhausted Claire and a doctor who spoke in virtually unintelligible English. Claire left, and I laid for what seemed an eternity, trying to control the thoughts—and fear—racing through my mind. I couldn't.

*   *   *   *

She returned as it was beginning to get dark, dressed in a beige skirt and forest green cashmere sweater, and wearing a London Fog rain coat. She took my hand, held it tight, and stared at me with sad eyes. In a hushed tone, she said, "Oh, Matt. Why—why this?"

I stared back, but couldn't answer.

"I checked us into the Excelsior," she said.

Hoarsely, I said, "Us?"

"Yes, us. Your chest and shoulder are bandaged tightly. The doctor tells me that you can leave the hospital. Matt, I know you are in pain. I won't leave you. But we'll be better off if we don't stay here. Don't you agree?"

I nodded slightly, and with the help of two nurses, dressed. Within fifteen minutes, I was helped into our hotel room by the bellman and Claire, and into the bed. The bright green and yellow furnishings couldn't relieve my feeling of hopelessness. She sat across from me, looking equally as despondent. Gently rubbing her eyes, she said in a hushed tone, "Who would want to do this?"

I had no answer.

"There was no reason to kill you, not now. We learned nothing."

"Maybe they think we're getting too close. Maybe the answer is at the Vatican and they don't want us to find it."

"Did you recognize who shot you?"

"No." I closed my eyes, silently reminding myself of two facts. We were no closer to the money, and we were not safe—anywhere.

"Claire, listen to me. I want you to leave—now. I never meant for it to go this far. I don't want you involved."

"Matt, it's too late. I am involved. If I hadn't been with you at the Vatican, I don't know what might have happened." She stopped, as if to catch her breath, and turned to look out the window. Then she turned back to face me, looking flushed and defiant. "I won't leave you, Matt. You might as well stop trying."

The next morning we had coffee in our room and I confronted her again with my fears. "You've got to go home. I can't protect you. I don't even have a gun."

"Well, let's get one."

"You've got to be kidding! I wouldn't know what to do with a gun if I had one, except maybe get arrested."

"Well I would," she said, with a sight smirk on her face.

"How do you know about guns?"

"I was president of the gun club in college, and a marksman to boot."

"I'm impressed. Do you have any ideas on what we do then?"

"Yes. Get away from here for several days, until we hear from the Vatican." She stood up, walked to the balcony, and then spun around to face me. "I've thought this through. Rome isn't safe for us. Let's rent a car and drive north, to Lake Como. There's a hotel there, the Villa d'Este, where I stayed with my husband. It's very remote and quiet— no one will find us there. We'll stay there until you feel better and we hear from the Vatican. At least we'll be safe."

I was warming up to her suggestion as she talked. Just being safe was extremely appealing. "OK", I agreed. "But we'll go by train. I can't drive, and cars can be traced. By the way, how are we registered in this hotel?"

"I thought of that, Matt. You'd be proud. Under my maiden name, Reynolds." She then picked up the phone and had the concierge reserve a private compartment for us on the 10:30 train to Como.

The next morning, after I had taken medicine for my pain, she helped me dress and we inconspicuously checked out. Thanks to Mussolini, Italy's national railway, the Ferrovie dello Stato, is efficient and runs on time. We boarded the Settebello Rapido thirty minutes early and went quickly to our private compartment. It was reminiscent of the 20's—dark red velvet seats trimmed with gold and walnut panels. After we were settled, I locked the door and laid back, feeling my wound and very dizzy. "No gun, Claire," I mentioned as I closed my eyes.

"What do you mean, no gun?" she asked.

"Don't you remember yesterday? We said we were going to get a gun."

The train lurched forward as Claire reached into her purse and displayed a small Beretta pistol. Will this do?" she asked.

I was momentarily speechless. "Where did you get that?"

"The concierge and I got to be good friends. It's amazing what good a little Lira will do in the right place. You see, he has a friend, who has a friend..."

"I get the picture. Is it loaded?"

"Of course. What good would it do us if it were not?"

I again closed my eyes, thinking of the clinking sound of the rails and this interesting woman sitting across from me. Our ride to Como was a most uneventful six hours, for which we were both grateful. I had a difficult time getting off the train—my chest and shoulder were very painful. But Claire arranged to have me wheeled into the station, where we got our luggage and caught a cab to the hotel.

Although it was the dead of winter, the pansies were in full bloom and the lake was overcast with a heavy mist that reminded me of a scene from an old mystery novel. The weather was brisk and cold—around 40 degrees.

Our room in the Grand Hotel Villa d'Este was on the second floor, facing the lake. Opening the drapes, we saw Lake Como unfold before us like a Renoir impression—it was spectacular. Our room was large, with a writing desk, sofa and separate sitting room. But most of all, it was peaceful and quiet. The next several days were a blur. I found myself wanting to do little other than sleep. Claire changed my bandages with the loving care of a trained nurse. Gradually, I could feel myself recovering. The pain slowly left, but the numbness remained.

We talked little. Claire kept to herself, reading books provided by the hotel. But she was always there if I needed her.

On the third day she called the Vatican and asked for Monsignor Bertellini. She was told that he was away. When she asked next for Mr. Braschi, they said he was busy but would return our call shortly. She frowned as she hung up. "Matt, there's something wrong. They're either intentionally avoiding us or they're trying to find out where we are. In either case, I'm worried." She turned and stared blankly out onto the lake.

"Aren't you looking for ghosts? The Vatican is a busy place."

She scowled at my remark. "You didn't hear the responses I did when I called. It was as if everything had been rehearsed and the secretary was reading from a script. Do you suppose the Vatican is somehow mixed up on the wrong end of this? Surely they couldn't be conspiring to keep the money."

"If they have it, why not? The Vatican has a very dubious reputation in the way they run their bank. So what do you think we should do?"

"You don't do," she answered. "You're still too weak. I'm going back to Rome, back to see Signore Braschi."

"Oh no you're not! Claire, you go nowhere without me. If my recovery takes two months, so be it. We go together."

She backed off and looked at me wistfully. "How can we just sit here for several weeks? We don't have the time."

"We don't have a choice, do we? Sorry, Claire, we're going to have to wait this one out until I'm well enough to go back to Rome with you."

CHAPTER 15

▼

On the fifth day I felt well enough to walk into Como with her. We strolled through the Piazza Cavour, down the Via Vittorio Emanuele and between the Porta Vittoria and its five tiers of arches.

We found a quaint little bistro in the square where we ordered beer and wine, and sat staring over the mist that covered the lake for several hours. She looked at me with a sheepish grin as she sipped on her wine. The tension of the past week had disappeared from her face, indicating a relief that our nerve-racking journey since the Vatican was slowly coming to an end. "How are your chest and shoulder?" she asked.

"Much, much better, thank you." As I answered, I became abruptly aware of our aloneness, and how time had somehow lost us. "Claire, what day is it?"

"December 22—almost Christmas?"

"We've missed the fall. Where has time gone?"

"Matt, have you thought about Angela? You must want to be with her for Christmas."

"What can I do? I can't go back, not yet. And we haven't found out anything at the Vatican."

"Let's call her, and have her meet us here. We never told her about your being shot. We must call her, tell her what's happened, and ask her to join us."

"Angela has been through so much. I'm not going to get her involved in this. Angela's had a tough time with her mother's death and her tough schedule as a news anchor. Her career is very important to her. I don't want to take her away from it, or have her worrying about me, particularly not now. We manage some telephone time—that's enough for now."

Claire fiddled with her wine glass. "Do you want to know something funny?" she said. "If all this intrigue ended, I think I would be disappointed. Oh it scares me, but it suddenly has made me think differently about my life. I'm beginning to think again about what's really important. And Matt, it's not charities and social gatherings—all the things I seem to have gotten myself so wrapped up in."

"What have you concluded—what is important?"

"I haven't decided that yet. But Matt, what about you? There are people out there who are trying to kill you, but you won't stop. Why?" She reached into her purse for her lipstick as she waited for my response.

"Shouldn't that be obvious by now? My wife is dead, my law career is finished, my reputation is shot because of Braxton, and someone is trying to kill me. Do you see any other choice for me?"

She shook her head no in frustration. As the sun was beginning to set, we boarded a water taxi for the return trip to the Villa d'Este. Our launch glided by the Villa Piniana on the east side of the lake as we watched its spring of mountainous water rise and fall in silence. I looked at Claire in the eerie emptiness of the boat as we passed Isola Comacina and its rustic small inn and restaurant, Locanda dell' Isola. She spotted the pink stucco buildings, cradled on the shore of Como between horse-chestnut trees. "Matt," she said with a lift in her voice, "let's have dinner there tonight—it's charming."

I nodded my approval.

At the hotel, I called Angela. It was late morning in Duluth, and I hoped to find her at home. I succeeded. She labored with my explanation of what had happened and expressed total disbelief when I told her someone had tried to kill me. When she asked when she could see me, I answered, "Sweetheart, I have to finish my business here, in Italy. It's literally a matter of life and death. Please understand. I'll see you soon." I was glad that we talked but knew I had frightened her. I hadn't wanted to do that. I had an overwhelming feeling of sadness.

The evening felt very chilly as we boarded the launch for the restaurant. Claire wore a long silk evening gown, laced in navy blue and silver, that caused her some difficulty in boarding. As she was assisted by a crew member, I noticed that the boat was empty except for a lone passenger, in the corner, who seemed buried in his newspaper.

Pointing in his direction, I said in a muffled voice, "There in the corner, does he look suspicious to you?"

She turned nonchalantly towards him, then back to me. "No…just an Italian businessman wrapped up in the day's news."

"Could you read in the dark?" I whispered back.

She turned to me, raising her eyebrows. "Come now. Surely you don't think that here, in the middle of nowhere, he's following us?"

"I don't know, but do you have your gun?"

Her inquisitive look vanished and she suddenly looked in his direction. "I do," she said. "Do you want me to shoot him?"

"Don't be cute."

We sat quietly, for the rest of the journey, observing our suspicious friend and the terraced gardens along the lake. When we docked at the Inn, we were relieved to see that the object of our concern stayed on board. We were escorted along the waterfront promenade to the Locanda, a 15th century villa nestled among private gardens and huge pine trees. There we were led through the Inn, a pre-World War II decorated restaurant that opened onto a glass enclosed dining terrace, overlooking the lake and the villas along its banks.

The restaurant was fairly crowded with well dressed, seemingly affluent Italians, with a sprinkling of German and English speaking couples. We were seated in a far corner having a magnificent view of the lake as the moon began to rise in the sky. The only light was afforded by a tall candle in the center of our table and a street lamp from the 19th century in a park across from the Inn.

"Tomorrow we go back on the quest," I said with a renewed conviction.

Claire's eyes lit up as she leaned slightly across the table to whisper, "Do you mean back to Rome and the Vatican?"

"Yes," I answered as quietly. "I don't have a choice—I must return."

"Well, I'm ready. But Matt, do you really believe they'll tell you anything? They have no reason to help you. In fact, they'll be motivated to do the opposite. What do you think you'll accomplish?"

We were suddenly interrupted by the waiter who presented us with our menus and mumbled something in Italian. Claire straightened up, directed her full attention to the waiter, and said, "Ci porti una bottiglia di buon vino locale, per favore." The waiter nodded and responded "grazie" as he walked away.

"Where in the world did you learn…."

"To speak Italian that well?" She smiled. "I studied Italian for several years—in between my marksmanship classes."

"What did you just say?"

"I just ordered our wine, a very good local wine. Are you pleased?"

"Yes, of course. You continue to amaze me. First, I learn you're proficient with guns, and now Italian. What next?"

"You had better not ask, or you might find out," she said with a wicked grin.

I began to study the menu when I spotted a man approaching our table. He was fairly husky, well groomed, with a long mustache and a full head of hair, and wearing dark tortoise-shell rimmed glasses. He looked very familiar. "Don't look now," I whispered, "but we are about to meet the newspaper reader on the boat."

Claire paused and then looked up into the face of our visitor as he pulled up a chair at our table. "Signore Lawrence, pardon my interruption," he said. "Let me introduce myself. I'm Helmut Schmidt, a member of the Swiss Guard. I was sent to see you by Monsignor Bertellini."

He spoke with a broken German accent. Claire gave him a frozen look and asked skeptically, "What's the Swiss Guard?"

He studied her expression before answering. "It's one hundred men, assigned to guard the Pope."

"But you're not Italian."

"You're very perceptive, madame," he said. "I'm not Italian and I don't even speak the language. For the most part, the men of the Swiss Guard are Frenchmen and Germans. The reason should be obvious— it protects His Holiness against eavesdropping."

He reached into his coat, pulled out his wallet, and displayed a red and green card, impressed with his picture and the apparently official seal of the Pope. "Will you accept this as proof that I'm telling you the truth?" he asked. "Time is short. I must speak to you."

"So speak," she said impatiently, peering at him with doubting eyes.

He spoke in a hushed voice. "Signore, you're into things that will cause great problems for the Vatican. You're creating danger not only for yourselves but for others. The Holy See cannot let you continue. Monsignor Bertellini asks that you cease your inquiries, immediately, and that you return to your country. We cannot help you, and we cannot take responsibility for your safety."

"Is that a threat?" I asked. "From the Roman Catholic Church, from the Pope? Mr. Schmidt, what in the world are you people trying to hide?"

"Signore Lawrence, we have nothing to hide, but this is beyond our control. I'm here because of the Monsignor's concern for the two of you. There has been too much scandal, too much violence. The Pope was almost assassinated. We can't let it continue. That's beyond question."

"Are you saying that the attempted assassination of the Pope is connected with Braxton?"

"Of course not, there's no relationship. But violence leads to violence. Someone tried to murder you, at the Vatican!"

Claire studied him intently, causing him to shift in discomfort. Narrowing her eyes, after a moment of silence she said, "Mr. Schmidt, if you're really here to help us, tell us what's going on. For starters, tell us what you know about the shooting of Matt. And then tell us about the Vatican's relationship with Mr. Braxton, and where the money went that he deposited with your bank."

"I don't have that information," he replied, peering at her over the top of his glasses. "Your answers can be found only at the highest levels of the Vatican, but any effort on your part to obtain them would be wasted. You must understand the Vatican is committed not to let this go any further."

"What if it does?" I asked. The waiter interrupted our conversation to pour the wine.

Looking frustrated, Schmidt stood up. "It's late. I have to leave." He hesitated, and then added, "You're making a mistake, a very grave one. I'm sorry for both of you."

"Tell me," Claire said, "you didn't really expect us to stop based on your warnings, now did you?"

"We hoped you would," he said, showing his feeling of futility with our response. "If you only knew the danger you're in."

"You must be joking! Matt was shot at your precious Vatican, and you say if we only knew."

He paused. "One thing," he said. "Before you go any further, talk to the Monsignor. Please do that," he pleaded.

Claire took a sip of wine, glanced over her glass, and asked, "You know who shot Matt, don't you?"

The light from the street lamp reflected in his glasses as he sat back and appeared troubled by the question. "We have our suspicions, but they're only suspicions. If they're correct, however, you're wasting your time. Believe me, you'll never find the money—never. Now, it's getting late and I've interfered with your dinner. Please excuse me, but I must go. Consider carefully what I've told you, and believe that it comes from the Monsignor only with the greatest concern for your well being."

Schmidt left, and we sat staring at each other. I could see Claire questioning, in her eyes, what I was thinking. "OK," she threw out, "let's have it. Now it's you who are thinking about quitting. Can't you see that's what they want. Matt, they're not concerned about our safety, they're concerned about the Vatican and the money! They have it, Matt. Now I know they do. The Monsignor, he's our answer."

"What if he won't see us?"

"He will. Remember, Schmidt said to see the Monsignor. He was giving us a message."

"Your bravery is commendable."

She stared at me, lost in deep thought. Then she refocused her eyes and asked softly, "Is it Jarrett and Bird Dog?" Studying my expression, she then added, "Or maybe Braxton?"

"No, it's not them," I answered, looking out the window at the street lamp that was now being leaned against by a tall man. "Jarrett has no reason to try to kill me. He still needs me. I don't think he has any hope of finding the money without me. As for Braxton, he never had those kinds of connections, and even if he did, what would be his motive? It's someone else."

"But the Vatican knows," she said with a serious look as she began to review her menu. "Matt, Schmidt all but told us they knew who was behind all of this."

"No, Claire, he said they had suspicions."

"We have to go back. Matt, we're smarter this time. If you're concerned about meeting the Monsignor at the Vatican, let's arrange to meet with him somewhere else, somewhere safe."

"I like your idea. Where? What if he won't meet us outside the Vatican?"

"How about in the middle of the Sistine Chapel. Or better yet, in a confessional." Her eyes lit up. "We'll wear disguises."

"Surely you're kidding. This is beginning to sound like Laurel and Hardy!"

"I'm not kidding. It's necessary and we must do it. And I've got the perfect disguises."

"What are they?"

I watched her contemplate my question and could almost hear the wheels turning. Here was a woman of grace and charm, in a setting of intrigue and murder, plotting like a spy. Her hands were in her lap, her eyes focused on the flickering candle as she answered. "What would be the most inconspicuous disguise you could imagine?" she asked.

"I have no idea, Lady Sherlock. You tell me."

How about a priest and a nun, in the Sistine Chapel. It would be perfect!"

"And where in the world would we get our robes?"

"Oh, that's simple. From the Monsignor. He'll want to meet with us without anyone knowing. It will be easy."

I thought about her plan as I reviewed my menu. "What will you have," I asked, again noticing the man against the lamp post.

"I'll begin with crostini—in your language, Matt, liver paté—and will have as my entré trota salmonata with asparagi. How do you like my plan?"

"I'm thinking," I said. "Have you by chance noticed that man outside against the post. He's been there for over an hour."

She looked up, somewhat startled, and put down her menu. "I thought we had eluded everyone until Schmidt, but now I would guess he's there watching us. Who do you suppose he is?"

"I don't know, but if he's still there after dinner, I'm going to find out."

I gazed around the glass enclosure as we talked, and for the first time noticed red and green lights on several boats in the lake. "What do you suppose those lights mean?" I asked.

She looked at me oddly. "You really are out of touch, aren't you? It's December 23. Those are Christmas lights!"

I shook my head and smiled.

Reality crept back when I saw the man outside staring at us through the mist. It was almost 11 P.M. when we finished, and it was time for me to meet him.

I walked slowly down the path, around to the side of the restaurant. He looked the other way as I approached. It was dark, but under the lamp post I could see well enough to make out his features. He was at least six feet two and must have weighed in excess of two hundred pounds. He appeared to be in his early thirties, and his coarse complexion and facial features added to his menacing appearance. When I was within fifteen feet, he spun around and raised towards me a long-nosed weapon, a pistol with a silencer.

"Buona sera, Signore Lawrence," he said in a husky voice with a hint of sarcasm. "I've been waiting for you. Did you think we wouldn't find you?"

A wave of terror came over me as my breath in the cold clouded my vision. It hit me how stupid I was to be out here with him alone. "What do you want?"

He saw my state of panic and grinned. "Want? We want you to die. That's not too complicated, is it?" He then leveled the gun at my head, and I found myself praying for salvation as I expected the shot. It came, but it wasn't silenced. A look of surprise and then terror came over his face as his coat began to turn red and he fell backward into the bushes behind the post.

There, behind him, was Claire, holding a gun and trembling in the cold. "Matt, I had to shoot him. He would have killed you. Let's get out of here, quickly, before the police are called."

I grabbed her hand and we ran through the dark, dragging each other to the dock where the ferry was waiting. She followed me to the back of the boat, where we sat in terrified silence. The diesel engines shook and the boat pulled away from the dock, cutting through the night back to Como.

"You saved my life. I never had a chance. If you hadn't been there, I'd be dead. Why did you follow me?"

"When you left I could see him holding something against his coat. It looked like a gun. I couldn't leave you there, not by yourself.... I feel sick inside. But I had to shoot him or he would have killed you."

"He was a professional, a hit man."

"A hit man?"

"Yes. Someone sent him to kill me." I took a long deep breath. "Maybe we should call the police."

"What will we tell them?" she asked, looking amazed at my suggestion. "That I just shot that man. They might arrest me. Matt, that's not a solution."

"I have an idea," I said, suddenly energized.

I could see that she was beginning to regain her composure as the ferry docked in Como. We left the boat quickly, looking for anyone who might look suspicious. At the end of the landing we stopped and looked back at the dark lake, with its flickering lights. "What's your idea?" she finally asked.

"Bird Dog! He hasn't been around, but suppose I call Jarrett, tell him where we are, and ask for Bird Dog's help?"

"Matt, we lost him days ago. This is not one of your great sleuths."

"He's tough—and mean as hell. You got a better idea?"

"But if you call Jarrett, you're going to end up working for him. Who's then going to protect us from Bird Dog?"

"I'll deal with Jarrett when I have to. For now, I'd like for us to just stay alive, and Bird Dog can help us do that."

At the Villa d'Este, I called Jarrett. His first words were expected. "Lawrence, you mutha-fucker, you ditched Bird Dog. Shouldn't have done that. Until then, we were partners."

"We were never partners! And by the way, Bird Dog got lost." I paused. "Jarrett, I need your help. I'm getting close to the money, but someone's trying to kill me. I was shot several weeks ago in Rome. You want to tell me where Bird Dog was then?"

I could hear the wheezing on the other end of the line, and could feel Jarrett's blood boiling. He coughed repeatedly, then inhaled as if he were sucking a cigarette, and said hoarsely, "Bird Dog can help you and me. Don't try to ditch him again. Where are you?"

"Tell Bird Dog to meet us at the Trevi Fountain in Rome. Three days from now, on Wednesday, December 26. Got it?"

"Where will you be?"

"You don't need to know." I hung up.

I turned and stared into Claire's angry eyes. She sat across from me in a big over-stuffed chair. "I don't agree with what you just did. How in the world can you trust a man like Jarrett?"

"Two tries to kill me. The third time may not be a charm. Trust me. Please?"

"I'll try."

"Good. Now, let's get out of here."

"Right now? It's after midnight."

"Right now. The man who tried to kill me knew who we were, and I'll bet where we're staying. He was working for somebody, and that somebody is still around. We can't stay here. Pack your things, quickly. I'll check us out. Then I'm going to rent a car."

CHAPTER 16

▼

Through an all night branch of EuropeCar, I rented a black Alpha Romeo 640. Claire was waiting in front of the hotel with our luggage when I pulled up at 1 A.M. The night was clear as we sped away down the Autrostrada on our journey to Rome. We both kept watch for a while in our rear view mirrors, looking for a sign of anyone following us. There was none.

The Autostrada del Sole, A2, crosses Italy from north to south, and connects the northern lake region with Rome. Our engine made a constant hum as the car moved at over 180 kilometers per hour along the gentle curves of the road. After some silence, she finally asked, "Are we going to drive all night to Rome?"

"Lord no," I answered. "Rome is a good fourteen hour drive. We'll stop in Milan. It's about two hours from here." I tried the radio, hungry for any news, but succeeded only in getting unintelligible gibberish. She laid back and closed her eyes as I noticed that the headlights on a car far behind us had suddenly switched to the high beam and was quickly gaining on us.

Claire continued to doze as we rounded a sharp bend. I spotted a small road off the right shoulder and veered off, turned off the headlights, and felt the car slipping along on what seemed to be crushed gravel. Pulling behind a large tree, I killed the engine and sat motionless, waiting to see what would happen. She was jolted awake.

"What is it?" she whispered.

"It's probably nothing. A car behind us flashed its bright lights, then suddenly picked up speed. I got worried and decided to pull off the road. Do you have your gun?"

"Yes." She reached into her purse and held it in front of me. "You really must learn to use this. I don't want a repeat of Lake Como. Next time, you do the killing." Somewhere in the near distance I could hear the whine of the oncoming car. We sat in silence as the car rounded the bend and its headlights momentarily caught us in their glare. We shielded our eyes as the car sped by and then seemed to slow down. We held our breaths—and waited.

"Claire," I said softly, "give me your gun. Quick!"

She handed it to me just as the car spun around and stopped. Several seconds went by, and then the car suddenly sped away.

"Oh my God, Matt, how in the world could they know where we are? We were so careful!"

A feeling of hopelessness consumed me. I couldn't answer. We sat there for at least ten minutes in silence. The only noise was the rustling of the wind in the underbrush and the occasional barking of a distant dog.

We had to go on, and sometime after 3 A.M. we drove into Milan and to the Duca di Milano, a small hotel recommended by the night clerk at the Villa d'Este. Our room was large, with a balcony overlooking the piazza. I pushed a chair against the door and laid Claire's gun on the night stand. We then collapsed on the bed—exhausted.

I awoke several times during the night, half expecting the door to be broken through and to find ourselves at the mercy of our stalker. But it didn't happen, and I was deep into a nightmare full of snakes when I felt a gentle nudging. My eyes slowly opened to see Claire, handing me a cup of coffee.

"You can't sleep all day, you know."

"What time is it?" I asked.

"Would you believe almost 11 A.M. I hated to wake you, but I couldn't let you sleep all day. Your breakfast is waiting."

She went back to the balcony while I lay in silence, trying to think. But everything was a blur. I couldn't get the image of the other car out of my mind. I opened my eyes slowly and said, "Please give me the phone. I'm going to call Dallas."

"They wouldn't appreciate your call, Matt. It's only 3 A.M. in the States. Please get up and have breakfast with me. Matt, you must look outside. It's absolutely lovely. We overlook the Piazza della Republica, and it's decorated from one end to the other with lights and Christmas ornaments.""

I stumbled into the bathroom, showered and shaved, and then slowly sipped my coffee with her. We had an uneasy silence, and then, looking perplexed, she offered an attempt at consolation. "Don't be so troubled. We're safe here. It's almost Christmas. Let's enjoy it while we can. Please forget the Vatican and the money, just until the 26th. Let's stay here until then and be as inconspicuous as possible."

At noon on the 26th Claire and I sat in a small café overlooking the Trevi Fountain in Rome. After almost two hours of waiting we spotted a muscular, beady eyed man leaning against the fountain. She saw him first and exclaimed, "Oh my God, he does look like a bird dog. Matt, that must be him!"

It was. I got up, motioned her to remain seated, and approached Bird Dog. The sun had come out and it began to feel warm. He turned quickly as I came near and gave me a look that sent chills down my spine.

"Whoa there!" were his first words. "Soun' like yo' got yo'self in a shitpot full of trouble. Yo' lose me, yo' son'bitch, and then yo' got nobody to come in and mop up yo' flow. How come—tell me that?"

"I didn't lose you, you got lost," I scoffed. "I never knew where you were. But I need you now."

"Say, how yo' like workin' with a bird—that's some great lookin' chick!"

"Leave her out of this. It's not her business, she's just a friend. Did Jarrett tell you what we need?"

"Mr. Jarrett to yo'. Yeah, he tole me to fin out what's goin' on and to try to save yo' sweet ass."

"I'm getting close to the money. I know it. But someone's trying to kill me." He looked at me, unimpressed by what I was saying. "Do you understand what I'm telling you?"

He smiled sarcastically. "Yo' still alive, ain' yo'?"

I looked away and stared at the sky, wondering if it was hopeless. "I won't be for long if you don't stop these people. And if I die, your boss can kiss the money goodbye. Do you get my point?"

He squinted at me. I could see he finally got it.

"An' when do Mr. Jarrett get the money?"

"When I find it, and then he gets half. He thinks we're partners—I'm going to deal with him that way. I need my half to save my skin. Does he understand that?"

"He understands. But let me tell yo' somethin'—don't try to double-cross him. Ever! If yo' do, yo'll never live to see yo' grandchillen."

"Do you have a gun?"

"Yeah."

"How did you get it in to Italy?"

"In pieces. Listen fella, no mo' questions. What's yo' plan?"

"Tomorrow we go back to the Vatican to talk to several priests we met with earlier. I think they know how to find the money."

"Priests! I ain' touchin' priests."

"No, you're missing the point! I'm not worried about the priests. You have to stay around and watch for whoever is trying to kill me. Outside the Vatican. Remember, if I die, Jarrett loses the money."

Bird Dog slowly moved around the large fountain, holding his hand inside his coat. He stopped, halfway around, and stared back at Claire and me. I felt someone grab my arm, and I spun around to see Claire.

"Matt, for God's sake, tell me what's going on. You've been talking forever!"

"I don't know. I think he's going to help us, but in the middle of our conversation he just walked away."

She shuddered slightly as the water from the fountains crashed down into the pool of pennies thrown by wishers for good luck over the years. After a time, Bird Dog walked back, showing a slight limp I hadn't noticed before.

"What time?" he mumbled.

"What time what?"

"What time yo' goin' to be at the Vatican?"

"At about ten in the morning."

"See yo' then."

"Matt," Claire said with questioning eyes, "God help us if he doesn't know what he's doing."

We took the long walk back to our hotel, studying the people of Rome. The weather was getting colder and small drops of rain began to fall on us. I remembered painfully that it was in the rain that I had been shot. Thoughts of running and never coming back were with me every step. Our walk took us down the via Giovanni Ciolitti, by the multi-colored shops of the Colonna. Claire suddenly stopped, grabbed my arm, and said, "Matt, look. The sign, on the one at the end."

It said "Armaiolo Competente."

"What's that?"

"If my Italian doesn't fail me, it's a gunsmith. Let's go in."

"We don't need a gunsmith."

"But Matt, we do. I told you that I wasn't going to be the one to shoot next time, and I'm not going to give up my gun. You have to have one."

"Why? We have Bird Dog."

"Especially now that we have Bird Dog."

After some discussion between Claire and the shop owner, which was totally unintelligible to me, we were asked to produce our passports because of restrictions on ownership of guns by Italians. Following some further discussion, I was handed a small black pistol and two boxes of ammunition.

"It's a Beretta semi-automatic pistol, like mine," Claire explained. "It's easy to shoot and will hold nine cartridges. The shells are the hollow point shells I told you about."

The gunsmith offered to instruct me on how to use the gun, and we were shown into his cellar where he strapped a black nylon holster on my waist and took me through the fine points of firing a Beretta. I was surprised at the ease with which it fired and at its accuracy. After I had counted out several million Lira, the shop owner smiled and said, "Grazie, bella signorina."

Claire stuffed the package in my coat pocket, returned the smile, and said, "Prego, arrivederci." And suddenly, as we stepped onto the street, I felt I could breathe again.

CHAPTER 17

▼

It was not until almost five in the afternoon that I was able to reach the Monsignor. "Monsignor Bertellini, this is Matthew Lawrence. Your Mr. Schmidt requested that I call you." The reception I got was cold. When I suggested that Claire and I, disguised as a priest and nun, meet with him in the Sistine Chapel, he was outraged.

"Signore Lawrence, do you know what you're asking? It is ridiculous to think I could give you the garments of a priest and nun and permit you to wear them into the Sistine Chapel. It would break every sacred vow I have made!"

"Monsignor Bertellini," I said, realizing that I had made a serious mistake, "please forgive the suggestion. It was meant with no harm, but only to protect you and us."

"From what?" he demanded.

"Someone tried to kill me outside the Vatican, right after we met with you several weeks ago." I paused for a few seconds. "You must have known about it or you wouldn't have sent Schmidt to see us at Lake Como."

There was a pause on his end. I heard only his heavy breathing. Finally, "Yes, I knew of it." His voice was both tired and without patience. "That's why I asked you not to come back, to stop what you're doing."

"I can't stop. You must know that. I have to learn the truth."

"What truth? Don't you know, Signore, that there are things into which we cannot inquire? What you do involves the innermost chambers of the Vatican. The damage you could do, if you continue, is incalculable."

"I'll make you a pledge," I offered. "Meet with us, tell us about Braxton and the Vatican, and what you know about the money, and we'll leave. You have my word." I lied.

"Impossible," he said. "If I told you anything about that relationship, I would be violating the proscriptions of the Shadow Committee and the Directorate of the Holy See itself. I cannot do that!"

"Then I assure you, Monsignor, that the Italian and American journalists will have a field day with what I'll tell them and I'll withhold nothing."

"You're bluffing. You know nothing!"

"I have documents in my files," I threatened, "which confirm transfers of enormous sums from Braxton to the Vatican, and memorandums of meetings between the Pope and Braxton. I'm sure the press can put two plus two together."

"Why would you do that?" he asked, concern beginning to show in his voice.

"Because it's too important to be left alone. Too many people are involved, and I can't let the money end up in the wrong hands."

"There was a deafening silence as I listened to him breathe deeply. "Do you know Janiculum Hill?" he asked.

"No."

"It's where the gardens of the Risorgimento are, on the hill overlooking the Vatican. Any cab driver can take you there. I'll meet you at 11 o'clock tonight."

"No," I said as I looked up into Claire's inquisitive eyes. "Tomorrow night, at 11. Come alone. It's important that we talk in private."

"Tomorrow then. The phone clicked and went dead.

Claire looked at me, frowning. She gave me an innocent look, raising her eyebrows and probing for an explanation. "What in the world are you doing? Tomorrow night? What about Bird Dog? We told him tomorrow morning. And why not tonight if it has to be at night?"

"I'm not very good at this," I admitted. "He wouldn't meet during the day, and particularly not in the Sistine Chapel. He got very angry at your suggestion of disguises."

"But why tomorrow?"

"So we'll have time to find Bird Dog and check out the place where he wants to meet."

We left our room and wandered several blocks from the hotel to an out of the way bistro, constantly on guard. But I could see no Bird Dog or anyone else. Following a dinner of minestrone and spaghetti alla carbonera for me, and tortellini al pomodoro for Claire, we gathered the courage to walk across the Sant' Angelo Bridge towards the Vatican and up the long walk to Janiculum Hill. The sun was slowly setting and dusk arriving as we quietly made our way along the old path, past the statues of the ten Bernini angels that lined the entrance to the gardens.

We walked in silence, feeling the cold evening air descend on us. As we approached the hill, I was surprised to see the flowers and the color, in the middle of winter. Looking down the path, past the multi-colored shrubs and trees, the world seemed to end in the white clouds that were drifting by the yellow moon, and by that incessant face staring at me.

Claire pulled her scarf tighter around her head and shoulders as we stopped by a 19th century park bench. She glared at the sky and then turned to me. "Matt, what is it that you think you'll achieve with the Monsignor? I'm beginning to think you won't be happy until you kill the men who are responsible for Julia's death. Will that make things right with you? I thought it was truth you were after, and justice. To do things right. What happened to all that?"

I shrugged. "I lost that a long time ago." We continued to walk. "What good are truth and justice when people you love are being murdered?"

"My mother always told me," she said, "that we're judged not by others, but by those inner voices we all hear, by our consciences. I really don't think you mean what you're saying. In my opinion, you're running and just don't know when to stop."

As we walked and I listened, I couldn't separate what was real and what was imagined. It was as if I was living in a dream, or a nightmare. Each shadow along the way seemed sinister and full of danger, when in another life shadows had only been the reflection of my happiness. "What choice do I have? I'm dealing with treachery everywhere. If I don't maintain my anger and my will to deal with these people, I won't survive.... Can't you see that?"

She turned and looked at me, with sadness in her eyes. "Matt," she said slowly and deliberately, "I can see it, but I don't like it. One day it may end, before we expect it and before you've come to terms with anything. Are you prepared for that?"

Before I could answer, I noticed we were being approached by a man in a dark overcoat. When he walked under the street lamp, I recognized Bird Dog. "Whoa," he said through his yellowed teeth. "What you nice refine peoples doing up here in the dark?"

"Scouting," I mumbled back.

He walked up, hands in his coat, and said with his nose not five inches from mine, "Yo' ain' no movie director. If there be a chang' of plans, it ain' healthy not to tell Bird Dog."

"We're meeting the Monsignor tomorrow night, here at eleven? Will you be here then?"

"Yo' bet yo' sweet ass—over there," he said, pointing to a thick cover of bushes. He shuffled around along the damp ground, half limping, surveying the area and occasionally looking back at us.

"Well, maybe he does know what he's doing," Claire whispered. "I just hope he doesn't ruin our meeting with the Monsignor."

*   *   *   *

At precisely eleven the next night we returned to the top of Janiculum Hill. The face in the moon had disappeared, as had the moon. The night was pitch black, and but for the lone street lamp near the bench, we wouldn't have seen the Monsignor. Each time I breathed, the cold stung my lungs. I quietly shivered in the cold, wondering why this meeting seemed so foreboding.

The Monsignor's silver gray hair stood out in the dark against his black robe. "Ah, Signore," he said as Claire and I slowly approached. We saw no sign of Bird Dog or anyone else for that matter. We were isolated, with one lone man in a priest's robe, and I felt something was terribly wrong.

"Please stay back," I said as I nodded for Claire to stand away from the bench. The Monsignor motioned me to sit, and I watched his breath dance through the night sky like clouds of smoke. "Monsignor, thank you for coming. Please tell me everything you know about Braxton and the Vatican," I said.

"Braxton," he mumbled, looking down at the damp walkway. "He fooled us all. We thought he was a good man, someone we could trust. We had no idea he was out to use us and the Holy See." He stopped, raised his head, and pointed at me. "You...you are his lawyer—at least you say you are. Why should we trust you or tell you anything?"

"Because there are evil men at work, and you and the Vatican are caught in the middle. You have no choice," I insisted. "Absolutely none."

He sighed deeply, showing his frustration. "And if we don't help you...then what?"

"If you don't, the Vatican will be exposed publicly in a scandal that will be your worst nightmare."

"It's not that simple," he insisted. "If it were, we would have ended it long ago. I can't give you what you want."

I looked directly into his eyes. "Yes you can," I answered quietly. "Monsignor, where is the money?"

His age was telling on him. I could hear his labored breathing. The slowness of his movements and his expression told me that he was in pain. "I have no idea," he answered. "But I would like to tell you a story, one that may help you understand why I can't help you."

He took a deep breath and looked up at the night sky. "Do you know of the scandal involving the Holy See and Banco Ambrosiano?" he began.

"I do," I said, "and about the man Roberto Calvi. Was he connected with Braxton?"

"No, no connection," he answered. "But Braxton had met with His Holiness. It was a very good meeting, one that resulted in a gift to the Holy See worth several millions. Braxton made a very good impression, Signore. A very good impression. Before he left, he had become good friends with not only the Pope and Cardinal Ramoni, but also Angelo Braschi."

"Tell me about Braschi." I interjected.

"You may remember from our meeting at the Vatican, several weeks ago, that he is the Controller for the I.O.R. He has enormous power with the Holy See."

"But he's a layman," I said. "Certainly a priest or other official of the Church should serve in that capacity."

"Ah, yes. But, you see, no one could be found with Mr. Braschi's particular talents. He has very special business skills. It's mainly because of him that the Holy See was able to avoid the scandal. His Holiness is most appreciative of that fact."

"But what has this got to do with Braxton?" I asked.

While he was trying to collect his thoughts, I felt a gentle nudging as Claire eased down next to me. She put a finger to her lips to silence me, and whispered, "I couldn't stand over there any longer. I want to hear what he has to say."

The Monsignor took notice of Claire, nodded his approval, and took a deep breath. "When the scandal broke, the Holy See was in a state of panic. Over a billion dollars had disappeared from Banco Ambrosiano, and more than three hundred million belonged to the Vatican bank. And worse, the newspapers were beginning to implicate the Vatican in the disappearance of the funds. We were desperate. But then Braxton contacted Signore Braschi and within hours over one hundred million dollars had been transferred to the Vatican."

"Braxton gave you one hundred million dollars!" Claire blurted out.

"No, of course not. He lent us the money, with the concurrence of the Holy See. His terms were most generous, and he required only that his loan be kept absolutely confidential. We quickly agreed. That loan kept the Vatican bank from collapsing. Surely you can imagine the gratitude felt by the Holy See."

"If he loaned you the money, did you pay it back?" I asked.

"Only His Holiness knows the answer to that question. Braxton insisted, as part of his conditions, that the terms be known only to the two of them."

"No one else?" Claire quizzed.

"Perhaps one, although I have no proof."

"Braschi?" I guessed.

"Yes, probably Braschi, because he was involved in all of it—from the very beginning."

"So you're telling us," I said, "that over one hundred million dollars was transferred to the Vatican bank several years ago and no one, not even you, knows what happened to it other than the Pope and possibly Braschi?"

"Yes, that's what I'm telling you. And I'm also telling you that His Holiness will never divulge to you or anyone else what happened to that money. His agreement with Signore Braxton is inviolate."

"But I'm his attorney...I'm acting for him," I pleaded with little hope of success.

"Unless you could convince His Holiness of your position, which I am sure you cannot, what you say means nothing."

I paused, collecting my thoughts. "Monsignor, the American Government wants that money and so do hardened criminals—and God knows who else. As long as you have it, the Vatican and those who live within its walls are in danger."

"You assume facts that may not be true." He stood to leave. "You and I have no idea where the money is, and there is no way we will find out. None! Do you understand me? I have come here at personal risk. I am under a directorate of the Holy See not to discuss this matter with anyone, and I have breached that directorate by speaking with you. You assured me, when we talked by phone, that if I met with you, you would leave. I expect you to keep your promise." With that, he turned and left.

Suddenly, we heard several muffled noises and then a gunshot. The Monsignor looked back at us briefly, then walked quickly into the darkness. "Get down!" I pushed Claire behind the bench. We tried to see through the overcast night into the bushes where Bird Dog was supposed to be. There was a sickening gurgling sound, a deep moan, and then ominous quiet. I reached for my gun and pulled the slide to load the chamber. I cursed myself for not doing it earlier.

"Hey Lawrence, get yo' ass over here." The familiar voice startled me.

I rose and walked cautiously towards the bushes. Behind the row where the noise had come from I noticed a moving light from a small flashlight. On the ground was a nearly decapitated man with what appeared to be a bullet hole in his head. Bird Dog was on the ground next to him, rifling through his clothes with blood soaked hands.

"Who is he?" I asked, feeling nauseated from the scene in front of me.

"A mailman."

"What do you mean a *mailman*?"

"No I.D. and a silencer. This cat was carrying yo' a message."

"What message?"

"If I hadn't been 'ere," he said with a sarcastic smile, "yo' and the bird would be dog meat. He was going to fry yo' ass."

The lifeless body of what was once a large man, with those transfixed eyes and blood around his neck and head, overwhelmed me. Death, the heart of my thousand fears, kept me paralyzed until Claire grabbed my arm and pulled me back.

"What happened?" she mumbled.

"Ripped 'im like a gator," he said, with an obvious amount of pride. "'Ere, take a look at that," he said as he handed me a bloodied piece of paper. On it was written a series of numbers. They were listed in two rows, of ten each. The first was 2078970778 and the second was 9364228401.

"What do these numbers mean?" I asked as he first shined his light on the paper and then in my eyes.

"Don' know," he said. "He was there to send yo' to never-never land. It's time to let those folks who hired 'im know this ain' open season."

Bird Dog grabbed the paper from my hands as we stumbled back, retreating quickly down the walk and away from the dead man. He stayed behind us, pushing us down the hill. "Yo' don' wanna waste yo' time thinking on that dead meat and have his friends hit yo'. Forget 'im, the street sweepers will clean 'im up."

"What now?" Claire asked with glazed eyes.

"Now yo' tell Bird Dog what that priest say."

I thought about what he said and didn't answer. I motioned Claire to the bottom of the hill, past the statues of the angels, and looked back on his sinister profile. Behind him, in the mist, was the lone light on Janiculum Hill. It was past midnight and the only sounds were our breathing and an occasional dog. Contemplating carefully my response, I said to him, "He confirmed that Braxton sent a lot of money to the Vatican, but that it was gone. No one knows where except the Pope and Braxton."

"No one?" He stood back and gave me an angry look. "I don' believe yo'!"

"I don't give a fuck if you believe me or not!"

Claire jabbed me in the ribs, pleading with her eyes for me not to antagonize him.

"He said," I continued, trying to control my temper, "that maybe one other person might know. A man named Angelo Braschi, the Controller for the bank."

"Braschi," Bird Dog mumbled to himself. "I'll call Mr. Jarrett and see yo' two later. Be at the fountains tomorrow noon." He then disappeared into the dark night.

Claire took my arm and we walked slowly back to the hotel in stark silence. When we had arrived safely in our room and had securely fastened the door, she sat me on the sofa and fixed us each a glass of cognac. "Well, what now? Shall we go see Braschi tomorrow?"

"No. It would be a waste of time. He's not about to talk to us. Remember our last meeting with him and the others? He was the most hostile."

"So where do we go?"

"Let's go to the Cotton Bowl. I'm absolutely worn out. A break would do us good."

"You've got to be kidding. The Cotton Bowl?"

"The Cotton Bowl. Claire, it's time to go back. We've found out as much as we can here. It's time to go home. I think we'll find more answers now back in Texas."

"Do you think so?"

"I know so. Braxton's the answer and he's there. He knows what happened to the money. I've got to find a way to make him tell me."

"He wouldn't talk to you before. What makes you think he'll talk now?"

"Because I know more now. The last time I was with him, I was in the dark and fishing. He knew it. Jarrett gave me an idea when he said that Braxton, in the long run, would do what was necessary to save his skin. Maybe I can play middleman."

"OK, let's go back," she said, sniffing her cognac. "I'm ready to escape this insanity."

CHAPTER 18

▼

Dallas, Texas, 1992

After an early morning flight from Rome to London, we boarded the British Air flight to Dallas at eleven o'clock the next morning. Standing in line to board, we were conscious of the 300 or so passengers around us, wondering who might be watching us. We didn't see Bird Dog. Once boarded, the 747 lifted off the runway at Heathrow, turning sharply to the left as it made its rapid ascent. Claire and I looked at each other, and both breathed a temporary sigh of relief.

The ground below disappeared as the 747 stabilized. The seat belt lights were quickly extinguished and the crew began to serve drinks to the passengers. Claire settled back in her seat and turned to me. She smiled. "Is it too early for a drink?"

"Not if it's coffee."

"You know that's not what I meant. Even if it is 11:30 in the morning, let's have a glass of wine to celebrate."

"Celebrate what?"

"Matt," she sighed, "we're alive and on our way home after all that's happened in the past three months. I don't ever want to relive that again."

We each ordered a glass of Chardonnay. When they arrived, Claire grabbed my hand and raised her glass. "Matt, I've learned a lot about me in Europe, but a whole lot more about you. You're amazing. I wish I had your strength."

I smiled. "Thank you, but you do. I'm so grateful for you, I don't know quite how to express it."

She squeezed my hand and refused to let go. "I think you just did."

We landed at DFW Airport at six o'clock in the evening. The airport was like a cavern, a huge building shell with few people. It was midnight in London, and we both felt exhausted from jet lag. Neither of us said much as we walked the long concourse, picked up our luggage, and headed for our cars. The garage was ominously empty. I scanned the parking area for any sign that someone was watching us. I saw no one. At Claire's black Mercedes, I put my arms around her and held her close for a few moments. She responded with her arms and whispered, "Will I see you soon?"

"You can count on it. I'm already beginning to miss you."

She brushed my lips with hers and then left me standing there alone watching her drive away.

Although it was late, I decided to drive to the home that Julia and I had shared for most of our married life. It was in a suburb of Dallas, called Highland Park, and was only five minutes from my apartment. Memories of Julia overwhelmed me as I pulled into the driveway. I hesitated—it had been almost nine months since I had been in that house, but I couldn't bring myself to sell it. I turned the key with misgiving, opened the door, and was engulfed by what had been my life. Everything was there, just as it had been when Julia died. I stayed for only several minutes, feeling the pain, and then left and drove to my apartment.

My answering machine flashed 30 messages. After methodically skipping through most of them, I heard a pleasant voice. "Mr. Lawrence, this is Martine Paulet. I've looked into your questions. I have no answers yet but will let you know when I do. A toute à l' heure." I thought to myself that her voice was as smooth as velvet. The next voice was not.

The message began with his clearing his throat and then wheezing violently. "Lawrence, if you're there you son-of-a bitch, whataya think you're doing. Bird Dog says you ducked out. You're out of time, fella. I'm taking this thing into my own hands. Stay away from it. Go back to your shyster practice." With that, the wheezing started again, and I listened to another few seconds of his coughing and wheezing before the phone clicked off.

New Year's day was brisk and sunny, perfect for the Cotton Bowl. I went by myself and watched Texas battle Miami throughout the game and win in the last second on a desperation pass. I adjusted my orange Longhorns cap and sat for several minutes after the game was over, realizing how desperate I had become for normality and how good it had felt.

In the parking lot I flipped open my cellphone and dialed Big Spring. After waiting ten minutes, I reached Braxton.

"Bic, what are you doing?"

"Watching football. What do you want, Matt?"

"I want to come see you."

"It's all over. You're wasting your time."

"What do you mean, it's all over?"

"I can't tell you on the phone, but believe me," he said, "you're wasting your time."

"It's not over, Bic. There are things I've got to clear up—for my own sanity. Can I come see you?"

"When?"

"Tonight."

"Sure," he said, "but after the Orange Bowl. Seven o'clock. See you then, Matt."

I looked at my watch and noted that it was around 3 P.M. I figured I could fly to Midland and be in Big Spring by seven. I arrived fifteen minutes late. On entering the prison, I was escorted by a burley guard to the visitors' area, which was empty and quiet. True to his word, Braxton didn't show up for almost an hour—at the end of the Orange Bowl. He looked healthy, relaxed and tanned. Incredible, I thought, for a Federal penitentiary.

"Matt," he said as he shook my hand, "you've come for nothing."

"I just came from the Vatican. I met with Cardinal Ramoni, Monsignor Bertellini and Angelo Braschi. Mean anything to you?"

He sat back trying to hide his surprise at what I had told him. "Names sound familiar. What were you doing there?"

"Getting information—and getting shot. Bic, you've been dealing with very dangerous characters."

"I tried to tell you that, didn't I?" He showed a slight smile. "It's ironic, isn't it? You go to all that trouble and almost get yourself killed, for nothing!"

"Why for nothing?"

"Why?" he repeated, scowling as he sat back and grabbed a cup of coffee. "What I'm going to say is for your ears only, do you understand? I owe you something, Matt, and this is for old times' sake. Between you and me, OK?"

"Yeah."

"This guy McAlister, who wanted to see me put away for life. Well, he made me an offer I couldn't refuse."

"He came to see you?"

"No, he wouldn't do that. He sent his assistant, Dawson. Very pleasant. It seems McAlister is willing to set me free for the money, or at least part of it."

"He's willing to let you keep part?"

"Oh yeah. Interesting, isn't it?"

"Why would he do that?" How do you know you can trust him?"

He leaned across the table. "Because, Matt, old buddy, he'll get a lot of money. A lot. But he won't see any of it until I'm out."

"Have you given any thought to your friend Jarrett and those others who tried to kill me in Rome? Whoever they are, Bic, these are dangerous people. They won't go away."

"You ever hear about the Witness Protection Program?"

"Of course I have, but not for people like you. You're serving time and you're not a witness."

"Part of my deal with McAlister," he said, lowering his voice, "is that I go into the program. I'll be long gone, and with millions."

"Where's the money, Bic?"

"Not on your life, buster. I've told you all you need to know. Any more, and I'll screw up my deal with McAlister."

"Just you and the Pope, right?"

"Why can't you leave it alone?" he said, showing his uneasiness with my remark.

"Don't worry, I'm not going to screw up your deal." I stared at him and he stared back. "But I'll promise you one thing. I'm going to find the people who killed Julia and tried to kill me in Rome. Whatever it takes—I'll find them."

"It won't bring her back!"

"It won't, but maybe I'll be able to sleep at night."

"You want some advice? Stop while you have a chance. If you find them, you may wish you hadn't." He stopped, lit a cigarette, and inhaled deeply. "You think you're dealing with boy scouts? Stop kidding yourself, Matt. You don't have a prayer against them. Leave it alone—and maybe they'll leave you alone."

"How do you know that?"

"I don't. But it makes sense. When I settle, they'll know it. What good will it do for them to try to get you then? Matt, they want the money, not you."

"Who are they, Bic? Tell me, and I'll leave."

"I told you the last time you were here—I don't know. Maybe Jarrett, maybe not. It could be some of the scum I dealt with in Sugar Daddy. Or it could be the Mafia. Hell, I don't know. That's why I'm going to settle and get into the Witness Protection Program."

He stood up, turned, and walked towards the door. "You leaving?" I asked.

Turning back to look at me, he said, "No, no I'm not leaving. Where am I going to go? Look, Matt, I trust you. Work with me to get this thing done. When I go free, I'll see that you get paid a bundle for your efforts."

"Help you with McAlister?"

"No, not McAlister. I'm sworn not to talk to anyone about my deal with him. Help me think this through…don't let him figure out a way to screw me."

I thought about his offer. It was attractive. In a temporary eerie silence in that big, gray empty room, we sat and looked hard at each other, both thinking of removing barriers. "How big a bundle?" I asked.

"Half a million, hard cash. Wherever you want it, tax free."

"Not enough. I know how much is involved. Make it $1 million."

He hesitated and then smiled. "You are good. Done!"

"Tell me about your so-called deal."

"In two weeks, McAlister gets Justice Department approval, releasing me from this hell hole. I get a new identity and head for parts unknown. Simple?"

"Yes, simple. So what are you worried about?"

He walked slowly across the creaking wood floor, gazed out the window for several minutes, and then turned and said, "You warned me about trusting him—and I don't. That's why it's not so simple."

"What have you told him?"

"Only that the money was safe, overseas."

"Does he know about the Vatican?"

"No, I don't think so. But so what. Matt, that's irrelevant."

"Why irrelevant. I thought that somehow the Pope had your money?"

"Matt, quit fishing. You're off base. Don't try to be so smart or you'll find you'll outsmart yourself."

"Then why did you mention the Pope in our last visit?"

"I was playing with your head. Drop it, Matt."

His eyes told me he was lying, but I dropped it. "Any way he can get to the money without you?"

He looked amused, smiled slightly, and mumbled, "No one can get to the money without me. That's my ticket—no fuckin' one!"

"What if something happens to you? Sterling could say goodbye to the money."

"I'll think about that," he said, sitting again to drink his coffee. "That's why I need your help, to guide me through that kind of thought process. It's been a long day. Go find a place to stay, and be back in the morning, at ten." We shook hands and he left.

I drove a few miles down the highway until I spotted a motel. After checking into my room, I unpacked my small case and laid out a note pad and pencil. Next to it I placed my Beretta in its holster. Rome seemed like only yesterday, and I found that I slept—and thought—better with my gun nearby. On the pad I outlined a chart. At the top I put Braxton. Underneath I wrote $200,000,000, followed by the names McAlister and Dawson. To the left, I wrote in the Pope, Ramoni, Bertellini and Braschi. Next, I wrote Jarrett and Bird Dog. To the right of all of that I put a large question mark.

After pouring a Dewars and soda from the small refrigerator in the corner, I pondered the diagram. It was the sum of my life over the last several months—and my fears. I then drew a series of arrows, through all the names and the money, to a name at the bottom—Matthew Lawrence.

*   *   *   *

I checked out at eight-thirty in the morning. The day was already beginning to melt into darkness as heavy black clouds began to drift across the sky. I ate breakfast in a nearby coffee house, bought a copy of *USA Today* and caught up on the news of the new year. As I read, I listened to the monotonous humming of the air conditioning compressors outside the window. The business section reviewed the financial disasters of the year, and in particular the huge Texas bank collapse. Just two years before, the President had assured the public that the loss would not amount to more than ten billion dollars. He had either lied or was stupid. The article pointed out that he had missed his estimate by four hundred and ninety billion!

As I drove to the prison, the sky turned so dark that my headlights automatically turned on. Beads of rain began to form on my windshield, and they quickly turned into a torrent. The weather continued to deteriorate rapidly as the winds blew at a steady twenty miles per hour. I pulled through the prison gates and thought of the fact that Braxton would be leaving in just two weeks, for a new life with apparently unlimited amounts of money—some justice! But he was still a convicted felon.

The visitors' area was surprisingly full of people when I entered. Braxton came in on time and we were given a small table in the corner. He immediately cautioned me not to say anything that might be overheard.

Whispering, he said, "This is what I want you to do. Outline for me a fool proof way out of here, one where McAlister won't be able to double cross me, and then put it in writing. I want his personal signature on this deal before I turn over the money."

"Fool proof, Bic, means getting a court order. Let's require that."

"Impossible. Dawson and I talked about that. He said my court order would be the Justice Department getting me released and relocated. He claimed no Federal judge would put his signature on a deal that would let me walk with millions, but that the Justice Department could handle it all internally."

"I'll have to think that through." I knew that providing him with what he wanted would be very difficult.

"One other thing," he said, sitting back and pulling lightly on his ear. "Don't make it look like a lawyer's involved. This has to look like I'm representing myself. That's a condition that Dawson pounded into me—no one can know about this deal."

"No one? Why?" Something was not right.

"Because he says it's too hot. No one in government wants to be associated with a deal with me. He says it's not politically expedient."

"Do you believe him?"

"I don't know. What choice do I have? Do you know any other way out of this place? If you do, tell me—but do it quickly."

I sat back in my chair and looked around the room. He didn't have any other choice. I knew it and he knew it. "Do you know what really bothers me?" I asked.

"What?"

"It's one thing to work out a deal with the government. But it's an entirely different thing to protect you from whoever is out there trying to get the money. I don't know that they'll stop when you leave this place. Let's rethink who knows about the money."

"I only have suspicions. Jarrett's at the top of the list."

"Good, let's start with him. He left me a message on my answering machine yesterday. He was angry as hell. He thinks you two had a deal. That he was to get eighty percent of what you got. Any truth to that?"

Braxton took a long sip of coffee. "Yeah, a fuckin' ridiculous deal. He squeezed me when I had no choice. By the way, it's unenforceable. It was illegal. He was trying to indirectly get into the banking business through me."

"But you made the deal."

"Yes, I made the deal."

"So what do we do with him now?"

"Forget him."

"You ever heard of Bird Dog, his hired help?" I asked.

"Yeah, I know Bird Dog. So what?"

"If you know him, you don't say so what. Jarrett's not someone you can forget."

"He'll never find me."

"You getting wishful, Bic. He'll find you. Who else?"

"I'm being honest—I don't know. I've dealt with a lot of people who would be very unfriendly to me now, but I don't think anyone knows about the money except Jarrett, the Pope, McAlister and you. Not even Sterling knows."

"The Pope."

"I said drop it, Matt."

"OK. What was your arrangement with Dawson?"

"He suggested," his voice in a bare whisper, "that I arrange to have the money wired to a Justice Department account in two weeks."

"Before or after you're out?"

"We didn't discuss that. But he did say they wanted absolute confirmation where the money was before my release becomes final and I'm given a new identity."

"What did you say to that?" I didn't like what I was hearing.

"I said that would be OK. Even when I tell them where it is, they won't be able to touch it."

I glanced at my watch. Visiting time was limited, and we had ten more minutes. Braxton then looked at his watch, stared off into the few visitors in the room, and leaned towards me. "I know what you're thinking, Matt. If I tell them where the money is, they may get it. Well they can't. And what if they try? I still control it and they would risk losing it all. They're not that dumb!"

"Are you going to stop talking in riddles and tell me where it is so I can help you?"

"No, not now. But I'll tell you this," he said, "it's not in the Vatican."

I felt like we were playing games, and I was beginning to wonder if any of this made any sense at all. "If you won't trust me, I can't help you."

"Matt, you're missing the point. What I don't tell you is for your own good. You said they tried to kill you, and you don't even know where the money is. Wherever it is, they don't want you to know. Forget where the money is. Just help me get out of here."

The visitors' time had ended. "I'll work on it. Can I call you tomorrow? Are the phones safe?"

"No," he whispered. "Work out a plan and be back here in two days. See ya, Matt." He rose and left.

*　　　*　　　*　　　*

I was rain soaked by the time I got back to my car. I sat for a few minutes in the lot, listening to the pelting rain and trying to add up everything Braxton had said. One thing kept echoing in my head—the money wasn't in the Vatican.

The drive back to Midland was treacherous in the strong winds and rain, and I found myself thinking of Julia and our intimate moments together. I turned on my tape player and listened to old songs I had recorded years before that Julia and I had never seemed to tire of. When "Along the Lonely Street of Memories" by Johnny Ray came on, I had difficulty keeping my eyes on the road.

CHAPTER 19

▼

When I returned to Dallas, I called Jarrett. Bixler answered and told me he wasn't in. I left my cellphone number and asked that he call me, only to get as a response a click and a dial tone. Then I called Leigh. "Matt," she exclaimed, "you haven't returned any of my calls or Mr. Stanton's. He's very anxious to talk to you."

"Sorry. I've been too busy."

"Doing what?"

I paused, wondering how to tell her what I had been through. "I've been in Europe for the past several weeks, trying to sort through the deaths of Julia and Marianne."

"Are they connected?"

"Yes. They're connected. Leigh, listen carefully to what I'm going to tell you. Someone involved in some way with Braxton and the bank scandal is trying to kill me."

"Oh my God! Why?"

"I don't know why, but I'm still alive. I need you to do some things for me. First, I want you to find out everything you can about a guy named Dawson. He works for the Justice Department, evidently for Buckroyd McAlister. So he's probably a licensed attorney. It's important, Leigh, that no one knows what you're doing."

"How do I do that and not have anyone know?"

"I don't know, be ingenious. First, check him out in Martindale Hubbell. Then call the Justice Department, anonymously, and find out what you can. Also, you might call Peter Segal in Washington. See if he has heard of Dawson, but tell him to keep it very confidential. This is very important to me. Will you do it, please?"

"Of course I'll do it. But, Matt, I'm not a detective. Anything else?"

"Yes there is. Please pull all of my personal files on Braxton and deliver them to my apartment."

"Are you serious? Those files will fill several boxes."

"I know that. Please do it."

"I will. Where can I reach you?"

"I'll be home for several days. You can leave any messages on my answering machine. Oh Leigh, one more thing. Have a paralegal check the Federal Witness Protection Program on our Lexis research system and find out all you can. How it's used, who's in charge, et cetera."

"I'll get to work on it right away. Take care, Matt. Please be careful."

I hung up and within minutes received Jarrett's call. "What is it? I thought I told you to back off," he said hoarsely.

"If you can tell me how, be my guest."

"Fuck you, Lawrence," he stammered. "We'll find the fuckin' money without you."

"No, no you won't. I can talk to people who wouldn't give you the time of day."

"You been to Bangor, Maine, lately?"

"What's in Bangor, Maine?"

He coughed for a minute, cleared his throat and said, "Your boy seems to have had connections there."

"What boy?"

"The boy that Bird Dog made short order of in Rome, that boy. One of the numbers in his pocket was a phone number to a Julius Freytag in Bangor. Mean anything?"

"No. Mean anything to you?"

I could hear his breathing increase rapidly as the coughing and the wheezing resumed.

"You don't know shit, Lawrence. There's someone out there trying to kill you, and you don't have a fuckin' clue who it is. You're in the wrong racket, fella. Go back to selling shoes." He hung up.

*   *   *   *

The next day I flew to Bangor, Maine, to confront Julius Freytag. On the flight back to Dallas, I read and reread the file he had given me. The wire transfer of funds was for $50,000 to an account at the Royal Bank of Canada. I suspected the account was now closed and the funds long gone. I also knew the Bank would never divulge to me the ownership of that account. The post office box, if it wasn't closed, was my only hope.

*   *   *   *

At the Athena, Frank had deposited three large boxes of papers in my apartment, all delivered by Leigh. They were the Braxton files. On top of one of the boxes was a large manilla envelope containing a thirty page copy of an annotation from American Law Reports dealing with the Federal Witness Protection Program. The envelope also contained a note that read "No Dawson—call me." I called her at home.

The voice I heard was groggy. "Yes," she said, "who is it?"

"Leigh…it's Matt. I'm sorry for waking you. I have to know what your note meant."

"Matt, it's almost midnight!" There was a pause as she collected her thoughts. "I checked out Dawson as best I could. He's not listed in Martindale Hubbell. When I called the Justice Department, they told me that they had no one there by that name. I don't think he's a lawyer. Do you want me to check anywhere else?"

"Did you talk to Peter Segal?"

"I tried. He wasn't in. Anything else?"

"No, you've done enough for now. I'll talk to you tomorrow. Thanks."

I settled at my desk with a large cup of coffee and began to read the annotation. It dealt with cases brought against the Federal government claiming that it had failed to properly administer the Witness Protection Program. There must have been over one hundred cases discussed. The pertinent provisions of the program were outlined at the beginning. It read-

"The Attorney General may provide for the relocation and other protection of a witness or a potential witness for the Federal Government or for a State government in an official proceeding concerning an organized criminal activity or other serious offense, if the Attorney General determines that an offense involving a crime of violence directed at the witness with respect to that proceeding is likely to be committed. The Attorney General may also provide for the relocation and other protection of the immediate family of, or a person otherwise closely associated with, such witness or potential witness if the family or person may also be endangered on account of the participation of the witness in the judicial proceeding."

I sipped on my coffee and tried to place the circumstances in which Braxton was involved within the provisions of the Act. I wasn't sure I could. I read on. It stated that the Attorney General is required to take such action as he feels is necessary to "protect the person involved from bodily injury and otherwise to assure the health, safety, and welfare of that person." It further provided that the Attorney General could provide a new identity and relocate the person involved to a new and secret location.

Then I stumbled on the condition to the protection of any person under this law. The Attorney General was "required" by law to enter into a written memorandum of understanding with each protected person, setting forth the arrangements to be made.

The next morning I called my friend in Washington, Peter Segal. "Peter, I'm in a lot of trouble. I need your help. I have a client who's dealing with a guy at the Justice Department named Dawson. We thought he worked out of the Dallas office, but there's no one there by that name. Could you very quietly check this guy out in Washington?"

"Trouble? What kind of trouble?"

"Someday, I'll tell you all about it. But I don't have the time now."

He hesitated. "Dawson. No first name?"

"That's all I know."

"Matt, we've known each other for a long time. What's this all about?"

"Peter…it's very complicated."

"Try me. I have to have more than just a last name."

"OK. The short story is Dawson is acting for a U.S. Attorney named Buckroyd McAlister. My client's serving time, and we're trying to work a deal that would free him under the Witness Protection Program. I need to know who Dawson is and if we can trust him."

"Trust? If he works for the Justice Department and is negotiating for the A.G., what makes you think you can't trust him?"

"For several reasons," I answered. "First, their proposal sounds fishy. And there's another point—I've dealt with his boss, McAlister. Peter, he's not your everyday prosecutor. There's something wrong. Last night I scanned over one hundred cases in American Law Reports dealing with witness protection. In many of them the Justice Department ultimately betrayed the witness it was supposed to protect."

"Do you realize how big the Department is?" he asked. "There could be a hundred Dawsons working there. Let me see what I can find out. Where can I reach you?"

"Call my apartment—522-6323 in Dallas. If I'm not there, leave a message on my answering machine."

"You won't be at the firm?"

"I left the firm. So I'm on my own. Peter, what I'm dealing with is very sensitive. Please keep all of this very confidential."

"Of course I will."

I next called the postal service and asked about box number 9112. The answer I got was not unexpected. The names of owners of post office boxes were kept strictly confidential. Under no circumstance could they be disclosed. Thumbing through the yellow pages under private detectives, I circled the name Jason Best and dialed his number. He answered on the first ring.

"Mr. Best, I'm a Dallas attorney. I need surveillance work."

The muffled voice on the other end asked, "How did you get my name?"

"The Yellow Pages."

"Then it was worth the hundred bucks," he mumbled.

"What?"

"Forget it. When can you be here?"

"I can't. I don't have the time. All I need is for you to find out who owns a post office box."

"That could be hard. You know those things are kept confidential by the Post Office."

"Yes I do. That's precisely why I need you."

"It'll cost you five hundred a day."

"It's no problem. I'll deposit a one thousand dollar retainer in the mail today. Will you start right away?"

"I'll start when I get your retainer." I could hear the clinking of ice against a glass in the background.

"OK, I'll have the check hand delivered. Write this down. The box number is 9112. As soon as you get any information, call me. If I'm not here, leave a message on my machine. Got it?"

"Got it," he confirmed. Hanging up, I silently wondered if I hadn't gone one step too far.

Five hours later I was back in Big Spring. The day was windy and sunny, and the prison took on an entirely different appearance from the last time I had been there. Braxton appeared rested, like a man who was about to gain his freedom. He came in wearing his prison fatigues, puffing on a large cigar. Blowing a ring of smoke in my direction, he sat across from me, placed his elbows on the table, and said, "You got it worked out?"

"Not quite. There are some loose ends that don't seem to fit."

"Like what?"

"Like whether you really fit into the Witness Protection Program, for starters. And why McAlister is working through Dawson. I'm try-ing to add two and two and I'm getting five."

"Give me a straight answer. What in the hell are you talking about?"

"I don't know if we can trust these people. The last time we talked, you told me you were worried about Sterling if the deal didn't go through. I can't help you, or Sterling, if you don't tell me the whole story. You've got me playing with half a deck. Confide in me, Bic."

"I am confiding in you, dammit. If I weren't, you wouldn't be here."

"No you're not. Bic, it's all about the money. I don't know how much there is or where it is. And I can't talk to McAlister or Dawson."

"My proof of trust is the $1 million you'll get when I'm out of here."

"That's not enough! I can't plan for the what ifs if I don't have the facts. And Bic, let me ask you again, what if something happens to you? There are people out there who will do anything to get their hands on the money. Don't ever forget that."

He stood up, walked slowly away from the table and looked out the window. I was wasting my time and I knew it. The money would remain his secret.

"Tell you what," he said as he returned and grabbed my arm across the table. "You give me a workable plan for my freedom and I'll give you information about the money—but only when you need it to get me out of this rat hole."

"This is ridiculous—no stupid! I'll give you a plan, but it may be half-baked based upon the wrong assumptions. What the hell do you think I'd do if I knew where the money was, for Christ's sake?"

"Maybe work your own deal," he answered. "I know the trouble you and your firm are in. I'm not going to chance someone taking your deposition or offering you a deal you can't refuse. No fuckin' way!"

"Just don't die on me Bic, because if you do that money will rot in Hell. Give me until Friday, and I'll have an answer for you."

Our meeting ended as abruptly as it had begun.

CHAPTER 20

▼

As hard as I tried, I couldn't stay away from Claire. Separation, I thought, would clear my head and help me see things better. It didn't. My thoughts kept drifting back to her.

When I called, she wasn't particularly friendly. "It's been a month, Matt, and not a word from you. We travel over Europe almost getting killed together, I nurse you back to health, and then you ignore me. I'm not sure I want to have anything more to do with you."

"I was wrong," I said apologetically. "I had things to do and I didn't want to get you any more involved."

"Any more involved? Is that really what you thought? How much more involved could I be than when we were in Europe? You have no idea how angry that makes me!"

"I think I do," I mumbled to myself. "I was wrong and I'm sorry. Can we have dinner tonight?"

"I don't think so," she said slowly as if planning her next sentence. "I didn't tell you this before, but I've dated a doctor, a friend of Roberts, and I'm serious about that relationship. Matt, you and I have no future. None!"

I was surprised. "Claire, I'm not trying to interfere with your relationship. I only asked you to have dinner with me."

"Matt, you just don't get it. Do you honestly believe it's that simple? It wasn't just you not calling," she said with an expression of hurt, "but it was your indifferent attitude. I didn't hide my feelings from you. I'm too old for this. I refuse to pursue a man searching for his own death. Let's call it quits, shall we?"

"Claire, I'm not asking you for anything other than dinner with me tonight."

"No! Don't you understand what I'm saying. It's pointless. There's no future."

"There is a future, Claire."

"I have a future, it's you who don't."

"What do you mean by that?"

"What do I mean?" she repeated. "What I mean is that I don't think you're going to live very long. And Matt, I don't want to be part of that. It's late. I must go." She hung up. I sat for several moments, holding the receiver and listening to the dial tone.

$$*\qquad*\qquad*\qquad*$$

After regaining my thoughts, I grabbed a pad and pen and began my outline for Braxton. At the top I sketched "Written Agreement" and then the following:

- new identities

- new location

- delivery of funds

- time

- test

- protection

For the next several hours I worked relentlessly, trying to fill in the gaps and holes of the plan. I found myself getting nowhere. I was mentally and physically exhausted, and I couldn't get what Claire had said out of my mind. My watch showed the time was just past eight. I fixed a martini, ordered a pizza, and thought about my predicament.

The silence was shattered by the phone. I let it ring four times and then listened to the caller as he was picked up by my answering machine. The voice was urgent. "Mr. Lawrence, this is Jason Best. We have a report for you. Call me."

Before he could disconnect, I picked up the phone, shut off the machine, and said, "Jason, this is Lawrence. What have you found out?"

"We staked out the box, but didn't expect an early result. Within hours it was visited by a heavy set man in his thirties."

"Did you find out who he was?"

"We followed him. He met a man in a coffee shop on Oak Lawn. A thin man, about five foot ten, thinning hair, in his fifties. He wore small glasses. Ring any bells?"

"No, not that I can think of. Do you have anything else for me to go on?

"How about photographs? We took this guy's picture. I'll drop them by your apartment in the morning. What else do you want us to do?"

"Stand by. I want to see those pictures."

"By the way, Mr. Lawrence," he volunteered, "if someone is trying to kill you, do you want to tell me what you're doing in your apartment answering your own phone?"

"I'm screening my calls through my answering machine," I said defensively.

"What good does that do when you're a sitting duck?"

"Jason, I don't want your protection. I only want information."

"Maybe you should want my protection. Let me tell you something—you're not using your head. It won't help you, or me, if you get yourself dead."

"So what do you recommend?"

"Get out of there is what I recommend. That's a no-brainer!"

I wasn't going to do that. "Call me as soon as you get an answer."

The next morning I received an 8:30 A.M. call from Frank at the security desk. "There's a man here to see you," he said. "Says he's got a package. Want me to let him come up?"

"What's his name?"

I heard Frank mumble something to my visitor, and then "Says his name is Best."

"Send him up."

Several minutes later I opened my door to meet Jason Best. His face looked like the road map for the Mojave Desert. His eyes appeared bloodshot and his posture was pathetic. I realized that this is what you get from the yellow pages. "Come in, Mr. Best," I said motioning him to my study. "Coffee?"

"Yeah." He sounded worn out.

"Work all night?" I asked.

"Played all night," he said. "The way I play, it's about the same. Here, take a look at this." He handed me a small manilla envelope. I opened it and saw two men through a window in the coffee house. There were a series of pictures, most very difficult to see.

Watching me struggle to identify the two men, he reached into his pocket and produced a magnifying glass. "Look through this," he suggested.

I studied each face carefully, and then it hit me like a two ton truck. "McAlister," I whispered.

"Mac who?"

"McAlister," I repeated. "Jason, this guy's a U.S. Attorney!" I nervously studied the picture again, feeling my pulse quicken.

"What would he be doing meeting with the guy with the P.O. box?"

"I don't know…. My God," I stammered, my heart pounding, "he has to be involved with the people trying to kill me."

"You got to be kidding!"

I waited for a moment, allowing my equilibrium to return to normal. "I only wish I were," I said with a sinking feeling in my stomach. "Try to get more information on these two. Also, see what you can find out about a man named Dawson, who's somehow tied in with McAlister."

"This will really cost you. Do you have any idea what's involved for me to be investigating a U.S. Attorney?"

"How much?"

"Another five thousand dollars."

"That's a lot. O.K., but for God's sake, limit it to five thousand unless I tell you otherwise."

He drank his coffee like someone trying to recover from a hangover, which I suspected he was. "Mr. Lawrence," he said preparing to leave, "do you know what you're getting involved with? You don't screw with U.S. Attorneys."

"I'm not getting involved—I'm there. And yes, I know all about U.S. Attorneys. Just do your job, and do it very discreetly."

"I'll be discreet to your last penny," he said with a sickening grin. "You'll hear from me in a couple of days." He left, and I wondered if I had made a good or bad choice. The results so far were impressive, but he wasn't.

*   *   *   *

On Sunday Claire gave in. We agreed to meet at Casa Olé, a Mexican restaurant in far north Dallas, for dinner. I wasn't quite sure what to say, but I knew it had better be good. It was decorated in white stucco with a dark red tile floor. Dark green glass lanterns hung from the heavy rafters on the ceiling, giving it an appearance that was more like Rick's Cafè Amèricain in Casablanca than a Mexican restaurant. A mustached waiter, speaking unintelligible English, brought me chips and hot sauce while I waited for her.

She came in twenty minutes late, looking stunning in a yellow and white tattersall silk blouse, a pleated blue skirt and gray cashmere sweater. She walked up to the table, pushed her brunette hair away from her eyes, and said unexpectedly, "I've missed you."

I stood quickly, showing my surprise with what she had said. I smiled.

She smiled back, slightly, masking any reaction to my response. "Don't misinterpret that, Matt." Her expression then changed. "Are you going to tell me what you've been doing?"

"In time. But first, can I order you a margarita?"

"Please." She settled in her chair, placed her purse on the table, and slowly twisted her pearl necklace between her thumb and forefinger.

"How was your date?" I asked.

"What date?"

"Robert's friend."

"That's none of your business," she answered curtly. "I don't ask you about your dates. Matt, let's not get this started on the wrong foot, shall we?"

"I'm sorry. It is none of my business. Since I saw you last, I've been to New England once and Big Spring twice."

"What's in New England?" She looked down and took a light sip of her drink.

"A man named Julius Freytag. He was involved with the man Bird Dog killed in Rome."

"Involved?"

"Yes, he was the broker. He served as a middleman between the killer and whoever hired him."

She put down her drink and stared at me for a moment in silence. "How did you find him?"

"Do you remember the numbers Bird Dog found in his pocket? One was Freytag's phone number."

"Who told you that?"

"Jarrett."

"This is incredible!" she said, fidgeting with her drink. "After all you've been through, I can't believe you'd take the risk of confronting the man who arranged for that killer to find us in Rome. Who did he say hired him?"

"You won't believe this. He didn't know. He's involved in an elaborate, and evidently very secretive, murder for hire business. He's amazingly detached from the people he acts for."

"You're telling me someone is secretly hiring killers to murder you. Matt, you've got to be scared to death! I am, just listening to you."

I took a large drink and mentally agreed with her. I was scared.

Before I could speak, she said, "Jarrett! Tell me you're not back working with him."

"No. Jarrett told me about Freytag to let me know how angry he is at me. He told me to buzz off."

"What else?"

"I hired a private detective to follow up on a lead I got from Freytag. It led to McAlister."

"You must be kidding," she said with a startled look on her face.

"I only wish I were."

"What does it mean?"

"I have no idea," I said. "You know, it never occurred to me that people from the Justice Department could have any involvement with Freytag."

She sighed and gave me a look of hopelessness. "If you can believe what you read, our government's capable of anything. But the real question is why—why would they want to do that? It just doesn't make any sense. Is it possible that your private detective is mistaken or that what he found was just a coincidence?"

"Anything's possible. But not likely. There's something going on that's terribly wrong, but I can't figure it out."

"Let's change the subject for a moment," she suggested. "Can we?"

"Yes, of course. What would you like to talk about?"

She took a deep breath and let it out slowly. "How are your chest and shoulder?"

"A little stiff, but healing miraculously. I still can't believe I was so lucky."

"I can't either, Matt. I sit here and look at you, and think that just two months ago you were lying in a wet street, apparently dying. I still have nightmares about that."

She took another sip of her margarita and we ordered dinner. I couldn't take my eyes off of her. She truly was more beautiful than I had remembered.

"I know you have this other relationship," I said as she handed her menu to the waiter, "but I really want to see you again."

She placed her elbows on the table, adjusted her gold bracelet, and gave me a long look. "This meeting is against my better judgment, but I'm here."

We each ordered another drink. Claire then gently closed her eyes and reached for my hand. "I honestly began to believe that I would never hear from you again."

"Please try to understand. That was not about you."

She looked at me, confused. "Then what was that about?"

I shrugged. "About my fixation on finding them, my complete pre-occupation with revenge for what they did."

She contemplated my answer with a questioning look in her eyes. "Does that mean you're ready to surrender this obsession you have?"

I hesitated, carefully weighing my answer. "Yes…and no."

"There's a catch, isn't there, Matt?"

"I can't quit—you know that. Whatever it takes, I will find them and they will pay."

"Matt, after what happened in Europe and what you just said, you're beyond hope. For a while, I felt as you do. But I don't agree anymore with what you're doing."

I stared at her, remaining silent. She continued, carefully measuring her words. "Why," she said slowly, "can't you change? Can't you see…what you're trying to do, what you've done, is futile? You won't find any more answers—only more pain."

"There is a purpose and a reason. For too long I've been following my instincts. It's gotten me in a lot of trouble. I've changed that. I believe now that if I follow the money, it will lead me to the truth."

She stared at me intensely. "The truth…Matt, is that really what you're after? You just used the word *revenge*. And why in the world do you think you can find the truth? Other people tried and they're dead. And it almost killed you."

"It's useless, Claire. You're wasting your time."

She let out a deep breath and said nothing for a few moments.

"That's what I've been trying to say. Maybe you do get it. So long, Matt."

"Can I see you again?"

"Not for a long time. I leave tomorrow for Houston to stay with my sick mother. I don't expect to be back for quite a while." And she was gone.

*   *   *   *

Thirty minutes later I arrived at my apartment. The first thing I saw was Frank, waiving to me as I pulled into the drive. I gave him my keys, got out, and was about to step into the elevator when Frank said, "Oh Mr. Lawrence, the officers came to talk to you while you were out. I showed them to your apartment. Hope I did right."

I stopped dead in my tracks and turned to face him. "You did what?"

"They didn't have uniforms, but they had badges. I made them show me their badges. They said they were investigating a murder, that it was important they talked to you. They said you knew they were coming."

I was incredulous at what he had done. "And you let them into my apartment?"

He detected my displeasure. "No, I wouldn't do that. They're waiting in the hallway for you, on your floor."

"Frank, do me a favor. Call the police and ask them if they sent plain clothes officers here."

Frank dialed 911 and told them the story. His call was quickly rerouted to police headquarters, where he was told by the Sergeant that the Dallas police had sent no one to my apartment. At my request, he asked them to send a squad car to investigate, and then turned to me. "Mr. Lawrence, don't go up there. The police will be here in a minute. Let them handle this."

I agreed with him and could see his embarrassment. "Frank, don't worry about it. You didn't do anything wrong. When the police get here, show them up. Call me on my cellphone when they've left. Here's the number." I handed him a piece of paper on which I had scribbled my cellphone number, got back in my car and drove to the Mansion Bar to wait for his call. An hour later he called and said the phony officers had left by the time the police arrived. I returned to my apartment, obsessed with the thought that *they* knew where I lived and had actually been there.

CHAPTER 21

▼

Big Spring, Texas, 1992

It was 6 A.M. when I awoke the next morning. I showered and dressed quickly and headed for Big Spring. Braxton wouldn't accept what I found out through Best.

"You're going to try to make me believe," he said, showing his utter frustration, "that McAlister and the Justice Department are trying to murder you. C'mon Matt, you're losing touch with reality. It doesn't make any sense. I won't accept that."

"Bic, stop and think this through with me. The detective I hired took pictures—it was McAlister."

"So what do you want me to do?" he demanded. "Give up my only chance to get out of this place because some schlock detective you hired took some pictures that you figured out, looking through a magnifying glass, are of McAlister and some other jerk. No way!"

"What if he were involved?"

"What if, what if!" he shouted back. "Don't you mouthpieces speak any other language. For Christ's sake, Matt, I can't deal with what ifs. Why do you think I agreed to pay you $1 million? You deal with the what ifs, but you better have a plan that works."

I glanced quickly around the room to see if anyone was listening. We were alone. I looked back to see him grimace. "OK." I said. "Relax. Let's start from square one. In two weeks or so you walk out of here. Where to?"

He paced the floor in front of me, showing his impatience. Lighting a cigar, he turned, leaned heavily against the wall, and said, "I've thought hard about that. South America is where. Quito, Ecuador, in fact. Sterling has relatives there. Its population is mostly European, and predominately German. Very secretive—but friendly."

"You'll get no protection there."

He ignored my comment and began pacing again. Puffing violently on the cigar, he stopped, leaned in front of me, and filled my face with disgusting smoke. "I'm not going to rely on some asshole from the Justice Department for my safety. I'll take care of myself. What's next?"

"Identities, that's what's next."

"What do you suggest?"

"Sit down and I'll tell you."

He sat, continuing to puff on the cigar. "Since you've decided on Ecuador, let's require citizenship there."

"Can they do that?"

"We can ask. I think they can do almost anything they want. Now, for the million dollar question. "When and how do you release the money?"

"When Sterling and I are in Ecuador, and not before. You get the picture?"

"It won't work. You told me that Dawson already laid out an absolute condition that you don't walk until they have the money."

"So what's the solution?"

"An escrow with a friendly third party."

"Like who?"

"You tell me who you trust?"

"No fucking one!"

"What about your buddies in the Vatican, like the Pope?"

"Damn it, Matt, forget it. They wouldn't lift a finger to help me."

The room was beginning to get crowded and I could see his discomfort increase. "Shall we finish this another time?" I asked.

"No, I'm running out of time. You come up with a fool proof escrow, but do it by tomorrow. In the meantime, what else do we have to deal with?"

"The old problem of double cross," I said, lowering my voice to stay below the noise in the visitor's area.

"Explain that."

"Use your brain, Bic. We're devising this elaborate scheme to get you out of here. What if it's a set up? We have to deal with that possibility."

He looked at me oddly, frowning. Before he could speak, a heavy-set guard came up, grabbed him by the arms and said "Time's up. Let's go. Prison activities are waiting."

"Matt," he said, looking over his shoulder as he was being taken away, "get this thing figured out, completely, and by tomorrow. I'm out of time. Be back here then."

On my flight from Midland back to Dallas, I accepted my complimentary Coke and began drafting. The agreement was between Henry David Braxton and Buckroyd McAlister, U.S. Attorney for the Northern District of Texas, acting for the United States of America. It provided for the complete release and discharge of Braxton from prison and from all crimes for which he was convicted or charged. I set the date of his release as the fifteenth day of January. I further provided for new identities, Ecuadorian citizenship and passports from Ecuador for Braxton and Sterling.

Next, I dealt with the funds. I required that a deposit be made with American Escrow of Dallas on the fourteenth day of January, leaving the amount blank. I underlined the blank space as I thought of Braxton's refusal to tell me anything about the money. Finally, I included provisions dealing with an unconditional guaranty of the Attorney General of the United States that the identity and location of Braxton and Sterling would at all times be kept strictly confidential, and that their safety and welfare would be guaranteed by the United States government.

In Dallas, I called an old friend at American Escrow, Dan Walsh, and posed a hypothetical question to him. "If a large sum of money, say $200 million, were deposited with you for delivery, upon certain conditions, to the U.S. Government, how would you account for those funds and how would you confirm to the U.S. Attorneys' office that it was in your possession?"

He thought for a minute, obviously impressed by the size of my hypothetical question, and answered, "By certified confirmation, typed on our letterhead, stating that we were holding the funds."

"That simple?"

"Yes, that simple."

"Dan, I need a favor. I need a pro forma confirmation to show to the Justice Department, with the amount left blank. Can you do it?"

"A pro forma. Explain."

"Give me an original but unsigned typed confirmation, showing all relevant information except the amount, so that I can get their approval. Can you do that?"

"Yes. Where do you want it delivered?"

"To Leigh, my secretary, marked confidential." I had the first leg of my "test".

The next day I delivered four typed copies of my draft agreement to Braxton. His had one comment. "They'll never sign it."

"You've got no choice," I said. "If you want any assurance that McAlister will live up to the deal, you've got to get it in writing."

"We'll see. By the way, I had visitors yesterday. You'll never guess who."

"Tell me."

"Jarrett and his gunny, Bird Dog."

"Why would they take a chance in coming here?" I wondered out loud.

"Because he's getting desperate, that's why. He knows he'll never see any part of the money without me. You know what," he added, "he's sweetening the deal. He says he'll split it, 50-50, if I'll cooperate."

"And what did you say?"

"I told him I'd think about it."

I got up, walked around the table, and sat squarely in front of him. He knew what I was going to say and slid his chair back to get some distance between us. "This man is dangerous. I can assure you he knew you were lying."

He blinked wide and then rubbed his eyes. "So what's he going to do?" he asked, taking issue with what I had said. "He can't get to me in here."

"Don't be so sure. And what about Sterling, or when you get out?"

"Sterling knows nothing, and he'll never find me once I'm out."

He got up, walked over to the window, and then turned. His uneasiness with Jarrett was obvious. "Do you think he might try to get to Sterling?"

"It's possible," I answered. "Do you want to consider compromising with Jarrett?"

"Hell no!" His words lashed out at me like a long whip. "I've got nothing to compromise with. After I pay Uncle Sam and you, I'll need the rest for my retirement. Do me a favor, Matt. Get Sterling away from our house, into a safe place until we finish our little exchange."

"Where?"

Her sister lives in Wichita Falls. Take her there."

"Alright. Now let's talk about the mechanics. When do you see Dawson next?"

"Tomorrow."

"When he gets here, Bic, give him the letter. Tell him it's a deal breaker—no money without it."

He lit a large Cuban cigar, contemplated my instructions, and began blowing rings. "Deal breaker? Fat chance. I'd kiss his ass to get out of here."

I looked at him, encircled in smoke, and knew why he needed me. "If that's your attitude—great! You'll get out of here, but it might be feet first. Use your head. They'll sign a letter, it's required by law."

"And what do I say when he asks where the money is?" He glared at me with raised eyebrows.

"That's elementary. You tell him we'll give him written confirmation of the escrow when you get the letter."

"You can't do that! I told you, I'm not telling anyone where the money is until I'm out of here."

"You don't have to," I said quietly.

"Then how do you give him the confirmation, counselor?"

"I've got that all worked out. We give him a confirmation, but not a real one."

"A fake? You've got to be crazy. They'll find out."

"I'm not sure they will. Unless they're playing games with you, I think they'll accept that letter and go forward. It sure as hell won't hurt to try."

"Let's do it," he answered, brightening to the challenge of my deception.

"I'm glad you agree." I removed an envelope from my pocket labeled American Escrow. It contained the pro forma letter, an official looking confirmation, emblazoned with a seal confirming authenticity, or appearing to do so. I handed it to him. "Give this to Dawson after he delivers a signed letter to you."

Braxton took the letter, examined it carefully, and said in a disappointed tone, "This won't work. It's not signed and the amount's not filled in."

"The amount's up to you. Remember, you wouldn't tell me how much you had agreed to pay."

"How do I get the amount filled in, and who's going to sign it?"

"Borrow the warden's typewriter and fill in the blank. As for the signature, give it to me."

"He returned the letter and watched in amazement as I took a pen from my pocket and signed the letter in the name of Charles Bickingham.

"Who's this guy?" he asked.

"One of the escrow officers at American Escrow. Don't worry, he's authorized to sign."

"Yeah, but you're not," he said.

"I've got that covered, too. Bickingham's on safari in Kenya for two weeks. If they call him to verify that he signed, that's what they'll hear."

Braxton rose, took another hard look at the letter, and shook his head. "This is fucking crazy. Where does this get me?"

"It gets you a signed commitment from McAlister, without you telling him where the money is. When the time comes, you can tell him about your little game. Then it won't make any difference to him— he'll have the money."

As I finished my explanation, two warning bells went off, signaling the end of our visit. "Bic, do this the way I planned it for you. It will work. And in the meantime, either start arranging to get the money or tell me where it is and I'll get it."

"Matt, I'm not going to say this again. Forget the money! I'll worry about that."

*   *   *   *

When I arrived back in Dallas at my apartment, I was met by Jason Best. Rumpled suit and stained tie—he looked like hell. "Do you buy your clothes at Neiman Marcus?" I asked when I first saw him.

"No," he answered, thinking I liked the way he dressed. "Clothes Warehouse, but they tell me the suits are the same sold by Neiman's, just one-third the price."

My humor had escaped him. I wondered silently about his basic intelligence. "What are you doing here?" I asked.

"Mr. Lawrence, I found out some things you should know. Let's go up to your apartment. We shouldn't talk here."

In my apartment he produced a logged time report of his activities for the past several days and a stack of photographs. "What's all this?" I asked.

"I'll tell you in a moment. First, you got a beer? I'm parched."

"Drinking on the job?" I half-heartedly asked.

"Not generally. Just today." I handed him a cold Amstel Light as he sifted through the pictures to produce several he wanted me to see. "Recognize anyone?" he asked.

I gazed at the pictures. They were taken in a parking lot and showed several men talking. None looked familiar. "How did you take these without being seen?"

"Telephoto lens. Look again," he asked. "Any familiar faces?"

"Sorry, Jason. I'm afraid you may have wasted your time. Who are they supposed to be?"

"The one on the left," he began, pointing to a rugged looking man evidently in his early forties and slightly balding, goes by the name Rudy Blair."

"How in the world can you know that?"

"That's the way he signs credit card bills. He met with McAlister on Tuesday morning and then had lunch with the other men in this picture. I simply told the cashier that I thought our bills had been mixed up and asked to see his. There it was, his calling card."

"So what? Jason, I'm impressed with your work, but it gets us nowhere."

"So this guy doesn't work for the Justice Department. Guess what he does?"

"You tell me."

He stooped to swallow half the bottle of beer in one drink. Letting out a low belch, he looked at me and said, "This guy's a private eye. Ain't that something. Now why would McAlister be working with a private dick when he's got the whole FBI at his beck and call?"

"That is interesting. You just may earn your keep after all. What else did you find out?"

"Only this. See the guy to the right of Blair, the one with the glasses?"

I struggled with the picture and then nodded my confirmation. "Who is he?"

"Dawson Henry. The guy you asked about."

I opened my eyes wide in disbelief. "So that's why I couldn't find him before. Dawson is his first name, not his last. But how do you know that's him?"

"I'm speculating, but just a little. We think we heard one of the others call him by that name."

"You think you heard that, in the parking lot at telephoto distance?"

"We have listening devices. Yeah, we think we heard that."

"So how can you put the name with the face?"

"He looks like a guy named Dawson Henry I met several years ago. He was an insurance investigator then. We're checking to see what he does now."

I let him out, thanking him and feeling relieved to have him out of my sight. My watch showed 5 P.M. on Wednesday, January 10. Five days until Braxton's release. I called Peter Segal.

"Peter," I asked, "Have you found out anything?"

"Yes, but it may not help you. We checked all the registries. There's no one with the name Dawson. With nothing more to go on, we're at a dead end."

"Sorry to put you through all this, but I just found out that Dawson is his first name, not his last. His last name is Henry."

"Don't worry about it. I'll check out Henry. By the way, Matt, did you know McAlister's leaving the Department?"

"You're kidding! When?"

"End of the year. He's been there over twenty years, evidently taking early retirement. I'll get back to you on Henry. Let me know if there's anything else you need." He hung up before waiting for my response.

CHAPTER 22

▼

The next Wednesday I found myself again seated at the end of a long table in the Federal Courts building. The room was cold and barren. Beige plaster walls, brightly lit with cheap exposed light fixtures, and inexpensive gray soiled carpet—it reeked with a musty smell and government frugality. The summons I received was signed personally by Buckroyd McAlister.

McAlister was seated directly across from me. "Cup of coffee?" he offered as he poured himself one from a plastic thermos.

"Thank you, I'd like one."

He slid a full cup in front of me, sat back and tilted his chair at a precarious backward angle. His gold rimmed glasses, on his slight frame, reminded me a little of Heinrich Himmler, the Nazi Gestapo chief. "Mr. Lawrence, you're a very lucky man. We have more than enough to implicate you in the schemes of your client, Braxton, but so far we have decided to leave you out of it. Frankly, I think you're an honest man, but you were in the wrong place at the wrong time."

"Braxton's not my client."

He sipped very slowly on his coffee, adjusted his glasses on his nose, and placed the sole of his shoe on the edge of the table. "If he's not your client, what have you been doing in Big Spring this past week?"

"Visiting an old friend."

"You're pushing your luck, Mr. Lawrence. What you're doing could be interpreted as obstructing justice. You don't need that."

"What do you mean, obstructing justice?" I took a deep breath to calm my anger.

"We know Braxton embezzled millions," he said, carefully measuring his words, "and we gave you limited immunity. You're not his counsel of record, we know that. But what you're doing is interfering with our investigation. Do you know what that means?"

He gave me a frozen look. He took another drink of coffee, refilled his cup, and softened his look. "I want to tell you something, Mr. Lawrence. You can walk out of here with my assurance that you will no longer be a target of our investigation. You can go on with your life, but I want your assurance that you will stop interfering with us. Do you get my point?"

I could feel my pulse quicken. "Are you telling me that I can have no contacts with Braxton?"

"I'm telling you," he said, tilting his chair back again, "that you're free to do as you wish. But know that what you do will have consequences. We will not tolerate interference from you or anyone else. You'd better think this over. We're not playing games!"

He continued to sip his coffee, rocking slowly in his chair as he watched my every move. "It's your choice, Mr. Lawrence. You won't have a second chance."

"Are you threatening me?"

He flashed a thin but arrogant smile. "Of course I'm threatening you! Either you stay away from Braxton and our investigation, or get ready for a felony indictment."

"You would do that?"

"Of course we would do that!" he said, slamming his coffee cup on the table. "If you don't stay away from Braxton, you'll have only yourself to blame for what happens."

I looked hard into his riveting eyes, feeling perspiration on my forehead. He stood up, adjusted his vest, and asked, "May I have your word?"

"You do." I never intended to carry out my promise.

"You've made a very wise choice, Mr. Lawrence. Let me remind you, that should you have any relapse in your commitment, you will seriously regret it. Consider that you have just gained your freedom. Understood?"

"Yes, understood."

*   *   *   *

I walked through the long corridor of the building, trying to reconstruct the meeting I had just had. When I reached the garage and my car, I sat for a moment in silence, unable to fully piece it all together. I then called Leigh.

"Leigh, please call Sterling and arrange to get her to her sister's house in Wichita Falls. Tell her it's important that she leave immediately."

"Matt, do you want me to drive her there?"

"Only if she wants your company. It's important that she not let anyone know where she'll be."

"Got it. Do you want to hear your messages?"

"Only the important ones."

She hesitated and then said, "I'm not sure what's important, but I'll try. One man has been calling, says his name is Best, and that it's important that he reach you. Do you know him?"

"Yes, unfortunately."

"Who is he, Matt? He's called before but never left a message."

I hesitated. "It's unimportant. Who else called?"

"You had a call from Martine someone in France, from several old clients, Charles Martin and Dick Millard, and from a man in Houston named Kirkendall. Other than that, nothing that can't wait. Matt, some of these calls are several days old. You know you have not been checking with me for your messages."

"I know. Sorry. I've had a lot to do. Leigh, did Martine say anything?"

"No, just to call her. Who is she, Matt?"

"Just a friend."

"A friend? She seemed very secretive."

"What about this guy Kirkendall. What did he want?"

"He wouldn't say either. He just asked that you call, but he did say that he had some information for you."

"Don't forget…"

"Sterling," she interrupted. "I know it's important—you don't have to tell me again."

"Sorry, I just wanted to be sure you would get her."

"Have I ever let you down?"

"No," I said apologetically.

$$* \quad * \quad * \quad *$$

The next morning I called Beaune, France, for the Hotel de la Poste. There I found Martine Paulet. "Martine, this is Matt Lawrence. You called."

"Yes. How are you?"

"Surviving."

"Mr. Lawrence, I talked to my stepfather. He said he would like very much to help you, but he can't. He has no close contacts with the French banks you mentioned, and has never heard of the Institute for Religious Works. I'm sorry."

"Thank you for trying. I have actually answered part of my question. The Institute is the Vatican bank."

"Oh, how interesting. Mr. Lawrence, I've thought about you and your wife. Again, I want to say how sorry I am. Perhaps you might want to get away and come to Beaune. It's beautiful this time of year."

"I may take you up on your suggestion. I do need to get away, but I might feel very lonely in Beaune."

"I'm here," she said. "Maybe I could be of help to you."

"Thank you. I'll let you know."

We hung up and I tried to reach Kirkendall and Best. But it was late that day before I could reach either of them. Kirkendall stepped out of a meeting to talk to me. "Ah, Mr. Lawrence. I was asked by Ms. Boles to contact you."

I paused and thought for a minute. "Ms. Boles? I don't think I know a Ms. Boles."

"That's quite strange," he said, "because she said she met with you in London several months ago. Well, it sounds as if she made a mistake."

"Wait a minute. You mentioned London. Is she the lady with Barclays Bank?"

"Then you do remember?"

"Yes, I'm sorry. It didn't register at first. What can I do for you?"

"Ms. Boles said you inquired about the meaning of a code. I believe it was YANOU. Well, she asked that I pass on to you the results of her inquiry. It seems that YANOU is the name of a lady in Italy."

I took a deep breath and let it out slowly. "Do you know her full name?"

"I do. Ms. Boles said it was Yanou Folare."

"What else did she say?"

"Nothing," he said. "She thought you might want to know more about her, but said she was sorry that she couldn't be of help. Our files indicated nothing else."

"Who are you with?"

"I'm with Barclays of course, here in Houston."

I replaced the receiver slowly, thinking...Yanou! It wasn't a code at all—it was a person. But I was no closer to her. One more lead, one more apparent dead end. I tried Best for a second time. Again, no answer.

The night sky was drifting in and the clouds were turning a hazy orange as the sun set below the horizon. Because of the time difference, I couldn't call France. I got in my car and drove to Travis Walk, a Moroccan style shopping area on the edge of downtown. There, I went into a small French restaurant, La Routhe. It was decorated with tapestries hanging from the walls, Persian rugs on a rust tile floor, and candle lit tables with soft pink table clothes. And it was filled with memories of Julia. I hesitated as I entered, trying to look away from those memories.

My nerves were jangled. I sat by the window with a double martini, pondering Yanou Folare. Who was she, and what was her connection with Braxton? And how could I find her? My head ached as I studied the menu, and I noticed that the light rain was beginning to turn to sleet. When the waiter approached, I was startled by a car which screeched to a halt at the stop light on the corner outside my window. The car looked very familiar, as did the woman in the front seat.

I couldn't make out the man next to her, but as she turned to say something to him, I caught a clearer glimpse of her profile. It was as if I were dreaming. It couldn't be true! The car was a black Mercedes, and the woman looked exactly like Claire. I looked again and they were gone. In the far distance, I heard a voice say, "Excuse me, sir, your menu," as my waiter tried to hand it to me.

My world seemed to spin out of control. I grabbed the menu for a touch of reality. "Are you alright?" he asked, showing his concern.

"Yes," I mumbled. "Please, leave me alone." I returned the menu and left for my apartment. Waiting for me was another bombshell—Best. "You look awful," he said, "like an old friend of mine just before he died of cancer."

"You could have said anything else. Jason, I don't know how much time you're spending on my affairs, but it's beginning to be too much. I can't afford to put your kids through college."

"It's O.K.," he said, holding up both hands to silence my concern. "I don't have any kids."

"I need a drink," I said. "Do you want one?"

He looked at me with his bloodshot eyes as if I were crazy. "Is the Pope catholic?"

"Scotch or bourbon?"

"Bring the bottles, then I'll tell you."

"Jason, I'm very tired."

"No problem," he said, unloosening his tie. He slouched back on my sofa, took a stiff drink of the scotch on the rocks I had fixed for him, and then said, "Mr. Lawrence, you're going to love what I'm about to tell you. This guy Dawson Henry—well that's just one of his names. We traced his fingerprints through a buddy at Dallas police. You're gonna love this," he said again proudly gulping his drink.

"For God's sake Jason, get to the point."

"He was a priest! When my buddy told me that, I said you're shittin' me. He wasn't. Henry went by another name as a priest, it's Kaletta. Evidently sort of a renegade in the Church—not well liked by the people we talked to."

"So where does all this lead?"

"You tell me," he answered. "What's a former priest doing in a deal like this? And what's he doing mixed up with McAlister?"

I took a sip of my drink, finding it difficult to get the couple at the stop sign out of my mind. I stared at Best, hardly taking in what he was saying. He took another large swallow of his drink, refilled his glass, and said, "You're in another world, aren't you?"

I considered how to answer his question, and then finally said, "I may need your help on another matter. There is this woman that I'm very fond of, but I'm not sure she's what she appears to be. Is it possible that you could find out for me where she's been in the past several days…without her knowing it? If she ever thought that I had her under surveillance, it would be the end of us."

"You think she's screwing around on you?"

I raised my eyes to catch his, and thought that's the kind of mind I'm dealing with. "No, it's nothing like that. She told me she would be in Houston with her sick mother, but I think I saw her here in Dallas, just thirty minutes ago."

"Yeah, I can do that. What's her name, and do you have any pictures?"

"No pictures. Her name is Claire Sorrell. She lives out on Meadow Lane, along the Bent Tree golf course. Jason, this woman is very important to me. You can't let her know you're watching her. That's critical! Do you understand?"

"She won't know anything. If she's in Houston, how do I find her?"

"You're the detective, do some detecting. All I want you to tell me is that she has been with her sick mother yesterday and today. That's all."

"What if she hasn't been? Then what?"

I poured myself another drink, kicked off my shoes and took a long sip. I wasn't sure that I really wanted to know. "If she hasn't been in Houston, see if you can find out where she's been and what she's been doing. Will you do that?"

"I'll do my best, but I'm no magician. You're giving me very little to go on. Where will you be?"

"I don't know. Leave any messages on my answering machine. And Jason, don't call my secretary. She's beginning to ask too many questions. I don't want her to know anything about this—or about you."

On Friday morning, Leigh told me she hadn't been able to reach Sterling. She also told me she had received a strange call from Braxton. He left no number but only a message. The letter was signed. I called him in Big Spring, and after what seemed to be an eternity, he was brought to the phone.

"Matt," he said in an excited voice, "they signed the letter, just as you wrote it. Can you believe it? I've got to hand it to you, it worked."

"Just a minute," I cautioned, "signing the letter doesn't get you out of there. How do they propose to get you to Ecuador?"

"Dawson said it would be no problem. That passports would be arranged and that we would become citizens within a short time."

"Dawson! Bic, this guy's a chameleon. I've had a private detective look into him. He was a priest!"

"That's great!" Braxton said, his voice rising. "When have you been screwed by a priest?"

"It's not that simple. He's evidently some sort of a renegade. Tell me, why would a priest be involved in this?"

"I don't care if he's a fuckin' dog catcher," he snapped back," as long as I'm safely out of here. The letter is signed by McAlister, that's all I want."

"What have you done about the money?"

"I followed your instructions to a tee. I gave them that phony letter. They took it hook, line and sinker!"

"This is the eighth of January, Bic. You are going to have to arrange for the money to be transferred to American Escrow in seven days. Can you do that?"

"They'll get the money…or its equivalent," he said casually. "By the way, Matt, did you take care of Sterling?"

I stopped dead in my tracks. "Or its equivalent? What the hell does that mean?"

I could hear him breathe deeply, showing his aggravation. "I've warned you, Matt," he said in a low voice. "Don't ask too many questions."

I suppressed my temper. "Sterling…my secretary couldn't reach her. I'll personally handle it today and get her to Wichita Falls. Don't worry, it'll be done. In the meantime, we have to nail down the arrangements with McAlister. Don't trust him. Until you and Sterling are safely relocated to Ecuador, we shouldn't assume he'll do what he promised."

"Even with the letter?"

"Even with the letter. That's just a first step."

Our conversation ended, and I turned on the radio as I prepared to find Sterling. According to the weather channel, the temperature had fallen during the night to an unseasonably low of 15 degrees. I dressed warmly in gray wool slacks and a heavy blue sweater. Walking out of the Athena, I was greeted by Frank. Sitting on the drive was my black Jaquar with the engine running. The exhaust fumes drifted slowly against the overcast sky which was layered with gray clouds.

"Thought you might want a warm car," Frank yelled out as I approached. "It's cold as hell!"

The wind whistled through the pine trees surrounding the building, making it seem ten degrees colder than it was. I quickly got into the car, nodding my thanks to Frank. The engine roared quietly as I pulled onto the Dallas Toll Road, heading north for Braxton's house. I could see flakes of snow begin to descend on my windshield as my mind drifted to thoughts of Julia and the last day we spent together.

The wail of a siren and flashing red and amber lights behind me put an end to my dreaming. I was approaching the Spring Creek cutoff, and quickly exited and pulled to a stop. The snow was now coming down in heavier drifts, blurring my vision. First a fire engine and then two police cars moved by me at rapid speed. I lowered the window slightly to be sure that they were far enough ahead, and then continued north. The cold air that came through as I raised the window was sharp and bitter.

Several blocks later I turned into Spring Dale Circle, the secluded alcove where Braxton had built his mansion in the eighties. It was a sprawling ranch style home situated behind a six foot high brick wall. I pulled up to the gate, pressed the button, and yelled for Sterling through the speaker. The rush of cold air stung my lungs when I lowered my window. Sitting there in silence, inhaling crystals of snow, I waited. There was no answer.

After ten minutes, I killed the engine and walked over to the heavy gate. It was not locked. I pushed and it opened enough for me to squeeze through. Standing in the shadows and the falling snow, I saw that twenty yards away from the house was Sterling's white Cadillac. Sucking in the cold air, I walked slowly towards the house, getting an ominous feeling of what I might find. The snow was blowing across the driveway in gusts when I reached the front door and rang several times. There was no answer. I tried the door and found that it was locked.

Moving to the side of the house, I saw what appeared to be a man standing in the shadows. I reached for my Beretta and released the safety. Walking slowly towards the back of the house, I was warned by a voice, off to the side, among some Poplar trees. "Hold it," he said. His outline seemed to fade in and out in the snow drifts. Wiping the snow from my eyes, I hesitated, and suddenly focused on a dark object he appeared to be holding in his hand.

"I'm here to see Mrs. Braxton," I yelled back. "Where is she?"

"Not here. You're trespassing."

"No, you're trespassing. Who are you?" I waited, feeling the cold wind bite at my nose and lips.

"A friend of the family."

"I don't believe you," I yelled back. "This family has no friends. Tell me where I can find her. I'm her attorney."

He slowly advanced towards me, keeping the object of my concern at his side. He was dressed in a heavy green parka, blue jeans and cowboy boots. I looked to see if he was alone and tried to prepare myself mentally for what might be coming. "Put down your gun," I demanded. "It's important that I see Mrs. Braxton."

He glared at me and shifted his stance, positioning himself at an angle, legs spread wide apart. "You've got ten seconds to get out of here."

"Or what?"

"Or you're a dead man."

I froze, nervously gripping my gun and pointing it towards him. Snow was beginning to blur my vision. "Who are you?" I asked.

"None of your business—" His voice trailed off as I saw him raise his gun. I pulled the trigger and the crack of my shot surprised him as he looked at me in amazement. It hit him between the eyes. His surprised expression quickly turned to one of fear, and then death. He fell backward into the snow, letting out a slight moan as he died. I felt a sickening feeling. This is what I had become—taking another man's life. I kept telling myself that I didn't have a choice. Probing the area with my eyes, I saw no one else.

I quickly searched his clothes, looking for some identification. In his wallet I found a Louisiana driver's license, almost $2000 in cash, some credit cards and a list of three phone numbers. His name was Robert Chandler, and the occupation shown on his license said photographer. I didn't believe it. I kept the wallet and looked towards the house. The back door was open.

The wind had blown snow onto the carpet, but the damage had already been done by Chandler. What was once a lavishly decorated house looked like a cyclone had hit it. Papers and books were strewn everywhere—the house had been professionally ransacked. I walked quietly from room to room, looking for Sterling. She wasn't there. Everywhere drawers had been emptied and the contents dumped.

Before I left the house, I looked one more time through the scattered papers and files, hoping for any clue that might tell me what Chandler was looking for, or where Braxton had hidden the money. Bank books, cancelled checks and statements all indicated that Sterling was living on very little. The bank accounts were all local, and there was no sign of foreign dealings or transactions with the Vatican bank or anyone else. I carefully wiped my fingerprints off of everything I had touched and returned to my car, dazed by the fact that I had just killed a man.

CHAPTER 23

▼

Braxton was stunned by the news that Sterling was missing and his house ransacked. After a long silence, he finally said, "Jarrett!"

"How do you know that?"

"Who else?"

I thought about the Louisiana driver's license I found on Chandler and mentally agreed with his conclusion. "What will he do with her?"

He shrugged. "Nothing—he won't harm her. He wants the money. When the money's delivered to McAlister, he'll have no reason to keep Sterling."

"Aren't you playing games with Sterling's life? And don't forget one fact, Bic. McAlister won't have all the money. You're keeping a bundle, so you tell me."

He rubbed his forehead, then pointed a finger at me. "Go see him, Matt. Find out what it will take to get Sterling back. I'll play his little game—but just for a while."

"What if he wants the money?"

"Fuck him—no way!"

"Wait a minute, Bic. I thought Sterling was important to you. What the hell do you think you'll accomplish with that attitude? I've met Jarrett. I wouldn't put anything past him. Not anything."

He glared at me. "Do it my way."

"If that's your decision, so be it. It's your funeral. Do you want to tell me what happens in the meantime?"

"Dawson told me the gates will open on the fifteenth, and I'll be on my way to South America with a new identity. Only when I arrive safely do they get the money. He agreed to that."

"Did you ask him who the hell he is and why he's negotiating for McAlister?"

"I know what you're thinking, Matt, but I'm not going to get into that. If he delivers, what difference does it make. If he doesn't, they'll never see the money. I've got to go. Call me when you talk to Jarrett. And, Matt," he added as he walked away, "get her back."

After many calls, the only thing I learned about Jarrett was that he was not in New Orleans or apparently anywhere else.

The next morning I met Best at the Good Eats Restaurant. He had promised information on Claire and McAlister. Good Eats was my choice, it seemed to fit him. He walked in wearing a two piece suit, each piece different. A blue suit coat and brown slacks. "Did you lose your razor?" I asked as he slid into the booth.

We were momentarily interrupted by an overweight waitress with uncombed hair, a swarthy complexion and an attitude, who wanted our orders. When she left, he answered, "It's my disguise. People think I'm an indigent. It works great. Who'd suspect I'm a private eye?"

"You sure have me fooled."

He grinned, wide and toothy.

"Claire Sorrell. What have you found out?"

He took a cup of coffee, lifted a folder and placed it on the table, and gave me a sympathetic look. "I hate like hell to be the one to tell you this. Your woman never went to Houston. We checked all the flights on the day you said she left. She wasn't on any of them. And off and on we spotted her car in her garage—she comes and goes."

"Then where was she?"

"I don't know. I couldn't have a man tailing her twenty-four hours a day. Too expensive. At this point, I just don't know."

I sat back, wondering if Claire's lies were really important. "What else you got?"

He looked around the room, gestured to the waitress, and said, "In a minute. This may take a while. You buying breakfast?"

"Yes, order what you want."

I couldn't eat, but watched him order half the menu. After the waitress had left, he returned his full attention to me. Opening the manilla folder, he said, "I want to show you a few things. First, here's a notice we picked up from our friend at Dallas police."

Best handed me a white sheet of paper. I stared at it for a minute, in disbelief. It said:

<u>WANTED BY U.S. MARSHALS</u>

Notice To Arresting Agency: Before arrest, validate warrant through National Crime Information Center (NCIC)-United States Marshals Service NCIC entry number (NIC/ W2335409873).

NAME: Henry, Dawson

ALIAS: Kaletta, Anthony; Alexander, Peter; Stewart, Robert; Ferdinand, Benjamin; "Kelso"; "Dawson"

DESCRIPTION:

Sex	Male
Race	White
Place of Birth	Santiago, Chile
Date of Birth	December 1, 1945;
Height	5'8"
Weight	165 lbs
Eyes	Brown
Hair	Brown
Skintone	Medium
Scars, Marks, Tattoos	1" Vertical Scar Left Cheek
Social Security no.	499-56-9081, 563-21-5443
NCIC Fingerprint C1.	P0 04 12 14 24 27 57 48 39 20

WANTED FOR:	FELONY THEFT, ASSAULT, MURDER
Warrant Issued:	District of New York
Warrant Number:	9020-0447-1111-G
DATE WARRANT ISSUED:	September 10, 1992

MISCELLANEOUS INFORMATION: Henry is a frequent traveler. He speaks fluent English, Spanish and Italian. He uses many disguises, including businessman, Catholic priest and private investigator

---

If arrested or whereabouts known, notify the local United States Marshals Office (Telephone: 212-342-5667)

"This is Dawson Henry?" I asked. "You can't be serious! This man's a dangerous criminal. What's he doing with McAlister?"

Best took a bite of his eggs, gulped down some coffee, and handed me the next piece of paper in the file. It showed an official "HOLD" that was put on the Marshals' notice by the U.S. Attorneys' office—in Dallas, signed by one Buckroyd McAlister.

"Can he do that?" I asked in amazement.

Trying to talk with a mouth full of toast, Best mumbled, "Looks like he did it, doesn't it."

He took another swig of coffee, moved his plate to the side, and belched quietly. He then handed me the final piece of paper, a computer printout of airline reservations in the name of Buckroyd McAlister to Rome, Italy, on January 16.

"How in the world did you get this?"

"A friend, at American Airlines. Just a hunch, but I asked this friend to tap into the Sabre reservations system, under McAlister's name, and that's what he came up with. Impressed?"

"Yes, enormously."

I thought about what he said. McAlister going to Rome, on the day after Braxton is to be released. And Henry, wanted for murder, was the contact point with Braxton. "Why?"

"I can't answer your question," he said. "But consider this. These are bad people—real bad. You know it, and they don't know that you know. That's critical. Whatever it is they're up to, at least you have a chance to see it coming. But you'd better not forget," he added, "that you've got a tiger by the tail."

I watched him drink his coffee, in silence, and wondered what was next. Finally, I said, "Jason, I get no comfort from that. It may be O.K. to have a tiger by the tail, but you'd better know what to do next. I don't."

He didn't respond. I watched him, inhaling a piece of toast. "You've spent a lot of time on this," I said, "and I'm very grateful. But to tell you the truth, I feel lost. You're giving me all this information, and I'm suddenly wondering what in the hell I can do with it."

"Why don't you tell me the whole story?" He stopped eating for a moment and looked up at me. "Isn't it about time?"

I thought about the "whole story" as I ordered more coffee. "I'm not sure you want to know more. And there are parts that I simply can't tell you, not now."

"Terrific! I work like hell to help you, and you can't tell me everything. Why?"

"Why? Because there are things that have been said to me in confidence—strict confidence. I'm a lawyer, and there are certain niceties that I have to observe."

"Like ethics?"

"Yes. I believe you get my point."

"Then tell me everything you can. When I was a small boy, my mother used to tell me that if I ever got lost, to head for the nearest exit. Have you tried that?"

I looked at him, puzzled. "What in the hell does that mean?"

He leaned across the table towards me and said in a sharp tone of voice, "It means to get your ass out before the alligators eat it. Now do you understand?"

"Impossible!" I took a deep breath and closed my eyes.

"I'm not saying to drop it, but just to stand back and take a better look at what's happening."

"O.K. Are you ready? Here goes." I told him my tale, all the way from my problems with the firm to Jarrett and to Braxton. I omitted, however, telling him about the money.

"So you're dedicated to getting this former client and friend out of jail and into a safe place, and this guy Jarrett, and maybe Dawson and McAlister, are dedicated to stopping you. Is that right?"

"That's right."

"It doesn't make any sense," he said. "Where's the bottom line? What are they after?"

"For now, that's not important to what I've asked you to do. Let's just say it has value to everyone. So, what do you think I should do?"

"For openers, tell your buddy in Big Spring not to trust anyone. Someone's got his wife, dead or alive, and he may be next. Until we find out who, he had better stay where he is. If he doesn't, you may be working on his obituary. Let me see if I can find out who has Braxton's wife."

"I know who," I mumbled to myself.

"Would you like to share that with me?"

I studied his expression. "No. I just had a terrible thought. How much is all this costing me?"

He crunched on his toast and said, with his mouth full, "Plenty".

"I'm serious Jason. How much?"

"So far, you owe me about ten grand."

"Jesus H.! In addition to what I've already spent?"

"In addition."

I smiled, very faintly, as it occurred to me that the money wouldn't do me any good if I were dead. "O.K. But for God's sake, watch the way you spend my money. And Jason, first try to find out what Claire Sorrell has been doing and where she's been."

He nodded that he would, and we parted.

*   *   *   *

When I called Braxton, his reaction to Best's revelations on Dawson Henry was not surprising. He refused to talk about it. "I don't care who he is or what he's done," he shouted at me, "I want out of here. And the only way out is through McAlister. So leave it alone, Matt. Just see that McAlister carries through with his part."

I was tired of arguing with him. "You're wrong. You should put this thing on hold until we know what we're dealing with."

"Forget it, Matt! Oh, by the way," he added in a calmer voice, "you can also forget about finding Sterling."

"Why?"

"Because she's safe with her sister. While you were screwing around trying to find her, she got herself out of Dallas."

I held the phone at a distance, feeling fairly stupid.

"Something else you should know. Dawson delivered to me today two passports and applications for citizenship in Ecuador, confirmed by the U.S. Consul in Quito. If these guys aren't for real, as you're trying to tell me, they sure as hell don't act like it."

I hung up, looked at myself in the mirror, and yelled "Fuck!" My rabbit trails were all leading nowhere. I walked out of my apartment feeling enormous frustration and was met by Frank.

"A gentleman here to see you," he said. I looked across the drive to see a heavy set man in a dark suit leaning on a black Ford. He motioned me over and extended his hand.

"Mr. Lawrence. Please join us for a minute."

"Who's us?" I suspiciously asked, peering into the car. He opened the door and I was pushed inside. There I saw the cold eyes of McAlister.

"We had a discussion, only two days ago," he began. "You agreed with me that you would stay away from Mr. Braxton. You've broken your word. Shall we take a short drive?"

His heavy set friend took the wheel and we drove off. McAlister was dressed in a dark gray wool overcoat and blue scarf. His gold rimmed glasses sat on the edge of his nose as he waited for me to speak.

I looked him squarely in the eyes. "You're not what you say you are, Mr. McAlister. Frankly, I don't trust you. You keep very strange company."

"Do you want to expain that?" He stared through me, showing his irritation as the car rounded a bend heading for downtown.

"This man Henry, who works for you. He's a pretty surly character."

"In what way?" he rasped.

"As in a wanted criminal."

He adjusted his glasses, gave me a thin arrogant smile, and said, "I don't know where you're getting your information, but it's wrong...dead wrong."

"Mr. McAlister, we're playing games. I've seen the U.S. Marshals' wanted poster on this man—he's a murderer."

I could see his patience wearing thin and wondered if I should have kept my mouth shut. He raised his hand and then slapped the leather seat between us. "That's precisely why I warned you to stay away from my investigation! Henry is a special agent for the Department of Justice. He operates undercover. Mr. Lawrence, the Marshals' wanted poster is his cover. Did you happen to find out that he is not being pursued by the Marshals' office?"

I stopped for a moment and thought about the hold that had been put on the search for Henry. Maybe he was telling the truth. I stared straight ahead, not knowing what to say and feeling somewhat embarrassed. He grabbed my arm and leaned towards me, saying in a rough tone, "Do you have any idea of the damage you are causing? This is not a game." He stopped, took a deep breath, and sat back as the car sped down the expressway. "I'll make a deal with you," he said. "I don't think I can rely on you not to talk to Braxton. So I suggest we agree that you'll limit your activities. My number one objective is to recover for the U.S. Government the money he embezzled."

"Do you intend to give Braxton his freedom…and a safe life in Ecuador?"

"Yes. We're going to do that, provided we get the money. If that happens, he'll be in the Witness Protection Program. But that's a big if!"

I sat back as we turned onto Main Street, watching the skyscrapers pass by. "What do you want me to do."

"I'm O.K. with your talking to Braxton, but only to help him make the arrangements to get the money transferred to me. That's all— nothing else. And no more games. Your last little trick wasn't amusing. Did you really believe you could fool us with those forged escrow papers? Do you know how many years I could nail you for forgery?"

I kept quiet.

"You'll cooperate with us? Yes or no?"

"It sounds like I don't have a choice."

"You damn sure don't!"

I nodded in resignation. He smiled. "Good! Now where can I let you off?"

"How about my old law firm?"

Several blocks later we pulled in front of Fountain Place and I was let out. I stood in the cold, watching as he drove away, trying to get my thoughts together. I entered the building, quickly took the elevator to the fifty-ninth floor, and walked down the empty corridor to my former office. There I was met by a surprised and shocked Leigh. "I never expected to see you again, at least not in the near future," she blurted out.

"Well you have. So tell me, what's left of the firm?"

"The latest count—about 400 lawyers. A lot of attorneys left because of the Government's law suit. But Mr. Stanton's still here. I'm sure he'll want to see you."

I went into my old office, removed my coat, and was offered a cup of coffee by Leigh, which I gratefully accepted. Most of the memories were gone. The papers and files, and the pictures of Julia and Angela, had disappeared. I sat at my old desk and closed my eyes, briefly feeling like a cornered animal. Within minutes I was joined by Harry. He had lost weight, had sunken eyes, and generally looked a lot worse than when I had last seen him.

"Hello, Matt." He stopped, closed the door with his foot, and focused on me. "You look like you've been hit by a train."

"Just a fast moving freight, Harry. And by the way, you don't look so terrific yourself."

"We're both alive. So what have you been up to?"

"For a time, Harry, I thought I could find out who killed Julia. But I think now that that's impossible."

He looked at me with his tired eyes and put his feet upon my desk. "Why?"

"Because it's too much for ordinary citizens to get mixed up in the business of government, intrigue and murder. I'm way over my head and don't stand a chance."

"Let's change the subject. How's Claire?"

His question took me by surprise. "Claire?"

"You were with her in Europe, weren't you? Is she alright?"

"Yes, I believe so."

He gave me a look of surprise, moved his feet off my desk, and said, "You believe so! What in the world does that mean? Matt, I thought that maybe you and Claire might hit it off, get married. You need someone like her."

"You're right that I need someone, but it's not Claire. It's too soon for me to think about that. Maybe what I need the most is just peace of mind."

We sat and looked at each other for a few moments, both tired and wanting something better. Our conversation was interrupted by Leigh.

"Matt," she said, "there's someone on the phone named Carol. She says she's got to talk to you."

"Who knows you're here?" Harry asked.

"No one. Will you excuse me for just a moment?"

"Of course," he said as he left and shut the door behind him.

I picked up the phone to hear a frantic voice. "Mr. Lawrence, my name is Carol Whitfield. I'm Sterling Braxton's sister. She asked that I call you. I'm sorry to interrupt you, but I have some terrible news. Bic Braxton's been stabbed at Big Spring. He's dying. He asked to see you...you'll have to hurry."

"Stabbed!" I sat back, in shock. "How, when did it happen?" I stammered.

"This morning. They say he was attacked by another inmate on his way to breakfast. They have no idea why he did it."

"How's Sterling taking it?"

"Very hard. She's beside herself. You know they were leaving the country in just five days."

"I know, I know." I hung up the phone, stunned and silent. Then I pushed the intercom button and said, "Leigh, please get me on the next Southwest flight to Midland."

"What's wrong, Matt?" she asked.

"Braxton's dying."

*   *   *   *

Two hours later I was in Midland. From there, I rented a car and made the 30 mile trip to the prison in 20 minutes. When I arrived, I was told that he was still alive but that he couldn't have visitors. After thirty minutes of pleading, I was taken to the hospital wing and given five minutes to see him. When I walked into his room, I was startled to see him wrapped in bandages and connected to a life support system.

I rushed to his bed. "Bic, what happened?" I received no response. "Can you hear me?" I said gently leaning towards him.

He mumbled something, and then whispered, "Yes."

His pale face was a death mask. "Bic, who did this?"

"Unimportant," he gasped. "I told them the Pope has the money. I lied."

"Where is it?"

He pushed a folded slip of paper into my hand, squeezed my palm closed, and whispered, "Matt, take this. Figure it out. See the Pope, tell him—the money." He began breathing convulsively, and a doctor quickly appeared to place oxygen over his face. "Please leave," he demanded. "This man is dying. Let me do what I can for him."

"Just a few more minutes," I protested.

"No, he doesn't have a few more minutes. Leave!"

I left Braxton and was taken to the exit. I glanced at the piece of paper. The writing was in French. I quickly put it back in my pocket before someone saw me. Before I got to my car, a guard came running to me and shouted that Braxton had died. I felt a deep sadness. He had committed so many wrongs, but he had done a lot for me. I sat for several minutes behind the wheel of my rented car, holding my head, and then drove back to Midland for my flight to Dallas.

CHAPTER 24

▼

Dallas, Texas, 1992

Best was piecing together a theory. I called him from the airport when I landed and told him about Braxton's murder. We agreed to meet at Roscoe's Easy Way, a slight notch up from Good Eats. He was squeezing a double martini when I arrived, as if it were his last drink. He looked up when I approached, smoke coming out of both nostrils. A cigarette in one hand, a drink in the other, and his seedy lavender tie dangling on the table. I looked around to be sure I didn't know anyone before I seated myself. The poorly lit, empty room was a welcome refuge.

"I'm not surprised he was killed," he mumbled without taking his attention away from his drink. It was late in the day, and I sat and watched the shadows made by the setting sun through the plantation shutters as he outlined his theory.

He looked at me, seemingly in a daze. "This is all about McAlister. He's the one. It's not Jarrett or anyone else. McAlister's behind it all!"

I focused my attention on him as he slouched in the booth and sipped on his drink. "Impossible! You're dead wrong. You were wrong about Dawson and you're wrong about McAlister. The man I shot at Braxton's house was from Louisiana. That means Jarrett."

"Not necessarily," he said. "Did you ever try those numbers you mentioned to me? They might tell us who he was working for."

"Yeah, I tried them."

"And?"

"A car rental agency and a stock broker."

He was not phased by my answer. "You said I was wrong about Dawson. Why do you think that?"

"McAlister told me that Dawson is working for the Justice Department, under cover, and that's why he put the hold on the arrest warrant."

"And you believed that bullshit?" he asked with an incredulous look on his face.

"Jason, it all adds up. They delivered what they promised to Braxton. They gave him passports and citizenship papers for Ecuador. Why would they have done that if they never intended to provide him with a safe home?"

"Put yourself in their place. What would you do?"

I sat in silence, listening to his theory. He continued. "I'll tell you what they would do. They would get Braxton to tell them how to find what they were looking for. They had to get his confidence, and when he told them what they wanted to know, they would have him killed."

"There's the flaw, Jason. He didn't tell them."

"You said he told them where they could find this thing they were after, which I presume is money, but that he told you he lied. What if they believed him and thought that he was of no further use." He continued to drink, slouching in his rumpled suit. "If that were the case," he continued, "they might have tried to kill him and then go after the money."

"And when they can't find it, then what?"

"Then they go after everyone who might know where it is, including Braxton's wife and you."

I still couldn't buy it. "They could have gotten the money the easy way when they delivered Braxton to freedom," I said challenging his analysis. "And it makes no sense that a U.S. Attorney would get involved with murder." I ordered my second martini, and Best ordered his third. Our logic and discussion were beginning to be affected by our inebriation. I slouched down to his level, peered at him through my glass, and said, "Claire."

"Claire what?" he responded.

"What have you found out about Claire?"

"Nada, zilch, zippo," he said. "We've watched her home for several days. As of three hours ago, she hadn't returned. Have you tried to call her?"

"No, I haven't had the nerve since I saw her at that stop sign. Why do you suppose she hasn't called me?"

"Maybe there's no phone where she is, or maybe she's tired of you. I dunno—you tell me."

I looked out through the shutters, watching the sky grow dark with the night. We were alone in the restaurant, except for one couple. I suddenly felt thankful to have him across from me. "Jason, how do you take care of your other clients? You've spent so much time on my problems—it must be hard on you."

He gave me a sheepish grin and took another sip of his drink. "What other clients?"

I looked at him and hoped he wasn't being cute. "Come on, Jason, how do you do it?"

"You're my first and only," he confessed. "Don't let that shake your confidence, though, because I spent ten years with Pinkertons. Any referrals you got, I'd appreciate."

I smiled and shrugged off his remark. "Let's get back to your theory. You never answered my question. If McAlister had an easy way to get the money by setting Braxton free, why kill him?"

"You got me, but I think I'm right. Maybe it was all a ruse. Maybe he didn't have the ability to set him free."

I was tempted to show him the paper Braxton gave me, but decided not to. We sat and bounced theories back and forth for over an hour, accomplishing nothing. He ended our meeting with a premonition. "Whoever is behind Braxton's murder—and I think in some way it's connected with McAlister," he said, "is going to come after you when they can't find the money. You can count on it. If I were you, I would make myself very scarce for a while."

"For how long? I just can't disappear indefinitely."

"Long enough for me to finish my investigation of Dawson and Blair. Maybe I can learn something from them."

"You would talk to them?"

"Why not?" he asked. "You want answers, you better ask questions. I might even talk to Jarrett."

I thought about the slip of paper and the Pope. "I could leave the country for a week or two. Maybe I'll go to France."

"Do it! Leave as soon as you can, and call me in several days after you get there."

I hesitated, finished my martini, and said, "What about Sterling. I owe something to Braxton."

"We'll get word to Sterling. I'll see to it that she gets far away."

"By the way, Jason, what is this 'we' stuff I keep hearing?"

"I have contract labor," he answered. "I can't be in two places at one time, so I hire retired friends from Pinkertons. They like the opportunity to get back to work, and they work cheap. Look, Mr. Lawrence, I'm telling you that you're making a mistake to stay around here. There are three dead people, according to my latest count, and I don't want there to be four."

I thought hard about his last words—three dead people—as I pulled away from the restaurant. What he didn't know was that there were more. The murders in Europe. The deaths of Alan Crone and the man Bird Dog killed in Rome had been kept secret. It was a carnage.

*   *   *   *

The whole city appeared ominous as I drove north, trying to shake the effects of two martinis and searching my rear view mirror for anyone who might be following me. Ten minutes later I pulled in front of Claire's house. The lights were on.

The humidity was turning to a dense fog in the dark evening sky. I sat for several minutes, watching through the haze for any sign of her. Finally, I dialed her number on my cellphone. After several rings, she answered.

"Matt," she said. "It's late. Are you O.K.?"

I paused. "Yes. Are you?."

There was momentary silence. "Matt, I'm not in the mood for this. What do you want?"

"How was Houston?"

"Please, no questions," she said.

"How is your mother? Can I ask that question?"

"Yes, you can, and she's doing much better."

"Can I see you tonight?"

"I'm very tired. Another time," she said.

"Did you go to Houston?"

My question was met with another moment of silence. "What business is that of yours? And why would you ask a question like that?"

"Because something's not right, and I'd like to know what it is."

"It's very complicated. Not tonight. Let's discuss this tomorrow."

"There won't be a tomorrow. I'm leaving for France."

The windows of my car had become completely steamed up, and I felt isolated as I sat and talked with her. My patience was wearing thin. "Tomorrow? Why?"

"I have to go on business."

"O.K. Come over for just for a short time."

"I'm here," I answered.

"You're here?"

"I'm sitting in front of your house. If you'll open the door, I'll come in." She hung up and appeared in seconds at the front door, dressed in loose fitting khaki cotton slacks, tied with a rope sash around her waist, and a white silk blouse.

"Come in." She gestured to me, trying to stay back from the cold wind that was blowing towards her house.

"So," I began, "will you tell me where you have been?" Why had even Claire now seemed to have become the enemy?

She motioned me to the sofa and sat at the end, crossing her legs underneath her. "Matt, there are things that should remain private between us. I'm touched by your concern over where I was, if that's what it is, but I don't feel that I have to account to you for everything I do."

Her statement was brisk and pointed. She lowered her eyes and then looked away. "Can I get you a drink?" she asked.

"No, not now. You're right, you know. You have no obligation to tell me a thing. But if you didn't go to Houston, I would like to know why you lied to me."

"I didn't lie to you. I intended to go to Houston, but something came up that I had to deal with. Matt, what's going on? You're acting as if I'm one of 'them'." Her eyes began to moisten as she sat back, crossed her arms in front of her, and gave me a distressed look.

I took a deep breath. "Braxton's dead. He was murdered in prison."

She stared at me with a shocked expression. "So how do you want me to react? What's the point? Matt, this only shows that now you have absolutely nothing to gain and everything to lose if you continue with what you're doing. There's no more Braxton to pay you a share of the money everyone seems so hell bent on finding. Can't you see what I'm telling you? I almost enjoyed Europe in some crazy kind of way. Everything happened so fast and nothing, not even danger and death, seemed to be real. But now they are, and I don't want any part of it. Not any more. I know you won't stop, even with everything stacked against you. But that's your choice. Keep in touch and try to stay safe, if that's remotely possible. Goodbye, Matt."

She showed me to the door, and I left, knowing she was right. My staying safe was very remote.

CHAPTER 25

▼

Beaune, France, 1992

Two days later I sat in the bar of the Hotel de la Poste all alone, except for the steady sound of the rain. The weather in Beaune was dreary. I gazed through my glass of white wine at the front desk, trying to sort through my emotions. Suddenly, a soft voice interrupted my trance. "Mr. Lawrence, I'm sorry I wasn't here when you checked in. Is there something I can do for you?"

I looked up and saw the deep blue eyes of Martine Paulet. "No, I'm fine. Why do you ask?"

"Because you've been sitting here, for quite some time, staring through your glass at me."

"I didn't recognize you from here, and I wasn't staring. I was thinking."

"You think through your glass?" she said, smiling softly.

"Alice did, why not me?"

"Alice?"

"Yes," I said, "in Wonderland. Don't you remember, Alice through the looking glass?"

She lowered herself into the chair next to me and smiled again. "I've never been told that I looked like an Alice. Could it be that you've had too much to drink?"

I laughed for the first time in days. "If only I had. But no, I haven't. Sorry."

She leaned forward. "I'm pleased that you've decided to come here. Can I help you with reservations for dinner tonight?"

"Yes, but only if you'll join me."

My suggestion took her completely by surprise. "I don't think so," she said with hesitancy. "It would be difficult to leave the hotel tonight. And besides, management frowns upon employees associating with guests."

"When I called, you said you'd try to be of some help to me. This is your chance. Martine, I don't want to be alone tonight. Consider it part of your job—guest entertainment. We'll make it an early evening. I promise." I could see that she was beginning to take pity on me.

Her eyes closed slightly and she pursed her lips. Opening her eyes, she looked into mine. "The restaurant Le Jardin des Ramparts is very nice. Shall we say eight o'clock?"

"By the way, my name's Matt. Please drop the Mr. Lawrence."

"I will."

At quarter till eight we met in the hotel lobby. She stood, motionless, watching me approach. Pulling at her gold necklace, she smiled softly.

I smiled back. "Hello."

"Shall we be off?" She tossed her blonde hair to the side, reaching for her purse.

I stared at her for a moment. A light pink dress trimmed with soft green—she looked like a Ralph Lauren advertisement. "You look different. Not like the hotel manager I met earlier." She frowned. "Actually, what I mean is that you look stunning."

She glanced at me with a slight smile, silently accepting my compliment as we walked from the hotel to the restaurant. The night air was crisp and invigorating. As we entered the restaurant, we were met by Mme. Chanliaud, its owner. "Bonsoir, monsieur et madame. I have a lovely table for you, by the garden." We were seated in a dimly lit dining room, whose only light came from the firelight of candles dancing off the green and white laced wallpaper.

"Martine, I thought you were French."

"Oh but I am," she said, looking down into her wine glass and then raising her eyes to look into mine. "I was born in Paris, but I attended the London School of Economics."

"Ah…. So that explains why you speak English so well."

"That and the fact that my stepfather is English."

"Your stepfather?"

"Yes. My real father died when I was very young, and my mother remarried. You may remember that I told you he is an editor with the *Economist*. He is the one who taught me to speak English. But it's the French language that I love. It's so much more beautiful."

Looking into her radiant blue eyes over the top of my glass, I saw that they sparkled with the reflection of the candle flame. She pushed back the wave of her hair that fell across her forehead and took a sip of wine.

"Your wife. When did she die?"

"Over a year ago." I took a deep breath but couldn't hide my anguish.

"I'm sorry, Matt. I shouldn't have brought that up."

"It's alright. You don't need to be sorry. It now seems like so long ago. Tell me about The London School of Economics? It doesn't seem to fit you."

"Should I resent that comment?"

"Absolutely not. What I meant to say is that you're so attractive. You just don't seem to fit the mold of an economist."

She looked up at me, eyes flashing, and then blushed. "Thank you for the compliment, but I do have a brain. I was not an economics major. I majored in hotel management and marketing. And what about you?"

"I think you know. I was a lawyer in Dallas. My life is pretty complicated right now. I took your suggestion and decided to come here to get a little distance and to clear my head."

"Distance?"

"Yes. From myself, and others."

"To get a better look? You can see yourself, and others, better from far away?"

"I had hoped so."

Her face in the dim light changed into a delicate smile, giving me a strong feeling that she knew what I was thinking. The evening passed much too fast, and we left the restaurant after eleven. "Will I see you tomorrow?" I asked when we had returned to the hotel."

She gave me a disappointed look. "I have to be in Paris in the morning to attend a hotel managers' meeting. After that I'll be in London for two weeks to attend a seminar. Is there a chance that you'll return soon?"

"I don't think so." I couldn't hide my disappointment. I could feel the pains of reality begin to creep back into my body.

Three days later I returned to Dallas. The loneliness of being alone in France was more than I could bear. There wasn't an escape.

CHAPTER 26

▼

Dallas, Texas, 1992

When I returned to the Athena, I was exhausted but couldn't sleep. At 1 A.M., I called Best. "Jason, sorry to disturb you so late, but I'm back from France and thought you might have something new to report."

I looked out my balcony doors as I heard him groan. The rain was slowly pounding the streets, glistening with the reflection of the street lamps. "Are you fuckin' crazy?" he mumbled. "It's after midnight. No, there's nothing new. And by the way, what in the hell are you doing back here? I thought we agreed that you'd be gone for at least two weeks."

I sat for a few moments in silence. "We did, but I couldn't stay over there, not by myself."

I could hear him take a drink and then exhale. "I feel sorry for you, Mr. Lawrence, but if you won't help yourself, then my hands are tied."

"I hear you," I said. Then the phone went dead.

During the next week, I unsuccessfully tried to see McAlister and Jarrett. Out of desperation, I finally called Best. I left a message on his answering machine to meet me at my apartment at five. When he arrived, I was in the middle of again sorting through my files on Braxton, looking for any clue that might explain the list. "Glad to see you're back," he said, looking at the maze of papers spread out across the room.

I looked up at him and was shocked at his appearance. "My God, Jason, you found a comb and shaved."

"Got a hot date. You finding anything?"

There was no place for him to sit, so I quickly moved some of the papers to a stack in the corner. After falling into a chair, he loosened his tie and gave me a wide grin. "How 'bout a drink? I'd hate to pick up my date sober."

"Jason, let's hold that for a while. I need your help. I've spent a good part of the day sifting through papers looking for answers that aren't there."

"What answers?"

"This piece of paper Braxton gave me," I answered, handing him a copy. "It's in French. A woman who lives in this building told me that it's a list of names and appears to be some sort of a receipt, all in French."

"What?" He jolted up, giving me his full attention. "When did he give you that?"

"Just before he died."

"And you're just now showing it to me. Why?"

"Because I wanted to find out what it meant first."

"Have you?"

"No. I thought maybe you could help." I decided it was time for a drink and went to the bar for the scotch. "How do you want yours?" I asked, swinging the bottle in his direction.

"In a glass—with ice. This piece of paper," he said, holding it above his head. "What did he tell you about it?"

"He was dying. He mumbled something about seeing the Pope, telling him about it. Oh, and he told me to figure it out."

Best motioned for his drink, which I handed to him, and took a big gulp. He choked momentarily, and then began coughing. "Are you all right?"

He stopped coughing, took another drink, and then smiled at me. "Scotch makes me sentimental—brings tears to my eyes."

"Be serious. Are you listening to what I'm saying?"

"I'm listening. So, did you?"

"Did I what?"

"Did you see the Pope and tell him about the paper?"

"Jason, are you crazy? You don't just see the Pope. And he's in Poland. I did the next best thing. I talked to one of his assistants about it."

"And?"

"And he had no idea what it meant. He said he didn't know any of the people named. Now what?"

"Do what Braxton said." He took another long drink.

"Didn't you hear me? I can't do that. The Pope's not in Rome. And even if he were, he wouldn't see me. It's like getting an audience with the President—impossible!"

"They don't have fax machines in Poland?"

"Fax machines?"

"Yeah, fax machines. Shit, they got faxes in Mongolia. Why don't you fax that list to your buddy in Rome and ask him to send it to the Pope. Maybe he'll tell you what it means."

His suggestion was too simple. I felt imbecilic for not having thought of it. "I'll do it," I murmured to myself, taking back the list.

"What else?"

"Nothing."

"Mr. Lawrence, it's late and I've got to pick up my date. What do you want me to do?"

"I don't know…I'll call tomorrow."

*   *   *   *

The fax I sent to Monsignor Bertellini was brief. It asked that he take Braxton's list, send it to the Pope, and ask the Pope what it meant. I promised it would be my last request. He wouldn't hear from me again. I lied one more time.

At first I thought it was a joke. Within two hours a return fax came through my machine. The letterhead looked authentic—it said The Vatican, and beneath it was the official seal of Pope John Paul II. In perfect English, it said that His Holiness had studied the Braxton list and did not understand its meaning or recognize any of the names. The signature appeared to be that of the Pope, and underneath it was a scribbled note, signed by the Monsignor, saying he was sorry and wished me luck, "with the grace of God."

CHAPTER 27

▼

Through the manager at the Hotel de la Poste, I was able to get Martine's phone number in Paris. I left a message for her saying I needed her help. Within hours, she returned my call. "Matt, it's so good to hear from you. How can I help you?" Her voice was soft and bore slightly her French accent.

"I'm coming back to Europe. I have some names I would like you to look at. I'm hoping that you can help me try to find those people."

"But, Matt, I leave Paris tomorrow for London. I won't be here."

I hesitated. "Could I meet you in London?"

"Well...I have a management seminar to attend. But I'll be free in the evenings. When will you be there?"

"I intend to leave tomorrow evening and should arrive the next morning around 10 A.M. I'll stay at the Inn on the Park. As soon as I check in, I'll call you."

"Matt, you can leave a message at my hotel and I'll call you when my seminar is over. I'm staying at the Intercontinental."

"Martine...."

"Oh, Matt."

"Yes?"

"I'm so glad you're coming."

I smiled. "I am too."

*   *   *   *

The weather had continued to deteriorate during the night and through the next day. I was met by strong winds as I stepped into a cab at four in the afternoon. My American Airlines flight had not made it in from Paris, and I was delayed for six hours and then moved to the British Air flight that arrived at Heathrow at eleven in the morning. Before leaving, I placed another call to Best.

"You're not going to like this," he said. "Your lady friend has been spending some time with a Charles Duggan. Do you know him?"

"No I don't. Why are you still following her? I thought I told you to leave her alone."

"We are leaving her alone. This report I'm looking at is from yesterday, but delivered to me this morning. If you don't want to hear any more, I'll tear the son-of-a-bitch up."

"No, don't do that. Tell me what else you know."

I could hear the announcement that my plane was boarding as he shuffled papers over the telephone. "All we've got is that this guy lives here in Dallas, and she spent the last two days with him."

I heard the last boarding call and asked quickly for anything else he had found out. There was nothing. I boarded, confused and tired. Why did I care who Claire was seeing? Why didn't I trust her anymore? Who could I trust?

PART II

CHAPTER 28

▼

England, 1992

British Air flight 210 was overbooked as a result of the cancellation of my earlier flight. Without thinking, I scanned the faces of the passengers as they boarded and was relieved to see no familiar ones. After a forty-five minute delay, the plane seemed to taxi forever, suddenly lurched violently from left to right, and then lifted quickly above the storm.

A hand tugged gently on my arm as I watched sheets of rain wash off the wings. Looking up, I saw a flight attendant offering snacks and drinks. "A dry martini. Beefeater gin on ice with an olive."

"Right away," she answered. "Can I bring you anything else?"

I hesitated for a minute and then asked, "Do you by chance speak French?"

"No, I don't, but I'm certain one of the other hostesses does. After we've finished serving, I'll try to send someone who does. Do you need anything in particular?"

"Yes, I need someone to interpret a note from a friend. It's in French."

I sipped my drink and studied the paper Braxton had given me. It was letter size and typed in fine print. I had already been told that it only seemed to be a list of names and some sort of receipt. But I wanted a second opinion. Within a few minutes I was joined by another flight attendant. "Are you the gentleman who asked for a French interpreter?"

"I am. Can you help?"

"Well," she hesitated, "I'm not an expert in French, but I do get by. Please show me what you want me to interpret."

I started to hand her the paper and was interrupted by a voice beside me. "I say, old chap, do you mind my requesting a drink?"

To my right was a man I hadn't noticed before. A fairly dumpy salesman type with a double chin and thin moustache. His hair was a curly black and he wore a turtle neck sweater under a brown corduroy sport jacket. He extended his hand, remarking, "I couldn't help but overhear. Sounds like you may need some of her time. Just a J&B and soda, if it wouldn't be too much trouble."

"No, of course not," I answered. "Please," I said looking at the flight attendant, "serve this man his drink first."

As she moved quickly down the aisle to the galley, I turned to apologize for monopolizing her time.

"It isn't necessary, not at all," he said. "Let me introduce myself. Alfred Peabody, from London. And you are..."

"I'm Matt Lawrence, an attorney from Dallas." We shook hands.

He temporarily unlocked his seat belt, removed his jacket, and then refocused his attention on me. "I just met with Dallas attorneys. Do you know the Crandall firm?"

"I don't." I didn't want to be drawn into a conversation.

"Copyright attorneys. I'm in the business of skin appliques—tatoos in the everyday world. They're assisting my company in the States."

"That's very interesting," I lied, "but if you'll excuse me, I would like to have the flight attendant take a look at my friend's note." She handed him his drink, and I handed her the note from Braxton.

She knelt down in the aisle next to me and began to study the paper. "The first sentence," she began, "says ce reçu, or this receipt. After that, there seems to be quite a list of names, including J. Camus, Drouhin-Laroze, L. Traper, et cetera. And then there seems to be a list of places, such as Clos des Porrets-Saint Georges, Les Varoilles, Les Amoureuses, et cetera. I'd like to help you, but frankly I don't have a clue as to what they mean or where they are."

"No indication of any other meaning? No sentences or instructions?" I was disappointed.

"Nothing. At the end is some reference to expéditions, which I believe means shipment. That's all." She rose and returned the letter to me. "I can only conclude that it's someone's list of people and places."

I thanked her and returned the paper to my wallet.

"See here," my seatmate blustered out. "Maybe I can make some sense of your friend's letter."

"No thank you. I think I've learned all that I need to know for now." I closed my eyes, laid back, and it suddenly hit me that I had made a showing of the letter to anyone within hearing distance on the plane. I felt like an idiot and quickly excused myself for the rest room. There I removed the letter, placed it inside my left sock, and returned to my seat.

Ten hours later I sipped on my orange juice and felt relieved to finally be rid of my chattering seat companion as we prepared to land at Heathrow.

*   *   *   *

The next thing I remembered were soft, mumbling voices as I felt someone trying to turn me over in a bed. I looked up and saw two bare light bulbs against a dark dingy ceiling. Sunlight was streaming through venetian blinds on the wall next to my bed, and I could barely make out faces staring at me. I tried to sit up and was helped by a hefty woman in a white nurse's outfit as she propped two large pillows behind me.

The voices had English accents.

"Don't try to move too quickly," the hefty nurse said to me. "Just lie back and rest. You've been quite ill. How do you feel?"

"Very dizzy…and light headed," I answered slowly.

I pushed myself up against the pillows, and my head began swimming again. "What—what happened? Where am I? How long…."

"Have you been here in the hospital?" she said, continuing my broken sentence. "You were brought here yesterday, from Heathrow. It seems you took sick on the British Air flight from Dallas and had to be rushed off the plane."

The dizziness overcame me again, and I found that focusing my eyes was impossible. "Please rest," she said. "You're going to be alright."

I fell back into a deep sleep. It must have been several hours later when I heard other voices, this time a man's deep voice asking if I could hear him. I answered I could. Then panic struck me. "Did you get my baggage and other things off the plane?"

"We did. But I'm sorry to tell you that your wallet is missing. I hope you won't think this hospital is responsible. It was gone when you were carried off the plane."

"No, of course not," I mumbled. "Listen to me…I had a piece of paper in my sock! Did you recover it?"

"Very strange indeed," he responded. "Got a few chuckles from our staff. Yes, we have your piece of paper."

Thank God, I thought as I peered up into the blinding lights of the bulbs on the ceiling. "You seem to have gotten food poisoning or something like that," he said. "Your eyes are very dilated and light sensitive. Don't try to look directly at the lights. It could be painful for you."

One day—gone! I felt a slight jostling of my arm and was asked if I wanted coffee. Nodding that I did, I was given several large swallows. I could feel my senses slowly returning.

"I'm Dr. Mannering," the deep voice said. "I must tell you that a young lady has been here inquiring about you. Extremely attractive. Said she would be back this afternoon."

I took another gulp of coffee, rubbed my eyes and peered at the doctor standing next to me. He had a curled mustache, wavy brown hair that looked as if it had hardly seen a comb, and wore a green doctor's robe over white trousers. He felt my pulse as I lay there and said I would live.

"You mentioned food poisoning," I remarked. "Could that really be possible—I mean, were any other passengers sick?"

"None that we know of," he answered. "But food poisoning seems a logical guess."

I stared at the ceiling, then at him. "Could I have been drugged?"

He appeared startled by my question. "Drugged? My Lord, who would do a thing like that?"

"I don't know, but could I have been?" I asked again.

He stepped away, walked to the window and adjusted the blinds. Turning back towards me, he confirmed my suspicion. "Yes, as a matter of fact, I somewhat suspected that you might have been. All the right indications, you know. As you Yankees say, you could have been slipped a Mickey Finn. Any idea who would do that to you?"

I breathed deeply to avoid another bout with nausea, exhaled slowly, and sighed. "Yes, I have an idea," thinking of the tatoo salesman. "When can I leave?"

"Within several hours, as long as you feel up to it. There should be no lasting effects. Perhaps when your lady friend returns, you can leave with her. It would be wise for you not to venture out by yourself, at least not until you feel fully recovered."

By three in the afternoon the doctor had returned. A warm shower and shave had done me a world of good. I sat, dressed in slacks and a sport coat, but feeling only half alive when he walked in. "You're looking much better," he said. "Any dizziness left?"

"No, I feel much better."

He felt my pulse, listened to my heart, and pronounced me well enough to leave. "Your friend is waiting outside," he remarked as he placed his instruments back in his bag. "Are you ready to see her?"

"Yes."

The door swung open when he left, then swung back to reveal Martine, dressed in a wine-colored suit. She looked like a burst of sunlight. Her blue and yellow striped satin blouse under the jacket was framed by the curls of her light blonde hair. She was more beautiful than I had remembered.

She gave me a captivating smile as she entered and placed her black alligator purse on the bed table. "They tell me you'll be alright."

"Yes. How did you find me?" I stood and gave her a gentle hug, which was returned with enormous warmth.

She stood back, flashed another smile and squeezed my hand. "I've been so worried about you. I must tell you that, at first, I thought you had stood me up. I decided to meet you at the airport, but your flight was canceled. It was only after I checked with the airlines, and I had to call several, that I was able to find out what flight you were on and what had happened. Matt, I never dreamed I would meet you at a hospital, but I'm so glad you're here."

I felt the affection in her voice. "Shall we leave this place?"

"Let's," she answered.

I was handed my luggage as we walked down the hallway to the exit. "Do we need a cab?" I asked.

"Oh no, I have my stepfather's car. Luck would have it that he's on vacation in Sicily, so for two weeks I have free transportation."

She led me to a blue BMW in the parking lot, unlocked the doors as I loaded my luggage, and offered me the keys. "Do you want to drive?"

"In my condition, and considering that my driver's license and wallet have been stolen, I'll leave that to you for now."

I sat to her left as she drove, feeling oddly out of place in her car. "Have you had lunch?" she asked as we sped along Knightsbridge, the main thoroughfare south of Hyde Park.

"No, but what about your seminar? Can you spare the time?"

She slowed as we approached a stop light and then turned and smiled. "Matt, I could care less about the seminar. If you weren't here, I would of course be there. But with you here, and assuming you have the time, I would much prefer to show you London. Do you have the time?"

The light changed and we sped forward, turning along the shops that decorated Kensington. I pondered her question so long that she asked it again. "Don't tell me that you don't," she protested. "I've so looked forward to spending time with you."

"I have some business, here in London and elsewhere in Europe. But I definitely have the time. In fact, I have all the time in the world. This is a great time to slow down my life, and doing it with you is perfect!"

From Chelsea Bridge we turned into Pimlico-Victoria, the district of the City of Westminster which reaches westward along the Thames. Her reaction to my answer was spontaneous, and she asked with her soft voice if Chelsea Inn would be satisfactory for lunch. I replied that it would.

Chelsea Inn appeared dark as we entered and were shown to our table. It was decorated with wood panels in rich gold and brown tones, scarlet carpets and mysterious looking dark tapestries. The restaurant was virtually deserted because of the late hour. We ordered a bottle of '82 Margaux.

"You're staring at me, you know."

I snapped out of a temporary trance and replied, "No…not you. I was lost in a trance."

She laughed slightly, raising her eyebrows. "A trance?" she whispered.

"Maybe not what you think," I scoffed. "Mayhem and murder."

She looked at me inquisitively, her smile vanishing. "Oh come now, Matt, surely you're not attributing more to what happened to you on that plane than was there."

I searched her face, wondering how she would react if I told her what did happen. "There's an old favorite song of mine," I said. "It goes something like 'When I'm with you, I'm lost in a trance over your charms—and I could waltz across Texas with you.' My mind was drifting back to Texas and the day I first heard that song."

"Waltz across Texas," she murmured. "Yes, I could do that with you." A loving smile crept across her face.

"Martine, you look so serene and beautiful. Being here with you means so much to me."

"And you," she said. "You look wonderful. You seem so much less troubled. Are you?"

I sniffed my wine, but could smell only her perfume. Staring at her through my glass, I hesitated to respond. "Truthfully—my life has been a living hell. But it's much better at the moment."

She opened her menu and looked up at me, smiling faintly. "I'm so sorry for what you've been through. It's very difficult for me to find the right words. But maybe I can help ease your pain."

I couldn't take my eyes off of her as she laid down her menu and took a slow sip of her wine. "Matt, do you want to tell me what you think happened to you on the plane?"

"I think I was drugged."

Her smile quickly faded and a horrified expression came over her face. "Surely you're not serious! Why would anyone want to drug you?"

"I've thought hard about that. It has to do with a lot of money that I and a number of other people are trying to find."

She smiled imperceptibly. "Isn't that the source of all evil?"

I momentarily closed my eyes, thinking of the irony of what she had said. "Yes, yes it is. Over $200 million of evil."

She put her glass down and stared at me in total disbelief. "You must be joking!"

"I'm not. Let me show you something." I reached into my pocket and removed the paper from Braxton. "Take a look at this and tell me what you think it means."

She unfolded it slowly, casting one eye on me and the other on the paper. "It's all in French. Where did you get this?"

"From a dying friend. This piece of paper, I believe, has the secret to an enormous amount of cash that he had before he died."

"Who does it belong to now?"

"That's a very good question. There are a lot of people out there who have laid a claim to it, including the people who had me drugged on the plane. I know they were after that piece of paper. Oh, and that reminds me, since they stole my wallet, do you mind paying for lunch until my bank wires me new funds?"

"No, of course not."

"So…what do you make of that piece of paper?"

She studied it intently for several minutes, then looked up with a puzzled expression. "This is just a long list of names and places, presumably French from their sound, but I'm not familiar with them. The first paragraph refers to a receipt, and the last seems to say that there will be no shipment, whatever that means. You say you got this from a dying friend?"

"Yes. My friend was evidently murdered because of what's on this paper."

"Murdered? Is that what you said?" She gave me a horrified look.

"Martine, I must tell you something. Almost four months ago, in Rome, I was shot outside the Vatican. And there have been other attempts on my life. You have to know that if you stay with me, you may be in danger."

The stark reality of what I was saying left her stunned. "What have you done? Why would someone want to kill you?" She leaned forward across the table and waited for my answer.

"It's nothing I've done, I assure you. This all revolves around a former client who got into a great deal of trouble. Over a period of time, he put away a large sum of money, money that he evidently embezzled from his bank. I've discovered that the money was transferred to the Vatican bank three or four years ago. My client's dead, his secretary's dead, and my wife is dead, all because of people out there who want that money."

Her mouth dropped open and she was unable to speak. She stared at me as if I were a zombie and then slowly took a drink of her wine. "All those people! And Julia? I thought it was an accident...an automobile...."

"I didn't know that until recently. Julia was evidently killed by mistake. They were trying to kill me."

"Did you call the police or the FBI? Surely they could help you."

I reached for my glass and inhaled the aroma. "Call the police or the FBI? It would be useless. The killings took place in Europe, San Antonio and a Federal penitentiary. My client was a convicted felon. Martine, I'm dealing with hired assassins—professionals." Her expression told me I had successfully cast a pall over our lunch.

"Explain to me," she asked, "why you don't get away from it all? Why you continue when all these people have been killed?" Before I could answer, we were interrupted by a very impatient waiter. "Pardon," he said, "but the kitchen is about to close. If you want to order anything, you must do it now."

She stared at her menu, without saying a word. "I'm not sure I can eat now," she finally said.

"Please, I'm sorry if I spoiled your appetite. Let me order a salad for each of us. O.K.?"

"Yes, O.K."

When the waiter left, I sat back and tried to gather my thoughts to respond clearly to her question. "I thought many times of going away, but it's not that simple. Wherever I go, it follows me. I can't escape it, so I have to face it."

"But why? Surely there is somewhere you could go where they won't find you."

"Why?" I repeated. "Because I have no choice and they won't stop. Because they've taken it upon themselves to kill people I loved, all for the money, and they want to kill me. I'm not going to let them succeed."

"If they knew you were on that plane, then they must know you're in London and where you're staying. We must move you immediately," she said.

"We?"

"Matt, when I first met you, I knew you were married but I couldn't get you out of my mind. I thought you were terribly handsome and mysterious. I'm so sorry Julia is dead, but I can't let you go now, not when we're finally here together."

"But you have to understand. You'll be in grave danger."

"Only if we stay around here," she said faintly. "Can you continue your search outside of London?"

I thought about her suggestion and back to a time when Claire and I had escaped Rome to go to Lake Como, only to be followed and almost killed there. "What makes you think we can go anywhere and not be followed?"

"It's simple," she retorted. "Whoever is chasing you doesn't know me. If you fail to check in to the Inn on the Park, they will have no idea what happened to you. Let's drive tonight to the Swiss Cottage at Endsleigh."

"The what?"

"It's a lovely little inn, about four hours from London, near Tavistock in Devon. I promise—you'll love it."

"But you hardly know me."

"That's not true. You forget the years that you and Julia stayed at the Hotel de la Poste. I got to know both of you very well then."

"But I've changed from what I was then."

"Matt, no you haven't, not to me. What I see is a very attractive man, with a lovely smile and dark brown eyes—gentle eyes. Eyes that don't lie. They don't turn away when you look at them. And I see a great amount of charm, humor and sincerity…. and pain." She paused and looked deeply into my eyes, as if she were looking for a reaction, and then said, "Matt, it should come as no surprise that I've become very fond of you. And I'm not sure how to deal with that."

I looked down at my wine, not expecting what she had said and uncertain how to respond.

I was saved by our waiter interrupting us again, this time with our salads and brown bread. He filled our wine glasses and then asked if we needed anything else. I said no, but thank you, and returned my attention to Martine. "Endsleigh. What is it?"

"It's a place I visited when I was very young, before my mother died. It sits on the banks of the Tamar River between Cornwall and Devon. It's an eighteenth century estate, built by the Duchess of Bedford. There are private cottages, lodges and pavilions. You'll adore it. I promise."

I thought about her suggestion, but just for a few moments, and then asked, "When?"

"As soon as we finish our salads," she said, "I'll return to the Intercontinental and check out—quietly. Then I'll return here for you and we'll be on our way. Agreed?"

"Yes."

*   *   *   *

It was beginning to get dark as we headed north on the motorway towards Devon. We reached the Swiss Cottage by 7:30. I was astonished at what I saw. Lichen-covered roofs, carved wood on eaves and beams, and a panoramic veranda. Mountain laurel and rhododendron surrounded the cottage to give it the appearance of a Swiss fable. Inside were stout pine furniture, Alpine scenes, and antique Swiss chests and bookcases. Martine grabbed my hand and led me to the veranda, where we stood and gazed upon a sweeping moon-lit view of the Tamar River.

"I hope you don't mind," she said, staring off into the evening mist, "but I reserved adjoining rooms for us. I think it's the proper thing to do. Don't you agree?"

"Yes, of course." I could feel the evening chill and pulled my coat tightly around me as we stood there.

"Are you cold?" she asked.

"A little. I'm not well dressed for your English weather. An open shirt and sport coat don't give much warmth. Let's go in."

Our rooms were small but charming, reminding me of an old Swiss chalet.

I unpacked my suitcase and carry-on bag, and carefully unwrapped the barrel, grips and magazine of my Beretta, which I had packed in separate compartments to avoid any problems with airport security. It had worked. I laid the barrel against the slide, inserted the recoil spring, attached the grips, and rotated the barrel to lock it into position.

"What in the world are you doing?"

I turned to see Martine's shocked expression. "I find this very necessary these days," I said. "It was a gift from a friend, in Rome. It's already saved my life once."

Her surprised look turned to fear, and she sat on the bed to study my weapon more carefully. "You really need this?"

"It's not just necessary, it's essential."

"And you know how to use it?"

"I'm proficient. Please try to understand. Someday it will please me greatly to throw it away. Until then, it's my only protection."

She sighed and returned to her room.

CHAPTER 29

▼

It was eight thirty when Martine appeared for dinner. She entered my room through our connecting doors, dressed in a soft blue silk dress that elegantly fit her shapely figure. A double strand of South Sea pearls hung from her neck. Her light blonde hair was brushed across her forehead, framing her luminous blue eyes and lying gently above her shoulders. She was dazzling. "Are you ready?" she softly asked.

"For what?"

"For danger and intrigue, what else?"

We walked, arm in arm, down the dark hallway into the lobby. The hotel hound, as if on cue, let out a long, low moan, which swelled into more of a roar, and then sank into a melancholy murmur. Our response was at first humorous and then shivers, reminding me of scary movies I had seen. She held my arm tighter as we passed into the dining room. Only one other couple was there, and they sat whispering in the far corner.

"You wanted privacy?" she rhetorically asked. "Well, what could be more secluded?"

Before we were seated, we were interrupted by the night manager. "Excuse me, sir, but you have a message. It appears rather important." He handed me a sheet of paper faxed by Jason Best.

Martine looked at me in total surprise—and dismay. "You told someone we were here?"

"Don't be alarmed. Only my private detective. He's sworn to secrecy. Believe me, he can be trusted. Remember, I told you I had to continue my business from here."

She assumed a more relaxed position. "I know you know what you're doing, but Matt, I hope you don't tell anyone else."

I began reading the FAX, and looked up momentarily to assure her. "No one else will know. I promise you."

"What does it say?" she curiously asked, peering at me over the paper.

"One minute," I responded, trying with great difficulty to read in the dim light. It said:

> *You were right. Chandler worked for Jarrett—on contract. Police report says he was shot by unknown assailant in the act of burglarizing Braxton's home. Regarding Dawson, my information is McAlister lied to you. He seems to be what Marshal's arrest notice says. Will have more information later. Note McAlister's in Rome. Regards, Best.*

"Interesting," I mumbled to myself.

"Interesting what?"

"Only that Mr. Best has confirmed that there may be no good guys left. It seems the U.S. Attorney may have the same objectives as a crook in New Orleans."

"This is too deep for me to understand, so I won't try. Wine?"

"Yes, how about a Puilly Fuissé?"

"My favorite," she answered with a casual smile. "How did you know?"

I returned her smile, feeling a momentary sense of euphoria.

We enjoyed a dinner of prawns with cream of watercress soup, Dover sole for Martine and pork with cider sauce for me, rutabaga, sugar snap peas and potatoes. We finished with Lemon Lush, the chef's surprise, and a strawberry tart. Over coffee, our discussion again turned to the money.

"What are your plans?" she asked as her tongue caressed her cup of espresso.

"As a beginning, to spend time with you. But in between that time, to try to locate a woman in Italy, named Yanou Folare, and talk to a priest at the Vatican."

"In person?"

"Only if I have to. I'm hoping to find these people by telephone."

After dinner we ventured out onto the road that led to the Haytor Rocks, which rise above the hills to give a view of the coast. We could hear the bleating of the blackfaced sheep that seemed to be all around us as we walked along the secluded road. The air was crisp and cold, and the mist rose above the Dartmoor Hills to give an illusion of clouds hugging the ground.

We climbed slowly to the top of the rocks, but from there could barely perceive the coastline because of the fog that was becoming more dense. We stood in perfect quiet, in the fog and mist, until I felt her reach out for my hand.

"I've hesitated to ask," she said as her gaze drifted from the moon and clouds into my eyes, "but I will. What has your life been like since we met last, in dealing with the death of your wife?"

"Difficult, but I'm coming to terms with it," I answered after a long pause.

We walked a little further, trying to get a better glimpse of the coast. "What I'm actually trying to say," she continued, "is what have you decided to do with your life. Is there anyone else?"

"I can ask you the same question," I said, drawing a deep breath of cold, damp air.

"You can and I'll answer. But don't avoid my question. Is there?"

"No, that's why I'm here with you. And you?"

"I was engaged once. It was a long time ago. I backed out. It just wasn't right. Since then I've dated many men, but I've had no feelings for any of them. I've never understood why. Not until now. I find myself very content to be with you."

"With me, a liability," I warned.

"I'm old enough to take risks," she said demurely. "Just imagine how boring life would be without them."

"Oh, I can imagine," I half-heartedly responded. "But there are risks and then there are risks. Martine," I continued, taking both of her hands in mine, "my risks involve life and death, and an enemy I can't put a face on. You don't want to be part of that."

"I'll make that decision, thank you," she quickly replied. "If I ever think the risks are too great, you'll be the first to know. In the meantime, what shall we do tomorrow? I feel like a school-girl playing hooky."

"After my calls, let's explore Devon."

We stared at each other, holding both hands, and kissed in the dark mist. The scent of her perfume and the softness of her lips left me groping for words. She stepped back, took my hand again, and said, "Comme tu es ravissant!"

I was startled by her French for a brief moment, and then reached and kissed her again, soft and lingering. Our tongues touched briefly. I was intoxicated by her warmth and exquisite beauty. I whispered, "Are you going to tell me what you just said?"

"Someday—maybe."

That night we stayed in separate rooms, but I laid awake for hours, unable to get her out of my thoughts. The next morning I couldn't take my eyes off her, but I knew it was the wrong time. After a breakfast of kippers, eggs, sausage and grapefruit juice, I took my third cup of coffee and called Rome. I was surprised at the speed at which Monsignor Bertellini came to the phone. "Monsignor," I said quickly, "this is Matt Lawrence. Please don't hang up."

After a short silence, his tired voice said, "I won't." Then he added, "What is it, Signore Lawrence? I thought we had satisfied you."

"Monsignor, have you been contacted by Buckroyd McAlister, a U.S. Attorney from Dallas?"

"Yes. He was here just a short while ago. A very difficult man."

"Can you tell me what he wanted?"

"I think you know," he replied. "It was the money that Signore Braxton had, that you seem to think we have."

I sat back, took a deep sip of hot coffee, and asked "Did he get it?"

"Please, Signore! Did you not believe me? Several days ago Signore McAlister called, introduced himself, and asked to speak to His Holiness. He was told that would be impossible. His Holiness is away from the Vatican now. He then asked if we would honor a U.S. order to turn over illegal funds held by the Vatican. We told him that if the funds were illegal and if his order was proper, we would of course comply with it. You understand, Signore Lawrence, that we have a treaty with your country. It would not permit us to keep such funds."

"Yes, of course I do. So did he send you such an order?"

"The next day," he continued, "we were visited by a representative of your government. He presented us with a document that was called, I believe, an arrest warrant. Could that be right?"

"Yes. So then what?"

"Well this arrest warrant said that your government was arresting all money owned by Signore Braxton and deposited in the Vatican bank. Can you arrest money?"

"Yes, you can do that. Please, continue."

I could hear his labored breathing, and remembered the weary and aged man I had met on the two occasions in Rome. The silence seemed to linger forever, and then he resumed. "This warrant was presented. We told them, as we told you, that we do not have Signore Braxton's money."

"What was their response?"

"Signore McAlister visited personally with the Cardinal and Braschi. He was impossible to deal with. No one has ever talked to Vatican officials like he did."

"Where is he now?"

"After some time, during which he claimed that the Vatican intentionally lied to your government, he left."

"Lied? Did you lie to him?"

"Of course not!" I could hear, following his answer, a staccato of coughs and difficult breathing.

"Forgive me if I've upset you. I didn't intend to."

"No," he said. "It's not you, but Signore McAlister. He said we told him we would comply with his order. We did. But he never asked if we had the money, and he did not mention Signore Braxton. If he had, we would have told him."

I had been taking notes, but put down my pad. I circled his last statement, and then asked, "When did he first call you to ask if you would comply?"

"I'm not sure," he said, hesitating with my question. "It was at least three or four days ago."

I looked at my calendar. "Maybe about January 13?"

"Yes, about that time."

January 13, I thought. Two days before Braxton was to be released. It was becoming obvious. McAlister never intended to let Braxton walk out of the prison."

"Signore, I must go. Is there anything else?"

"Nothing. Monsignor, I know this has been very unpleasant for you, but I appreciate more than you'll know your patience and willingness to help me. I know you've been sick. I hope that you are well soon. I wish you the best of good health."

*　　　*　　　*　　　*

"You're in a quandary," she concluded as I hung up.

She sat next to me, in her silk beige robe, and sneaked a look at my note pad. "No good answers?"

"Oh, I got some good answers," I said, "but the riddle is still there. I can't figure out," I wondered out loud, "why McAlister didn't ask the Monsignor if they had the money. Why would he not do that before going to the trouble of getting an arrest warrant?"

"Maybe he thought he knew the answer."

She caught my grin.

"Martine, you're an absolute genius! He did think he knew the answer. Braxton told him the Pope had the money. It all adds up."

She smiled and intertwined her fingers with mine, announcing that she was returning to her room to dress for the day. I was left to call Clarissa Boles at Barclays. I poured my fourth cup of coffee as I waited for her to come to the phone. Eventually, the voice said, "Yes, this is Ms. Boles. How may I be of help?"

"Ms. Boles, this is Matthew Lawrence. We met several months ago in your offices regarding Mr. Braxton from Dallas and some wire transfers. You may recall that I'm his attorney."

"Ah, yes I do," she answered. "But Mr. Lawrence, did you not get my message from our Mr. Kirkendall in Houston concerning Yanou Folare?"

"I did," I replied, taking another drink of coffee. "But he gave me no information other than that she's a lady living in Italy. Can't you tell me more? It's very important that I find her."

"Well," she said, "Italy is a very big place. Our files showed no address or way to communicate with her. She was simply a code name, for contact purposes. We put her name on the wire transfers only because we were asked to."

I studied her response and my dilemma. I asked again. "Can't you give me any idea, any lead, on how I might find her?"

"If I were you," she said, "I would begin in Vatican City, and then possibly in Rome. It's likely that she had some connection with the Vatican bank, since it was the ultimate recipient of the funds."

"I asked at the bank," I said feeling very puzzled. "They said that they never heard of her."

"Mr. Lawrence, I'm very sorry, but I'm afraid I've done all that I can. If you can think of anything else, feel free to call me."

I hung up, wondering how to make connections in Rome to search for Yanou Folare. My thought process was interrupted by the return of Martine, dressed in a blue crew sweater and camel colored corduroy pants. "The day is getting by us," she announced. "Hurry. Let's be on our way."

"How would you go about locating a woman in Rome?"

"You might try calling Rome information," she answered.

"I speak very little Italian," I said with a frustrated expression.

"Maybe the front desk can help," she suggested. "Now, let's go."

I dressed quickly, zipped up my sailor's windbreaker, and headed with her to the lobby. An enormous black Newfoundland hound was lying in front of the desk. We both recognized it as the baying hound from the night before. The clerk was a kindly looking and very elderly lady who must have been there when the hotel was built in the nineteenth century. She offered to help with our search for Yanou Folare through the Italian phone system while we were out for the day. Before leaving, I had her make two copies of Braxton's list. I placed the original in the hotel safe, gave one copy to Martine and kept the third.

The day was overcast and damp, and a chill breeze was blowing as we pulled away from the hotel. Martine pushed her blonde hair back over her eyes, snapped her navy jacket closed to the top, and grabbed my hand.

"Do you want to tell me where we're headed?" I asked.

"First stop is the Moorland, just beyond that rise." She pointed as we wound down the narrow road, across a centuries old bridge, and up a sharp incline. Over the top I spotted it.

"What a dark and dreary place," I mumbled, wondering what we were doing here. We drove through an iron gate, over a grate-covered moat, and onto the front drive. There I saw a manicured lawn extending the length of three football fields, and in the center a formal English garden. Beyond the garden was a pasture, littered with black-nosed sheep, and beyond that the domed moors that seemed to roll forever into the horizon.

We parked and walked what seemed to be a hundred yards to the lobby. A huge portrait of a domineering woman hung over the main sitting area, and Martine pointed in its direction as we entered, whispering, "Agatha Christie."

We were escorted beyond the main area, onto a porch, where we sat and ordered coffee and tea. "Agatha Christie?"

"She stayed here for years and wrote a number of her books here."

"No wonder so many people got murdered in her books."

Next to us was an elderly couple, finishing their breakfast. The man turned and said, "A bit of a beautiful mess out there, wouldn't you say gov'ner?"

I peered outside into the back gardens and could see the rain beginning to fall. I nodded my agreement with his remark and then turned my eyes to Martine, who was breathtakingly beautiful. She sipped on her tea, occasionally smiling at me as if to say, "I know what you're thinking."

"Here's my plan," she finally said. "We'll have the hotel fix two box lunches, together with wine and a pint of beer, if you want one. Then we'll plunge into the moors, through those woods over there, and to the top of that hill where we'll have lunch."

"In the rain?"

"Oh, it rains every day, but only lightly. It won't last into the afternoon."

*   *   *   *

Several hours later we were on the top of moss-covered rocks, some two thousand feet above sea level, gazing over the misty English countryside. We sat drinking a French Merlot and eating our packed lunch—pork pie and potato chips—lost to civilization. I was at total peace, gazing first into Martine's deep blue eyes and then off into the horizon. Far in the distance, I watched a helicopter weave its way among the hills, circling back and forth, and then disappear out of sight to the west.

"What would a helicopter be doing out here?" she asked.

"I have no idea, but if by chance it's for hire, we're going to see the countryside from up there."

We returned late in the day as it was getting dark, and we again saw the helicopter hovering when we drove up to our hotel. "It must be someone important," I remarked as we walked up the path to the front entrance.

At the front desk, I inquired if there were any messages. I was referred to the elderly lady I had spoken to earlier. "Mr. Lawrence," she said, "I'm Matilda Havisham. You asked this morning if we could help you find Ms. Folare. I'm sorry to say that so far we've had no luck. Shall I keep trying?"

I unzipped my jacket and reflected on her question. "It may be a waste of time, but if you could continue trying, I would be very grateful," I said, gazing at the old Swiss furniture that occupied the massive lobby area. I noticed a man in the corner, reading the London Financial Times. He was dressed in a heavy wool jacket and hunting boots, and seemed to be oblivious to my staring at him. Then it hit me. He was the double chinned, tatoo salesman I met on British Air. Peabody!

I felt a tug on my jacket and turned to see Martine. "Anything wrong?" she asked. "You look as if you've seen a ghost."

"Get away from here, quickly," I whispered. "Go to the room."

"Why? I'm not going to just leave you here. What's wrong?"

"That man, there in the corner. He's the one who drugged me on the plane. He's dangerous. Please leave. I'll be there shortly."

She hurried off to the room while I stood there, for several minutes, trying to determine what to do next. Finally, I walked over to him and sat down. "Peabody," I said. "What are you doing here? And don't tell me it's a coincidence."

He shifted his gaze slowly from the newspaper to me, put the paper down, and sat up to give me his full attention. "Mr. Lawrence, my employer wants that piece of paper. You'll save you and your lady friend a lot of misery if you'll hand it over."

"Misery? Are you threatening me?"

"Consider it whatever you like. You've caused me personally a great deal of embarrassment. I want that paper."

"And then what? You kill us?"

"I assure you," he continued, "my employer has no desire to see you dead unless it's absolutely necessary. Now why don't you save us all a lot of trouble and give it to me?" He stared at me with naked eyes.

The sparks from the fireplace to his right roared up and caught my attention for a moment. His ruthless lack of emotion left me cold. "Well?" he asked.

I was beginning to break into a sweat. My thoughts for a second shifted to Martine and that I had sent her to the room—alone. "Who's your employer and how did you find me?"

He chuckled and then paused, taking a deep breath. "You didn't really think you could avoid us, now did you? As for my employer, his identity is not for you to know. Suffice it to say, and lest I repeat myself, you have a simple choice. You and your lady friend can continue your holiday, free from interruption, or you can choose to die. It's your choice. I'm running out of time."

"And what's my guarantee that you won't harm us?" I asked again.

"If my instructions had been to kill you, I wouldn't have just slipped you knock-out drops on the plane. I could easily have poisoned you, but I didn't. That's your assurance."

Outside I could hear the wind beginning to pick up and the shutters bang lightly against the Inn. The flames in the fireplace flickered higher as I watched his faint smile come and go. "Times up," he said. "Make your death wish."

I had no choice and I knew it. Reaching into my side pocket, I pulled out a copy of the list and handed it to him. He examined it carefully to verify it was authentic, looked up and said, "Wise choice!" He stood up, folded his newspaper, and gave me a disdainful look. "Butt out," he warned, walking across the lobby to the exit. Before reaching the door, he spun around and said, "My employer has one more message. You've had nine lives and used eight! Don't interfere again!"

A chill ran down the back of my neck. I sat there, not knowing what to do next.

"What was that all about?"

A hand grabbed mine, and I raised my head to see Martine. "I didn't go to the room," she said. "Don't be angry. I watched from over there, in the corner. I couldn't leave you alone."

"They found us," I uttered. "I don't know how, but they did. I'm not sure we're safe anywhere."

"What did he want?"

"The piece of paper."

"Did you give it to him?"

"Just a copy. What difference would it make?" I said, trying to rationalize what I had done. "If we can't make heads or tails out of it, how can they? And I still have the original."

"Come," she motioned. "Let's get a drink. I think you can use one."

After my first martini, I repeated several times the word "how", and then it hit me. "Only one person in the world knew how to find us. Jason Best!"

"But he wouldn't tell them," she insisted. "You said he could be trusted."

I thought he could. Maybe he has his price like everyone else."

She flicked her blonde locks over her shoulder, tightened her full lips as if in deep thought, and nodded.

"It's been a long day. Tomorrow, let's get away from here. Got any ideas?"

"It's already planned! We'll drive south, through the woods and on to Bigby on the Sea. It's a delightful little village on the Channel. On the way, we'll stop at Grimpen Mire, where Arthur Conan Doyle set the story for the Hound of the Baskervilles."

After trying unsuccessfully to find Best that evening and the next morning, we stepped out after breakfast into a blustering gale and frigid temperatures. The clock was ticking away, but it made little difference while I was with Martine. The elderly lady Havisham reported that she had contacted an affiliated hotel in Rome, and they were searching for Yanou Folare. She also offered to have our car brought to the front and warmed for our days' venture.

Martine appeared in a green pleated skirt, yellow turtle neck sweater and dark brown leather jacket. She was stunning with her golden hair and sparkling blue eyes. We sat in the lobby mapping our destination when suddenly we were startled by a low roar, then a flash of light and an explosion that rocked the hotel and shattered windows everywhere. The explosion ripped the front of the hotel apart, leaving a gaping hole that exposed searing flames and billows of dark smoke.

Soot and debris filled my eyes, blurring my vision, but I could see Martine. She had been flung across the sofa and was lying against the wall, blood from several cuts showing on her face. I ran over and grabbed her, lifted her up and carried her away from the flames to the back of the hotel. I screamed for help. All around me I could hear more screams as people ran for safety. Martine shivered as I laid her in a safe corner. I fought a foul taste in my mouth and the urge to vomit, but it was the intense anger that overwhelmed me.

Within minutes I was offered a wet towel and told a doctor was on his way. I gently wiped Martine's face as tears welled up in my eyes. I begged God that she would be alright. Her eyes slowly opened and she squeezed my hand. "What happened?" she whispered.

"How do you feel?" I asked, ignoring her question. "Can you move your arms and legs?"

She nodded that she could and mumbled that she wasn't in much pain. The shattered glass left several cuts and abrasions across her forehead and arms. After what seemed to be forever, I heard the wail of sirens and saw policemen and medics rush through what had been the entrance to the hotel. A young doctor pushed me away from Martine and very efficiently cleaned her wounds. I fell back against the wall, holding a towel to my head, feeling tears well up inside.

"Sir," a voice above me shouted. "Let me look at your wounds." A kindly looking older man, with rumpled hair and a white jacket, removed particles of glass from my face and arms and swabbed the wounds with a burning ointment. "The lady there, will she be alright?" I begged.

"She'll live," he answered. "Her wounds were superficial. Quite lucky, I would say, being in the line of the blast as she was. Other people were not so lucky, though. Old Mrs. Havisham and two others are dead. Several are seriously wounded."

"Do you have any idea what happened?" I asked.

He continued working on my face, and then turned his attention to my question. "Seems to have been a car blast," he said. "It looks like the IRA is back to its rotten tricks. Puzzling, though, that they would be in business here. This far removed from London—no real reason why they'd be killing people down here. But I'll leave that to Scotland Yard."

Sergeant Patrick Egan made his rounds among the guests remaining in the blackened lobby, listening to the moans and despair while trying to piece together what had happened. Eventually he made his way to Martine and me. "Do you want transportation to the hospital?" he first asked.

"My friend," I answered, pointing to Martine. "Please arrange to take her as quickly as possible. I'm alright. Can you tell me what happened?"

"Well sir, it appears to have been a car bomb, set on some sort of a timer. Placed in what's left of a blue BMW."

"Jesus!" I mumbled to myself, having my suspicions verified.

""What was that?" he asked.

"It was my friend's father's car," I answered.

He removed his note pad, pulled a pen from his jacket, and pulled up a chair next to where I was sitting. "If you don't mind, sir, I must ask you a few questions."

"Of course, go ahead."

"Do you have any idea why the IRA, or anyone else, would want to harm you or the lady?"

I thought about his question, and the obvious answer, as I watched the medics carry Martine to the waiting ambulance. Before I could speak, he said, "Don't worry, sir, they tell me she'll be alright. Just a few cuts and bruises. She won't look spiffy for a while, but I would say she was quite fortunate."

"Where will they take her?" I asked.

"To Devonshire County Hospital. She'll be well cared for. You can join her shortly. I'll be glad to drop you off there when we're finished here."

"Thank you," I muttered. "Now, your question. I flew in to London, several days ago, on British Air flight 210 from Dallas. On that flight was a man, sitting next to me, named Albert—no Alfred—Peabody. Claimed he was a tatoo salesman based in London. He took a great interest in a piece of paper I had, thought it would lead him to some lost money."

"A piece of paper? Lost money? Please, be more explicit."

"Sergeant, it's very complicated. If I can try to summarize what happened-"

"Please—" he interrupted again.

"I'm an attorney, from Dallas. A client of mine serving time in prison was murdered, just last week. He gave me a piece of paper that I'm sure this Mr. Peabody thought would lead him to the money he was looking for."

"How much money?"

"I don't know, but it seems my client had stashed some money somewhere before he died."

"Did this piece of paper say where this money is?" he asked, furiously taking notes.

"That's the irony. No, no it didn't. When Peabody asked for it, I gave it to him."

"And you think," he continued, "that this Alfred Peabody tried to kill you and the lady?"

"I don't think, I know he tried to kill us."

His attention had become riveted on me, and I could see his expression become hardened. As he looked around the burnt out lobby, contemplating what I had told him, I took in his ruddy complexion, manicured black mustache and dark eye sockets. He was a moderately built man, overweight in the wrong places, but his lack of build was fairly well covered by his blue uniform. Redirecting his attention to me, he asked, "This man Peabody, was he acting alone or working for someone?"

"For someone. I'm sure of that. He mentioned his employer several times when we talked."

"And when was that?"

"On the plane and yesterday."

"Yesterday?"

"Yes, he was here yesterday. That's when he demanded the piece of paper and I gave it to him. He threatened to kill us if I failed to hand it over."

"And who was his employer?"

"He wouldn't tell me."

"Do you know where this Peabody is now?"

"I don't have the slightest idea. Sergeant, you have to understand that I had never seen this man before until my flight from Dallas. I don't know anything about him, except that he's violent and thinks that I have information about the money he's searching for."

He stroked his mustache, then removed a curved pipe from his breast pocket. "Mind if I light up?" he asked not waiting for my answer. Removing a tin of tobacco, he filled the pipe, packed it tightly, and struck a match. Sucking in deeply, he turned back and next asked, "And you don't?"

"Don't what?"

He puffed several times, removed the pipe from his mouth, and said, "Don't know where this money is?"

"Of course not," I emphatically pronounced. "Believe me, Sergeant, I've told you everything I know. You're wasting a lot of time. Shouldn't you get moving to find this man?"

He closed his notebook, returned the pen to his coat, and nodded his concurrence. "We'll find him. You can bloody well count on it." Turning back to face me, he added, "Now, I must ask you to come with me to the station. The Chief Inspector will want to ask you more questions, and we'll need a good identification of this Peabody."

It was past four in the afternoon when I was released from the county police station. Before leaving, Sergeant Egan informed me that Peabody was not Peabody. Whoever he was, he had traveled on the passport of a dead man.

CHAPTER 30

▼

Devonshire County Hospital reminded me of a mental institution—dark gray walls with a massive iron gate protecting its entrance, and situated in a bleak neighborhood on the edge of the town. Martine was sitting in a large room with several other patients, attended to by a single nurse. She rushed to me when our eyes met.

"Matt, you're O.K.?"

"I'm fine. But Martine, this can't go on. I will not put you in any more danger." She had several bandages on her forehead, one directly above her right eye, and cuts and abrasions on her cheeks and chin.

She gave me a sullen look and said, "That's not your choice—it's mine. And I'm fine. We were very lucky, you know," she said, holding tightly onto my arm. "People died, including that poor Mrs. Havisham!"

"I know. I want to get you out of here and back to London as soon as possible. Are you ready to leave?"

"Yes—all checked out."

We rented a white Ford Escort, picked up our baggage and the original Braxton list at what was left of the Swiss Inn, and headed north on the autoway to London. Driving through the fog on the rain-slicked highway was difficult as night fell, so I kept our speed at a slow one-hundred kilometers per hour. I intermittently shifted my gaze from the road to my rear-view mirror, taking every precaution to be sure that we weren't being followed.

"You're going to have a problem in London," I said. She turned towards me, peering beneath the bandage over her eye, and gave me a quizzical stare.

"What problem?"

"Your father's BMW, or what's left of it. I hope he wasn't too attached to it."

"I'm sure it's covered by insurance. And he's not my father. He's my stepfather. What will I tell him?"

"The truth wouldn't hurt."

"He'll never believe it. Who would?"

"In London," I said, "I want to deposit you in a safe place. Do you want to go back to your seminar at the Intercontinental?"

She flashed a very perturbed expression at me and released my hand. "I thought we discussed that. I'm free for the next ten days and I want to help you. Why don't we go to my stepfather's apartment in Kensington for tonight, and then tomorrow make our plans?"

I took a deep breath and thought carefully about my response. "I've got things to do that I must do by myself," I said. "Give me two or three days. Then we'll meet again."

"No! Matt, I won't do that. What's so important that I can't go with you?"

"Your life, that's what's so important. I almost got you killed back there. That's not going to happen again. I've got to find that woman in Italy, Yanou Folare, and then those men on Braxton's list."

"But you don't speak French," she implored. "You'll get nowhere. Please let me help."

"Absolutely not. I'm not going to take any more risks with you. Martine, it's too-"

Before I could finish, she placed her finger gently on my lips. "Please let me help?" she again quietly asked. "If you ever think it's getting too dangerous for me, then I'll go away. I promise."

"We'll discuss it in the morning," I said. She closed her eyes and rested her head back on the seat. I knew I had a problem.

Everything at the apartment was too big. The ceilings were at least fifteen feet high, the living room would have taken in my whole apartment, and the king-sized bed in the bedroom seemed lost. I turned to Martine and said, "Your stepfather must be very successful. I'm overwhelmed."

"Not quite. Some just marry wealthy women. My stepfather's first wife was part of the royal family. A distant cousin of the Queen, or something like that."

The apartment was shades of Victorian England. Edwardian sofas and tables sat on turn-of-the-century oriental rugs, in colors of blue, deep red and gold. It was elegant but overdone from another time.

"This apartment," Martine pointed out, "has unbelievable conveniences, like two bathtubs. Shall we each retire to one and meet later for a rendezvous?"

"On one condition," I said, watching her flinch. "Only if mine has a telephone."

"Only you!" she said with a warm grin. "There's a portable phone, there in the corner. Help yourself, but don't get electrocuted."

After submerging my battered body in three feet of hot water, I dialed my one-time friend, Best. I lay there, hot water running down my cuts and bruises, and finally heard at last his familiar voice. "Yeah?"

"Jason, it's Lawrence. What are you up to?"

"Where are you?"

"Before I tell you that, you tell me something," I demanded, holding a hot washcloth against my forehead. "Did you tell anyone, and I mean anyone, where I was yesterday?"

"No, why'd you ask?"

"Why? Because someone tried to kill me and a friend, and in the process they blew up three other people."

I sank lower in the tub and heard nothing but a strange silence. Finally, the silence was broken. "Are you fuckin' crazy!" he yelled.

"How could you possibly think that I would set you up! Jesus, that pisses me off!"

"Easy Jason. Nobody knew but you. Explain that to me."

"I don't have to explain anything to you. Did you think I would sell you out? Is it possible, just maybe, that you told someone else, or maybe that you were followed?"

Water eased down my head, creating beads on my forehead, as I thought about his question. "No," I said, "that's not possible. Look, Jason, I trust you, but someone followed us straight to the hotel and blew the son-of-a-bitch to smithereens. It wasn't a coincidence. Are you sure, absolutely, that you didn't tell anyone where we were?"

"No one! I swear to God. You're looking in the wrong direction. If you want to get rid of me, just say so. But don't accuse me of disloyalty. That's fuckin' insulting!"

He sounded convincing, and it occurred to me that I was wrong. "Can you cool down enough," I asked, "to give me a report?"

I could hear the jingle of ice in a glass near the phone, and the sound of Best gulping down a drink. "A report?" he repeated. "Well, how about this one. Your lady friend's friend, this guy Charles Duggan, is a neurologist. How does that strike you?"

My skin was beginning to wrinkle in the water and I could feel my brain going to sleep. "It makes sense," I answered lazily. "Her husband was a doctor. This guy is probably someone she met through him. For the last time, forget about her. What else?"

"McAlister sent the twins on a trip—to France."

"The twins? What are you talking about?"

"The boys—Dawson Henry and Rudy Blair."

"How in the hell do you know that?"

"Simple. I called Blair's office, told his receptionist I was an old friend and had to see him. She said impossible, that he was out of the country. I asked where, and I'll be damned if she didn't say he went to France, for several weeks. So I said, 'vacation?' and she said 'no, just business.'"

"But you don't know that Henry was with him."

"Like hell I don't! I popped the question to her. Did he go with my good friend, Dawson Henry? Guess what? She says yes. How did I know?"

I almost laughed out loud. "I've got to hand it to you, Jason. You're good, real good. Anything else?"

"No. You sound like you're in a hurry to go."

"Only because I'll drown if I stay here another sixty seconds."

"What?"

"I'm taking a hot bath. It's good for bruises. I'll call you later. Oh Jason, don't do anything else until I call you again."

"Like what? There's not much else I can do. If you can decide who your friends are," he added sarcastically, "I'll be around."

I slowly got up, dried off, and put on a terry cloth robe hanging behind the door. After shaving and trying to repair some of my damaged face, I collapsed on the bed and made one more call, this time to Vatican City. My eyes involuntarily closed while I waited for an answer, listening to the intermittent beeping of the Italian phone system. A woman's voice finally answered and told me the Monsignor was not available. I told her that it was a matter of life and death, that he must call me as soon as possible. She said nothing and then I heard a dial tone. I closed my eyes again, exhausted.

My dreams in troubled times are troubled dreams. But this time it was quirky. I was driving in a small sports car with a Mack Truck bearing down behind me. On my right was a woman in a convertible, beckoning me to follow her. And on my left, I saw another woman in a jeep, telling me to follow her. In front, there was a brick wall. Then I heard a shrill sound, a beeping followed by a loud ring. My dream was shattered and I awoke to hear the phone.

Flipping the on switch, I mumbled, "Yes?"

"Signore, what is life or death?"

"A figure of speech," I answered, suddenly coming to my senses. "Sixty seconds of your time," I pleaded. "That's all."

"It's past ten. Please, leave me alone!"

"Monsignor, listen to these names," I began, grabbing for Braxton's list. "Just tell me if you know any of them." Before he could interrupt to protest, I rattled off ten of the names on the list.

"I know none of them," he answered when I was through. "They are all French. I don't know these men. Now, will you leave me alone?"

"Yes, now I will," I answered, and listened for the dial tone which came quickly.

I flipped the switch to off, laid back and almost drifted back into my dream when I was gently nudged by Martine. She was in her beige silk robe and looked irresistible, bandages and all. "Any results?" I looked up at her, squinting through my half-closed eyes, and knew that I recognized her from my dream.

"Zippo," I answered.

"Zippo? Is that some sort of American slang?"

"It means nothing," I interpreted.

"So—tomorrow. What's on?"

"Tomorrow, I enter a race."

"A race?"

"Yes, against two thugs who are in France. I think they have the Braxton list, and I'm going to try to beat them to the punch. I've got to find some of those names before they do."

"But how? You don't have any idea where they are."

"Yes I do," I said. "I know where they come from. Didn't you say these other names on the list are places?"

"I said they sound like places, but I don't know how to find them."

"Then how do I put them together?"

She adjusted her robe, stood up and pushed her hair back. "You're not much fun, you know," she said. "How about a drink?"

"Dewars and soda, please."

When she returned, I hit her with my suggestion. "Your stepfather, would he know?"

She delivered my drink, sipped on a tall glass of champagne she had poured for herself, and gave me a stark "No!"

"Why?"

"Because he lived in France for only a short time. He's English."

"But the *Economist* has a Paris bureau, correct?"

She sat down, next to the bed in an oversized chair, and gave me one of her perturbed looks. "Matt, I can't get him involved in this."

"Don't get him involved," I pleaded, "just have him run the names and places through their computer system. That's all."

"That's all?"

"Yes."

"O.K. But don't ask me for more, not from him. Matt, I don't have that sort of relationship with him. What I mean is that we're not that close. Do you see?"

"Yes, I think I do."

CHAPTER 31

▼

The Médoc Region, France, 1992

"He knows two of them! Can you hear me?"

I slowly opened my eyes, focused them on Martine, and asked, "What time is it?"

"It's almost eleven in the morning! Did you hear me? He knows two of them."

"He does?"

"Yes. Before I had finished reading the list to him, he said he had met two of the men while in France. They own vineyards in the Bordeaux wine region. He says they live about four hours from Paris, near each other."

*   *   *   *

By three in the afternoon we had boarded Air France to Paris, armed with information that I knew would tell me what happened to the money. London had its usual gloomy cast, and gave an appearance of an all gray city as we rose into the clouds. I sat, studying the paper with Braxton's names, when Martine asked a question that had somehow not occurred to me.

"Suppose," she asked, "that one of these men tells you precisely what happened to the money. Then what?"

Her question pierced me like the point of an arrow. "Then what?" I repeated. "I don't have the slightest idea," I confessed. "As a matter of fact, the money may be untouchable."

"Untouchable?"

"Yes, beyond my reach. It may be in some Swiss account, or who knows where. I admit it. I'm flying blind."

Our destination in France was Gilbert Renaud at St. Estephe and Henri Gras-Doisson at Beychevelle. I had decided not to announce our coming. I felt the element of surprise would be important in learning the truth.

Paris Orly airport was jammed at five in the afternoon. We weren't able to begin our journey—east from Paris on the autoroute to Bordeaux—until after six. The wind in February was brisk as we drove our small Puegot through the environs of Paris eastward to the autoroute and then along N-10 to Bordeaux.

Martine was dressed in a black knit skirt and creamy yellow sweater. She had covered her cuts and bruises with makeup, and they were becoming less noticeable. With the roadmap in her lap, she ran her finger along our route and then glanced over at me as we sped along the four-lane freeway at over one-hundred and fifty kilometers per hour.

"It's almost six hundred kilometers to Bordeaux," she announced. "We go through Tours and Poitiers. Matt, let's not drive through tonight. It's late and I'm tired. In Bouliac there's a pleasant small hotel, owned by a woman I know, Madame Flourens. Let's stop there. Then, in the morning, we'll have only an hour or so drive to St. Estephe."

I'd heard her suggestion but was lost in thoughts of what was ahead. "Well?" she asked.

"What happens if Renaud or Gras-Boisson won't see us, or if they're away?"

"It was your idea," she reminded me, "to appear unannounced. If we can't see them, we'll search out other names on that list."

"Other names—how in the world can we do that?"

"I'll just bet you," she said, "that there are other men in the same area—the Médoc."

"The Médoc?"

"Matt, it's the entire wine region. The men my stepfather knew own vineyards. Wouldn't it be logical to assume that other vineyard owners might also be named?"

I shot her a puzzled look, and asked, "If they are, what would be the connection?"

"I don't know," she answered. "Isn't that why we're going to Bordeaux?"

*   *   *   *

Three hours later we diverted from our course onto Route de Latresne, along a country road and to Bouliac. There we drove to Auberge du Marais, a small stone, manor-like chateau hotel buried among pine trees off to the left of the road. The lobby was dark and dank, reminding me of an old medieval castle. The ceiling was supported by large wood beams, and an old red frayed rug covered the gray stone floor. Madame Flourens recognized Martine at once and met us with "Bonsoir, Martine."

"C'est mon ami, Matt Lawrence," Martine said extending her hand and nodding in my direction.

I smiled and heard Madame Flourens say "Enchantée".

After a flow of unintelligible French between the two of them, we were shown to our rooms. They were each decorated in white and green flowered wallpaper. Cream colored sheets with blue velvet quilts and ruffled shams covered the large double beds. Each room had adjoining doors and balconies that overlooked an expanse of vineyards barren in the winter landscape. I opened the balcony doors and breathed in the chill evening air, wondering how long the peace would last.

With the help of Madame Flourens the next morning, we marked our map to lead us first to Henri Gras-Boisson and then to Gilbert Renaud. At her suggestion, she called each man to confirm he would be in and would see us. I was surprised at how easily our meetings were arranged. By 9:30, we left the hotel and wound along the Gironde River through the vineyards.

At Chateau Beychevelle we came upon a medieval fortress that dominated the banks of the river. Driving into Beychevelle, we passed rows of vineyards, lying nearly on top of each other, all grouped on the highest ground possible. In the low lying areas of the approach, we saw herds of cows grazing in the fields. The narrow, winding road led us to a gray stone chateau, with large French windows and doors surrounded by climbing Ivy—the home of Henri Gras-Boisson.

Monsieur Gras-Boisson, we were told, would meet with us in the cellar. We were taken into a dimly-lit cellar on the side of a hill, with a long, central colonnade and whitewashed walls. Inside, we saw thousands of barrels of wine, stacked two and three high and arranged in long, neat rows. There was a cathedral-like silence in the cellar, and an overwhelming aroma that reminded me of grapes and vinegar.

Near the end of the cellar, we were met by a tall, lanky man in his fifties, wearing a black wool cardigan over a gray turtleneck sweater and blue jeans. He was bald except for a whiff of white hair in the center of his forehead that was combed back into a curl. His dark rimmed glasses accentuated a sharp nose and deep brown eyes, framed by bushy white eyebrows. He ignored us as we approached, and then suddenly turned to extend his hand.

"Bonjour, Monsieur et Madame," he said in a resonant voice.

Martine stepped forward and said, "Bonjour, Monsieur. Comment allez-vous?"

Before I could say anything, he responded, "Bien, merci," and then, "You are Mr. Lawrence and Ms. Paulet, I presume."

"You speak English," I said, feeling immediately relieved.

"Oh yes," he said. "It's quite indispensable in this region. Too many foreigners to deal with. Madame Flourens said you were inquiring about my connection with a Mr. Braxton, I believe. Is that correct?"

I could feel the damp cold penetrating my jacket as I nodded my confirmation. "Mr. Braxton was a client of mine, in the United States," I began. "We're attempting to settle his estate. In the course of assembling his properties and interests, we were told that he may have some involvement here in the Medoc. We thought you might be of some help."

He slowly removed his glasses and motioned us into a small office between two enormous casks. There he propped himself against a massive oak desk, lit a cigarette, and offered one to each of us. "Mr. Braxton," he said again, rubbing his chin. "I don't have any recollection of that name. Was he ever here?"

"Not that I know of," I replied. "Do you know of any interests he might have had in your vineyard or with others here in the area?"

"None," he quickly answered. "My family has owned this vineyard for centuries, and it's the same throughout most of the Medoc. Tell me again, what makes you think he had interests here?"

I hesitated, then reached into my pocket and removed the list, and said, "I was given this list of names by him when he died. As you can see, you and your chateau are named."

He studied the list for some time and then looked up and smiled. "This list," he said, "could be the table of contents of a book on the wine country. I'm afraid someone has played a joke on you, and a very bad one at that. I'm sorry, but I can't be of help to you."

Martine and I looked at each other, in total frustration, as he handed back the list. "I really am sorry," he added, "but you've made your long trip for nothing."

He rose to leave, again extending his hand. "Monsieur Gras-Boisson," Martine said, "have you been contacted by anyone else concerning this list of names?"

He stopped, gave her a puzzling stare, and asked, "Why would anyone else want to contact me?"

"We don't know for sure that they would," I answered, "but this list is important in settling Mr. Braxton's estate. It's a possibility that you will hear from other people."

"If I do, they'll be wasting their time the same way you have," he said, turning his back to us and walking down the long corridor. We thanked him for his time and walked slowly back to our car.

Martine smiled as I reached for my keys to let her in. "And what's so funny?" I asked.

"Wild geese."

"Wild geese?"

"Yes," she said sarcastically, "it's what you chase. Can't you see how futile this is? I have this strong premonition—no, I have a prediction," she said correcting herself, "that if we were able to talk to every man on that list, the answer would be the same—they don't know anything."

"O.K.," I said with an enormous sense of hopelessness. "If that's the case, then why are men dying, and killing others, over this piece of paper?"

"Matt, you're not thinking logically. You don't know that the piece of paper has anything to do with anything. You're just guessing. Maybe this was your Mr. Braxton's final joke on everyone. Maybe he was trying to throw you off the track."

"Why would he do that?" I asked, starting the car and backing out of the drive. "He was dying!"

"I'm just here for the ride," she curtly answered. "I don't have the slightest idea." She buttoned her beige wool coat, tied the sash tightly around her waist, and settled back, waiting for my response.

I pulled over at the end of the road and turned to face her. She looked at me and smiled. I couldn't help myself. With her luminous blue eyes, enchanting smile and delicate features, I found her serenely irresistible. I rubbed my nose against hers and couldn't help but smile.

"Now you tell me what's so funny," she demanded.

"Maybe you're right," I admitted. "Maybe this is all very humorous. However," I said, pulling back and adjusting my seat belt, "why don't we go and meet Monsieur Gilbert Renaud, just for the fun of it?"

"I'm game," she replied. "If my map is correct, his chateau is about fifteen kilometers to the right. Shall we?"

The road to Monsieur Renaud was lined with massive pine trees, reminding me a little of New England. After ten minutes the trees abruptly ended and we came upon open fields and vineyards, as far as our eyes could see. We were on the Route des Grands Crus, D-2e, and signs pointed to the vineyard tours. When we reached the sign that said St. Estephe, we turned left down a gravel road and followed the sign to Chateau le Cortdier.

The chateau was actually two separate buildings, joined by a treillage, built on two levels, both of dark beige stucco with red tile roofs. It sat in a tranquil valley along the Gironde River. The river wound through the narrow valley to a far off village, screened by willows and poplar trees. We pulled into the main drive of the chateau and immediately came upon a courtyard and stables. Heather and ivy lined the drive and the walls of the stables, and massive dark green doors, surrounded by six-foot tall shrubs with red berries, were opened to expose an enormous array of equipment and horses.

Pulling up near the house, we were met by two large Alsatian hounds, showing their ill-tempered nature. Saliva dripped from their fangs while we sat, pinned in the car, wondering what to do. Our thoughts were interrupted by a shrill whistle, and the dogs quickly retreated to the stables. "Is it safe?" Martine asked, showing me that she wanted to be the last person out of the car.

Before I could answer, a plump man wearing brown coveralls and a hunting jacket, walked up to the car and motioned us out. "Pardon, Monsieur et Madame," he said.

"Bonjour, Monsieur," Martine replied. "Parlez-vous anglais?"

"Oui. Please, come in."

He led us into a large drawing room having a red brick floor and dark green painted walls. The ceiling was massive, at least twenty feet tall, and was supported by heavy wood beams. Against the wall was a large gun case, filled with shotguns, muskets and war relics. A huge stone fireplace with a five foot high iron grate was on the opposite wall, billowing smoke that burned our eyes when we entered.

Gilbert Renaud gave every appearance of a man who liked food. His stomach protruded beyond his blue plaid shirt as he sat in a large rocking chair next to the fire. He brushed back the hair on the side of his head, accentuating a slick bald area on top, and removed his glasses. "Pardon le chien," he said, smiling through uneven teeth that extended beneath a dark brunette mustache.

I turned to Martine, hoping for an interpretation, but he quickly corrected himself. "Forgive me," he said, "But I must remember to speak English. Please," he added, motioning us to a small sofa opposite his chair, "tell me what I can do for you."

"Monsieur Renaud," I said, "I'm the attorney for the estate of a man from Dallas, Texas, a Mr. David Henry Braxton. We believe he might have had some business dealings here, in Bordeaux, and hoped that you could be of some help."

"Ah, Mr. Braxton," he said.

Martine and I looked at each other at the same moment, in stark surprise. She was the first to blurt out, "You knew him?"

"Yes, not well, but we met."

"When?" I asked.

"Two days ago, here at my chateau."

I stared at him while he rocked gently, waiting for my response. "Impossible!" I said.

He stopped rocking, pulled his chair forward, and glared at both of us. "Do you say I am lying?"

"No, no," I quickly said. "But Monsieur Renaud, Mr. Braxton was murdered, in a federal penitentiary, a week ago. You could not have met him."

"He was here!" he insisted.

Martine sensed his irritation growing and motioned me with her hand to be quiet. "Vous avez raison," she said softly to him.

"It's O.K.," he responded. "I will speak English. But you must know that your Mr. Braxton was here."

"What did he want?" I asked.

He hesitated, stood and poked the fire. He then turned to Martine and asked, "Voulez-vous du café?"

"Oui, merci."

"Attendez ici jusqu'à ce que je revienne," he replied and left the room.

I sat, totally puzzled. "Can you tell me what's happening, if it wouldn't be too much trouble," I said.

Martine leaned towards me and whispered, "He went to get us coffee. If you're smart, you'll leave this to me. Matt, he got very upset when you questioned his integrity."

"I didn't question his integrity."

"But you did," she said. "You said he couldn't have met with Braxton, when he assured you that he had."

"But he couldn't have," I protested.

Martine adjusted her skirt, looked to the door to be sure he hadn't returned, and then fixed her eyes on me. "He may not have met with Braxton, but he met with someone who said he was Braxton. Wouldn't you like to know more about that someone?"

Before I could answer, the door swung open and he entered with a pot of coffee and three cups. After pouring cups for each of us, he returned to the rocking chair with his cap. "Monsieur," he began, "let me repeat myself. I met with Monsieur Braxton, here, just two days ago. Now, what is it you want to know?"

The coffee tasted extremely bitter, and I winced as I thought about his question. Noticing my reaction, Martine offered cream, which I declined. "Can you describe this man you met?" I asked.

He paused, took a sip of his cup, and placed it on a precarious table next to his chair. "Rather rough features, I would say. Shorter than you. Dark black hair and a thin mustache, fairly overweight. He wore brown frame glasses. A very pleasant man."

He had not described Braxton. It sounded more like he was describing Peabody. "Can you tell me what he wanted?"

Renaud adjusted his glasses and peered at me as if I were crazy. "You're his lawyer," he said. "Why should I tell you what he wanted. Don't you know?"

"Monsieur," I said with a great amount of caution, "the man you met with was not my client. He was an imposter. He lied to you."

He looked stunned. "Not Monsieur Braxton?" he said. "Why would he lie to me?"

"I don't know. Tell us what he wanted. Maybe then we can find some answers."

Renaud stood up and walked to the fireplace. There he turned and stoked the coals, massaging his forehead. Gazing at Martine, he said, "Voulez-vous encore du cafe?"

"No, merci," she responded.

"He said he was interested in buying a vineyard, and asked which ones might be for sale. He wanted to know who the owners were."

"And what did you tell him?" Martine asked.

"I told him," he said, scratching his forehead, "that none were for sale—at least none that I knew of. I told him they had been owned by the same families for years, that it would be difficult for him to buy one."

"Anything else?" I quizzed.

"No, nothing. Just a friendly conversation, and then he left."

"Nothing?" I said in disbelief.

"Nothing," he repeated. He paused and then held up a finger. "Oh, there was one other thing."

"What?" I waited.

"He asked about a list of names he had."

"And?"

"I told him they were chateau owners, here in the Medoc. My name was on the list. It meant nothing."

We finished our coffee, thanked him for his time, and left. "What was all the talk in French?" I asked as we pulled out of the drive.

"Just small talk. Now what?"

The feeling of reality slipping away was beginning to come over me. I looked at Martine's cuts and bruises, and felt hopeless. "Someone's lying," was all that I could say.

Martine smiled, looking straight ahead while we sped away from the chateau. She turned, leaned against the door, and reached for my hand. "Matt, why would any of these men lie to you? They wouldn't. Is it possible that your list doesn't mean anything, that's it's a big hoax perpetrated by your dead client? After all, it certainly looks to me as if a lot of people are chasing the wind."

"It's not possible. People died because of that list. It means something! But I don't have the slightest idea what."

CHAPTER 32

▼

Dallas, Texas, 1992

"Sterling Braxton is dead, but Braxton's not!" The message from Best was unbelievable.

"What! That's impossible."

"No," he said, "this is the truth. She was murdered Sunday night, at her sister's house. But we found out that while everyone assumed that Braxton died, he didn't."

"They told me he was dead!"

"They told you wrong. He's not, but he ain't saying much. He's been in a coma since he was stabbed. But he's definitely alive. Mr. Lawrence, I'll tell you this. Whoever tried to kill him, when they find out, they'll try again!"

"Jesus."

I closed my eyes and held the phone against my chest, not wanting to believe what I had just heard. "Jason, I'm coming back, tomorrow. Meet me at my apartment Tuesday night at nine."

"See you then." I stared at the phone, listening to the dial tone in a daze after he hung up.

Martine sat wide eyed across from me. "You didn't mean that? You're not going back to Dallas?"

"I have to. Bic Braxton is alive."

I watched the wave of disappointment flash over her face. "Just like that," she said. "Don't you know how much I care for you?"

"I do," I said, taking her head into my hands and softly kissing her. "And I care that much for you, but I'm not leaving you for good. It will only be for a short time. Tomorrow," I said, "I'll drive you back to Paris and then I'll catch the flight to Dallas."

"I'll go with you."

"No, Martine. I have to do this alone."

*   *   *   *

The pavement moved in a blur beneath my feet as I walked quickly down the concourse after landing in Dallas. My gloom had turned to rage and anger when I arrived at my apartment. The echo of the word "why" wouldn't stop pounding in my head.

The next morning I was seething with anger. I called Jarrett. He began by shouting at me, but it stopped when I said as loudly, "Listen, you fat-ass son-of-a-bitch. Your days are over. You've tried once too often to get me. Now it's your turn, do you hear me!"

My shout was met with silence, and then wheezing and coughing, which seemed endless. Eventually, a hoarse voice came through. "Whatdaya mean?"

"Bird Dog, Peabody and all those assassins, that's what I mean," I shouted. "It's over, Jarrett. Either you stop or you're a dead man."

"I don't know any Peabody! You little chicken shit threaten me! Who the hell do you think you are!"

I held the phone back and wondered if he was lying. Then, more calmly, I said, "I don't have the money, I don't want it, and I'm sick and tired of the trail of murder and mayhem your people are leaving behind me."

I could hear deep sucking and then more wheezing. "Who do you think I've killed?" he asked in a quieter voice.

"How about Braxton's secretary, Marianne, for starters. And Braxton, and his wife. And what about Julia!" My rage was again becoming intense.

"You're fucking crazy!" he yelled. "I didn't touch any of those people—ya think I'm a lunatic. Why would I do that?"

"Because you goddamn threatened to. Do you remember what you told me? Anyone who got in your way would be dead meat."

"That was a figure of speech. I don't kill people!"

"You sure as hell fooled me. Who is doing it then?"

"You tell me!" he shouted again.

I sat speechless and then heard him say, "Lawrence, I told you before that you didn't know shit! You're a child in a man's game. I want the money, not a life sentence for murder. We saved your life, or can't you remember Bird Dog in Rome. And by the way, you still don't have a fuckin' clue as to what's going on."

"Do you?" The phone went dead.

I had gambled that Peabody worked for Jarrett, and that Jarrett would admit it. Maybe I was wrong.

*   *   *   *

I met with Best the next morning. Scratching his day old beard, he said, "Look's like you're barking up the wrong tree."

"Jason, someone's lying. Braxton gave me that list of names and places when he thought he was dying, and he told me to go see the Pope. There's no way that he would have misled me. Not under those circumstances."

"You got a drink?"

"Are you kidding?" I said. "For God's sake Jason, it's eight in the morning—you haven't even had breakfast."

"It's too early for breakfast."

"Let's get back to the list, shall we?"

"What's there to get back to? This ain't no problem for a physics genius. You say Braxton's not lying. O.K. Then it must be either the Monsignor or the Pope. It can't be the Pope—Popes don't lie. So, we have the Monsignor."

"I've met with him. I just can't believe he'd lie to me. It doesn't add up."

Best got up and wandered over to my liquor cabinet. "Do you mind?" he asked, not waiting for my answer before he poured a scotch over ice.

"You've got a problem, Jason."

"Easy for you to say," he responded with a grin on his face. "Could it be," he continued while swirling his drink, "that Braxton wanted you to see the Pope, but not about that piece of paper. What if the paper holds a key to the mystery, but it's just an unconnected key. Suppose the Pope has another, and Braxton wanted you to put all the pieces together."

"Interesting theory," I said. "But it's too complicated. Why didn't he just lay it out for me?"

"So you wouldn't have anything to say that was meaningful if the wrong person wanted to know what you knew. Maybe Braxton doesn't trust anyone. Maybe that list of names will somehow get him his money without anyone understanding it. Didn't you say it had the word receipt on it?"

"Yes, that's what I was told. But it's not a receipt. It's just a list with the word receipt on it. And I'll say again—he was dying. Why play games?"

He finished his drink and rose to leave. "You got me," he said, throwing his hands in the air.

"Where are you going?"

"Where do you want me to go?"

"Go find Dawson Henry and this guy Peabody. Maybe they've got some pieces. Remember what you told me—you can't get answers unless you ask questions."

He opened the door and mumbled as he left, "I'll be back in touch."

After he left, I was thoroughly confused. Then it suddenly hit me. Henri Gras-Boisson had said the list could be the table of contents of a book on the wine country. I pulled down from the shelves a book written by Etienne LaFonne, *The Definitive Guide to the French Wine Country*. Flipping through its pages, I looked for a list of the wine chateau owners. All the names on Braxton's list were there, and more. I turned the pages, one by one, searching for the slightest clue. There was nothing. I closed the book after forty-five minutes of wasted time, remembering not so affectionately that it had been a gift from Braxton. In better days.

Thirty minutes later I stood in front of my bathroom mirror, wrapped in a towel, shaving. My thoughts were interrupted by a buzz on the intercom. "Yeah," I screamed. "Who is it?"

Frank yelled back. "Says his name is Peabody. Want me to send him up?"

My hand jerked when I heard his message, and a thin line of blood began to form across my cheek. I froze momentarily, unable to speak. "Tell him to wait. I'll be down in ten minutes."

"You got it."

I nervously dressed and then grabbed my Beretta and its holster. The holster made a loud click as I snapped the straps together under my arm. I next pushed the safety of the gun up with my thumb, and depressed the magazine release button. The magazine fell loose and I quickly loaded nine shells. Then I pulled the slide, loaded the chamber, and slid the gun into the holster.

Warning bells went off in my head, telling me it was idiotic to meet again with Peabody. I ignored them and grabbed a sport coat to conceal the gun.

It seemed a lifetime for the elevator to descend to the lobby. The door opened slowly. Except for Frank, the lobby was empty. "Where'd he go?"

Frank looked up from his newspaper and nodded his head towards the doors. "Across the street. Said he'd meet you in the park. A friend of yours?"

"I wish," I mumbled. "Frank, keep an eye on me. This man's no friend. If I call, come."

Frank abruptly closed his newspaper. "You want me to call the cops?"

"No, not now. Just watch."

On the other side of the road I could make out a man, sitting on a park bench along the creek. The wind was brisk, and he held his coat closed as I approached.

"You've got a lot of guts, Peabody, or whatever your name is. What makes you think I haven't called the police?"

He smirked and gestured me to sit down. "And tell them what? I knew you'd be here, and alone."

I sat on a bench directly opposite his, squinting to avoid the direct glare of the sun. "How, how did you know?"

"Because you're curious—and stupid! Can't stop, can you?"

"You killed all those people. You bastard! I don't know who you work for, but they'll pay, every one of them."

"How do you know I killed anyone?"

"Scotland Yard knows you, and they'll find you."

He kept his coat held tightly against his body and glared at me through the sunlight. "Regard me as your emissary," he said. "There won't be another. I suggest you take what I'm about to say to heart."

"Why should I accept anything you say? If you expect me to talk, you're wasting your time."

An almost imperceptible smile crept across his face and then quickly disappeared. "We don't expect you to talk. We expect you to keep your mouth shut."

I sat frozen in the cold breeze and blinding sun. He studied my confused expression. "There are people you hold dear. Let me name a few. For starters, there's Ms. Paulet and Ms. Sorrel. Two at a time—we're impressed."

"Go to hell," I countered, reaching into my coat for my gun.

"Pull it out," he said quietly. "Shoot me. I'm unarmed. But consider this. I don't work alone. You kill me and those two women will be dead by in the morning. It's your choice."

"What do you want?" I asked, my mood tumbling. "The last time we met, you promised you wouldn't harm us. You lied."

"You lied—I lied. You didn't give me that list in England, you gave me a copy. A very bad move on your part. What we want isn't complicated. You back off, for good, and we spare your friends."

"Back off from what? I don't know what it is you people are after."

"Come now, Mr. Lawrence. You're smarter than that."

"You O.K., Mr. Lawrence?"

I spun around to see Frank. Shifting my eyes between Frank and Peabody, I said, "Call the police, Frank."

"What?"

"You heard me, Frank. Call the police. This man's a wanted fugitive."

Frank moved quickly back across the street, and Peabody glared at me. "You just made a big fucking mistake." He stood up.

"Stop!" I demanded, removing my gun and pointing it at his head.

"You won't shoot!" He turned and walked to a waiting car, gave me a contemptuous look, and drove off. I then noticed Jason Best, in his broken down Ford. He shot a thumb's up sign in my direction and sped down the road after Peabody.

*   *   *   *

Best returned at five in the afternoon. He looked better. "Room 311 in the Stoneleigh."

"What?" I said as he threw his wet raincoat across my sofa.

"He's staying at the Stoneleigh Hotel—room 311," he repeated.

"How did you know to follow him?"

"Just returning from breakfast, and there you were, crossing Cedar Springs Road in front of me. You were in a daze. Lucky you weren't hit by a car. I figured something wasn't right, so I pulled over and watched. When I saw you draw your gun, I guessed you might want to know where he was going."

"Prophetic!" I said, amazed at his foresight. "Jason, it was Peabody. He threatened to kill Martine and Claire if I continued."

Best watched me intently and then said, "There's something here I'm missing. Did he ask you if you knew where the money was?"

"No. In fact, he said they didn't want me to talk. They wanted me not to talk. I don't get it."

A smile crossed his face. "I do. They don't need you to tell them how to find the money. They know where it is!"

"Then why chase me across the ocean to be sure I didn't tell anyone something I don't know?"

"Think this through with me," he said. "First, let's assume they know you don't know. O.K. Then, let's assume another point. They believe you can stop them from getting to the money."

"But I can't," I protested.

"You don't think you can, but maybe you're wrong. Maybe you're the one person who is standing in their way."

"Then why haven't they killed me?"

"Don't take comfort in that," he said. "They've sure tried."

"I'm worried, Jason. Not about me. They know where to find Martine and Claire. I can't risk their lives. What do I do?"

"Find them first. I don't know an easier solution," he said.

"That's impossible!"

"Is it?" he questioned. "We're making a lot of headway."

He suddenly got my full attention. "Headway? How?"

"We're watching Peabody. All we need is one phone call to the people he's working for."

"You're tapping his phone?"

"We don't have to. There are other ways."

"Do it quickly. I'm running out of time."

He brushed back his uncombed hair with his hand and reached for his coat. "Call your two lady friends and warn them. Then meet me at the Stoneleigh Bar at 11 P.M."

"Is it safe?"

"Hell if I know," he said, leaving without turning to look back.

Martine was groggy when she picked up the phone. "Allô."

"Martine, it's Matt."

"Oh darling," she said softly. "It's so late. What's the matter?"

"I'm sorry for calling you now, but I had to. Peabody found me here in Dallas. I'm worried about you. He knows where you are—you're not safe. Please be careful."

She responded, a little breathlessly. "But you said he's there, in Dallas. How can I be in danger? It's you who must be careful."

"Martine," I said cautiously. "There are others. I don't know what they're up to, but I'm trying to find out. Until I do, can you go somewhere where they can't find you?"

I could hear her gentle breathing. "Je t'aime—I love you, Matt," she said.

"And I love you too," I answered. "But tell me, can you do that?"

"I'll be careful. But I can't drop out of sight. I have my job."

"Watch for anyone suspicious. Don't take any chances," I begged.

"And you also," she said sleepily.

CHAPTER 33

▼

Best was late. I sat in the dark bar of the Stoneleigh for fifteen minutes before he arrived. "I thought you said eleven," I said as he sat down.

"I did, but business held me up."

"She wouldn't let you leave?"

He smiled without answering. My fixation on him was briefly interrupted by the waitress. "Scotch on the rocks—cheapest you have," he ordered. "And hold it for five minutes. We have a quick errand. We'll be back then."

"Errand?"

"Follow me," he motioned, and we headed for the front desk. There, he addressed the hotel operator. "Excuse me, I'm Mr. Peabody, room 311. I made a call earlier. Can you give the amount of the charges. It was long distance."

She looked up with a broad smile. "Actually," she said, "you made three calls. Do you want all charges?"

"Yes," he said. I watched him, incredulous.

"Here you are," she said, returning shortly and presenting him with a print-out of the calls. "That one to Rome was particularly expensive."

"Rome," I mumbled. "Jesus!"

"Shh…," he whispered, nodding for me to return to the bar.

Walking back, he leaned towards me and said, "You're not very discreet. I had her going there. Next time, act dumb."

In the bar we jointly studied the print-out. There were three calls, two international and one in the U.S. The international calls were to Rome and Paris, and the third was to a 207 area code. "What's 207?" I asked.

"I dunno," he said. "This call to Rome lasted thirty-five minutes. Someone had a lot to say."

"Excuse me," I heard. The waitress had returned with Jason's drink.

"You got a phone book?" he asked.

"Behind the bar. I'll get it for you."

She returned a second time with a local phone book. "Don't we need something other than a local phone book?"

"No," he answered, gesturing me to keep quiet.

He opened the front of the book and displayed a map of the U.S., dotted with area codes. Running his finger rapidly across the map, he moved it from west to east and pointed to the northeast. "There—207!"

I caught a glimpse of what he was pointing at. "Mean anything to you?"

I was shocked. "Let me see the phone numbers again." He handed them to me, and my worst fears proved to be true.

"207," I muttered.

"207?"

"Yes. It's the bastard, Freytag."

"The middleman in Bangor," he said, his eyes lighting up. "I told you we were making headway."

"Yes, but didn't you trace him to McAlister?"

"No," he corrected. "We traced him to a man who was seen with McAlister. Not necessarily McAlister. Let's call that number in Rome."

He motioned the waitress for a phone, and she promptly responded with a portable phone that was brought to our table.

"Can I dial out on a credit card?" he asked, taking a huge sip of his drink.

She nodded yes, and he held his hand out, towards me. "What do you want?" I asked.

"Credit card."

I handed it over and he dialed. There was no answer. "Who were you calling, Jason?"

"Rome."

"Don't you know? With the time difference, it's 7 A.M. there. Wait two hours."

He finished his drink and then handed me the print-out. "You call tomorrow," he said. "But for God's sake, don't let them know who you are. Now, let's go see our friend."

Room 311 was at the far end of the hall, in the corner. The hallway was dimly lit, and Best flashed a pocket light to verify the correct room. Standing in front of the door, he motioned me to the side. "You stay there," he whispered, "out of sight. He knows you, but not me. I'll do the talking. You just listen."

"Don't do anything stupid," I whispered back.

"You got your gun?"

I patted the left side of my coat and nodded yes.

Best knocked lightly three times on the door. A voice inside said "Yes?"

"Message from the front desk!" Best answered.

There was a moment of silence, and then, "Slip it under the door."

"Can't. Have to deliver it in person."

Another period of silence followed. I could hear my heart pounding in my head as we waited. A muffled voice then said, "The door's open."

I reached inside my coat for the comfort of my gun, impressed with Best's show of bravery. Best turned the knob and pushed the door open. It was pitch black inside. Best stood for a second, exposed in the middle of the door frame, and then cupped his hand over his eyes.

"Do you want to turn on the light?" he asked.

"What's the message?" came the reply.

"The message is from Rome. If you'll turn on the light, I'll give it to you."

I peered through the door jam and saw the neon lights on the side of the building reflect on a dark figure seated in a chair in the corner. It held an oblong object, with perforations. A silencer! "He's got a gun," I yelled quietly to Best. "Get out of the doorway."

Two pops broke the silence. I saw Best spin around, look at me with sad eyes, and arch violently backward. His throat was torn open. He grabbed it in anguish, blood streaming down his hands, and tried to speak. There was only silence as he collapsed in a heap at my feet.

Without thinking, I stepped around him into the doorway, raised my gun at the figure in the corner, and pulled the trigger twice. Peabody's eyes gleamed at me in the darkness, wide with terror, and the gun fell from his hands. Blood streamed from his forehead and he fell forward onto the carpet.

Unable to move, I stood looking down the corridor, waiting for footsteps. There were none. I stepped quickly inside, turned on a light, and stared at the corpse of Alfred Peabody. Reaching inside his jacket, I pulled out his wallet. Quickly, I moved to his luggage on the bed and rifled through his clothes, looking for anything that might help. Nothing!

I slipped out into the still quiet corridor and walked quickly to the back staircase. Reaching the bottom of the stairs, I opened the emergency door and walked in a daze through the lobby, past the concierge. He sat on a stool behind a marble counter and barely looked up. I reached my car, breathless, rain drizzling down my forehead.

I slid behind the wheel and sat there, trying to catch my breath. When the pounding of my heart stopped, I started the engine and drove slowly down the rain-soaked streets.

CHAPTER 34

▼

I returned to my apartment in a daze, too stunned to notice if I was being followed. Waiting for the hysteria to pass, my mind played tricks. It happened. It didn't. It wasn't real. At eighteen minutes past three, I lay in my bed, counting the minutes tick off the clock, in dark silence. It was nine in the morning in London and ten in Paris. What time was it in Bangor? Or in Rome? My mind was a blur.

*   *   *   *

The bleak headlines of the newspaper the next morning brought me back to stark reality. It had happened. Jason Best was dead.

DOUBLE MURDER AT STONELEIGH HOTEL
Police Searching For Suspects

Under the headlines were two pictures. Jason and a second man identified only as Alfred Peabody, "thought to be from Louisiana." I knew he wasn't.

I threw the paper across the room. The intercom buzzed, intermittently. "Mr. Lawrence, a lady's here to see you."

"Who is she?"

A long silence followed. "Says her name's Claire. She insists on seeing you," he said.

"O.K. Send her up."

I opened the door to see Claire. She stared at me with pale eyes. "What have you done?"

"Come in and I'll tell you," I answered.

Her face softened. She sat across from me, her chin in her hand. "That was your private detective, wasn't it?"

"He was my friend, Claire. Only one of a few. I'll miss him more than you'll ever know."

"Why would they kill him?" she said softly.

"It was dark…Peabody didn't know who was standing in the doorway."

"My God!" she said, covering her mouth with her hand. "Can I help in any way?"

"It's devastating," I said. "Living with the knowledge and fear that someone is trying to kill you. And watching them, helplessly, while people around you are killed."

She watched me, silently. Finally, she asked, "When can you find peace?"

"When I know all the reasons why. When 'they' are stopped. That's when."

"So…" she let drag from her lips. "There is no end. I've prayed for you, I hope you know. Every day."

"Thank you," I said. "Please take care of yourself. I'll always be here if you need me."

"That's what I pray about, Matt. That you'll live. May God help you."

She left.

*   *   *   *

After sitting, lost in silence, I dialed the phone number in Rome that Peabody had called. The first sound I heard when I finished dialing was the intermittent beeping of the international line. After that the loud, spaced sound telling me I had connected with the Italian phone system. Then came a soft voice. "Buon giorno, potrei aiutarie?"

"C'è qualcuno qui che parla inglese?" I asked.

"Speak slowly," the voice answered. "Who do you want?"

"Where are you?"

"Non capisco—I do not understand."

"What is the place I have called?"

"It is Italy, of course," she answered, assuming I was stupid.

"No, you misunderstand. What is the name of your company?"

I heard a slight giggle. "It is no company," she said, "it is the Vatican."

"The Vatican?"

"Well, it's the bank," she clarified. "May I help you?"

"No," I said. "I'll call back."

I struggled with what I had heard. Peabody, the assassin, had talked to the Vatican Bank for thirty-five minutes. But to whom? I leapt for my coat and removed the wallet I had lifted from Peabody's corpse. I shook out its contents and threw the empty wallet in the corner.

He hadn't expected to die. The contents included several thousand dollars, credit cards, three business cards, a driver's license, a prayer card with a cross at the top, and a picture of two little children. I felt a twinge of remorse for what I had done, but it only lasted a few seconds.

One of the business cards had the name Instituto per le Opere di Religione printed in large black lettering, and underneath it, in fine print, the name Angelo Braschi, Controllè. In the opposite corner was a telephone number, the one I had just dialed.

I had to return to the Vatican. But first I faxed to Monsignor Bertellini a copy of the article on the two murders at the Stoneleigh, with the business card of Braschi at the bottom. I scribbled on it "Don't show this to anyone. Call me A.S.A.P. Matt Lawrence."

Within thirty minutes the phone rang. "What's the meaning of this, Signore Lawrence?" he asked.

"Monsignor, the man named Peabody is a hired assassin. He killed three people in England and a close associate of mine in Dallas, the other man in the picture. He carried the card of Mr. Braschi. He was somehow connected with the Vatican!"

The sound of labored breathing held my attention for several minutes while he considered what I had said. "I've been afraid of something like this," he finally said.

"Afraid?"

"Yes," his hoarse voice said. "We have swept too much under the rug. Braschi had too much authority. I never trusted him."

"Do you think he's behind this?" I asked, totally surprised by his admission.

"It's possible," he answered in a restrained voice.

"The money, Monsignor. This has to do with the money. I'm sure of it."

"Signore, listen to me carefully. The Vatican bank does not have the money!"

"Then why were all those people killed?"

"I don't...know," he said painfully. "I just don't know."

"Will you see me if I return to Italy?"

"When?"

"In two days."

"Yes, I'll be here. Arrivederla."

Conspiracy, murder and the Vatican. The minutes passed while I tried to regain my thoughts.

My next call was to Bangor, Maine. "What is it?" I heard the deep, calm voice say.

"Mr. Freytag. This is Matt Lawrence."

"Ah, Mr. Lawrence. I thought our business was put to bed during your visit here."

"I thought so too. It evidently wasn't."

"It wasn't?"

"No, it wasn't. A man named Peabody called you last night, just before he died. Do you remember him?"

"No, I don't," he answered impatiently. "Get to the point, Mr. Lawrence. No more games."

"The point. It's that he was a hired assassin, staying at the Stoneleigh Hotel in Dallas. He killed a close friend of mine. I'm sure he would have killed me had he had the chance."

I heard a gentle tapping over the line, then a deep sucking sound. "Did you hear me?" I asked.

"Pardon me," he said. "Lighting my pipe. You were saying...."

"I was saying he was a murderer. He's dead. He called you, Mr. Freytag, before he died. Why?"

"It had nothing to do with you, Mr. Lawrence. I assure you of that."

"Then what did it involve?"

He hesitated. "Actually," he said, "none of your business."

"It is my business, all of it," I said. "Either you tell me or you'll explain it to the police. I'm sure they'll want to know about your connection with Peabody."

He let out a deep breath and tapped the phone several times. "I'll tell you this much, and no more. It involved a matter in France, thousands of miles from you. Is that sufficient?"

A chill crept down my spine. "France!"

"What's your connection with France?" he asked.

Without answering his question, I said, "Where?"

"What do you mean where?"

"Goddamn it, Freytag, answer the goddamn question!"

Silence. And then, "Beaune. Ever heard of it?"

"A woman I care deeply about is there," I stammered. "She's there!"

"What did you say?"

"Is there a contract on her?"

"Look, Mr. Lawrence," he tried to explain, "I didn't—"

"Answer me," I shouted. "Is there?"

"Maybe," was his whispered answer.

"Stop it! Now! If you don't, I swear to God I will hunt you down and kill you, if it's the last thing I do!"

"I'll try. Call her, tell her to get away. Do it now. Give me time."

I slammed the phone down and frantically dialed Martine. "Allô," the voice said. "S'il vous plaît laissez un pétit mot."

Her answering machine! "Martine, this is Matt. I'll be in Paris in the morning. At Orly. 9 A.M. Please meet me. Get away from Beaune— now! Don't stay there. You're in danger. Please!" I begged, and was cut off by the beep.

CHAPTER 35

▼

France, 1993

Martine met me the next morning at Orly. She looked at me, wide eyed, when I walked through the gate. Then she rushed forward, taking my hands and saying, "You don't know how good it is to see you!"

"And you!" I said.

"I got your message on my answering machine late last night, just in time to book a flight to Paris. Why didn't you call me sooner?"

"I have a lot of explaining to do…but later."

I felt the ache of being near her, of feeling the memory of holding her. And knowing she was safe. The pain slowly disappeared. "I've missed you," I whispered as we walked hand in hand to the car.

She stopped and gently kissed me. "Is that all?"

"No, not all. I love and adore you! That's all."

She smiled a broad smile. It overcame Paris in March—cold and gloomy. A heavy overcast had begun to descend, and the morning was taking on the appearance of night. We made it to the car just as the dampness turned to rain.

We drove into Paris through a downpour. There we took a suite at the Plaza Athèneè, overlooking what seemed to be a watercolor of Paris. Martine flipped through the latest edition of L' Express as I told the room clerk that we did not want to be disturbed, by anyone. Her wet blonde hair glistened under the overhead lights against her dark green raincoat.

In the room, we stood for a moment, holding each other and looking at the Eiffel Tower, surrounded by black storm clouds. She turned, kissed me lovingly, and said, "Now what's this danger I'm in?"

"After."

"After what?" she asked.

"After I make love to you." The moment was all I wanted. We kissed and loved, completely in the warmth of the bed, and held each other close afterwards, both escaping the darkness of the world outside. Exhausted, we fell asleep in each other's arms. I woke first, aware of sirens on the Avenue Montaigne. Martine was beside me, breathing deeply, her soft yellow curls wrapped around her blue eyes and slightly parted lips. I kissed her. Her arms reached up, her eyes still closed, and held me tight.

"Am I dreaming?" she said in a sleep-filled voice.

"Only if you want to be."

"What time is it?"

I strained to see the clock on the desk across from me and answered, "Five o'clock."

"In the afternoon?"

"Of course. Did you think the morning?"

"I can't believe it," she said, slowly opening her eyes. "We've slept most of the day."

"Yes," I said groggily. "Let's get dressed."

She blinked twice and then said, staring into the ceiling, "Matt, my stepfather. I talked to him again about those names."

I sat up. "And what did he say?"

"He said a friend of his, Etienne LaFonne, knows most of them. He lives near Bordeaux, in the heart of the Medoc."

"LaFonne," I said. "A strange coincidence. I was reading his book last week. Could your stepfather arrange for a meeting?"

"Yes. He's very willing to help. Shall I call him?"

"Yes, while I jump into the shower. Tell him we would like to meet Mr. LaFonne tomorrow—anytime during the day."

Thirty minutes later I stood wrapped in a towel, trying desperately to shave in front of a steamed-up mirror. I wiped the steam only to find it quickly reappear. I could hear Martine, standing behind me, laughing to herself. "Men!" I heard her say.

"Women steam mirrors too," I countered.

"If you won't cut yourself shaving, I'll tell you what my stepfather said."

"You called him again?"

"You asked me to, didn't you?"

"Yes," I said, straining to avoid nicks.

"He's arranged for us to meet Mr. LaFonne, tomorrow night."

"Why night?"

"Because we've been invited to his chateau for dinner."

"Evidently a special invitation—he's a very important man in the wine country."

"Where is his chateau?"

"It's at Milly Lamartine, in the Saone-et-Loire region. About four hours from here—if we drive."

"What is your wish, my darling?" I asked, now trying to stop the bleeding from three cuts.

"It's a lovely drive. We can take the Autoroute from Paris. But if you'd rather, we can get there on the TGV—the bullet train."

"Let's skip the bullets," I said without much humor. "The Autoroute will do fine. And tonight?"

"Tonight let's eat in the Cour-jardin and then go dancing at the Bar Anglais."

I turned around and stared into her blue eyes. Her hair was disheveled and her yellow silk robe was loosely tied around her waist, slightly exposing her full breasts.

"You're staring at me, you know," she purred softly.

"I know. "I was just thinking…"

"What?"

"How you have saved my life—and how much I love you."

She didn't answer, but stepped towards me and engulfed me in her arms. Her cheek rubbed gently against mine, and she kissed me for what seemed a lifetime. When she pulled away, we were both smeared with shaving cream. I couldn't help but laugh.

Attempting to wipe the foam from her face, she smiled broadly. "In my whole life," she said, "I've never been in love like now. Where have you been?"

"Just waiting for you."

✳   ✳   ✳   ✳

Night had fallen when we arrived at Milly Lamartine. Along the tree shrouded road that led to the chateau, the houses were all dark. The chateau was magnificent. It was a two-story Spanish house, light beige stucco with a red tile roof, hidden among large trees, banks of veronica and rows of azaleas. The moon cast shadows among the trees, giving everything an other-worldly glow.

We were led through a pair of massive French doors onto the veranda. There stood Monsieur LaFonne and several guests. "Monsieur et madame. Bonsoir." He extended his hand to me and I took it, shaking vigorously. LaFonne was tall and robust, in excess of six foot two inches. His tanned skin was highlighted by his perfect teeth and bushy eyebrows. He was everything a wealthy Frenchman in his early sixties should be.

"Please," he said, "join me in the dining room." He motioned us to a large room with heavy wood rafters. The table was a massive oak table set for ten guests. We were seated on either side of him.

LaFonne directed everyone to sit and then tapped lightly on his wine glass. "Prière de…."

The room suddenly quieted down, and he turned and smiled at me. "For the benefit of our guests here, I will ask each of you to speak English. Let me introduce everyone. To my right is Madame Martine Paulet, daughter of my good friend, Sidney Harrison. On her right is

Monsieur Bernard D'Amacord and his lovely femme, Colette. And then my arch rival all these years, the singlemost reason why I have not the only Grand Cru in this area, Pierre Morillon. His wife of course, Jean, should have been mine."

Pierre Morillon smiled and showed his approval. His wife looked down at her napkin.

"Continuing," he said, "we have that noted wine connoisseur Gèrard Labarrère and Madame Labarrère, René. Finally, my erstwhile companion all these years, Edith Jobert. And on her right, Monsieur Matt Lawrence from Dallas, who is Madame Paulet's companion."

He then leaned towards Martine and whispered, "C'est un bel homme."

She winked at me and said to him, "Je l'aime."

LaFonne then snapped his fingers and his servants hurriedly appeared. "Apportez-moi du vin."

They bowed slightly and quickly returned with several large bottles of wine, methodically filling every glass. LaFonne turned to me and said, "It's so nice of you and Martine to join us. Monsieur Harrison said you needed some information from me."

"Yes," I said. "Did he mention the list of names?"

"He did," he confirmed. "Each of them is a highly respected wine merchant in this region."

"Is there any connection between them?"

He scratched his chin and raised his glass. Sniffing the bouquet of the wine, he mumbled, "Excellent!" He then rolled a sip of the wine around his tongue and refocused his attention on me. "Each has a vineyard and winery in the Bordeaux area, and each produces a substantial volume of wine."

Across from me, I watched Martine gently rub her forefinger across the top of her glass. Her black silk evening gown was stunning. She was elegant and gorgeous. She smiled thinly, knowing I had a difficult time keeping my eyes off of her.

"Please, Monsieur Lawrence," LaFonne said with a wide smile, aware of my preoccupation with Martine. I smiled back. The other guests seemed consumed in conversation with each other as I continued my questioning.

"I'm very interested in their business—the wine business," I said, prying as subtly as I could.

Martine interrupted, breaking her silence. "Monsieur LaFonne, do these men have any common business, any close connection with one another?"

"No," he answered, "not that I'm aware of. Let me tell you a little about what they do. Perhaps that will help you."

His explanation was temporarily stopped by the entrance of his servants, bearing large silver plates of roast pork, potatoes and green beans. While they were serving, he resumed his explanation. "Bordeaux chateau proprietors long have known that it takes more than the rocky soil to produce an excellent vintage," he said. "These men led the way in technological winemaking advances. Together they sponsored extensive studies into the climatic patterns of the region, and they lengthened the growing season."

"Lengthened?" I interrupted. "How could they lengthen the season?"

He smiled. "No, they didn't get control over that mademoiselle you Americans call Mother Nature. They changed the old rule that governed harvests in Bordeaux."

"The rule?" Martine asked.

"Yes. It was that grapes must be harvested 100 days after flowering. They extended that rule, based on their studies, to 110 or 120 days, depending on the weather. The result—full-bodied, richer and less acidic wines."

"That doesn't seem very revolutionary," Martine commented.

"Oh, but it was," he assured. "Until then, when the weather was abnormally cool and even worse, it uniformly meant a poor harvest—

and disaster. Now it means an excellent vintage. It was monumental for this region when that mindset was changed."

Just then we heard a clinking of a glass, and Monsieur Labarrère loudly cleared his throat. "Excusez-moi," he said.

"Parlez anglais, s'il vous plait," LaFonne interrupted.

"Pardon," Labarrère said. "May I propose a toast to our host, His Holiness."

All glasses were simultaneously raised. "To years of friendship. May they continue forever!"

"Hear, hear," I heard several voices say as everyone took a sip.

Martine looked at our host, smiling, and said, "His Holiness?"

"Oh yes," he said. "Quite embarrassing. Monsieur Labarrère is a critic and an author. Years ago he labeled me the Wine Pope of France, a label I have not yet been able to escape."

I spilled my glass of wine down my chin and onto my tie.

Edith Jobert quickly took her napkin and wiped the wine from my tie. She smiled, as if to say it happens to us all, and said, "Je suis désolée."

I nodded my appreciation for whatever it was that she had said, and then turned my attention back to LaFonne. "They call you the Wine Pope?" I repeated.

"Just an expression," he said apologetically.

"Etienne," interrupted Madame Jobert, "you are much too modest. It fits you very well. You see, Monsieur Lawrence, Etienne is regarded as the mystical head of the French wine region—his knowledge of wines is extraordinaire. He would not tell you that, but it is true!"

LaFonne blushed slightly, and then held up his hand towards Madame Jobert. "Enough," he said. "We mustn't bore our guests."

"I'm not bored, I assure you," I said. He began to take a bite of his food, and I asked the question that had been troubling me since Labarrère's revelation. "Monsieur LaFonne, did you ever meet my client, a man named Bic Braxton?"

He immediately stopped eating, put down his fork, and looked at me in total surprise. He remained quiet for several seconds, and then said, "Later."

"Later?"

"Yes. After dinner, in my study, I will discuss Monsieur Braxton with you."

I had a difficult time finishing my dinner, anticipating my meeting with LaFonne.

After we finished, LaFonne politely excused us from his guests, saying that we had a small business matter to discuss, and led me to his study. It was at the back of the chateau and reminded me of a wildlife kingdom. "Trophies," he said, "from many trips to Kenya. In my heart, I'm a wild game hunter—first and foremost."

The study was dimly lit. The smoldering embers in the fireplace cast shadows on the stuffed animal heads, occasionally wheezing from a spark or flame. He motioned me to sit near his massive oak desk, under the head of what must have been an elderly zebra. He then leaned back in his chair and lit up a cigarette.

"You say you are Monsieur Braxton's attorney. Can you provide me with any evidence of that?"

"Only this," I said, handing him my business card.

He looked at it, turned it over to see there was nothing on the reverse side, and focused again on me. "I suppose I can rely on my old friend Sidney Harrison and his beautiful daughter, Martine, to know you're not a fraud. Now, what is it you want to know?"

"Mr. Braxton sent over $200 million to France several years ago."

"Four years to be exact," he said.

I suddenly had difficulty getting my breath. Inhaling deeply, I said, "Yes, four years. He asked me to assure him that everything was in order."

"Assure him? He knows very well where his money is," he said, wrinkling his brow.

"For my edification," I said, "could you fill me in on what you know?"

He took a long drag on his cigarette, let the smoke drift out of his nostrils, and addressed my question. "It's all there, sitting in stainless steel vats."

I was stunned. "Vats?"

"Yes, waiting for the bottling process. As you may know, the bottling of a chateau's entire production can take up to three months, even with our modern bottling equipment."

I lightly rubbed my chin, trying not to show my shocked reaction.

"I can see you're confused," he continued. "I'm not sure how much your client told you. When he purchased futures to the entire production of some twenty vineyards, he understood that he wouldn't realize his profit for some four years. That was our understanding from the beginning."

"When will this profit be realized?" I asked.

"Let me see," he said, flipping through a calendar on his desk. "I would say the bulk of it will be bottled and sold within the next forty-five days. And let me add, you can report to your client that his timing was impeccable. His profit should be at least seventy percent of his investment."

"Impressive," I said, trying to act as if I knew what I was saying. "And what would be the total amount due him then?" I held my breath.

He pulled a small calculator from his desk drawer and punched in some numbers. After several minutes, he looked up and narrowed his eyes. "About $325 million, but that's just an estimate, mind you. I don't want to be held to that."

He waited for a reaction. I was speechless.

"I would say," he continued, "that we should have cash funds to Mr. Braxton within sixty days from now."

"How do you intend to do that?"

"In accordance with his instructions, of course," he answered as if I knew.

"Refresh me, Monsieur LaFonne, if you will. What were those instructions?"

"Why do you ask?" he said, now showing a little suspicion at my line of questions.

I leaned forward and said, "We may have a change of instructions—that's the reason for my visit. It's important that we discuss this."

He studied my face intently for a moment, causing my heart to flutter. "The funds will be wired to his account at the bank. It's all arranged."

"What bank?" I asked.

"His bank—the Vatican bank."

I took several deep breaths, trying to digest all he was telling me. He detected my uneasiness and shifted in his chair.

He lit another cigarette, and I watched a thin stream of smoke go up into the air.

"I'm afraid you're leaving me somewhat in the dark," he said. "Suppose you explain to me what this change is you're referring to." His cynical look left me slightly unnerved.

"Mr. Braxton is in the federal penitentiary," I said.

"I'm aware of that. We have newspapers here. That fact doesn't change a thing."

"He asked me to alter the wiring instructions and to advise you of the change."

"Why doesn't Monsieur Braxton tell me himself. They have telephones in the prisons."

"Because someone tried to kill him. He's been in a coma for several months. This matter is now totally in my hands."

He gasped and turned away, sickened by what I had just told him. "I liked your client—very much," he said. "A very intelligent and kind man. Why did this happen?"

"I think because of the money," I answered. "It's for that reason we must change the payment instructions. I believe whoever tried to kill Monsieur Braxton has arranged to take the money when it reaches the Vatican bank. So it's of the utmost importance that the money not be sent there."

"If you can show me proper authority and provide me with your new instructions, you will have my cooperation," he assured me.

"I am his attorney," I reminded him.

"Yes, you said that. But you must understand. I will need written authorization that my attorneys tell me is proper and that I should act upon. Can you give that to me?"

"Yes, of course," I answered, doubting I could provide him with what he wanted. "Within the next week you'll have the necessary papers."

"Very good," he said. "Now shall we rejoin our guests?"

CHAPTER 36

▼

A cold wind blew into my face as we left LaFonne's chateau and returned to our rented car. Watching through the windshield as he said goodbye to his guests, Martine nudged me slightly. She leaned over, kissed me softly, and asked, "Are you going to tell me about your private conversation with Monsieur LaFonne?"

I looked up to see the rows of trees lining the countryside, swaying gently in the wind, creating an image of ballet dancers on a moonlit night.

"Well?" she asked again, as I started the engine.

"I found the money," I whispered.

"I don't believe it!" she exclaimed.

"Believe it," I said.

"Where is it?"

"In stainless steel vats of wine, waiting to be bottled and sold."

She sat motionless. "I don't understand."

"Martine, he invested the money in wine futures, four years ago. That's why Monsignor Bertellini has insisted that the Vatican didn't have it. He was telling the truth."

"Then what is the Vatican's connection with all this?"

"Simple. Braxton's instructions to LaFonne are that the money will be automatically deposited to his account in the Vatican bank when the wine is sold. In sixty days, the Vatican will have the money!"

She sat back, eyes glazed, and then blinked twice at me. "Tell me, then," she said, gently holding my hand, "why have so many people been killed? And why have they tried to kill you?"

I took a deep breath. "It's obvious to me. Whoever knows that the money will be deposited back to the bank has plans to take it."

"Who are they?"

"I have only one guess—and it's a good one. Angelo Braschi."

"But Matt, he works for the Pope. How could he do a thing like that?"

I laughed sarcastically. "Who knows what evil lurks in the hearts of men?"

Without conscious intent, I began cataloguing everything I had learned from LaFonne as we headed down narrow country roads to the autoroute. The light from the moon cast shadows that danced back and forth across the windshield, faintly reflecting in my eyes. Martine held my hand, looking at me inquisitively.

"Are you lost to me?" she finally asked.

"I could never be lost to you...never. I was just thinking—how very close but yet so far away."

"From the money?"

"What else?" She squeezed my hand and momentarily closed her eyes.

"I've never been involved in this sort of thing before. You're getting very close, Matt. Doesn't that have you worried?"

I sensed what she was thinking and answered with an innocent shrug. "Matt, I'm petrified. We could both be dead tomorrow. You know that, don't you?"

I stared at the road moving rapidly beneath our small car. "Yes we could. But I have to finish what was started—not by me, but by others.

And to tell you the truth, I honestly don't believe we'd ever be safe until we find out who's behind all of this."

"Matt, if you could just listen to yourself. You're not James Bond. You're just an ordinary man."

"Ordinary?"

"Well, you know what I mean. Why don't we escape, just the two of us, to South America, or somewhere, and live happily ever after?"

"That's very tempting. And don't think it hasn't occurred to me. But I can't."

"I know that," she said, sighing deeply. She looked away, surveying the fast changing landscape that moved along the highway. "So much for my suggestion. Now what?"

"Now I have to talk to Monsignor Bertellini, in total privacy, if he'll do that. I'm hoping that he'll accept what I tell him. If he does, I may be able to stop Braschi and then get my hands on the money."

"And if he won't talk to you?"

I sighed. "I don't know."

"You've never told me one important thing," she added. "If with God's grace—and you're going to need it—you find the money, what will you do with it?"

"I remember hearing once that he who has little money is nobody very much. Need I say more?"

She sat up and looked at me—startled. "Matt! You don't mean that. Do you intend to keep it?"

"I can't think of anyone else more deserving. If we're going to risk our lives, I think we're entitled to it, don't you?"

Her frown changed to a soft smile. "Would it be legal?"

"It will be the way I'll do it."

"I don't know if that's good or bad," she said, closing her eyes and laying her head back. After a few moments she raised up and looked at me. "Matt, there's a trick to getting what you want. You know that, don't you?"

"I have no idea what you're talking about."

"The trick is wanting it when you get it. You'd better think hard about that."

*   *   *   *

We didn't arrive back in Paris until after three in the morning. We slept until ten. Had we not been jolted awake by the sound of the telephone, we might have slept until noon.

"Is this Monsieur Lawrence?" I heard a woman's voice ask.

I was immediately struck by the thought that no one should have known where we were. Following a sharp pang of fear, I answered hesitantly. "It is. What can I do for you?"

"Hold please."

I waited. My fears were immediately calmed when LaFonne came on the line. "Monsieur Lawrence," he began. "Sorry to bother you, but I was wrong in what I told you last night."

"Wrong?" I asked in a louder tone than I intended, bracing for the worst.

"Yes. It seems that my calculations were in error. I checked this morning with my agents, and they tell me the bottling process is ahead of schedule. The wine will be sold not later than thirty days from today. The money will then be transferred to Rome. So I urge you to provide me with the necessary documents changing the instructions without delay."

"I'll do my best," was all I could say.

He cleared his throat and then said, "I understand your predicament, but you must understand mine. Without your client's signature, I don't know how you can redirect the funds. Please understand that what happens now is not within my control. Monsieur Braxton was very explicit in his instructions. They are in writing and provide for no change without his express written approval. Those instructions have been filed with the central wine clearing house and with the Vatican."

"I understand," I mumbled, feeling an enormous sense of hopelessness.

"Then I'll wait to hear from you?"

"Yes. Thank you."

I stared out the window, past the figure of Martine in her robe, to the Eiffel Tower. "Incredible view," I said, placing the receiver back on the phone.

"That's sweet of you to say," Martine said with a bright smile.

I laughed. "You too."

"What?" she asked, showing her confusion.

"It's unimportant. But what is, is that LaFonne needs Braxton's change of instructions immediately, in writing. It's impossible!"

"Why?" she asked innocently.

"Martine, he's in a coma. You know that."

"Isn't there someone who can act for him?"

The sudden shock of what she said left me speechless.

"You look white as a ghost," she exclaimed. "What did I say?"

I jumped up, grabbed her hands, and sang, "She's got it. By God, I think she's got it."

"You are crazy!" she said, pulling away.

"By Jove," I answered, "not if you know Henry Higgins. Martine, it was as close as the nose on my face, but I couldn't see it."

I had her complete attention. "What, for God's sake?"

"In Dallas I have three boxes of files. All personal, and all dealing with Braxton. He may be a crook, but he's thorough. Every time he took a trip, he signed a general and irrevocable power of attorney authorizing me to act on his behalf if something happened—like a crash. Martine, those powers of attorney are still good and they give me the right to sign documents, on his behalf and in his name! Don't you see, there is a way!"

"But they were intended only for you to use if he was involved in an accident."

"Only he and I know that, and he can't talk."

She walked over to the bar, poured a cup of coffee, and handed it to me. "Aren't you overlooking a small fact?" she asked.

"A small fact? What?"

"That man Braschi isn't going to just sit there and let you take that money. If what you think is true, he's already killed a lot of people to be sure no one gets in his way."

I took a sip and burned my tongue. "The Monsignor—he'll stop Braschi."

"Why? Because you tell him to?"

I picked up the receiver and dialed Rome. After several minutes, I heard the voice of the Monsignor. "Can you see me tomorrow?" I asked.

"At four," he said hoarsely. "I'll meet you in my office, on the second floor of the Vatican."

"No. That won't work. It must be in complete privacy. No one must know about our meeting."

I could hear his intermittent deep breathing. Finally, "Do you know St. Peter's Basilica, at the square?"

"Of course."

"Go into the church, take the aisle on the right to the far back. There you will find a small room, beyond the statue of our Holy Mother. I'll meet you there."

"Tell no one, please."

"No one will know."

CHAPTER 37

▼

The Vatican, 1993

Leigh promised to sort through the documents at my apartment and to send the powers of attorney to me. Martine promised to wait for me in Paris, after protesting angrily. And I returned to the Vatican, alone.

The chill from the thousand-year old stone walls of St. Peters gave me shivers as I walked silently through the dark passageway to the small meeting room. I pushed the old wooden door open to see the Monsignor, standing in a flowing black robe with a sash tied at his waist. He said nothing when I entered, but simply motioned me to a chair in the corner. He pushed the door closed, bolted it from the inside, and stared at me with a wrinkled brow.

Sitting on a small wooden table across from me, he removed his glasses to expose bloodshot eyes in deep sockets. He looked very tired and very old.

"The committee was formed," he began, "to protect the Holy See from the bank scandal. It had no other purpose. None! But it operated free of control from anyone; it had too much power. Braschi answered only to His Holiness, no one else."

I interrupted. "What are you talking about? What is this committee you're referring to?"

He rubbed his eyes and looked at me with a painful expression. "You have a short memory. It's the Shadow Committee."

"Please start from the beginning," I implored. "Tell me what connection this man Braschi had with Braxton—and with the assassin in Dallas, Peabody."

"You said this Peabody carried a card with him—Signore Braschi's card?"

"Yes. I found it in his wallet."

"You found it?"

"Monsignor," I said with enormous reluctance, "I shot and killed him."

"Oh heavenly Father," he whispered, holding his head in both hands.

"I had no choice," I quickly added. "He would have killed me. He had just murdered a friend of mine."

He paused for a deafening period of silence.

"Are you alright?"

He slowly lowered his hands and blinked, narrowing his eyes towards me. "Braschi had dealings. He met with people, people the Vatican should have had nothing to do with. But we let him—we ignored what he was doing."

"Why?"

He lightly cleared his throat and then shrugged. "We didn't want to know, so we didn't ask questions. He did, or we thought he did, what we asked. The Holy See avoided the scandal, and His Holiness was enormously grateful. Braschi took advantage."

He stood up and threw a black wool coat around his shoulders. "These old cathedrals are too cold for a man of my age."

"How? How did Braschi take advantage?"

"Millions—hundreds of millions of dollars disappeared. They belonged to the Holy See. They have never been found."

"Did Braschi steal them?"

"We don't know," he answered, his voice trailing off. He coughed and then turned back towards me. "Secret meetings, people we didn't know, and violence. Suicides and murder. It was all investigated, but no one was ever found responsible."

"My concern is with Signore Braxton's money. The funds will be returned to the Vatican bank in less than thirty days. My fear is that they will also disappear."

He held his head down, shaking it in futility. "I can't help you—I'm sorry."

"Why?" I implored.

He looked up, directly into my eyes, fixing his attention on me. "Because only His Holiness knows about the Vatican's arrangements with Signore Braxton."

"And Braschi?"

He let out a deep breath of air. "Yes, and Braschi," he said softly.

"Monsignor, this man has had many people killed. He has tried to kill me—twice. I beg you to confide in the Pope. Stop Braschi before it's too late."

"Can you prove what you have just said?"

I considered his question, wondering what I could say to convince him. "No direct proof—but I'm certain of what I'm telling you."

"I want to believe you," he said. "But I cannot go to His Holiness with accusations against Signore Braschi. I must have more."

"How about pictures of his victims? Will that do?" I said angrily. "Do you want the woman he had strangled and dumped in a canal in San Antonio?"

"Enough!" he said, wearily holding up his hand. "If you want my help, you must do it my way." He turned, unlocked the door, and then turned back to face me. "Do you have that card?"

"Card?" I said, more calmly but confused.

"Braschi's card."

I reached into my wallet and removed the business card I found on Peabody. The Monsignor pulled back when he saw it, hesitated, and then reluctantly took it. Holding it by the corner, he quickly put it into his robe. Inhaling deeply to catch his breath, he said, "I will talk to His Holiness. Give me a little time."

"Thank you," I said, slowly extending my hand. I reached the street by a side entrance within minutes.

CHAPTER 38

▼

Paris, 1993

Four hours later I was with Martine in Paris. The first thing she said was, "I have the papers from your secretary."

"So soon?"

"Yes. She called while you were away and gave me the shipping information. I hope you don't mind."

"Mind—how could I?"

"I've done one other thing," she added. "I moved us to a small hotel on the Avenue Friedland—the Royal."

"Why? The Plaza was perfect."

"Too many people knew where we were. I just didn't feel safe."

"Martine, the documents-"

"Are safe in the hotel."

At the Royal, I called Peter Segal. He agreed to do what I asked. Then I called the Monsignor. Martine stood on the small balcony outside our room, watching the lights go on at the Arc de Triomphe. I waited and waited for him to come to the phone. "Matt, you must see this," she said.

"Shh—" I whispered, pointing to the receiver in my hand.

Finally, a man's voice, not the Monsignor. He spoke rapidly in thick English for three to four minutes. When he finished, I replaced the phone.

"Matt—what is it?"

"Get me a drink, please."

When she returned, I closed my eyes and took a long sip of straight gin. I opened them to see her, patiently waiting.

"They said it happened like this," I said. "The Monsignor received a call an hour ago from someone he evidently knew. He was asked to meet that person in the gardens of the Vatican. He never came back. An hour later they found him dead."

"How could that have happened?"

I swallowed hard, trying to contain my emotions. "Martine, there are no sanctuaries—not even the Vatican gardens."

"Who? My God, who would have done something like that?"

"They don't know! There, in the center of the Vatican, he was murdered, and they don't have a single damned clue."

"But why him—he was an old man?"

"Why? Because he was trying to help me. If it hadn't been for me, he'd still be alive."

She gazed at me with sympathetic eyes. "Matt, you musn't blame yourself. Talk to the Pope. Now you have to see him."

I took another sip, beginning to feel the gin having its effect. "I'm not sure he'll see me. And if he does, why would he believe me?"

"Because you're telling the truth. That's why."

"It's not enough. Braschi is very close to the Pope. He'll poison his mind against me."

"Then what's the alternative?" she asked.

"Intercept the money, before it gets to the Vatican bank."

Martine looked anxiously at her watch. "It's nine o'clock on the third of March," she said. "There isn't much time."

"The documents. Where are they?"

She reached into her suitcase and produced an Airborne package, labeled "Highest Priority", and handed it to me. Inside were three powers of attorney, all originals and all signed by Braxton. The most recent was dated in 1989, the year before he was sent to prison. It was labeled irrevocable and gave me the power to sign whatever documents

I deemed necessary in his name, for whatever purpose. It also provided that anything I signed would have the same force as his signature. He wanted it that way. He had absolute trust in me, and I was preparing to violate that trust.

Martine sat patiently, waiting for me to explain what I was up to. "This is the first piece," I said.

"The first?"

"Yes. My friend in Washington, Peter Segal, is sending me the next two pieces. The last is the list Braxton gave me."

"Then what?"

"Then I present them to Monsieur LaFonne and his attorney, and hold my breath."

*   *   *   *

We stood at the Air France counter under a sign that read "Consigne", anxiously waiting for Segal's delivery. We'd been there for over half an hour. Eventually, a young woman appeared in a blue uniform and said "Rien." I looked at Martine for an interpretation, and she whispered, "Nothing."

The woman then said, "Je suis désolée."

Martine responded, "A demain. Au revoir," and motioned me to leave with her.

I followed but protested. "What about the package? We're running out of time."

"It didn't come in. She said come back tomorrow. We have no choice."

When we arrived back at the hotel, I immediately called Peter. "There's a problem with what you want," he said. "That power of attorney you have automatically expires on death, as a matter of law. To give you a legal opinion of this firm, addressed to LaFonne, we'd need absolute proof that Braxton is still alive."

"What kind of proof? How about my affidavit?"

"Sorry, old friend—you're an interested party. Won't work. I'm afraid we'll need an affidavit of the prison doctor. Can you get that?"

I sat silently, thinking of the time involved in going back to Big Spring and the ticking clock. "Prepare your affidavit and fax copies to both me and my secretary in Dallas, Leigh."

"Leigh? I thought you left the firm."

"I have, but she still works for me, at least for a while. Part of my severance package."

"What about wire rerouting instructions? Has someone prepared them?"

"Done," he answered. "You'll have them with our opinion, when we get the affidavit of the prison doctor."

Leigh was very reluctant to do what I asked. "Matt," she argued, "Big Spring is four hundred miles from here. What if he refuses to sign the affidavit? Then what?"

"Leigh, this is critical to me. It's the most important thing I've ever asked you to do."

She took a deep breath and then asked, "Is it dangerous? I want the truth, Matt."

"Why do you ask that?"

She paused, and then said, "I really shouldn't have to ask that question, should I? You're asking me to verify that a man who was stabbed and left for dead, and is in a coma, is still alive. His wife and secretary were both murdered, and God knows who else. Why should I risk my life?"

I sensed I was losing the battle. "I have a reason."

"What is it?" she sighed.

"Twenty five thousand dollars, in cash, when you get the affidavit and deliver it to Peter Segal."

"Are you serious? Really?"

"Very."

"Then I'll do it…. I'll try to catch the next flight to Midland."

"Leigh, I'll never forget this. Wait until you get Peter's affidavit. It won't be long."

✳   ✳   ✳   ✳

Bordeaux, France, 1993

Two days later Martine and I were on our way to meet LaFonne in Bordeaux, armed with documents I hoped would radically change the events facing me.

LaFonne met us at his attorney's office in Bordeaux. Charles Musigny was a sole practitioner. He appeared to be in his late sixties and was dressed in clothes from the late forties. He sat next to his roll-top desk, with Lafonne on his right. When I presented the package of documents, I could see the early skepticism in their eyes. Martine sat quietly next to me, holding her breath as they examined each document, one at a time.

Musigny eventually looked up at me, holding the legal opinion of Segal's law firm. "Williams, Kaplan and Segal," he proclaimed, "a very fine firm. Do you mind if I call the author of this opinion—in private?"

"No, of course not."

LaFonne then interrupted. "You must pardon us," he said, "but these are only precautions. This money belongs to Monsieur Braxton, and it's my responsibility to be sure it is paid in accordance with his wishes. That's our agreement. I'm sure you understand that."

"Of course," I said.

Musigny then flipped through the rerouting instructions and noted that the funds were to be wired to the account of Braxton International at the Union Bank of Switzerland. "And what is Braxton International?" he asked.

"It's a Netherlands Antilles limited liability company."

"And its shareholders?"

"That should be obvious," I answered.

He squinted at me, looked again at the instructions, and mumbled, "Yes, of course."

They both excused themselves and moved into an adjacent conference room.

"They're not going to do it," Martine whispered. "It's not going to work."

I smiled lovingly at her. "Have a little faith. Of course they'll do it."

"What makes you think that?"

"Because I'm a very good lawyer. They have no choice. Those instructions are perfect."

A clock ticked loudly in the waiting room as we sat, in silence, for over ten minutes. Doubt crept through my mind as we sat there, and I began to feel something was wrong. Tick…tick….

When the door finally opened, our eyes were met with the stern gaze of Musigny, waving the documents in front of him. "Monsieur Segal has confirmed to us that everything is in good order. We will file these instructions immediately with the central wine clearing house in Bordeaux. The money should arrive in Monsieur Braxton's account within the next three to four weeks. If you'll tell us where we can reach you, we'll tell you the exact date."

I breathed an enormous, but very silent, sigh of relief. "I'll call you in a week."

"Very good," he confirmed. "Au revoir."

"Au revoir," we both echoed, thanked Musigny and LaFonne, and left.

Martine jabbed me hard in the ribs when we got into the car. "What was that for?"

"Because you think you're so smart! Tell me this. If the funds are wired to Braxton's company, how in the world do you expect to get them?"

"Who said it was Braxton's company?"

She looked surprised. "Well, you said back there-"

"That it was obvious?"

"Yes. It is Braxton International."

"That damn sure doesn't make it his company," I answered. "As a matter of fact, Braxton International is owned by a gentleman named Bluhdorne."

"Bluhdorne?" I could see she was totally confused.

"Yes. He's an attorney in the Netherlands Antilles—a good friend of mine. Companies formed there issue bearer certificates."

"What does that mean?" she asked as we passed by the Grand Theatre and drove along the wharves of the Port de la Lune.

"It means that the owner is not registered. No one can know who he is!"

"But you just said the owner is Bluhdorne."

"A nominee," I answered, winking gently at her.

"For whom?" she asked, showing heightened interest.

"As they say in French, moi."

"You own that company?"

"Yes, of course. Do you think I would have the money transferred to a company owned by Braxton?"

"But then what? A Swiss bank account. Can't that be traced?"

"They can try, but the money won't be there for more than ten seconds. It will immediately be sent to another destination. And that's where you come in. What do you suggest?"

"I'll have to think about that," she murmured softly.

CHAPTER 39

▼

Paris, France, 1993

Darkness was falling over Paris when we returned to the Royal. The spring storms had arrived, and sheets of rain blown by strong winds soaked the streets. As we rushed for the shelter of the hotel, our entrance was blocked by a large bearded man. He refused to move. I glanced at Martine, sensing that we were about to face another threat against our lives. My heart began to pound, standing there in the downpour, when suddenly he gestured to us to go inside. There we saw two men sitting in a small room to the side of the entry, Jarrett and Bird Dog.

I stood motionless, in total disbelief. Martine, her wet hair dangling about her eyes, whispered, "Who are they?"

"Trouble. I'll meet you in the room. Go!"

"How-?" I began to ask.

Jarrett gave me a cryptic smile. "You getting close, fella?"

Bird Dog sat on a sofa across from him. One hand was settled on his lap, the other held inside his coat. He said nothing.

I walked over to stand directly in front of Jarrett. His eyes followed me while he flicked the ashes from his cigarette onto the carpet. He gasped several times and then coughed loudly. "Didn't think we could find you, huh?"

"How did you?" I mumbled, feeling a combination of anger and fear.

He laughed out loud. "Now if I told you, it might spoil the fun. It might also give you the idea that you could avoid us next time. Let's get to the point. Sit," he said, pointing to a chair next to his.

"What point?"

"The one you're missing," he said between clenched teeth. He took a deep drag on his cigarette, wretched several times, and then blew the smoke in my face.

"And what's that?"

"It's self-preservation. Yours! I get the feeling you're on to something. Could it be my money?"

I sat, looking first at Bird Dog and then Jarrett. They showed no emotion, but waited in eerie silence for my answer. The light was dimmer than in the entry hall, and the burning tip of his cigarette reflected in the mirror behind him.

"I don't have your money."

Jarrett leaned over, blew more smoke in my direction, and snapped, "Listen fuck-face! I'm not playing games, you hear. Bird Dog tells me you and the little woman have been to Bordeaux." His massive hand reached out and grabbed my arm. Gripping it with enormous force, he tightened his lips.

"I want a fuckin' answer. Now!"

I noticed the night clerk was watching intensely what was happening. Yanking my arm up and freeing it from Jarrett's grip, I yelled out, "Police!"

The clerk immediately reached for the phone and dialed a number. Jarrett buried his cigarette in the palm of my hand and showed his teeth. "Either you tell me where the money is in the morning or you're dead meat. Don't fuck with me, boy!"

He stood, motioned Bird Dog to the door, and walked into the rain.

*   *   *   *

I was painfully tired when I knocked on the door to our room. After no response, I repeated "Martine" several times. Still no response. Questions began to quickly turn into fear. She had the only key. I ran down two flights of stairs. Within less than a minute I had a second key and stood, out of breath, in front of the door. Fumbling with the key, I whispered a prayer and pushed the door open.

The room was dark. I reached for a light switch and gazed upon clothing strewn across the room, overturned drawers and the mattress ripped off the bed. I stood, paralyzed, pleading silently that it wasn't true. Then I saw the note. It was pinned to a lamp shade.

> *We have your girl friend. No interference, for thirty days, and she lives. You try to stop us, and she dies. Your choice.*

Oh my God, I thought, I've killed her! A sound, shrill and then louder. Reality slowly came back into focus. I reached for the phone. "Yes—"

"Lawrence," a raspy voice said. "Did you lose your woman?"

"You bastard, Jarrett. I'll kill you, if it's the last thing I do. If you do anything to—"

"Whoa," he shouted. "I don't have her!"

I stopped, silently. "You have her, Jarrett. How else did you know she was gone?" I struggled, trying to breathe.

"In front of the hotel. In the rain. We saw them take her away in a white van."

"Why didn't you stop them?" I screamed.

"There wasn't time. Hey fella, would you like to know where she is?"

"Tell me, dammit!"

"First," he said, "a little understanding. The money." He suddenly stopped and began to cough, and then wheeze. The phone dropped, I could hear him struggling for something, and then a heavy sucking sound. After several minutes, he continued. "Fifty million!"

I heard more sucking and hard breathing. "That's what you want?"

"That's it," he said, gasping for breaths.

"And you'll tell me where she is?"

"Is that a yes?" he asked hoarsely.

"If I get it, goddamn it! Where is she?"

"33 Avenue Montaigne. Second floor."

"How do you know she's still there?"

"Bird Dog's watching them. They're still there."

I sat on the edge of a table, holding my head with one hand and the phone with the other. "How do you know all this?"

"You're wasting time," he said. "Bird Dog followed them. They know you, but not Bird Dog." The wheezing began again.

"Who are they?"

"I don't have a fuckin' idea. You tell me."

I hung the phone up and closed my eyes, unable to think clearly. It was now past ten. My thoughts raced between Martine and Julia—I couldn't let it happen again! What if it was a trap? If they meant to kill both of us. The Beretta! I rushed to my suitcase, removed the extra pair of shoes at the bottom, and turned them over. Pieces of metal clanked to the floor.

I examined each of the parts to be sure they were all there. I nervously fit each one into place. Depressing the magazine release, the clip fell loose. Five shells remained. Reaching into my dop kit, I grabbed a handful of extra shells and shoved four into the clip. The rest I put in my jacket and shoved the gun in its holster.

"I won't let them hurt you," I whispered to myself, stepping into the corridor. Waiting for the old elevator, the silence was unbearable. The metal cage rattled noisily as it descended.

Minutes later I sat in the back of a taxi, watching the rain splash off the windshield. The driver was lightly humming to himself. Hearing nothing from me, he turned and asked, "Où désirez-vous aller?"

"33 Avenue Montaigne," I answered. "Hurry!"

"Pardon?"

I quickly grabbed a piece of paper and wrote it down. He nodded his understanding. Ten minutes later he pulled into a parking space, diagonally across the street from a row of old apartments. I asked him to cut his lights. My head ached as we sat there in the dark, peering through the rain at those dimly-lit apartments. There was no movement outside, just silence.

When the empty cab had left, I stood in the drizzling rain, away from the only street lamp, watching for any sign of Martine. Nothing! The block was dark and heavily littered with trash. I noticed decaying fronts and burglar grills along the street. Moving quickly across the street, staying in the shadows, I saw a large man seated in the doorway. He had a beard. It was the man who blocked us at the Royal. I prayed he hadn't seen me.

He was barely twenty feet from me. Holding my breath as long as I could, I waited for any reaction. The only sound was rain hitting the metal gutters. Running quietly along the row of iron grills, I turned into an alley and stopped. He stood up and began to walk in my direction. Stepping over debris, I grabbed a brick and moved against the wall, hoping I had escaped his eyes. Suddenly there was a sound above me. I looked up, startled to see an old couple closing their shutters.

Rain was now pounding in my face. When I looked down, he was there. Less than six feet away, but miraculously looking at the couple above me. I moved quickly. Once, and then twice, I brought the brick down on his head with all the force I could muster. He turned to me, raised his arm, and I hit him again, and again. Finally, he slumped silently beside me, his face resting in wet garbage.

Headlights! Moving slowly down the street. I pressed back against the wall. First one and then two cars drove by. Then it was dark again—and silent. Number 33 was indistinguishable from all the others.

I walked nervously to the doorway and stood there quietly for several seconds, listening and watching. The street lamp across from me highlighted the torrent of rain that continued to fall. It was getting much colder.

Water dripped on my head from a faulty gutter. The smell was acidic and disgusting, reminding me of the alley I had just left. The door squeaked and then groaned when I pushed it open. The light from the street cast a shadow up a dark staircase. Focusing my eyes through the dark and up the steps, I could barely make out a dim light reflecting under a closed door. I stepped inside the hallway and left the front door open.

A pounding, throbbing sound filled my ears. I listened. My hands were clammy as I reached for my gun and started the long climb up the stairs. There was a smell of food, and then I heard whispering voices. Then they stopped.

Two more steps. The door suddenly opened, and I saw a familiar face. My presence surprised him. Before he could raise his gun, I fired twice. My breathing stopped and I rushed quickly into the room. A figure blurred out of a side room when I entered. Another familiar face. I fired three more times and he collapsed in a pool of blood. I looked around. There was no one else.

And then I heard muffled sounds in the adjoining room. I saw Martine, bound and gagged, in a seedy bed in the corner. Her terrified eyes were wide and moving frantically. I rushed to her and removed her gag. She laid there, motionless, her breathing erratic. "Matt!" she gasped, staring beyond me.

I felt a cord wrapped around my throat as I was pulled to the floor. I flailed desperately with my hands, but it was no use. As I was losing consciousness, I heard a knife click open and three slashing sounds.

Then I could feel the cord being removed. Retching violently, I was lifted to my feet and laid on a bed. I heard Martine's voice, quietly sobbing.

Slowly opening my eyes, I saw her, alive. Then the bearded man, lying in a pool of blood. His throat had been cut from ear to ear. My dazed vision was partially blocked by a wet towel that was offered to me.

"Yo' sho' got Mr. Jarrett to thank for yo' life," I heard Bird Dog's distant voice say.

I tried to sit up. "Easy," he said. "Yo's lucky to be alive. Don' push it." He clicked the blood soaked knife closed, and then stood to face Martine. "Some chick," he said, untying her ropes. "Yo'all betta get outa 'ere."

He helped me up. I was overcome with nausea and fell against a table. He then grabbed my arms and propelled me out the door to the staircase. "Som' mess yo' got yo'self into," he mumbled, dragging me down the stairs. At the bottom I leaned against the wall and waited while he went for a cab. Martine stood next to me, pale and frightened.

"Why?" she begged. "Who were they?"

I held up my hand, stopping any further questions. "Wait until later. Then I'll tell you all about it."

Just then a car pulled up, its lights flashing twice. I put my arms around her and helped her through the downpour to the cab.

No one spoke as we drove back to the Royal. When we got out, I leaned back into the cab and looked at Bird Dog. "Tell Mr. Jarrett he has a deal."

Bird Dog smiled, and for the first time didn't look so ominous. "He know that." I watched his cab pull away, into the storm, and then turned to Martine. She was shaking slightly and sobbing. "Will you be alright?"

She seized my hand and stared into my eyes, as if in a trance. "Matt," she said softly, the hysteria fading. "I must go home, back to London. Will you help me get there?"

"Yes, of course," I said, holding her tight.

The next morning I put her on the Air France flight to London. There, her stepfather would be waiting. My throat was raw, making it difficult to eat anything without pain. Calmer, but confused and angry, I had the driver drop me at the Pierre, a small left-bank hotel where I was sure no one could find me.

Three hours later the phone in my room rang. I was told my party in London was on the line.

"Mr. Harrison, this is Matt Lawrence. You have Martine?"

"Yes, Mr. Lawrence, I have her. The doctor just left. He tells me she is suffering from shock. She won't tell us much. Could you please tell me what happened?"

I took a deep breath, overwhelmed by feelings of guilt and pain for the woman I loved so much. "I got her involved," I began, "in a terrible situation. At first it was innocent. Neither of us had any idea what would happen."

I could sense his impatience. "You're telling me nothing. Would you please get to the point!"

"The point is murder. Martine was kidnapped yesterday, and three men were killed when we freed her."

"We?"

I knew he would never understand Bird Dog. "Another gentleman and myself."

I heard several deep breaths. "You've created a lot of problems for my daughter," he said. "I don't know what it is you're up to, but I want you to leave her alone. She's going through a severe emotional trauma. I just can't permit any more of this. I love my daughter very much."

"And I love her also. More than you could know."

"If you love her, as you say you do, then will you agree to leave her alone? May I have your word?"

I held the receiver down, feeling numbness take over my body. Reluctantly, I answered, "Yes, you have my word. Please tell Martine how terribly sorry I am, that I love her with all my heart. Will you tell her that?"

"Yes—I'll tell her. But when she regains her senses. Now, she is heavily sedated. Good day, Mr. Lawrence."

The phone went dead.

*   *   *   *

My breakfast was delivered the next morning with a copy of L' Express. There, on the front page, was a picture of three men—the bearded assassin, Dawson Henry and Rudy Blair. I couldn't understand the full article, but its meaning was clear. Three men had been found murdered at 33 Avenue Montaigne. Something very rare for Paris.

I studied the picture and thought about McAlister. What was his connection? Until I found Henry and Blair, I was certain that Braschi was behind everything. Now I didn't know.

Exiting the Pierre, I walked to Notre Dame Cathedral. Paris was bitterly cold for March. Inside, I knelt and prayed, for Martine and Julia, and for my sanity. After an hour I left, caught a taxi, and was able to say, "Je veux aller à l'aéroport, Orly." From there, I returned to Rome.

CHAPTER 40

▼

The Vatican, 1993

Vatican City was a melange of red-robed cardinals, nuns dressed in an assortment of white and black habits, monks in brown frocks, and a wide variety of people speaking almost every language of the continent. I cleared the inspections of the Swiss Guard at the Vatican's main entrance, the Bronze Door, and was ushered into the Sala Regia. There, I waited.

Forty-five minutes later a man entered, dressed in a uniform of red and green from another century. I stepped forward and extended my hand.

"Signore Lawrence. How are you?"

"Alive, which is a lot. And you, Captain Schmidt?"

"Not so well," he said, removing his beret. "The death of Monsignor Bertellini—it was an enormous loss for us all, and for the Holy See."

He motioned me to sit on a marble bench near the end of the antechamber. "He was a very kind man," I responded. "I feel responsible for his death. If I had not—"

He stopped me with his hand. "You are not to blame, Signore. The cause of the Monsignor's death is the cancer that has been growing here in the Vatican. We have no one to blame but ourselves. Now, your note. Please explain what you meant."

Our voices echoed slightly off the walls, and I hesitated when he finished speaking, fearful that someone could hear us.

"Is it safe to talk here?" I asked.

"We are totally alone, I assure you. This is the antechamber to the Sistine and the Pauline Chapels. They are both closed today to the public. No one has access. Don't be concerned."

"My note," I said, clearing my throat. "Before the Monsignor was murdered, I told him that I believed Angelo Braschi was involved in the murder of people in England and in Dallas. I offered him proof, and he promised me that he would speak to the Pope. He told me confidentially that he shared my belief that Braschi was a very dangerous man."

He stared at me. "Why have you waited until now? Why not when the Monsignor was murdered?"

"Because I was afraid no one would believe me. Braschi has a great deal of influence in the Vatican. I know that. I couldn't risk confronting him. Don't forget that someone tried to kill me here, just five months ago. It happened after I had left a meeting with the Monsignor, Braschi and Cardinal Ramoni."

He stood, stretched his legs, and walked to the end of the bench. Placing his foot on one end, he looked at me suspiciously. "What is it that you want us to do?"

"Accept what I'm telling you, as a beginning. And then I suggest you put Braschi under arrest until you can sort through the Monsignor's murder, before he can arrange to have anyone else killed."

"These are incredible accusations you make," he whispered. "We can't have the controller of the Vatican bank arrested without more evidence."

"How ironic," I said sarcastically. "That's what the Monsignor said. Now he's dead."

He stared at me wide-eyed and took a deep breath of air. There was no response.

"Was anything found on the body of the Monsignor?"

He looked surprised. "I don't know. It's not customary to search the body of a dead priest at the Vatican."

"I suggest you make it customary. If you still have access to his robe, the one he was wearing the night he was murdered, you'll find a tattered business card."

"Who's card?"

"Signore Braschi. The card was found on the body of a dead assassin in Dallas, a man responsible for the deaths of at least six people. He made a call the night he was shot. It was to the Vatican Bank."

He rubbed his eyes and then looked squarely back into mine. "Why? You've not told me why you think he did all this."

"Greed and avarice. He did it for the money Bic Braxton sent here to the Vatican."

"But you must know that Signore Braxton's money isn't here!"

He looked at me with a twinge of exasperation.

"Not now. But it's to be returned here, in the very near future."

"How do you know that?" he suspiciously asked.

"You have to trust me. I know."

"If that were the case," he said slowly, "I would know. The Monsignor and I discussed this matter at great length, on more than one occasion."

I smiled. "He never knew."

"Then who—"

"Only two people. The Pope and Signore Braschi."

"The Pope," he mumbled to himself. "Then Braschi must be working alone."

"That may be a wrong assumption," I said. "There's a committee that the Monsignor referred to, the Shadow Committee. Have you heard of it?"

"Yes," he answered, shaking his head. "Five individuals. They have the highest respect of the Holy See."

"And Braschi is a member?"

"Yes, of course." He paced back and forth, rubbing his chin. "But the other members are priests, every one. Three are Cardinals. They could not be involved in this. I'm sure of it. Is there anyone else you suspect?"

The sun was beginning to disappear beneath the skylight at the end of the hall and my vision was temporarily blinded. Shielding my eyes, I thought of Paris. "There's a man in Dallas, a Federal Prosecutor named McAlister. He's connected in some way with three assassins who were killed several days ago in Paris."

"Vatican officials and a U.S. Prosecutor! It's impossible to believe," he exclaimed.

"But I'm telling you the truth."

He sat, stunned. "And now what?"

"You tell me. A lot of people have died because of Braschi. It won't stop until he's stopped."

He stared down the long hall, past the huge painting of the Battle of Lepanto, and remained silent. Finally, he turned and said, "I'll talk to Cardinal Ramoni. He'll listen to me. Together, we'll then try to get an audience with the Pope. It may take time."

"We may not have much time," I said, letting out a deep breath.

He nodded his understanding and left. I sat for several minutes in that enormous marble cavern, feeling the chill of the conspiracy I knew was at work in the Vatican. I wondered if they would find out I had rerouted the money, and what they would do if they did.

*　　　*　　　*　　　*

Three blocks from the Vatican I found a phone booth. There, I placed a call to the Redattore of Il Progresso, the highly political daily newspaper of Rome. When I advised them of the subject matter, the editor was immediately brought to the phone.

"Buon giorno," I heard him say.

"C'è qualcuno qui che parla inglese?" I asked.

"I speak your language," he said. "How can I help you?"

"The murder of Monsignor Bertellini, at the Vatican last week. It's linked to the murders of three men in Paris two days ago."

"Linked?"

I heard him mumble to someone near him, and then a soft click, as if someone else were picking up a line. Reaching into my pocket, I quickly removed a handkerchief and placed it over the receiver.

In a muffled voice, I continued. "There's a conspiracy at work in the Vatican. Angelo Braschi, Controller of the Bank, is behind it all. He's responsible for the disappearance of hundreds of millions of dollars and for the murders of a number of people, including Monsignor Bertellini. I suggest you put your best reporters on this story. And I wouldn't waste any time if I were you."

"Who is this?" he yelled into the phone.

"That's unimportant. I just handed you the story of the decade. Do what I said," I answered, and disconnected the phone. After wiping my fingerprints off the receiver, I replaced it in its cradle and hurriedly walked down the Via Crescenzio to a waiting cab.

CHAPTER 41

▼

Duluth, Minnesota, 1993

A week later I stood at the far end of the Duluth airport, anxiously looking for Angela. My eyes were burning from exhaustion. It was ten minutes past six. I had waited for over thirty minutes—she wasn't there. A bus rumbled by, covering me with diesel fumes. Instinctively, I turned away and closed my eyes. Seconds later, when I turned back, my gaze was met with a white Volvo.

The horn beeped twice, and Angela stepped out. "Dad," she yelled as she ran to meet me.

We hugged for what seemed an eternity. She pulled back, and we looked hard at each other. "Well," she said with her hands on her hips, "you don't look too much older for what you've been through."

"Is that supposed to be a compliment?" I asked, grabbing my bags.

"You know it is. It's so good to have you here!"

We quickly loaded the luggage and pulled into the heavy airport traffic. "Until you called," she said, flipping on her headlights, "I'd almost forgotten how long it's been since we've seen each other. Do you realize it's been over six months?"

"I do," I admitted.

"How long can you stay?"

"Not long—several days."

"Perfect," she said. "I've got three days off."

I had difficulty not staring at her. Her long blonde hair draping a navy turtle-neck sweater brought back painful memories of Julia.

"What are you thinking?" she asked, sensing I was in a daydream.

I closed my eyes momentarily, and then said very softly, "Your mother."

"I know how terribly you miss her. I do too, and I think of her often. But Dad, she's gone. We'll be with her someday. Until then, we both must go on with our lives. She would have wanted it that way."

I held back my emotions and nodded my understanding. The countryside was bleak as we drove into Duluth. Snow flurries swirled across the frozen pastures, virtually blotting out the lights in front of us.

"Is it always this bad?" I asked.

She turned and smiled broadly. "Dad, this is Minnesota. It's still winter here. Did you expect to see the beach?"

We were greeted by a crackling fire in her two story townhouse. My heart sank for a moment when I saw the furnishings, largely from past homes Julia had decorated for us.

"Sad memories?"

I looked up to be handed a cup of coffee by Angela. "Some sad," I admitted, "but mostly happy."

"I'm glad," she said, sitting across from me. "So tell me, what have you been doing for the past six months. Anything exciting?"

I shrugged and smiled, having no idea where to begin. "If you only knew."

"I know one thing," she said. "I know there's something between you and Claire."

I took a long sip of coffee and stared into the fire. "If there was ever anything between us, it's over now."

"Over? I adore Claire."

"I do too," I said, fumbling for words. "But it wasn't to be."

"And what about you? Is there a life for you out there?"

"Sweetheart," I said, stirring my coffee, "it would take a millennium for me to tell you what's going on in my life."

"Is it about Mom, you're being fired, and the Government's suit against the firm? Is that what's been so difficult?"

"Oh, I'll learn to come to grips with that, in time. Since I saw you last, I've been looking for money taken by Bic Braxton."

She placed her chin in her hand and mumbled, "Interesting. I've done several stories about the banking crisis. Did you know over $500 billion has been lost?"

"Yes, I knew that. My search involves a lot less money. But I've uncovered a conspiracy that involves a Federal Prosecutor in Dallas and the Vatican."

Wide-eyed, she stared at me. "That's incredible!"

"And more," I added. "It involves the murder of more than ten people."

She stood up and poked the fire, and then turned, probing my face for understanding. "Are you in danger?"

"I have been," I admitted. "But not now, not here. And there's one other thing—"

"A woman?"

"How did you know?"

She showed a fleeting smile. "I know you pretty well."

There was a moment of awkward pause, when I wasn't sure what to say next, or how to say it. "You know how much I loved your mom—"

"It's O.K., Dad," she broke in. "It's been over a year and a half since she died. It's O.K. Tell me about her."

"I met her in France, last January, when I went to Beaune."

"But you only stayed there three days."

"It was on the first day," I tried to explain with a weak smile. "She's the assistant manager at the hotel where I stayed. We only had dinner then. It was not until several months later, when I was with her in London, that I fell in love with her."

"Love?" she asked softly, with a bright sparkle in her eyes.

"Yes."

She could sense the deflation in my voice. "So what's happened between the two of you?"

"I almost got her killed—twice. She's with her stepfather in London. He tells me she's in shock. I've agreed not to see her."

Her mouth flew open, as if to say something, and then stopped. "This is the most bizarre story I've ever heard. If I put this on the wires, they wouldn't believe it."

"That's one of the reasons I'm here," I said.

"What?" She was thoroughly confused.

"Angela, I'm looking for a lot of answers in my life. I need your help, but I'll explain that later. For the time being, I want you to understand that what I've become involved in, because of my past dealings with Bic Braxton, has resulted in the murders of some people I cared greatly about."

"Who?"

I hesitated to mention Julia, and decided not to. "A woman named Marianne Sandler, Braxton's former secretary. And Braxton's wife, Sterling. And a private detective I hired named Jason Best. You would've loved him. In addition to them, an attempt was made on Braxton's life. He's in a coma and is not expected to live."

"Stop," she protested. "I don't want to hear any more. Just tell me, who's doing this and why?"

I took a deep breath of air and exhaled slowly. "I believe a man who's the Controller of the Vatican bank is the one responsible. There may be others, but I'm not sure. And somewhere in this maze is the U.S. Attorney in Dallas I mentioned. His name is Buckroyd McAlister. He's a genuine bastard."

"That can't be! Not the Vatican and the U.S. Government! You must be wrong," she said, showing her total disbelief.

"You're right," I said. "It's not the Vatican or the U.S. Government. It's the people who work for them."

"The people," she repeated, rubbing her eyes. She sat silently, trying to accept what I had said.

"You still haven't told me why," she said.

"It's all about $235 million—money invested by Braxton in wine futures in France over four years ago."

"Illegally?"

"That's a matter of interpretation. My former client and the government have different views about that."

"And they're all after the money?"

Just then I noticed the bright lights of a car pull up in front of her large bay window, then suddenly go off. I briefly panicked when I realized the danger I was putting her in. She saw my concern, stood up quickly and peeked through the shutters.

She turned and smiled, and then walked over to take my hand. "It's just my neighbor," she said softly. "Relax."

"I don't want you involved in this. When it's over, I'll tell you everything. For now, I need you to do two things."

She was surprisingly calm, waiting for my request.

"First, please call London. Find out how the woman I mentioned to you is doing. Her name is Martine Paulet. I'm very worried about her. Will you do that?"

"Yes, of course," she agreed. "And the second?"

"Is there a way for you to put a story on the newswire that would be picked up nationwide? And without anyone knowing the source?"

Tightening her lips, she said, "It would have to be done very carefully, but I think I can do it. If it's anonymous, though, it probably won't be aired by many stations. What's the story?"

I handed her my briefcase. "It's all in there. Put it in the form of a news story, but don't release it until I tell you. O.K.?"

She nodded yes. "And the woman in London?"

I hesitated, and then handed her a slip of paper with Martine's telephone number.

She made the call, and after several minutes of talking to someone on the other end, hung up. A puzzled look came over her face. "I talked to a housekeeper," she said. "Ms. Paulet is gone. She wouldn't say where."

"No message?"

"No message."

"A final question," she said, her eyebrows raised in an attempt to change the subject. "Why have you persisted? Why not stop?"

I contemplated her question as I had done every day for the past year. "Justice, revenge and—"

"And?"

"Greed. And don't ask any more questions."

"Those aren't great motives," she observed.

I smiled. "They'll do."

*　　*　　*　　*

The rain was pounding the pavement, turning the snow to slush, three days later when I returned to the airport. From there, I made two phone calls before boarding my plane. The first, to Helmut Schmidt, left us at odds with each other. He somehow knew of my call to Il Progresso. The story had resulted in a full investigation of the Vatican bank and its Controller, and had led to his arrest. It promised a scandal of the proportions of Banco Ambrosiano.

The second call was to McAlister. I asked that he check his fax machine for an exclusive story that would be released across national newswires.

*　　*　　*　　*

Dallas, Texas, 1993

Somewhere over the Midwest, on my return flight to Dallas, I came to grips with the pieces to the puzzle and knew they were fitting together. It was in Dallas that the doubts crept back in. Awaiting me on my answering machine was a message. Schmidt, in his heavy German accent, gave me notice that Braschi had been released on bail and had disappeared. My calendar showed seven days until the wine would be sold. Visions of Martine blurred all my thoughts.

The next day I found myself again seated at that long table in the offices of the U.S. Department of Justice. Across from me was McAlister, on the brink of exploding. He held up the ten page fax he had been sent, his eyes bristling.

"What is this?" he demanded. "Blackmail! Do you have any idea what you're getting yourself into?"

"Not blackmail," I assured him. "It's journalism. And it tells the truth. Would you like to give me your side of the story?"

He threw the fax across the table and then leaned his chair back against the wall. His gold glasses slid to the end of his nose. "If this thing gets out, you'll spend the rest of your life in a Federal prison. I can promise you that."

"You're misreading the story," I pointed out. "It's not about me—it's about you. Did you read it?"

His face appeared confused, as if torn between an urge to kill and one of self preservation. The bluntness of what I had said left him stunned. "This would ruin me," he finally mumbled.

"As it should," I quickly responded.

His hand brushed across his face several times, shaking noticeably. "Has this been released?" he asked, pointing to the fax.

"Not yet. Do you want it to be?"

He paused, trying to catch his breath.

"This is an outrage," he finally mumbled.

"No, what you've done is an outrage. Intimidation and murder!"

"I was never involved in murder!"

"The people who worked for you were."

"Who?" he said impatiently.

"Dawson Henry and Rudy Blair. Didn't they work for you?"

He struggled with what I had said. "They provided us with information—undercover. They didn't work for me."

"Who'd they work for then?"

"I don't know."

"Somehow, I don't believe you," I shot back. "Read the article—you knew."

Humbled slightly, he said, "It went too far. What this article says they did…I never authorized that!" His icy stare changed to indignation.

I took a deep breath and tried to suppress my rage. "They almost killed a woman I love. They didn't do that on their own. Why…? Do you want to tell me?"

He turned his palms toward me, in a defeated gesture. "The money. All I wanted was the money. Those were their only instructions. There was to be no violence."

"But you…you're a U.S. Attorney. It doesn't make sense."

"I let it get out of control—maybe I got out of control. That money wasn't Braxton's, it didn't belong to anyone. It was a chance for me—" He paused and looked down, in silence. Then, returning his eyes to me, he said with resignation, "What do you want me to do?"

"Drop any investigation and charges against me. Immediately. And make it irrevocable."

"What about your firm?"

"Screw my firm. I left it long ago. Just leave me out of it."

"How do I know this story won't make it on the news wires if I do what you ask?"

I stood up, gave him a contemptuous look, and said, "Trust me." Turning to leave, I added, "By the way, did you know a man named Peabody?"

He paused and shook his head no. I left him there, sitting at the end of that long table, and walked out.

CHAPTER 42

▼

Istanbul, Turkey, 1993

On Tuesday, April 3rd, four days before the money was to be transferred, I received a travel brochure from a London agent. It was titled "The Pearls of a Necklace", and the cover showed parasols in every color imaginable. Inside were descriptions of cafés, guest houses and the last home of the Viceroy of Egypt, built in the 1800's, known as the Summer Palace of the Khedive. They were all in Istanbul.

Two days later, in Paris, I boarded the Istanbul Express and began a forty-eight hour journey across two continents and through six countries. Throughout the trip, I kept as secluded in my private compartment as I could. Only on rare occasions did I see anyone. There were no familiar faces.

Hour after hour, my thoughts were occupied with the sounds of the train—and Martine. What would Julia think? All the memories, and the difficulty of separating what was real and what was imagined, continued to haunt me.

By 7:30 in the morning on the second day we reached the Black Sea, which lies to the northeast of the Aegean and Mediterranean. Forty-five minutes later, we sped along the Bosphorus, the channel which separates Europe from Asia.

Approaching Istanbul, I lowered the window and felt the chill but clear and crisp air. We moved at over one hundred miles per hour past ancient mosques and palaces, at times providing me spectacular views of the city I remembered from my old history books as Constantinople.

The monotonous clanking of the rails had a hypnotic effect as I stood there, hoping my nightmare was finally coming to an end. Suddenly, the train rounded a bend. Spread before me were curved domes in layers and soaring minarets, as far as I could see. The city seemed to drowse behind a gauzy veil. Progressively, as the sun came up, it emerged as an endless array of changing colors, first from twilight shades of plum and purple and then multi-colors of the rainbow.

Flashes of light hit my eyes from the spires and windows of centuries old buildings as the train lurched and then settled on its route into the station. And then the soot and smell of a very old and dirty city confronted me. Sirkeci Station looked unchanged since World War I. An odor of lamb being cooked on skewers permeated the air. Everywhere there were Turkish men, in beards and mustaches, with black and red turbans, and women in black silk robes and colorful dresses.

It was almost ten when I stood somewhere near the middle of the old Galata Bridge, giving me a commanding view of the entire city and its natural harbor, the Golden Horn. I stared silently at the Blue Mosque of Sultan Ahmet, obscured by the swirling clouds of pigeons that were everywhere. Beneath them lines of white ferry boats moved through belching smoke.

Beyond the stark walls of Topkapi, I searched for signs and caught the needle-like minarets and huge domes of the St. Sophia Mosque. There, to the left of the conical Galata Tower, I saw it—Banka Turkey. A dull thumping filled the air as I walked the two blocks to the bank. It was the sound of dozens of ancient looms clawing away at ells of wool in small shops that lined the streets.

Inside the bank, I was directed to the office of Mehmed Ali Yashik. It reeked of stale pipe smoke and old furnishings. Oriental rugs in bright blue, crimson and gold were placed between heavily upholstered red chairs and sofas, lined with fringe. Vases of colorful flowers sat on his desk and credenza. Yashik entered dressed in a black suit and matching tie, and wearing a red turban which he quickly removed.

Yashik was relatively young, probably in his middle forties. He had a dark, well-manicured mustache, soft brown eyes and a very fair complexion. He was a hugely overweight man.

"Efendim. Merhaba," he said with a thick accent, extending his hand. "You are Mr. Lawrence?"

"I am," I said. "You're aware of my business with your bank?"

"Evet," he said, nodding his head. "The papers," he continued, pointing to a stack of documents on his desk.

I flipped quickly through them, noting they were partly in English and partly in Turkish.

"Counterparts, in both languages, as you requested," he said, anticipating my question. "All in the name Kultur Bakanhgi. You have registered that name with the Government?"

"Yes I have. I understand that no one will know. Am I correct?"

"Yes, of course you are. A registered name is your own here, and your true name must by law remain confidential. Now, if you will sign these documents, we can complete our business."

"In my assumed name?"

"Evet, please."

I signed and he watched. When I finished, he pushed a button and we were joined by a young man in a robe and black turban. "Will you have a cup of tea with me, Mr. Lawrence?"

I nodded yes and he turned to the servant. "Cay lutfen, mersi." The servant quickly disappeared.

"Para. The money will arrive today, from Switzerland?"

"The Union Bank," I responded.

"Over three hundred million U.S. dollars. Is that correct?"

"Yes it is. From here, monies are to be wired to ten other banks as provided in my instructions, with $20 million to remain here."

He smiled, showing his obvious pleasure at the size of the deposit. "And what shall we do with those remaining funds?"

"Convert them all into Turkish lira. Then deposit one million dollars U.S. in a checking account with your bank and invest the balance in Turkish government obligations."

He scratched his chin and then pulled a writing board from his desk. Taped to it was a sheet of codes and numbers.

Studying it for several minutes, he looked up. "The current interest rate for both our account and Turkish bonds will be about 8%. Is that satisfactory?"

Before I could answer, we were again interrupted by the servant, carrying miniature cups of hot spicy tea and small cookies. As he placed them on small tables, Yashik lit his pipe. The aroma was strong and pungent, and quickly filled the room with a cloud of smoke.

"Eight percent is very satisfactory," I said. "May I call you at the end of today to confirm that all arrangements have been made and the money is safe in my account?"

"You have nothing to worry about," he assured me. "I will call you. Where can I reach you?"

Temporarily, I'm at the Para Palas. But do you know the Summer Palace of the Khedive?" I asked.

"Of course," he nodded. "It's on the hills overlooking the Bosphorus. Beautiful! Do you have a room there?"

"No, that's my problem. Can you arrange one?"

He narrowed his eyes and studied my request. "It has only fifty rooms," he said with a worried look on his face. "It could be very difficult. I will try."

"Try!" I repeated, holding up the papers I had just signed. He understood the meaning.

"You will have a room tomorrow," he promised. We shook hands, he said, "Gunaydin," and I exited onto the street.

The city was becoming enveloped in fog. The lignite dust from a million coal burning apartment buildings burned my eyes as I turned and walked towards the Kapali Carsi, the Big Bazaar.

The Bazaar was a labyrinth of dimly lit alleyways, cul de sacs and narrow winding streets. The people who lined the shops would have made Alice of Wonderland green with envy. They were an assortment of hookah-smoking merchants, hamals or porters bent like hinges under incredible loads of fruit, carpets or spice, women hidden in black shrouds, and wide-eyed tourists. Among this melee, for the first time in months I felt safe.

Without warning, a large hand reached out from behind a doorway and grabbed my arm, pulling me with enormous force. I felt panic stricken, struggling to get free. A deep voice, on the other end of the arm, whispered, "American, don't struggle."

I looked up into the beady eyes of a massive Turk, dressed in a dark gown and a red turban. I cursed for not having my gun. "What do you want?"

He showed a wide grin and a number of missing teeth. "You look at our rugs. Big savings."

I stepped back, loosened his grip, and shook my head to indicate a vigorous no. Moving quickly away, I heard the call of the muezzin to the faithful for prayer—the center of the Islamic culture. All around me small carpets were thrown to the ground, and the owners knelt facing east, oblivious to the hustle of the Bazaar. Unnerved, I hastily left and returned to the hotel.

Thirty minutes later, I sat alone in the notorious bar of the Para Palas, waiting to hear from Yashik. The bar was famous for singing duels between German and British delegations. It was the center of spying activity in the 1930's and 1940's. The wood paneling, marble floor and wicker furnishings were in stark white, reminiscent of British colonial days.

After two martinis, the white blended to soft pink and I heard a low voice say "Kultur Bakanhgi. Mr. Bakanhgi."

I slightly raised my hand and motioned to the clerk. He handed me a note, folded once. Opening it only enough to see the message, I read,

"We have the wire transfer. Funds have been rewired and invested as you instructed. Tesekkur ederim. Mehmed Ali Yashik."

Refolding the paper, I slid it into my shirt pocket and broke into a cold sweat. Could it be possible? I hadn't allowed myself to believe it could really be done. It was a prayer and a wish—no more. But it had happened. I had the money!

I closed my eyes in a daze over what I had accomplished. When I opened them, my stare was met by that of a woman sitting alone across the room. She was dressed in a long creamy silk gown with a multi-colored necklace. Her hair was jet black and straight, combed under at her shoulders to give a Mata Hari effect. Without meaning to, I became transfixed looking into her dark brown eyes. Her full lips turned upward as she smiled at me, giving the impression of a fine china doll.

Squinting, I caught myself and instantly motioned to the waiter for another drink. Her expression changed quickly and she looked away. After my third martini, my vision and my brain began to get cloudy, and I returned to my room.

Undressing slowly, I stepped into a cold shower and gradually felt the return of sanity. The taste of that third martini lingered with me. Wrapped in my towel, I stepped out and fell onto the bed. All the fears and insecurities seemed to fade while I lay there, staring at the cracks around the steam pipe on the ceiling.

The next day was an Occidental day—intensely colored in the sun with a maze of white clouds drifting through a bleached indigo sky. A stiff breeze was blowing and the crystal blue of the Bosphorus was broken only by the white crests made by the constant stream of boats traveling through the channel.

At 11 in the morning I boarded the Guzen Kitap to cross the sea from the Occident to the Orient. The ship was a small ferry, used only for transporting people across the narrow straits. The hull dipped and rose, lifting clouds of spray across its bow, which were then whipped by the strong winds into the faces of the passengers on board. The steward pointed to the Palace of the Khedive as we plowed through the turbulent waters along our two-hour voyage.

There were four other persons on my side of the deck, a man and three women steadying themselves against the rail. One of them was the woman from the bar the night before. This time she was dressed in a beige rain coat and dark scarf. I could not make out the features of the other three, but she didn't seem to be with them.

My mind wandered away, listening to the steady throb of the engines. The man had turned into the alley-way between the captain's bridge and the passengers' cabin, and disappeared. She remained, talking to one of the boat's crew. I closed my eyes and could hear the sound of laughing children from the far side of the boat. I opened them and she was still there, but now alone. Drawing a deep breath, I walked over to her.

"You are from the Para Palas," I said.

She turned to face me, staring blankly. "Haki efendi evde midir," she mumbled indifferently.

I looked into her eyes, knowing it was hopeless. The boat rolled slightly and then pitched in a high wave from side to side. Grabbing the railing for balance, she said "Efendi var-dir. Gunaydin." She then turned and walked to the stairway leading to the lower deck, while I wondered who she was.

Looking around, I braced myself against the wind and sprays of water by holding firmly to the deck railing. Except for the whine of the diesel engines and the splashing of water on the deck, there was no sound other than my breathing. After almost an hour, I decided to seek the refuge of the cabin.

The alley-way which led to the doors was only wide enough for one person to pass. Holding onto the railing, I inched slowly into the corridor. The ferry swayed from left to right, making it difficult for me to maintain my balance. I could hear the clanging and whining of the engines through the vibrating floor. Before I had gone less than ten feet, I saw that the passageway was blocked by a small man coming the other way. I backed up to allow him access to the deck.

When we were clear of the corridor, he looked up, glaring at me with insolent eyes. My heart suddenly began pounding against my ribs when I recognized who it was. The small eyes didn't flinch, but an ugly little smile said, "Buona sera, Signori."

"Signore Braschi," I said calmly. "How did you know I was here?"

He glanced over his shoulder to be sure we were alone, and then redirected his attention to me. "The money was diverted from our bank. You stole it. I want it back!"

I stared at him for a moment, not knowing what to say. Then it came to me. "Fuck you," I mumbled softly.

"What?" he shouted, the anger rising in his face. Before I could react, he pulled a revolver from his coat and pushed it into my stomach. I felt the blood drain from my face as the spray from breaking waves blew into my eyes.

"You killed all those people, didn't you? And the Monsignor?"

His face, thick with Italian features, broadened into a wide grin. "And you, Signore Lawrence, how many did you kill?"

I watched him, stunned, not knowing what to do next. "Self-defense," I answered, stalling for time.

The grin quickly disappeared and his face hardened. For a moment, he stared icily at me, sending a chill down my spine. Then, waving his gun, he motioned me over to the railing. I looked around, hoping to see anyone on the deck. It was empty.

"They'll never find you," he said calmly, raising his gun to point at my eyes.

"And you'll never get the money," I said, fumbling for a response.

He pulled back the hammer and grimaced. "It's unimportant now. You've destroyed everything—years of waiting. All I have left is to watch you die."

My heart was pounding. I tried to plan a way out, but I couldn't think. Then I saw her standing behind him. The woman from the Para

Palas. She had a gun, also pointed at me. I was flabbergasted when I realized who she must be—Yanou Folare. He saw my eyes drift to her and stared blankly at me. "So it's the two of you," I mumbled. "How many others? Peabody?"

He smiled again. "Others? I didn't need others. They trusted me, those Cardinals and the Pope. They're too busy saving souls." He cackled. "They left the money to me. As for Peabody, you did me a favor. A freelancer—too free. I couldn't trust him."

I shook my head, feeling the throbbing in my temples. "Trust? You use that word a lot. But you abused it."

His eyes became angry. "Used!" he said in a raspy voice. "Not abused! The money wasn't theirs, it never would have been theirs." And then he said in an almost inaudible voice, "As you die, think of this. I will find the money! All of your efforts have been wasted."

"You or the two of you?" I shifted my eyes to the woman I knew was Yanou Folare.

"No more time and no more tricks," he said with an expression that left me grappling for understanding.

I couldn't overwhelm both of them. Finally, with resignation I asked, "Are you both going to shoot me?"

"What?" he said, spinning around to see the woman behind him.

She fired twice. I waited, motionless, for death. Braschi gave me a confused stare and then slowly dropped his gun. I stood in shock as she moved quickly to him. He was now slumping against the rail, blood seeping from his head and coat. She bent over, grabbed his legs, and lifted him over the rail. Steadying her gun at me, she watched his body fall into the heavy current and sink beneath the boat.

I involuntarily closed my eyes and waited for the next shot. It didn't come. She peered at me for a moment, and then said in broken English, "Monsieur Freytag says the contract is done." She turned and walked away, leaving me standing there, staring at the blood spattered deck which was gradually washed clean by the water splashing from the waves.

CHAPTER 43

▼

The sun had disappeared from the sky when we reached the shores of Asia. Dark gray clouds layered the hills overlooking the Sea of Marmara. The hazy blue waters were dotted with silhouettes of freighters, tankers and cruisers waiting their turn to navigate the tricky currents of the Bosphorus towards the Black Sea.

I tried to think of them during the long taxi ride up the hill to the Summer Palace. The sudden panic and then numbness from what I had just been through left me wondering. Was it really over? Could it ever be?

We drove through the empty parks, past nineteenth century lamps and spacious lawns and gardens. In the hotel, I was taken to a room on the second floor with a view of the park and blue waters of the straits of the Bosphorus. There, I placed a call.

After an interminable number of rings, the voice on the other end said, "Yes, what is it?"

"Mr. Freytag, this is your friend from Istanbul. How did you know where he was?"

"You told me," he said in a low voice. There was a pause, and then he continued. "He booked a flight to Istanbul two days ago. When you said you'd be at the Para Palas, I passed that to my agent."

He cleared his throat, and then I heard several taps against the phone. "Sorry," he said softly. "A bad habit, I'm afraid. Emptying my pipe against the phone. She found you in the bar. From there, she simply stayed with you."

"Why a woman?"

"Why not? She's one of the best. Was she not efficient?"

I let out a deep sigh. "Too efficient. I thought she was there to kill me. I didn't know who she was."

"Regretful," was all he could say. "By the way," he added, "the fifty thousand arrived as you promised. I believe our bargain is complete."

"One last question," I said. "How did Braschi know where to find me?"

He cleared his throat again. "You have a history, Mr. Lawrence, of leaving trails. I don't have an answer to your question, but I expect you will find it if you search your memory. Now, I must excuse myself. Other business is waiting." He hung up.

I hesitated, took a stiff drink, and then made my next call. Sidney Harrison was direct and to the point. Martine had left London and returned to France. He expected me to leave her alone. I mumbled something and hung up, feeling very sad.

The next morning I arrived back at Banka Turkey just as it opened. There I was met by Mehmed Ali Yashik. "Merhaba," he said, ushering me to the back of the bank and into his office. He smiled broadly as he presented me with a stack of wire-transfer confirmations. After I had reviewed and confirmed the transfer of funds to my accounts around the globe, he gave me a detailed statement of his bank.

Sitting down, the full impact of the transfers hit me. From an account in the Union Bank of Switzerland, $348 million had been transferred to the account of Kultur Bakanhgi at Banka Turkey. From there, $280 million had been sent to accounts held by me, under various fictitious names, in the Cayman Islands, Bermuda, Chile, the Netherlands Antilles, Costa Rica, Hungary, Lithuania, Australia and Argentina. Then $50 million had been sent to Hibernia Bank in New

Orleans, for the account of Raymond Jarrett. That left $18 million in my account at Banka Turkey. It was perfect!

I looked up at him, returning his broad smile. Using the few words of his language I had learned from a travel brochure, I said, "Tesekkur ederim!"

He bowed his head and acknowledged my appreciation. "Is there anything else?"

"Yes," I said. "A checkbook for my account, and the equivalent of $10,000, in Turkish lira."

He was momentarily startled by my request. "Cash?"

"Yes. Spending money."

"Of course." He left and within thirty minutes returned with a checkbook in the name Kultur Bakanghi and a small box containing stacks of neatly tied bundles of cash.

It was nearly 2 P.M. when I returned to the Summer Palace. I deposited the box of money in the hotel safe and walked into the Somineli Salon, the crescent shaped dining room that extends almost 180 degrees around the exterior wall of the building.

I sat alone, peering down the huge expanse of the restaurant that must have provided seating for 100 people. From left to right, dark marble pillars separated the hardwood floors from the engraved wood ceilings. The floors were softened by a thick creamy Turkish rug that extended from one end of the room to the other, adding to the deafening silence. Along the outside wall, I stared through the enormous floor to ceiling windows at the view of the junction of the Bosphorus with the Sea of Marmara.

When the waiter approached, I ordered a large bottle of Kavaklidere, a crimson red wine. Then I waited. Fixing my eyes on the billowing gray clouds that clung to the hills, I thought of all the people who had died since I left the firm. It was inescapable that I was responsible for many of them.

There was Peabody, who deserved to die. And Chandler, who I shot at Braxton's house. And the Monsignor, Sterling, Marianne, the assassin on Janiculum Hill, Dawson Henry and Rudy Blair, the man with the beard—and Julia. Last, I thought of Best. I felt a wave of sadness and aloneness.

I looked up to see the waiter pour a glass of the wine. After studying the color, I drank the entire glass and poured another. My grief was less intense. Glancing from one end of the empty restaurant to the other, I finished off the second glass and poured a third.

I felt elated—and desolate. Everything had worked out. I had $298 million. It meant very little. I finished the entire bottle of wine. The room and my life were fast becoming a blur. It was then that the waiter handed me a note. It said, "Look to the right, through your glass." My eyes wouldn't focus, so I rubbed them. Holding the glass up at eye level, I peered to the right. There was nothing. Spinning back around, I caught a glimpse of a woman, dressed in a soft beige wool dress with a navy and gold silk scarf, sitting across from me.

She smiled. "You used to be good at that—looking through glasses. Weather got you down?"

I gently placed my wine glass on the table and took a deep breath. "And who might you be?"

"Alice," she said softly.

"Hmmm…You recovered?"

"What do you see?"

"A difficult question. May I have a few minutes?"

She leaned across the table and took my hand. "I'll give you a life-time."

The wine and my vision of her were causing my head to spin. I held onto the table for balance. "It's O.K.," I answered. "I only need a few minutes. What I see is the love of my life and the woman I almost got killed—not once but twice."

"Not you…never you. It was those people. You saved me, in case you can't remember."

"But I promised your father…."

"That you would leave me alone? Some promise! Did you ever think to ask me?"

"You could've called."

She took a sip of my wine and blinked at me. "I did call, a number of times, but you were never there."

I looked down, thinking of Rome, Paris and Istanbul. "Well you might have left a message on my answering machine."

She shook her head in dismay. "I was afraid to. I didn't know where you were or who might hear the message."

"So how did you find me?"

We were briefly interrupted by the waiter, who at my urging brought another bottle of wine and a glass for Martine. When he left, a faint smile dawned on her lips and a gleam came to her beautiful eyes. "Matt, I'm in love with you. I believe we were meant to be soul mates."

"Soul mates?"

"Yes. Who do you think sent you that travel brochure for this hotel. The postal department?"

"Surely you couldn't have thought I would simply take that brochure and come here?" My brain was again getting cloudy.

She flashed a beautiful smile and held my hand again. "You're here, aren't you?"

"Yes…a long way from Texas."

And then she said, under her breath, "It was so far away—another world. I never thought anyone would find you here, except me."

"But they did, didn't they?"

She shook her head in disbelief and muttered apologetically, "It didn't seem possible, but yes, they did. But you're safe and we're together."

I nodded yes.

"I love you passionately," she said. "I knew you'd come here! Don't ask me how, but I just knew it."

I pulled myself up. "Isn't that interesting."

"That I knew you'd be here?"

"No, that you love me passionately. Because that's how I love you."

Her blue eyes stared at me, softly, and she placed her hands together. "If you love me that much, would you do one little thing for me?"

I put my hands over hers, leaned over the table, and whispered, "Martine, I love you so much. I'll do anything, if—"

"If?"

"You'll marry me."

"First, you'd better hear what I want you to do."

I sat back and waited.

"Give up the money."

"What...?" I was totally speechless. The room suddenly came back into focus.

"Matt, it will only come between us. We don't need it. Can't you see I'm right?"

Studying her expression, I knew she was deadly serious. I considered it and winced. "Could I keep a few million?"

She smiled very tenderly. "You will do it then?"

"If I can keep three or four million, give or take a few."

"We'll discuss that later," she said, as three violinists began to play a song that sounded vaguely familiar.

"Let's dance," she said.

We rose and I heard a satiny voice in the background, sing in distorted English-

> *When we dance together, my world's in disguise,*
> *It's a fairy land tale that's come true.*
> *And when you look at me with those stars in your eyes,*
> *I could waltz across Texas with you....*

"Why in the world are they playing that song—and here in Turkey?" I whispered.

She opened her half-closed eyes and smiled, lovingly, and I knew.

I held her close and we glided across the wood floor, as they continued-

> *Like a story book ending I'm lost in your charms,*
> *And I could waltz across Texas with you....*

0-595-66671-X

Printed in the United States
23199LVS00002B/160-186